MR. POTTERMACK'S OVERSIGHT

MR. POTTERMACK'S OVERSIGHT

R. Austin Freeman

with an introduction by
MARTIN EDWARDS

This edition published 2024 by
The British Library
96 Euston Road
London NW1 2DB

Mr. Pottermack's Oversight was originally published in Britain
in 1931 by Hodder and Stoughton, Ltd, London.

Introduction © 2024 Martin Edwards
Volume Copyright © The British Library Board

Cataloguing in Publication Data
A catalogue record for this book is available from the British Library

ISBN 978 0 7123 5546 9
eISBN 978 0 7123 6887 2

Original front cover image © Bridgeman images

Typeset by Tetragon, London
Printed in England by TJ Books Limited, Padstow, Cornwall

CONTENTS

Introduction   7

A Note from the Publisher   13

MR. POTTERMACK'S OVERSIGHT   15

INTRODUCTION

Mr. Pottermack's Oversight is one of the most enjoyable "inverted mysteries" ever written. Perhaps that isn't entirely surprising, given that the author, Richard Austin Freeman, was the man who created the "inverted mystery". This is a form of detective fiction that has entertained readers for more than a century, as well as appealing to television viewers of such series as *Columbo* and, more recently, Rian Johnson's *Poker Face*.

The novel begins with a prologue in which an escaped prisoner manages to elude the pursuing warders. The main narrative, set years later, begins with a discovery made by an amiable man called Marcus Pottermack. He comes across a sun-dial which takes his fancy and, having bought it, decides to install it in his garden, to cover an open and potentially dangerous well.

Pottermack is visited at home by a woman called Mrs Bellard, with whom he is on very good terms. The pair are "curiously alike in one respect; they both looked older to the casual stranger than they appeared on closer inspection". There is also something else, "something really rather odd. Each of the two cronies seemed to have a way of furtively examining the other. There was nothing unfriendly or suspicious... But they conveyed a queer impression of curiosity and doubt."

Pottermack's mood darkens, however, when he reads a letter which is addressed to him but begins: "Dear Jeff." It is clear at once that he is being blackmailed by someone who has black-mailed him in the past. This time his oppressor wants a hundred pounds in notes: *"I've got to have it.* No need to dwell on unpleasant alternatives."

It's abundantly clear to Pottermack that he is at the mercy of someone who will never let him go, whose attitude is: "the money that you have earned by unstinted labour and saved by self-denial has got to be handed to me that I may drop it into the bottomless pit that swallows up the gambler's losings." At the present rate, Pottermack fears he will soon be sucked dry and "reduced to stark poverty. And even then he would be no safer."

Before the night is over, however, Pottermack has come to a decision: "All the anxiety and bewilderment had passed out of his face... [he had] the calm of a man who has made up his mind." So ends the first chapter, and the scene is set for an excellent mystery.

Although we know at the outset that Mr. Pottermack is a man with a secret who is bent on murder, Freeman enlists our sympathy for him. This novel provides an early example of a type of story which became increasingly popular during the 1930s, where the author posed two compelling questions. First, can murder ever be justified? And second, if a murder can be morally justified, what then should happen to the murderer?

Pottermack is clever and his plan is so ingenious that it appears to be foolproof. But then Dr. Thorndyke, Freeman's brilliant detective, an expert in medical jurisprudence, comes on to the scene. The novel turns into a game of cat-and-mouse, with Freeman making splendid use of his technical expertise.

Richard Austin Freeman (1862–1943) had written a couple of non-fiction books before his first collection of detective stories was published in 1902. *The Adventures of Romney Pringle* was co-written with J. J. Pitcairn—who, like Freeman, was medically qualified—and published under the pen-name Clifford Ashdown. Dr. John Evelyn

Thorndyke made his debut in *The Red Thumb-Mark* (1907) and rapidly established himself as one of fiction's great detectives.

Shortly afterwards, in a short story called "The Case of Oscar Brodski", Freeman broke fresh and significant ground in the genre—something that few authors can claim. His starting point was to ask himself: "Would it be possible to write a detective story in which from the outset the reader was taken entirely into the author's confidence, was made an actual witness of the crime and furnished with every fact that could possibly be used in its detection? Would there be any story left when the reader had all the facts?"

He demonstrated in "The Case of Oscar Brodski" that the answer was "yes". The reader knew everything about the murder committed by Brodski, and Thorndyke knew nothing, so the fascination lay in seeing how apparently trivial points proved to be important as the detective strove to deduce what had happened. Freeman's meticulous approach to his craft meant that his description of the process of detection was not only credible and accurate but also fascinating. In 1912 he published *The Singing Bone*, which contained "The Case of Oscar Brodski" and five more stories constructed in the same intricate way.

Although he returned to this method of storytelling once or twice after the First World War, in *Mr. Pottermack's Oversight* he set out to write a full-length novel in the "inverted" style. As the late Norman Donaldson rightly said in his book *In Search of Dr. Thorndyke*, "Although the *quantity* of Thorndyke offered in *Pottermack* is somewhat less than average, the quality leaves nothing to be desired."

Once Freeman had shown the way, other Golden Age novelists followed his lead and wrote inverted mystery novels. Among the best are *The 12.30 from Croydon* and *Antidote to Venom* by Freeman Wills Crofts (both published as British Library Crime Classics) and *End of an Ancient Mariner* by G. D. H. and Margaret Cole.

The unfenced chalk pit in this novel was thought by the author's son John to have been inspired by a chalk pit in the vicinity of Gravesend, where Freeman lived for many years. David Chapman, the leading contemporary expert on Freeman and author of an excellent bibliography of the author's work, believes that this is Swanscombe Wood, which is today a nature reserve located between Gravesend and the Bluewater Shopping Centre.

A periscope disguised as a walking-stick like the one Thorndyke uses in the story was actually constructed by Freeman, who often conducted medical and other experiments to make sure that his stories were accurate. It is this scrupulous attention to detail that sets him apart from most other writers of the Golden Age who made use of scientific devices and know-how in their mysteries.

David Chapman suggests—plausibly, I think—that the relationship at the heart of this novel was inspired by a real life romance of Freeman's:

"The essence of the good fortune lay in the fact that Jeffrey Brandon and Alice Bentley were not merely lovers; they were staunch friends and sympathetic companions, with so many interests in common that it was incredible that they should ever tire of each other's society."

The real-life model for Alice Bentley, David Chapman believes, was Alice Bishop, to whom he dedicated one of his books. But Freeman and Alice were married to other people and their relationship became increasingly distant long before *Mr. Pottermack's Oversight* was written, so perhaps his description of the relationship is overlaid with regret as well as nostalgia.

Richard Austin Freeman was a major detective writer, accomplished enough to earn the approval of such astute judges (and superb prose stylists) as Dorothy L. Sayers, Raymond Chandler, and George Orwell. He was referenced in no fewer than three of Sayers' eleven Lord Peter Wimsey novels, while Chandler said in a letter to his British publisher that Freeman "is a wonderful performer. He has no equal in his genre". Orwell praised Freeman in print on several occasions, saying in the *New English Review* of 23 July 1936 that he was one of three detective writers worth reading (the others being Sir Arthur Conan Doyle and, rather less predictably, Ernest Bramah).

In *The Box Office Murders*, Freeman Wills Crofts' series detective Inspector French wishes that he had Thorndyke's skills, while Agatha Christie parodied Thorndyke's methods in "The Affair of the Pink Pearl", a story in *Partners in Crime*. Julian Symons, often an acerbic critic, was dismissive of Freeman's literary skills, but even he name-checked *Mr. Pottermack's Oversight* as one of Freeman's novels that was comparable in quality to his short stories. What is more, Freeman's reputation did not fade away following his death. A successful pilot in the BBC Television anthology series *Detective* led to a six-episode TV series in 1964; *Thorndyke* starred Peter Copley as the great man, with Paul Williamson and Patrick Newell as Dr. Jervis and Nathaniel Polton, his usual sidekicks.

More than seventy years after his death, Freeman's fiction continues to attract admirers. There is a Dr. John Thorndyke Appreciation Group on Facebook and David Chapman has recently relaunched the periodical *John Thorndyke's Journal* after a hiatus of several years. Nevertheless, in recent times Freeman has not received as much attention as perhaps he deserves. It would be good to think that the reprinting of this entertaining novel helps to gain him wider recognition as a master of the well-crafted classic crime story.

MARTIN EDWARDS

www.martinedwards.com

A NOTE FROM THE PUBLISHER

To my friend the honourable Lady Lynden-Bell

PROLOGUE

The afternoon of a sultry day near the end of July was beginning to merge into evening. The crimson eye of the declining sun peered out through chinks in a bank of slaty cloud as if taking a last look at the great level of land and water before retiring for the night; while already, in the soft, greenish grey of the eastern sky, the new-risen moon hung like a globe of pearl.

It was a solitary scene; desolate, if you will, or peaceful. On the one hand the quiet waters of a broad estuary; on the other a great stretch of marshes; and between them the sea wall, following faithfully the curves and indentations of the shore and fading away at either end into invisibility.

A great stillness brooded over the place. On the calm water, far out beyond the shallows, one or two coasting craft lay at anchor, and yet farther out a schooner and a couple of barges crept up on the flood tide. On the land side in the marshy meadows a few sheep grazed sedately, and in the ditch that bordered the sea wall the water-voles swam to and fro or sat on the banks and combed their hair. Sound there was none save the half-audible wash of the little waves upon the shore and now and again the querulous call of a sea-gull.

In strange contrast to the peaceful stillness that prevailed around was the aspect of the one human creature that was visible. Tragedy was written in every line of his figure; tragedy and fear and breathless haste. He was running—so far as it was possible to run among the rough stones and the high grass—at the foot of the sea wall on the seaward side; stumbling onward desperately, breathing hard, and constantly brushing away with his hand the sweat that streamed down his forehead into his eyes. At intervals he paused to scramble up the slope of the wall among the thistles and ragwort, and with infinite caution, to avoid even showing his head on the skyline, peered over the top backwards and forwards, but especially backwards where, in the far distance, the grey mass of a town loomed beyond the marshes.

There was no mystery about the man's movements. A glance at his clothing explained everything. For he was dressed in prison grey, branded with the broad arrow and still bearing the cell number. Obviously, he was an escaped convict.

Criminologists of certain Continental schools are able to give us with remarkable exactness the facial and other characteristics by which the criminal may be infallibly recognized. Possibly these convenient "stigmata" may actually occur in the criminals of those favoured regions. But in this backward country it is otherwise; and we have to admit the regrettable fact that the British criminal inconsiderately persists in being a good deal like other people. Not that the criminal class is, even here, distinguished by personal beauty or fine physique. The criminal is a low-grade man; but he is not markedly different from other low-grade men.

But the fugitive whose flight in the shelter of the sea wall we are watching did not conform even to the more generalized type. On the contrary, he was a definitely good-looking young man; rather small and slight yet athletic and well-knit, with a face not only intelligent and refined but, despite the anxious and even terrified expression, suggestive of a courageous, resolute personality. Whatever had brought him to a convict prison, he was not of the rank and file of its inmates.

Presently, as he approached a bluff which concealed a stretch of the sea wall ahead, he slowed down into a quick walk, stooping slightly and peering forward cautiously to get a view of the shore beyond the promontory, until, as he reached the most projecting point of the wall, he paused for a moment and then crept stealthily forward, alert and watchful for any unexpected thing that might be lurking round the promontory.

Suddenly he stopped dead and then drew back a pace, craning up to peer over the high, rushy grass, and casting a glance of intense scrutiny along the stretch of shore that had come into view. After a few moments he again crept forward slowly and silently, still gazing intently along the shore and the face of the sea wall that was now visible for nearly a mile ahead. And still he could see nothing but that which had met his eyes as he crept round the bluff. He drew himself up and looked down at it with eager interest.

A little heap of clothes; evidently the shed raiment of a bather, as the completeness of the outfit testified. And in confirmation, just across the narrow strip of "saltings," on the smooth expanse of muddy sand the prints of a pair of naked feet extended in a line towards the water. But where was the bather? There was only a single set of footprints, so that he must be still in the water or have come ashore farther down. Yet neither on the calm water nor on the open, solitary shore was any sign of him to be seen.

It was very strange. On that smooth water a man swimming would be a conspicuous object, and a naked man on that low, open shore would be still more conspicuous. The fugitive looked around with growing agitation. From the shore and the water his glance came back to the line of footprints; and now, for the first time, he noticed something very remarkable about them. They did not extend to the water. Starting from the edge of the saltings, they took a straight line across the sand, every footprint deep and distinct, to within twenty yards of the water's edge; and there they ended abruptly. Between the last footprint and the little waves that broke on the shore was a space of sand perfectly smooth and untouched.

What could be the meaning of this? The fugitive gazed with knitted brows at that space of smooth sand; and even as he gazed, the explanation flashed upon him. The tide was now coming in, as he could see by the anchored vessels. But when these footprints were made, the tide was going out. The spot where the footprints ended was the spot where the bather had entered the water. Then—since the tide had gone out to the low-water mark and had risen again to nearly half-tide—some five hours must have passed since that man had walked down into the water.

All this flashed through the fugitive's brain in a matter of seconds. In those seconds he realized that the priceless heap of clothing was derelict. As to what had become of the owner, he gave no thought but that in some mysterious way he had apparently vanished for good. Scrambling up the slope of the sea wall, he once more scanned the path on its summit in both directions; and still there was not a living soul in sight. Then he slid down, and breathlessly and with trembling hands stripped off the hated livery of dishonour and, not without a certain incongruous distaste, struggled into the derelict garments.

A good deal has been said—with somewhat obvious truth—about the influence of clothes upon the self-respect of the wearer. But surely there could be no more extreme instance than the present one, which, in less than one brief minute, transformed a manifest convict into a respectable artisan. The change took effect immediately. As the fugitive resumed his flight he still kept off the skyline; but he no longer hugged the base of the wall, he no longer crouched nor did he run. He walked upright out on the more or less level saltings, swinging along at a good pace but without excessive haste. And as he went he explored the pockets of the strange clothes to ascertain what bequests the late owner had made to him, and brought up at the first cast a pipe, a tobacco-pouch, and a box of matches. At the first he looked a little dubiously, but could not resist the temptation; and when he had dipped the mouthpiece in a little salt pool and scrubbed it with a handful of grass, he charged the bowl from the well-filled pouch, lighted it and smoked with an ecstasy of pleasure born of long deprivation.

Next, his eye began to travel over the abundant jetsam that the last spring-tide had strewn upon the saltings. He found a short length of old rope, and then he picked up from time to time a scrap of drift-wood. Not that he wanted the fuel, but that a bundle of driftwood seemed a convincing addition to his make-up and would explain his presence on the shore if he should be seen. When he had made up a small bundle with the aid of the rope, he swung it over his shoulder and collected no more.

He still climbed up the wall now and again to keep a look-out for possible pursuers, and at length, in the course of one of these observations, he espied a stout plank set across the ditch and con-nected with a footpath that meandered away across the marshes. In an instant he decided to follow that path, whithersoever it might lead. With a last glance towards the town, he boldly stepped up to the top of the wall, crossed the path at its summit, descended the landward side, walked across the little bridge and strode away swiftly along the footpath across the marshes.

He was none too soon. At the moment when he stepped off the bridge, three men emerged from the waterside alley that led to the sea wall and began to move rapidly along the rough path. Two of them were prison warders, and the third, who trundled a bicycle, was a police patrol.

"Pity we didn't get the tip a bit sooner," grumbled one of the warders. "The daylight's going fast, and he's got a devil of a start."

"Still," said the constable cheerfully, "it isn't much of a place to hide in. The wall's a regular trap; sea one side and a deep ditch the other. We shall get him all right, or else the patrol from Clifton will. I expect he has started by now."

"What did you tell the sergeant when you spoke to him on the 'phone?"

"I told him there was a runaway coming along the wall. He said he would send a cyclist patrol along to meet us."

The warder grunted. "A cyclist might easily miss him if he was hiding in the grass or in the rushes by the ditch. But we must see that we don't miss him. Two of us had better take the two sides of the wall so as to get a clear view."

His suggestion was adopted at once. One warder climbed down and marched along the saltings, the other followed a sort of sheep-track by the side of the ditch, while the constable wheeled his bicycle along the top of the wall. In this way they advanced as quickly as was possible to the two men stumbling over the rough ground at the base of the wall, searching the steep sides, with their rank vegetation, for any trace of the lost sheep, and making as little noise as they could. So for over a mile they toiled on, scanning every foot of the rough ground as they passed but uttering no word. Each of the warders could see the constable on the path above, and thus the party was enabled to keep together.

Suddenly the warder on the saltings stopped dead and emitted a shout of triumph. Instantly the constable laid his bicycle on the path and slithered down the bank, while the other warder came scrambling over the wall, twittering with excitement. Then the three men gathered together and looked down at the little heap of clothes, from which the discoverer had already detached the jacket and was inspecting it.

"They're his duds all right," said he. "Of course, they couldn't be anybody else's. But here's his number. So that's that."

"Yes," agreed the other, "they're his clothes right enough. But the question is, Where's my nabs himself?"

They stepped over to the edge of the saltings and gazed at the line of footprints. By this time the rising tide had covered up the strip of smooth, unmarked sand and was already eating away the footprints, which now led directly to the water's edge.

"Rum go," commented the constable, looking steadily over the waste of smooth water. "He isn't out there. If he was, you'd see him easily, even in this light. The water's as smooth as oil."

"Perhaps he's landed farther down," suggested the younger warder.

"What for?" demanded the constable.

"Might mean to cross the ditch and get away over the marshes."

The constable laughed scornfully. "What, in his birthday suit? I don't think. No, I reckon he had his reasons for taking to the water, and those reasons would probably be a barge sailing fairly close inshore. They'd have to take him on board, you know; and from my experience of bargees, I should say they'd probably give him a suit of togs and keep their mouths shut."

The elder warder looked meditatively across the water.

"Maybe you are right," said he, "but barges don't usually come in here very close. The fairway is right out the other side. And, for my part, I should be mighty sorry to start on a swim out to a sailing vessel."

"You might think differently if you'd just hopped out of the jug," the constable remarked as he lit a cigarette.

"Yes, I suppose I should be ready to take a bit of a risk. Well," he concluded, "if that was his lay, I hope he got picked up. I shouldn't like to think of the poor beggar drifting about the bottom of the river. He was a decent, civil little chap."

There was silence for a minute or two as the three men smoked reflectively. Then the constable proposed, as a matter of form, to cycle along the wall and make sure that the fugitive was not lurking farther down. But before he had time to start, a figure appeared in the distance, apparently mounted on a bicycle and advancing rapidly towards them. In a few minutes he arrived and dismounted on the path above them, glancing down curiously at the jacket which the warder still held.

"Those his togs?" he asked.

"Yes," replied the constable. "I suppose you haven't seen a gent bathing anywhere along here?"

The newcomer shook his head. "No," said he. "I have patrolled the whole wall from Clifton to here and I haven't seen a soul excepting old Barnett, the shepherd."

The elder warder gathered up the rest of the clothes and handed them to his junior. "Well," he said, "we must take it that he's gone to sea. All that we can do is to get the Customs people to give us a passage on their launch to make the round of all the vessels anchored about here. And if we don't find him on any of them, we shall have to hand the case over to the police."

The three men climbed to the top of the wall and turned their faces towards the town; and the Clifton patrol, having turned his bicycle about, mounted expertly and pedalled away at a smart pace to get back to his station before the twilight merged into night.

At that very moment, the fugitive was stepping over a stile that gave access from the marshes to a narrow, tree-shaded lane. Here he paused for a few moments to fling away the bundle of driftwood into the hedge and refill and light his pipe. Then, with a springy step, he strode away into the gathering moonlit dusk.

I

MR. POTTERMACK MAKES A DISCOVERY

A CONSCIENTIOUS DESIRE ON THE PART OF THE PRESENT HIS-
torian to tell his story in a complete and workmanlike fashion
from the very beginning raises the inevitable question, What was
the beginning? Not always an easy question to answer offhand; for
if we reflect upon certain episodes in our lives and try to track them
to their beginnings, we are apt, on further cogitation, to discover
behind those beginnings antecedents yet more remote which have
played an indispensable part in the evolution of events.

As to this present history, the whole train of cause and consequence might fairly be supposed to have been started by Mr.
Pottermack's singular discovery in his garden. Yet, when we consider
the matter more closely, we may doubt if that discovery would
ever have been made if it had not been for the sun-dial. Certainly it
would not have been made at that critical point in Mr. Pottermack's
life; and if it had not—but we will not waste our energies on vain
speculations. We will take the safe and simple course. We will begin
with the sun-dial.

It stood, when Mr. Pottermack's eyes first beheld it, in a mason's
yard at the outskirts of the town. It was obviously of some age, and
therefore could not have been the production of Mr. Gallett, the
owner of the yard; and standing amidst the almost garishly new
monuments and blocks of freshly hewn stone, it had in its aspect
something rather downfallen and forlorn. Now Mr. Pottermack had

often had secret hankerings for a sun-dial. His big walled garden seemed to cry out for some central feature of interest; and what more charming ornament could there be than a dial which, like the flowers and trees amidst which it would stand, lived and had its being solely by virtue of the golden sunshine?

Mr. Pottermack halted at the wide-open gate and looked at the dial (I use the word, for convenience, to include the stone support). It was a graceful structure, with a twisted shaft like that of a Norman column, a broad base and a square capital. It was nicely lichened and weathered, and yet in quite good condition. Mr. Pottermack found something very prepossessing in its comely antiquity. It had a motto, too, incised on the sides of the capital; and when he had strolled into the yard, and, circumnavigating the sun-dial, had read it, he was more than ever pleased. He liked the motto. It struck a sympathetic chord. *Sole orto: spes: decedente pax.* It might have been his own personal motto. At the rising of the sun, hope: at the going down thereof, peace. On his life the sun had risen in hope: and peace at eventide was his chief desire. And the motto was discreetly reticent about the intervening period. So, too, were there passages in the past which he was very willing to forget so that the hope of the morning might be crowned by peace when the shadows of life were lengthening.

"Having a look at the old dial, Mr. Pottermack?" said the mason, crossing the yard and disposing himself for conversation. "Nice bit of carving, that, and wonderful well preserved. He's counted out a good many hours in his time, he has. Seventeen thirty-four. And ready to count out as many again. No wheels to go rusty. All done with a shadder. No wear and tear about a shadder. And never runs down and never wants winding up. There's points about a sun-dial."

"Where did it come from?"

"I took it from the garden of Apsley Manor House, what's being rebuilt and brought up to date. New owner told me to take it away.

Hadn't any use for sun-dials in these days, he said. More hasn't any-body else. So I've got him on my hands. Wouldn't like him for your garden, I suppose? He's going cheap."

It appeared, on enquiry, that he was going ridiculously cheap. So cheap that Mr. Pottermack closed with the offer there and then.

"You will bring it along and fix it for me?" said he.

"I will, sir. Don't want much fixing. If you will settle where he is to stand, I'll bring him and set him up. But you'd better prepare the site. Dig well down into the subsoil and make a level surface. Then I can put a brick foundation and there will be no fear of his settling out of the upright."

That was how it began. And on the knife-edge of such trivial chances is human destiny balanced. From the mason's yard Mr. Pottermack sped homeward with springy step, visualizing the ground-plan of his garden as he went; and by the time that he let himself into his house by the front door within the rose-embowered porch he was ready to make a bee-line for the site of his proposed excavation.

He did not, however; for, as he opened the door, he became aware of voices in the adjacent room and his housekeeper came forth to inform him that Mrs. Bellard had called to see him, and was waiting within. Apparently the announcement was not unwelcome, for Mr. Pottermack's cheerfulness was in nowise clouded thereby. We might even go so far as to say that his countenance brightened.

Mrs. Bellard was obviously a widow. That is not to say that she was arrayed in the hideous "weeds" with which, a generation ago, women used to make their persons revolting and insult the memory of the deceased. But she was obviously a widow. More obviously than is usual in these latter days. Nevertheless her sombre raiment was well-considered, tasteful and becoming; indeed the severity of her dress seemed rather to enhance her quiet, dignified comeliness.

She greeted Mr. Pottermack with a frank smile, and as they shook hands she said in a singularly pleasant, musical voice:

"It is too bad of me to come worrying you like this. But you said I was to."

"Of course I did," was the hearty response; and as the lady produced from her basket a small tin box, he enquired: "Snails?"

"Snails," she replied; and they both laughed.

"I know," she continued, "it is very silly of me. I quite believe that, as you say, they die instantaneously when you drop them into boiling water. But I really can't bring myself to do it."

"Very natural, too," said Pottermack. "Why should you, when you have a fellow conchologist to do it for you? I will slaughter them this evening and extract them from their shells, and you shall have their empty residences to-morrow. Shall I leave them at your house?"

"You needn't trouble to do that. Give them to your housekeeper and I will call for them on my way home from the shops. But I really do impose on you most shamefully. You kill the poor little beasts, you clean out the shells, you find out their names and you leave me nothing to do but stick them on card, write their names under them, and put them in the cabinet. I feel a most horrid impostor when I show them at the Naturalists' Club as my own specimens."

"But, my dear Mrs. Bellard," protested Pottermack, "you are forgetting that you collect them, that you discover them in their secret haunts and drag them out to the light of day. That is the really scientific part of conchology. The preparation of the shells and their identification are mere journeyman's work. The real naturalist's job is the field work; and you are a positive genius in finding these minute shells—the pupas and cochlicopas and such like."

The lady rewarded him with a grateful and gratified smile, and, opening the little box, exhibited her "catch" and recounted some of the thrilling incidents of the chase, to which Pottermack listened with eager interest. And as they chatted, but half seriously, an observer would have noted that they were obviously the best of friends, and might have suspected that the natural history researches were, perhaps, somewhat in the nature of a plausible and convenient pretext for their enjoying a good deal of each other's society. These little precautions are sometimes necessary in a country district where people take an exaggerated interest in one another and tongues are apt to wag rather freely.

But a close observer would have noted certain other facts. For instance, these two persons were curiously alike in one respect: they both looked older to the casual stranger than they appeared on closer inspection. At a first glance, Mr. Pottermack, spectacled, bearded, and grave, seemed not far short of fifty. But a more critical examination showed that first impression to be erroneous. The quick, easy movements and the supple strength that they implied in the rather small figure, as well as the brightness of the alert, attentive eyes behind the spectacles, suggested that the lines upon the face and the white powdering of the hair owed their existence to something other than the mere effluxion of time. So, too, with Mrs. Bellard. On a chance meeting she would have passed for a well-preserved middle-aged woman. But now, as she chatted smilingly with her friend, the years dropped from her until, despite the white hairs that gleamed among the brown and a faint hint of crow's-feet, she seemed almost girlish.

But there was something else; something really rather odd. Each of the two cronies seemed to have a way of furtively examining the other. There was nothing unfriendly or suspicious in these regards. Quite the contrary, indeed. But they conveyed a queer impression of curiosity and doubt, differently manifested, however, in each. In Mr. Pottermack's expression there was something expectant. He had the air of waiting for some anticipated word or action; but the expression

vanished instantly when his companion looked in his direction. The
widow's manner was different, but it had the same curious furtive
quality. When Pottermack's attention was occupied, she would cast
a steady glance at him; and then the lines would come back upon her
forehead, her lips would set, and there would steal across her face
a look at once sad, anxious, and puzzled. Especially puzzled. And if
the direction of her glance had been followed, it would have been
traced more particularly to his profile and his right ear. It is true that
both these features were a little unusual. The profile was almost the
conventional profile of the Greek sculptors—the nose continuing
the line of the forehead with no appreciable notch—a character
very seldom seen in real persons. As to the ear, it was a perfectly
well-shaped, proportionate ear. It would have been of no interest
to Lombroso. But it had one remarkable peculiarity: on its lobule
was what doctors call a "diffuse nævus" and common folk describe
as a "port-wine mark." It was quite small, but very distinct; as if the
lobule had been dipped into damson juice. Still, it hardly seemed to
justify such anxious and puzzled consideration.

"What a dreadful pair of gossips we are!" Mrs. Bellard exclaimed,
taking her basket up from the table. "I've been here half an hour by
the clock, and I know I have been hindering you from some important
work. You looked full of business as you came up the garden path."

"I have been full of business ever since—land and fresh-water
mollusca. We have had a most instructive talk."

"So we have," she agreed, with a smile. "We are always instructive; especially you. But I must really take myself off now and leave
you to your other business."

Mr. Pottermack held the door open for her and followed her down
the hall to the garden path, delaying her for a few moments to fill
her basket with roses from the porch. When he had let her out at
the gate, he lingered to watch her as she walked away towards the

village; noting how the dignified, matronly bearing seemed to contrast with the springy tread and youthful lissomness of movement.

As he turned away to re-enter the house he saw the postman approaching; but as he was not expecting any letters, and his mind was still occupied with his late visitor, he did not wait. Nor when, a minute later, he heard the characteristic knock did he return to inspect the letter-box; which was, perhaps, just as well in the circumstances. Instead, he made his way out by the back door into the large kitchen garden and orchard and followed the long, central path which brought him at length to a high red brick wall, in which was a door furnished with a knocker and flanked by an electric bell. This he opened with a latchkey of the Yale pattern, and, having passed through, carefully shut it behind him.

He was now in what had probably been originally the orchard and kitchen garden of the old house in which he lived, but which had since been converted into a flower garden, though many of the old fruit trees still remained. It was a large oblong space, more than a quarter of an acre in extent, and enclosed on all sides by a massive old wall nearly seven feet high, in which were only two openings: the door by which he had just entered and another door at one side, also fitted with a Yale lock and guarded, in addition, by two bolts.

It was a pleasant place if quiet and seclusion were the chief desire of the occupant—as they apparently were, to judge by Mr. Pottermack's arrangements. The central space was occupied by a large, smooth grass plot, surrounded by well-made paths, between which and the wall were wide flower borders. In one corner was a brick-built summer-house; quite a commodious affair, with a good tiled roof, a boarded floor, and space enough inside for a couple of armchairs and a fair-sized table. Against the wall opposite to the summer-house was a long shed or outhouse with glass lights in the roof, evidently a recently built structure and just a little unsightly—but that would be remedied when the yew hedge that had been planted before it grew high enough to screen it from view. This was the workshop, or rather a range of workshops; for Mr. Pottermack was a man of many occupations, and, being also a tidy, methodical man, he liked to keep the premises appertaining to those occupations separate.

On the present occasion he made his way to the end compartment, in which were kept the gardening tools and appliances, and having provided himself with a spade, a mallet, a long length of cord, and a half-dozen pointed stakes, walked out to the grass plot and looked about him. He was quite clear in his mind as to where the sun-dial was to stand, but it was necessary to fix the spot with precision. Hence the stakes and the measuring-line, which came into use when he had paced out the distances approximately and enabled him, at length, to drive a stake into the ground and thereby mark the exact spot which would be occupied by the centre of the dial.

From this centre, with the aid of the cord, he drew a circle some four yards in diameter and began at once to take up the turf, rolling it up tidily and setting it apart ready for relaying. And now he came to the real job. He had to dig right down to the subsoil. Well, how far down was that? He took off his coat, and, grasping the spade with a resolute air, gave a vigorous drive into the soil at the edge of the circle. That carried him through the garden mould down into a fine, yellowish, sandy loam, a small quantity of which came up on the spade. He noted its appearance with some interest but went on digging, opening up a shallow trench round the circumference of the circle.

By the time that he had made a second complete circuit and carried his trench to a depth of some eight inches, the circle was surrounded by a ring of the yellow loam, surprisingly bulky in proportion to the shallow cavity from which it had been derived. And once more his attention was attracted by its appearance. For Mr. Pottermack amongst his various occupations included occasionally that of metal-casting. Hitherto he had been in the habit of buying his casting-sand by the bag. But this loam, judging by the sharp impressions of his feet where he had trodden in it, was a perfect casting-sand, and to be had for the taking at his very door. By way of testing its cohesiveness, he took up a large handful and squeezed it tightly. When he opened his hand the mass remained hard and firm and showed the impressions of his fingers perfectly to the very creases of the skin.

Very pleased with his discovery, and resolving to secure a supply of the loam for his workshop, he resumed his digging, and presently came down to a stratum where the loam was quite dense and solid and came up on the spade in definite coherent lumps like pieces of a soft rock. This, he decided, was the true subsoil and was as deep as he need go; and having decided this, he proceeded to dig out the rest of the circle to the same depth.

The work was hard and, after a time, extremely monotonous. Still Mr. Pottermack laboured steadily with no tendency to slacking. But the monotony exhausted his attention, and while he worked on mechanically with unabated vigour his thoughts wandered away from his task; now in the direction of the sun-dial, and now—at, perhaps, rather more length—in that of his pretty neighbour and her spoils, which were still awaiting his attentions in the tin box.

He was getting near the centre of the circle when his spade cut through and brought up a piece of spongy, fungus-eaten wood. He glanced at it absently, and having flung it outside the circle, entered his spade at the same spot and gave a vigorous drive. As the spade met with more than usual resistance, he threw a little extra weight on it. And then, suddenly, the resistance gave way; the spade drove through, apparently into vacant space. Mr. Pottermack uttered a

startled cry, and after an instant's precarious balancing saved himself
by a hair's breadth from going through after it.

For a moment he was quite shaken—and no wonder. He had
staggered back a pace or two and now stood, still grasping the spade,
and gazing with horror at the black, yawning hole that had so nearly
swallowed him up. But as, after all, it had not, he presently pulled
himself together and began cautiously to investigate. A very little
tentative probing with the spade made everything clear. The hole
which he had uncovered was the mouth of an old well: one of those
pernicious wells which have no protective coping but of which the
opening, flush with the surface of the ground, is ordinarily closed by
a hinged flap. The rotten timber that he had struck was part of this
flap, and he could now see the rusty remains of the hinges. When
the well had gone out of use, some one, with incredible folly, had
simply covered it up by heaping earth on the closed flap.

Mr. Pottermack, having made these observations, proceeded
methodically to clear away the soil until the entire mouth of the well
was exposed. Then, going down on hands and knees, he approached,
and cautiously advancing his head over the edge, peered down
into the dark cavity. It was not quite dark, however, for though the
slimy brick cylinder faded after a few feet into profound gloom, Mr.
Pottermack could see, far down, as it seemed in the very bowels of the
earth, a little circular spot of light on which was the dark silhouette
of a tiny head. He picked up a pebble, and, holding it at the centre
of the opening, let it drop. After a brief interval the bright spot grew
suddenly dim and the little head vanished; and after another brief
interval there came up to his ear a hollow "plop" followed by a faint,
sepulchral splash.

There was, then, water in the well; not that it mattered to him, as
he was going to cover it up again. But he was a man with a healthy
curiosity and he felt that he would like to know all about this well

before he once more consigned it to oblivion. Walking across to the workshop, he entered the metalwork section and cast his eye around for a suitable sinker. Presently, in the "oddments" drawer, he found a big iron clock-weight. It was heavier than was necessary, but he took it in default of anything more suitable, and going back to the well, he tied it to one end of the measuring-cord. The latter, being already marked in fathoms by means of a series of knots, required no further preparation. Lying full-length by the brink of the well, Mr. Pottermack dropped the weight over and let the cord slip through his hands, counting the knots as it ran out and moving it up and down as the weight neared the water.

The hollow splash for which he was listening came to his ear when the hand that grasped the cord was between the fourth and fifth knots. The depth, therefore, of the well to the surface of the water was about twenty-seven feet. He made a mental note of the number and then let the cord slip more rapidly through his hands. It was just after the seventh knot had passed that the tension of the cord suddenly relaxed, telling him that the weight now rested on the bottom. This gave a depth of sixteen feet of water and a total depth of about forty-three feet. And to think that, but for the merest chance, he would now have been down there where the clock-weight was resting!

With a slight shudder he rose, and, hauling up the cord, coiled it neatly and laid it down, with the weight still attached, a few feet away on the cleared ground. The question that he now had to settle was how far the existence of the well would interfere with the placing of the sun-dial. It did not seem to him that it interfered at all. On the contrary; the well had to be securely covered up in any case, and the sun-dial on top of the covering would make it safe for ever. For it happened that the position of the well coincided within a foot with the chosen site of the dial; which seemed quite an odd coincidence until one remembered that the position of both had probably been determined by identical sets of measurements, based on the ground-plan of the garden.

One thing, however, was obvious. Mr. Gallett would have to be informed of the discovery without delay, for something different from the proposed brickwork foundation would be required. Accordingly, Mr. Pottermack slipped on his coat, and, having sought out a hurdle and laid it over the well—for you can't be too careful in such a case—set off without delay for the mason's yard. As he opened the front door, he observed the letter still lying in the wire basket under the letter-slit. But he did not take it out. It could wait until he came back.

Mr. Gallett was deeply interested, but he was also a little regretful. The altered arrangements would cause delay and increase the cost of the job. He would want two biggish slabs of stone, which would take some time to prepare.

"But why cover the well at all?" said he. "A good well with sixteen feet of water in it is not to be sneezed at if you gets a hard frost and all the pipes is bunged up and busted."

But Mr. Pottermack shook his head. Like most town-bred men, he had rather a dislike to wells, and his own recent narrow escape had done nothing to diminish his prejudice. He would have no open well in his garden.

"The only question is," he concluded, "whether the sun-dial will be safe right over the well. Will a stone slab bear the weight?"

"Lor' bless you," replied Gallett, "a good thick slab of flagstone would bear St. Paul's Cathedral. And we are going to put two, one on top of the other to form a step; and the base of the dial itself a good two foot wide. It will be as strong as a house."

"And when do you think you'll be able to fix it?"

Mr. Gallett reflected. "Let's see. To-day's Toos-day. It will take a full day to get them two slabs sawn off the block and trimmed to shape. Shall we say Friday?"

"Friday will do perfectly. There is really no hurry, though I shall be glad to get the well covered and made safe. But don't put yourself out."

Mr. Gallett promised that he would not, and Pottermack then departed homeward to resume his labours.

As he re-entered his house, he picked the letter out of the letter-cage, and, holding it unopened in his hand, walked through to the garden. Emerging into the open air, he turned the letter over and glanced at the address; and in an instant a most remarkable change came over him. The quiet gaiety faded from his face and he stopped dead, gazing at the superscription with a frown of angry apprehension. Tearing open the envelope, he drew out the letter, unfolded it and glanced quickly through the contents. Apparently it was quite short, for, almost immediately, he refolded it, returned it to its envelope and slipped the latter into his pocket.

Passing through into the walled garden, he took off his coat, laid it down in the summer-house and fell to work on the excavation, extending the circle into a square and levelling the space around the well to make a bed for the stone slab. But all his enthusiasm had evaporated. He worked steadily and with care; but his usually cheerful face was gloomy and stern, and a certain faraway look in his eyes hinted that his thoughts were not on what he was doing but on something suggested by the ill-omened missive.

When the light failed, he replaced the hurdle, cleaned and put away the spade, and then went indoors with his coat on his arm to wash and take his solitary supper; of which he made short work, eating and drinking mechanically and gazing before him with gloomy preoccupation. Supper being finished and cleared away, he called for a kettle of boiling water and a basin, and, taking from a cupboard a handled needle, a pair of fine forceps, and a sheet of blotting-paper, laid them on the table with Mrs. Bellard's tin box. The latter he opened and very carefully transferred the imprisoned snails to the basin, which he then filled with boiling water; whereupon the unfortunate molluscs each emitted a stream of bubbles and shrank instantly into the recesses of its shell.

Having deposited the kettle in the fireplace, Mr. Pottermack drew a chair up to the table and seated himself with the basin before him and the blotting-paper at his right hand. But before beginning his work he drew forth the letter, straightened it out and, laying it on the table, read it through slowly. It bore no address and no signature; and though the envelope was addressed to Marcus Pottermack, Esq., it began, oddly enough, "Dear Jeff."

"I send you this little billy doo," it ran on, "with deep regret, which I know you will share. But it can't be helped. I had hoped that the last one would be, in fact, the last one, whereas it turns out to have been the last but one. This is positively my final effort, so keep up your pecker. And it is only a small affair this time. A hundred—in notes, of course. Fivers are safest. I shall call at the usual place on Wednesday at 8 p.m. ('In the gloaming, O! my darling!') This will give you time to hop up to town in the morning to collect the rhino. And mind *I've got to have it.* No need to dwell on unpleasant alternatives. Necessity knows no law. I am in a devil of a tight corner and you have got to help me out. So adieu until Wednesday evening."

Mr. Pottermack turned from the letter, and, taking up the mounted needle, with the other hand picked out of the basin a snail with a delicate yellow shell (*Helix hortensis,* var. *arenicola*) and, regarding it reflectively, proceeded with expert care to extract the shrivelled body of the mollusc. But though his attention seemed to be concentrated on his task, his thoughts were far away, and his eyes strayed now and again to the letter at his side.

"I am in a devil of a tight corner." Of course he was. The incurable plunger is always getting into tight corners. "And you have got to help me out." Exactly. In effect, the money that you have earned by unstinted labour and saved by self-denial has got to be handed to me that I may drop it into the bottomless pit that swallows up the gambler's losings. "This is positively my final effort." Yes. So was the last one, and the one before that; and so would be the next, and the one that would follow it, and so on without end. Mr. Pottermack saw it all clearly; realized, as so many other sufferers have realized, that there is about a blackmailer something hopelessly elusive. No transaction with him has any finality. He has something to sell, and he sells it; but behold! even as the money passes the thing sold is back in the hand of the vendor, to be sold again and yet again. No covenant with him is binding; no agreement can be enforced. There can be no question of cutting a loss, for, no matter how drastic the sacrifice, it is no sooner made than the *status quo ante* reappears.

On these truths Mr. Pottermack cogitated gloomily and asked himself, as such victims often do, whether it would not have been better in the first place to tell this ruffian to go to the devil and do his worst. Yet that had hardly seemed practicable. For the fellow would probably have done his worst; and his worst was so extremely bad. On the other hand, it was impossible that this state of affairs should be allowed to go on indefinitely. He was not by any means a rich man, though this parasite persisted in assuming that he was. At the present rate he would soon be sucked dry—reduced to stark poverty. And even then he would be no safer.

The intensity of his revolt against his intolerable position was emphasized by his very occupation. The woman for whom he was preparing these specimens was very dear to him. In any pictures that his fancy painted of the hoped-for future, hers was the principal figure. His fondest wish was to ask her to be his wife, and he felt a modest confidence that she would not say him nay. But how could he ask any woman to marry him while this vampire clung to his body?

Marriage was not for him—a slave to-day, a pauper to-morrow, at the best; and at the worst—

The evening had lapsed into night by the time that all the specimens had been cleaned and made presentable for the cabinet. It remained to write a little name-ticket for each with the aid, when necessary, of a handbook of the British Mollusca, and then to wrap each separate shell, with its ticket, in tissue paper and pack it tenderly in the small tin box. Thus was he occupied when his housekeeper, Mrs. Gadby, "reported off duty" and retired; and the clock in the hall was striking eleven when, having packed the last of the shells, he made the tin box into a neat little parcel with the consignee's name legibly written on the cover.

The house was profoundly quiet. Usually Mr. Pottermack was deeply appreciative of the restful silence that settles down upon the haunts of men when darkness has fallen upon field and hedgerow and the village has gone to sleep. Very pleasant it was then to reach down from the bookshelves some trusty companion and draw the big easy-chair up to the fireplace, even though, as to-night, the night was warm and the grate empty. The force of habit did, indeed, even now, lead him to the bookshelves. But no book was taken down. He had no inclination for reading to-night. Neither had he any inclination for sleep. Instead, he lit a pipe and walked softly up and down the room, stern and gloomy of face, yet with a look of concentration as if he were considering a difficult problem.

Up and down, up and down he paced, hardly making a sound. And as the time passed, the expression of his face underwent a subtle change. It lost none of its sternness, but yet it seemed to clear, as if a solution of the problem were coming into sight.

The striking of the clock in the hall, proclaiming the end of the day, brought him to a halt. He glanced at his watch, knocked out his empty pipe, lit a candle and blew out the lamp. As he turned to pass out to the stairs, something in his expression seemed to hint at a conclusion reached. All the anxiety and bewilderment had passed out of his face. Stern it was still; but there had come into it a certain resolute calm; the calm of a man who has made up his mind.

II

THE SECRET VISITOR

THE FOLLOWING MORNING FOUND MR. POTTERMACK IN AN undeniably restless mood. For a time he could settle down to no occupation, but strayed about the house and garden with an air of such gravity and abstraction that Mrs. Gadby looked at him askance and inwardly wondered what had come over her usually buoyant and cheerful employer.

One thing, however, was clear. He was not going to "hop up to town." Of the previous expeditions of that kind he had a vivid and unpleasant recollection; the big "bearer" cheque sheepishly pushed across the counter, the cashier's astonished glance at it, the careful examination of books, and then the great bundle of five-pound notes, which he counted, at the cashier's request, with burning cheeks; and his ignominious departure with the notes buttoned into an inside pocket and an uncomfortable suspicion in his mind that the ostentatiously unobservant cashier had guessed at once the nature of the transaction. Well, that experience was not going to be repeated on this occasion. There was going to be a change of procedure.

As he could fix his attention on nothing more definite, he decided to devote the day to a thorough clear-up of his workshops: a useful and necessary work, which had the added advantage of refreshing his memory as to the abiding-places of rarely used appliances and materials. And an excellent distraction he found it; so much so that several times, in the interest of rediscovering some long-forgotten tool or stock of material, he was able to forget for a while the critical interview that loomed before him.

So the day passed. The mid-day meal was consumed mechanically—under the furtive and disapproving observation of Mrs. Gadby—and dispatched with indecent haste. He was conscious of an inclination to lurk about the house on the chance of a brief gossip with his fair friend; but he resisted it, and, when he came in to tea, the housekeeper reported that the little package had been duly collected.

He lingered over his tea as if he were purposely consuming time, and when at last he rose from the table, he informed Mrs. Gadby that he had some important work to do and was under no circumstances to be disturbed. Then once more he retired to the walled garden, and having shut himself in, dropped the key into his pocket. He did not, however, resume his labours in the workshop. He merely called in there for an eight-inch steel bolt and a small electric lamp, both of which he bestowed in his pockets. Then he came out and walked slowly up and down the grass plot with his hands behind him and his chin on his breast as if immersed in thought, but glancing from time to time at his watch. At a quarter to eight he took off his spectacles and put them in his pocket, stepped across to the well, and picking up the hurdle that still lay over the dark cavity, carried it away and stood it against the wall. Then he softly unbolted the side gate, turned the handle of the latch, drew the gate open a bare inch, and, leaving it thus ajar, walked to the summer-house, and, entering it, sat down in one of the chairs.

His visitor, if deficient in some of the virtues, had at least that of punctuality; for the clock of the village church had barely finished striking the hour when the gate opened noiselessly and the watcher in the summer-house saw, through the gathering gloom, a large, portly man enter with stealthy step, close the gate silently behind him and softly shoot the upper bolt.

Pottermack rose as his visitor approached, and the two men met just outside the summer-house. There was a striking contrast between them in every respect, in build, in countenance, and in manner. The newcomer was a big, powerful man, heavy and dis-tinctly over-fat, whose sly, shifty face—at present exhibiting an uneasy smile—showed evident traces of what is commonly miscalled "good living," especially as to the liquid element thereof; whereas his host, smallish, light, spare, with clean-cut features expressive of lively intelligence, preserved a stony calm as he looked steadily into his visitor's evasive eyes.

"Well, Jeff," the latter began in a deprecating tone, "you don't seem overjoyed to see me. Not an effusive welcome. Aren't you going to shake hands with an old pal?"

"It doesn't seem necessary," Pottermack replied coldly.

"Oh, very well," the other retorted. "Perhaps you'd like to kiss me instead." He sniggered foolishly, and, entering the summer-house, dropped into one of the armchairs and continued: "What about a mild refresher while we discuss our little business? Looks like being a dry job, to judge by your mug."

Without replying, Pottermack opened a small cupboard, and taking out a decanter, a siphon, and a tumbler, placed them on the table by his guest. It was not difficult to see that the latter had already fortified himself with one or two refreshers, mild or otherwise, but that was not Pottermack's affair. He was going to keep his own brain clear. The other might do as he pleased.

"Not going to join me, Jeff?" the visitor protested. "Oh, buck up, old chap! It's no use getting peevish about parting with a few pounds. You won't miss a little donation to help a pal out of a difficulty."

As Pottermack made no reply but sat down and gazed stonily before him, the other poured out half a tumblerful of whisky, filled up with soda, and took a substantial gulp. Then he, too, sat silent for a time, gazing out into the darkening garden. And gradually the smile faded from his face, leaving it sullen and a little anxious.

"So you've been digging up your lawn," he remarked presently. "What's the game? Going to set up a flagstaff?"

"No. I am going to have a sun-dial there."

"A sun-dial, hey? Going to get your time on the cheap? Good. I like sun-dials. Do their job without ticking. Suppose you'll have a motto on it. *Tempus fugit* is the usual thing. Always appropriate, but especially so in the case of a man who has 'done time' and fugitted. It will help to remind you of olden days, 'the days that are no more.'" He finished with a mirthless cackle and cast a malignant glance at the silent and wooden-faced Pottermack. There was another interval of strained, uncomfortable silence, during which the visitor took periodic gulps from his tumbler and eyed his companion with sullen perplexity. At length, having finished his liquor, he set down the empty tumbler and turned towards Pottermack.

"You got my letter, I suppose, as you left the gate ajar?"

"Yes," was the laconic reply.

"Been up to town to-day?"

"No."

"Well, I suppose you have got the money?"

"No, I have not."

The big man sat up stiffly and stared at his companion in dismay.

"But, damn it, man!" he exclaimed, "didn't I tell you it was urgent? I'm in a devil of a fix. I've got to pay that hundred to-morrow. Must pay it, you understand. I'm going up to town in the morning to pay. As I hadn't got the money myself, I've had to borrow it from—you know where; and I was looking to you to enable me to put it back at once. I must have that money to-morrow at the latest. You'd better run up to town in the morning and I'll meet you outside your bank."

Pottermack shook his head. "It can't be done, Lewson. You'll have to make some other arrangements."

Lewson stared at him in mingled amazement and fury. For a moment he was too astonished for speech. At length he burst out:

"Can't be done! What the devil do you mean? You've got the money in your bank and you are going to hand it over, or I'll know the reason why. What do you imagine you are going to do?"

"I am going," said Pottermack, "to hold you to your agreement, or at least to part of it. You demanded a sum of money—a large sum—as the price of your silence. It was to be a single payment, once for all, and I paid it. You promised solemnly to make no further demands; yet, within a couple of months, you did make further demands, and I paid again. Since then you have made demands at intervals, regardless of your solemn undertaking. Now this has got to stop. There must be an end to it, and this has got to be the end."

As he spoke, quietly but firmly, Lewson gazed at him as if he could not trust the evidence of his senses. This was quite a new Pottermack. At length, suppressing his anger, he replied in a conciliatory tone:

"Very well, Jeff. It shall be the end. Help me out just this time and you shall hear no more from me. I promise you that on my word of honour."

At this last word Pottermack smiled grimly. But he answered in the same quiet, resolute manner:

"It is no use, Lewson. You said that last time and the time before that, and, in fact, time after time. You have always sworn that each demand should be positively the last. And so you will go on, if I let you, until you have squeezed me dry."

On this Lewson threw off all disguise. Thrusting out his chin at Pottermack, he exclaimed furiously: "If you let me! And how do you think you are going to prevent me? You are quite right. I've got you, and I'm going to squeeze you, so now you know. And look here, young fellow, if that money isn't handed out to me to-morrow morning, something is going to happen. A very surprised gentleman at Scotland Yard will get a letter informing him that the late Jeffrey Brandon, run-away convict, is not the late J. B. but is alive and kicking, and that his present name and address is Marcus Pottermack, Esquire, of 'The Chestnuts,' Borley, Bucks. How will that suit you?"

"It wouldn't suit me at all," Mr. Pottermack replied, with unruffled calm; "but before you do it, let me remind you of one or two facts. First, the run-away convict, once your closest friend, was to your knowledge an innocent man—"

"That's no affair of mine," Lewson interrupted. "He was a convict, and is one still. Besides, how do I know he was innocent? A jury of his fellow-countrymen found him guilty—"

"Don't talk rubbish, Lewson," Pottermack broke in impatiently. "There is no one here but ourselves. We both know that I didn't do those forgeries and we both know who did."

Lewson grinned as he reached out for the decanter and poured out another half-tumblerful of whisky. "If you knew who did it," he chuckled, "you must have been a blooming mug not to say."

"I didn't know then," Pottermack rejoined bitterly. "I thought you were a decent, honest fellow, fool that I was."

"Yes," Lewson agreed, with a low, cackling laugh, "you were a blooming mug and that's a fact. Well, well; we live and learn."

Still sniggering foolishly, he took a long pull at the tumbler, leering into the flushed, angry face that confronted him across the table. Suddenly Pottermack rose from his chair, and, striding out into the garden, halted some dozen paces away and stood with his back to the summer-house, looking steadily across the lawn. It was now quite dark, though the moon showed dimly from time to time through a thinning of the overcast sky; but still, through the gloom, he could make out faintly the glimmer of lighter-coloured soil where it had been turned up to level the ground for the sun-dial. The well was invisible, but he knew exactly where the black cavity yawned, and his eye, locating the spot, rested on it with gloomy fixity.

His reverie was interrupted by Lewson's voice, now pitched in a more ingratiating key.

"Well, Jeff; thinking it over? That's right, old chap. No use getting pippy."

He paused, and as there was no reply he continued: "Come now, dear boy, let's settle the business amicably as old pals should. Pity for you to go back to the jug when there's no need. You just help me out of this hole, and I will give you my solemn word of honour that it shall be the very last time. Won't that satisfy you?"

Pottermack turned his head slightly, and speaking over his shoulder, replied: "Your word of honour! The honour of a blackmailer, a thief and a liar. It isn't exactly what you would call a gilt-edged security."

"Well," the other retorted thickly, "gilt-edged or not, you had better take it and shell out. Now, what do you say?"

"I say," Pottermack replied with quiet decision, "that I am not going to give you another farthing on any condition whatever."

For several seconds Lewson gazed in silent dismay at the shadowy figure on the lawn. This final, definite refusal was a contingency that he had never dreamed of, and was utterly unprovided for, and it filled him, for the moment, with consternation. Then, suddenly, his dismay changed to fury. Starting up from his chair, he shouted huskily:

"Oh, you won't, won't you? We'll see about that! You'll either pay up or I'll give you the finest hammering that you've ever had in your life. When I've done with you, they'll want your finger-prints to find out who you are."

He paused to watch the effect of this terrifying proposal and to listen for a reply. Then, as the dim figure remained unmoved and no

answer came, he bellowed: "D'you hear? Are you going to pay up
or take a hammering?"

Pottermack turned his head slightly and replied in a quiet, almost
a gentle tone: "I don't think I'm going to do either."

The reply and the quiet, unalarmed tone were not quite what
Lewson had expected. Trusting to the moral effect of his greatly
superior size and weight, he had bluffed confidently. Now it seemed
that he had got to make good his threat, and the truth is that he
was not eager for the fray. However, it had to be done, and done as
impressively as possible. After pausing for another couple of seconds,
he proceeded, with a formidable air (but unobserved by Pottermack,
whose back was still turned to him), to take off his coat and fling it
on the table, whence it slipped down on to the floor. Then, stepping
outside the summer-house, he bent forward, and, with an intimidat-
ing roar, charged like an angry rhinoceros.

At the sound of his stamping feet Pottermack spun round and
faced him, but then stood motionless until his assailant was within a
yard of him, when he sprang lightly aside, and as the big, unwieldy
bully lumbered past him, he followed him closely. As soon as Lewson
could overcome the momentum of his charge, he halted and turned;
and instantly a smart left-hander alighted on his cheek and a heavy
right-hander impinged on his ribs just below the armpit. Furious
with the pain, and utterly taken aback, he cursed and grunted, hit-
ting out wildly with all the viciousness of mingled rage and fear; for
now he realized with amazement that he was hopelessly outclassed
by his intended victim. Not one of his sledge-hammer blows took
effect on that agile adversary, whereas his own person seemed to be
but an unprotected target on which the stinging blows fell in endless
and intolerable succession. Slowly at first, and then more quickly, he
backed away from that terrific bombardment, followed inexorably by
the calm and scientific Pottermack, who seemed to guide and direct

his backward course as a skilful drover directs the movements of a refractory bullock.

Gradually the pair moved away from the vicinity of the summer-house across the dark lawn, the demoralized bully, breathing hard and sweating profusely, reduced to mere defence and evasion while his light-footed antagonist plied him unceasingly with feint or blow. Presently Lewson stumbled backward as his foot sank into the loose, heaped earth at the margin of the cleared space; but Pottermack did not press his advantage, renewing his attack only when Lewson had recovered his balance. Then the movement began again, growing faster as the big man became more and more terrified and his evasion passed into undissembled retreat; deviously and with many a zig-zag but always tending towards the centre of the cleared area. Suddenly Pottermack's tactics changed. The rapid succession of light blows ceased for an instant and he seemed to gather himself up as if for a decisive effort. There was a quick feint with the left; then his right fist shot out like lightning and drove straight on to the point of the other man's jaw, and as his teeth clicked together with an audible snap, Lewson dropped like a pole-axed ox, falling with his body from the waist upwards across the mouth of the well and his head on the brick edge, on which it struck with a sickening thud.

So he lay for a second or two until the limp trunk began to sag and the chin came forward on to the breast. Suddenly the head slipped off the brick edge and dropped into the cavity, shedding its cap and carrying the trunk with it. The heavy jerk started the rest of the body sliding forward, slowly at first, then with increasing swiftness until the feet rose for an instant, kicked at the farther edge and were gone. From the black pit issued vague, echoing murmurs, followed presently by a hollow, reverberating splash; and after that, silence.

It had been but a matter of seconds. Even as those cavernous echoes were muttering in the unseen depths, Pottermack's knuckles were still tingling from the final blow. From the moment when that blow had been struck he had made no move. He had seen his enemy fall, had heard the impact of the head on the brick edge, and had stood looking down with grim composure on the body as it sagged, slid forward, and at last made its dreadful dive down into the depths of its sepulchre. But he had moved not a muscle. It was a horrible affair. But it had to be. Not he, but Lewson had made the decision.

As the last reverberations died away he approached the forbidding circle of blackness, and kneeling down at its edge, peered into the void. Of course, he could see nothing; and when he listened intently, not a sound came to his ear. From his pocket he brought out his little electric lamp and threw a beam of light down into the dark cavity. The effect was very strange and uncanny. He found himself looking down a tube of seemingly interminable length while from somewhere far away, down in the very bowels of the earth, a tiny spark of light glowed steadily. So even the last ripples had died away and all was still down in that underworld.

He replaced the lamp in his pocket, but nevertheless he remained kneeling by the well-mouth, resting on one hand, gazing down into the black void and unconsciously listening for some sound from below. Despite his outward composure, he was severely shaken. His heart still raced, his forehead was damp with sweat, his body and limbs were pervaded by a fine, nervous tremor.

Yet he was sensible of a feeling of relief. The dreadful thing that he had nerved himself to do, that he had looked forward to with shuddering horror, was done. And the doing of it might have been so much worse. He was relieved to feel the screw-bolt in his pocket—unused; to think that the body had slipped down into its grave without the need of any hideous dragging or thrusting. Almost, he began to persuade himself that it had been more or less of an accident. At any rate, it was over and done with. His merciless enemy was gone. The menace to his liberty, the constant fear that had haunted him were no more. At last—at long last—he was free.

Fear of discovery he had none; for Lewson, in his own interests, had insisted on strict secrecy as to their acquaintance with each other. In his own words, "he preferred to sit on his own nest-egg." Hence to all the world they were strangers, not necessarily even aware of each other's existence. And the blackmailer's stealthy arrival and his care in silently shutting the gate gave a guarantee that no one had seen him enter.

While these thoughts passed somewhat confusedly through his mind, he remained in the same posture; still unconsciously listening and still gazing, as if with a certain expectancy, into the black hole before him, or letting his eyes travel, now and again, round the dark garden. Presently an opening in the dense pall of cloud that obscured the sky uncovered the moon and flooded the garden with light. The transition from darkness to brilliant light—for it was full moon—was so sudden that Pottermack looked up with a nervous start, as though to see who had thrown the light on him; and in his overwrought state he even found something disquieting in the pale, bright disc with its queer, dim, impassive face that seemed to be looking down on him through the rent in the cloud like some secret watcher peeping from behind a curtain. He rose to his feet, and, drawing a deep breath, looked around him; and then his glance fell on something more real and more justly disquieting. From the edge of the grass to the brink of the well was a double track of footprints, meandering to and fro, zig-zagging hither and thither, but undeniably ending at the well.

Their appearance was sinister in the extreme. In the bright moonlight they stared up from the pale buff soil, and they shouted of tragedy. To the police eye they would have been the typical "signs of a struggle"; the tracks of two men facing one another and moving towards the well with, presently, a single track coming away from it. No one could mistake the meaning of those tracks; nothing could explain them away—especially in view of what was at the bottom of the well.

The first glance at those tracks gave Pottermack a severe shock. But he recovered from it in a moment. For they were mere transitory marks that could be obliterated in a minute or two by a few strokes of a rake and a few sweeps of a besom; and meanwhile he stooped over them, examining them with a curious interest not unmixed with a certain vague uneasiness. They were very remarkable impressions. He had already noted the peculiar quality of this loamy soil; its extraordinary suitability for making casting-moulds. And here was a most striking illustration of this property. The prints of his own feet were so perfect that the very brads in his soles were quite clear and distinct, while as to Lewson's, they were positively ridiculous. Every detail of the rubber soles and the circular rubber heels came out as sharply as if the impressions had been taken in moulding-wax. There was the prancing horse of Kent—the soles were of the Invicta brand and practically new—with the appropriate legend and the manufacturers' name, and in the central star-shaped space of the heels was the perfect impression of the screw. No doubt the singular sharpness of the prints was due to the fact that a heavy shower in the previous night had brought the loam to that particular state of dampness that the professional moulder seeks to produce with his watering-pot.

However, interesting as the prints were to the mechanic's eye, the sooner they were got rid of the better. Thus reflecting, Pottermack strode away towards the workshop in quest of a rake and a besom; and he was, in fact, reaching out to grasp the handle of the door when he stopped dead and stood for some seconds rigid and still with outstretched arm and dropped jaw. For in that moment a thought which had, no doubt, been stirring in his subconscious mind had come to the surface, and for the first time the chill of real terror came over him. Suddenly he realized that he had no monopoly of this remarkable loam. It was the soil of the neighbourhood—and incidentally of the little lane that led from the town and passed along beside his wall. In that lane there must be a single track of footprints—big, staring footprints, and every one of them as good as a signature of James Lewson—leading from the town and stopping at his gate!

After a few moments of horror-stricken reflection he darted into the tool-house and brought out a short ladder. His first impulse had been to open the gate and peer out, but an instant's reflection had shown him the folly of exposing himself to the risk of being seen— especially at the very gate to which the tracks led. He now carried the ladder across to an old pear tree which thrust its branches over the wall, and, planting it silently where the foliage was densest, crept softly up and listened awhile. As no sound of footsteps was audible, and as the moon had for the moment retired behind the bank of cloud, he cautiously advanced his head over the wall and looked down into the lane. It was too dark to see far in either direction, but apparently there was no one about; and as the country quiet was unbroken by any sound, he ventured to crane farther forward to inspect the path below.

The light was very dim; but even so he could make out faintly a single track of footprints—large footprints, widely spaced, the footprints of a tall man. But even as he was peering down at them through the darkness, trying to distinguish in the vaguely seen shapes some recognizable features, the moon burst forth again and the light became almost as that of broad day. Instantly the half-seen shapes started up with a horrid distinctness that made him catch his breath. There was the preposterous prancing horse with the legend "Invicta," there was the makers' name, actually legible from the height of the wall, and there were the circular heels with their raised central stars and the very screws clearly visible even to their slots!

Pottermack was profoundly alarmed. But he was not a panicky man. There, in those footprints, was evidence enough to hang him. But he was not hanged yet; and he did not mean to be, if the unpleasantness could be avoided. Perched on the ladder, with his eyes riveted on the tracks of the man who had come to "squeeze" him, he reviewed the situation with cool concentration, and considered the best way to deal with it.

The obvious thing was to go out and trample on those footprints until they were quite obliterated. But to this plan there were several objections. In the first place, those enormous impressions would take a deal of trampling out. Walking over them once would be quite useless, for his own feet were comparatively small, and even a fragment of one of Lewson's footprints would be easily recognizable. Moreover, the trampling process would involve the leaving of his own footprints in evidence; which might be disastrous if it should happen—as it easily might—that Lewson had been seen starting along the footpath. For this path, unfrequented as it was, turned off from the main road at the outskirts of the town where wayfarers were numerous enough. The reason that it was unfrequented was that it led only to a wood and a stretch of heath which were more easily approached by a by-road. Finally, he himself might quite possibly be seen performing the trampling operations, and that would never do. In short, the trampling scheme was not practicable at all.

But what alternative was there? Something must be done. Very soon the man would be missed and there would be a search for him; and as things stood there was a set of tracks ready to guide the searchers from the town to his—Pottermack's—very gate. And inside the gate was the open well. Clearly, something must be done, and done at once. But what?

As he asked himself this question again and again he was half-consciously noting the conditions. Hitherto, no one had seen Lewson's footprints at this part of the path. That was evident from the fact that there were no other fresh footprints—none that trod on Lewson's. Then, in half an hour at the most, the shadow of the wall would be thrown over the path and the tracks would then be quite inconspicuous. And, again, it was now past nine o'clock and his neighbours were early folk. It was extremely unlikely that any one would pass along that path until the morning. So there was still time. But time for what?

One excellent plan occurred to him, but, alas! he had not the means to carry it out. If only he had possession of Lewson's shoes he could put them on, slip out at the gate and continue the tracks to some distant spot well out of his neighbourhood. That would be a perfect solution of the problem. But Lewson's shoes had vanished for ever from human ken—at least, he hoped they had. So that plan was impracticable.

And yet, was it? As he put the question to himself his whole demeanour changed. He stood up on his perch with a new eagerness in his face; the eagerness of a man who has struck a brilliant idea. For that was what he had done. This excellent plan, which yielded the perfect solution, was practicable after all. Lewson's shoes were indeed beyond his reach. But he had a fine assortment of Lewson's footprints. Now footprints are made by the soles of shoes. That is the normal process. But by the exercise of a little ingenuity the process could be reversed; shoe-soles could be made from footprints.

He descended the ladder, thinking hard; and as the cloud once more closed over the moon, he fetched the hurdle and placed it carefully over the mouth of the well. Then he walked slowly towards the workshop—avoiding the now invaluable footprints—shaping his plan as he went.

III

THE EFFICIENT WORKMAN SAVES A VAST AMOUNT OF TIME BY so planning out his job in advance that intervals of waiting are eliminated. Now Mr. Pottermack was an eminently methodical man and he was very sensible that, in the existing circumstances, time was precious. Accordingly, although his plan was but roughly sketched out in his mind, he proceeded forthwith to execute that part of it which could be clearly visualized, filling in the further details mentally as he worked.

The first thing to be done was, obviously, to convert the perishable, ephemeral footprints, which a light shower would destroy, into solid, durable models. To this end, he fetched from the workshop the tin of fine plaster of Paris which he kept for making small or delicate moulds. By the aid of his little lamp he selected a specially deep and perfect impression of Lewson's right foot, and into this he lightly dusted the fine powder, continuing the process until the surface was covered with an even layer of about half an inch thick. This he pressed down very gently with the flat end of the lamp, and then went in search of a suitable impression of the left foot, which he treated in like manner. He next selected a second pair of prints, but instead of dusting the dry plaster into them he merely dropped into each a pinch to serve as a mark for identifying it. His reason for thus varying the method was that he was doubtful whether it was possible to pour liquid plaster into a loam mould (for that was what the footprint actually was) without disturbing the surface and injuring the pattern.

Returning to the workshop, he mixed a good-sized bowl of plaster, stirring and beating the creamy liquid with a large spoon. Still stirring, he carried it out, and, going first to the prints which contained the dry plaster, he carefully ladled into them with the spoon small quantities of the liquid plaster until they were well filled. By this time the liquid was growing appreciably thicker and more suitable for the unprotected prints, to which he accordingly hastened, and proceeded quickly, but with extreme care, to fill them until the now rapidly thickening plaster was well heaped up above the surface.

He had now at least a quarter of an hour to wait while the plaster was setting, but this he occupied in cleaning out the bowl and spoon ready for the next mixing, placing the brush and plaster tools in readiness and pouring out a saucerful of soap-size. When he had made these preparations, he filled a small jug with water, and making his way to the first two impressions, poured the water on to them to make up for that which would have been absorbed by the dry plaster underneath. In the second pair of impressions, which he ventured to test by a light touch of the finger, the plaster was already quite solid, and he was strongly tempted to raise them and see what luck he had had; but he resisted the temptation and went back to the workshop, leaving them to harden completely.

All this time, although he had given the closest attention to what he was doing, his mind had been working actively, and already the sketch-plan was beginning to shape into a complete and detailed scheme; for he had suddenly remembered a supply of sheet gutta-percha which he had unearthed when he turned out the workshop, and this discovery disposed of what had been his chief difficulty. Now, in readiness for a later stage of his work, he lighted his Primus stove, and having filled a good-sized saucepan with water, placed it on the

stove to heat. This consumed the rest of the time that he had allot-
ted for the hardening of the plaster, and he now went forth with no
little anxiety to see what the casts were like. For they were the really
essential element of his plan on which success or failure depended.
If he could get a perfect reproduction of the footprints, the rest of
his task, troublesome as it promised to be, would be plain sailing.

Very gingerly he insinuated his finger under one of the casts of
the second pair and gently turned it over. And then, as he threw the
light of his lamp on it, all his misgivings vanished in respect of that
foot—the right. The aspect of the cast was positively ridiculous. It
was just the sole of a shoe; snow-white, but otherwise completely
realistic, and perfect in every detail and marking, even to the makers'
name. And the second cast was equally good; so his special precautions had been unnecessary. Nevertheless, he went on to the first
pair, and they proved to be, if anything, sharper and cleaner, more
free from adherent particles of earth than the others. With a sigh
of relief he picked up the four casts and bore them tenderly to the
workshop, where he deposited them on the bench. There, under the
bright electric light, their appearance was even more striking. But
he did not stop to gloat. He could do that while he was working.

The first proceeding was to trim off the ragged edges with a
scraper, and then came the process of "sizing"—painting with a
boiled solution of soft soap—which also cleaned away the adherent
particles of loam. When the soap had soaked in and "stopped" the
surface, the surplus was washed away under the tap, and then, with
a soft brush, an infinitesimal coating of olive oil was applied. The
casts were now ready for the next stage—the making of the moulds.
First, Pottermack filled a shallow tray with loam from the garden,
striking the surface level with a straight-edge. On this surface the
two best casts were laid, sole upwards, and pressed down until they
were slightly embedded. Then came the mixing of another bowl of

plaster, and this was "gauged" extra stiff in order that it should set quickly and set hard. By the time this had been poured on—rapidly, but with infinite care to avoid bubbles, which would have marred the perfection of the moulds—the water in the saucepan was boiling. Having cleaned out the bowl and spoon, Pottermack fetched the pieces of gutta-percha from their drawer and dropped them into the saucepan, replacing the lid. Then he put on his spectacles, extinguished the lamp, switched off the light, and, passing out of the workshop, walked quickly towards the house.

As he let himself out of the walled garden and closed the door behind him, he had a strange feeling as of one awakening from a dream. The familiar orchard and kitchen garden through which he was now passing, and the lighted windows of the house which twinkled through the trees, brought him back to the realities of his quiet, usually uneventful life and made the tragic interlude of the past hour seem incredible and unreal. He pondered on it with a sort of dull surprise as he walked up the long path; on all that had happened since he had last walked along it a few hours ago. How changed since then was his world—and himself! Then, he was an innocent man over whom yet hung the menace of the convict prison. Now, that menace was lifted, but he was an innocent man no more. Legally—technically, he put it to himself—he was a murderer; and the menace of the prison was exchanged for that of the rope. But there was this difference: the one had been an abiding menace that had been with him for the term of his life; the other was a temporary peril from which, when he had once freed himself, he would be free for ever.

His appearance in the house was hailed by Mrs. Gadby with a sigh of relief. It seemed that she had made a special effort in the matter of supper and had feared lest her trouble should be wasted after all. Very complacently she inducted him into the dining-room and awaited, with confidence born of much experience, his appreciative comments.

"Why, bless my soul, Mrs. Gadby!" he exclaimed, gazing at the display on the table, "it's a regular banquet! Roses, too! And do I see a bottle under that shawl?"

Mrs. Gadby smilingly raised the shawl, revealing a small wooden tub in which a bottle of white wine stood embedded in ice. "I thought," she explained, "that a glass of Chablis would go rather well with the lobster."

"Rather well!" exclaimed Pottermack. "I should think it will. But why these extraordinary festivities?"

"Well, sir," said Mrs. Gadby, "you haven't seemed to be quite yourself the last day or two. Not in your usual spirits. So I thought a nice little supper and a glass of wine might pick you up a bit."

"And so it will, I am sure," affirmed Pottermack. "To-morrow you will find me as lively as a cricket and as gay as a lark. And, by the way, Mrs. Gadby, don't clear the table to-night. I am going out sugaring presently, and as I may be late getting back I shall probably be ready for another little meal before turning in. And of course you won't bolt the door—but I expect you will have gone to bed before I start."

Mrs. Gadby acknowledged these instructions and retired in sedate triumph. Particularly gratified was she at the evident satisfaction with which her employer had regarded the Chablis. A happy thought of hers, that had been. In which she was right in general though mistaken in one particular. For it was not the wine that had brought that look of satisfaction to Pottermack's face. It was the ice. Mrs. Gadby's kindly forethought had disposed of the last of his difficulties.

Before sitting down to supper, he ran up to his bedroom, ostensibly for the necessary wash and brush up; but first he visited a spacious cupboard from the ground floor of which he presently took a pair of over-shoes that he was accustomed to wear in very rainy or snowy weather. Their upper parts were of strong waterproof cloth and their soles of balata, cemented on to leather inner soles. He had, in fact, cemented them on himself when the original soles had worn through, and he still had, in the workshop, a large tin nearly full of the cement. He now inspected the soles critically, and when, after having washed and made himself tidy, he went down to the dining-room, he carried the over-shoes down with him and slipped them out of sight under the table.

Although he was pretty sharp-set after his strenuous and laborious evening, he made but a hasty meal; for time was precious and he could dispose of the balance of the feast when he had finished his task. Rising from the table, he picked up the over-shoes, and, stealing softly out into the garden, laid them down beside the path. Then he stole back to the dining-room, whence he walked briskly to the kitchen and tapped at the door.

"Good-night, Mrs. Gadby," he called out cheerfully. "I shall be starting when I've got my traps together. Leave everything as it is in the dining-room so that I can have a snack when I come in. Good-night!"

"Good-night, sir," the housekeeper responded cordially, presenting a smiling countenance at the door, "and good luck with the moths, though I must admit, sir, that they don't seem to me worth all the trouble of catching them."

"Ah, Mrs. Gadby," said Pottermack, "but you see you are not a naturalist. You would think better of the moths, I expect, if they were good to eat." With this and a chuckle, in which the housekeeper joined, he turned away and went forth into the garden, where, having picked up the over-shoes, he made his way up the long path to the door of the walled garden. As he unlocked the door and let himself into the enclosure, he was again sensible of a change of atmosphere. The vision of that fatal combat rose before him with

horrid vividness and once more he felt the menace of the rope hanging over him. He went to the ladder and looked over the wall to see
if any new tracks had appeared on the path to tell of some wayfarer
who might hereafter become a witness. But the path was shrouded
in darkness so profound that he could not even see the tracks that
he knew were there; so he descended, and, crossing the lawn by the
well—where some unaccountable impulse led him to stop for a while
and listen—re-entered the workshop, switched on the light and laid
the over-shoes on the bench.

First, he assured himself by a touch that the saucepan was still
hot. Then he turned his attention to the moulds. They were as hard
as stone, and, as he had made them thick and solid, he ventured to
use some little force in trying to separate them from the casts; but
all his efforts failed. Then, since he could not prise them open with
a knife for fear of marking them, he filled a bucket with water and
in this immersed each of the moulds with its adherent cast, when,
after a few seconds' soaking, they came apart quite easily.

He stood for a few moments with the cast of the right foot in
one hand and its mould in the other, looking at them with a sort
of amused surprise. They were so absurdly realistic in spite of their
staring whiteness. The cast was simply a white shoe-sole; the mould
an exact reproduction of the original footprint; and both were pre-
posterously complete, not only in respect of the actual pattern and
lettering but even of the little trivial accidental characters such as
a clean cut—probably made by a sharp stone—across the neck of
the prancing horse and a tiny angular fragment of gravel which had
become embedded in the rubber heel. However, this was no time
for contemplation. The important fact was that both the moulds
appeared to be quite perfect. If the rest of the operations should
be as successful, he would be in a fair way of winning through this
present danger to find a permanent security.

He began with the right mould. Having first poured into it a little of the hot water from the saucepan, to take the chill off the surface, he laid it on a carefully folded towel, spread on the bench. Then with a pair of tongs he picked out of the saucepan one of the pieces of gutta-percha—now quite soft and plastic—and laid it in the mould, which it filled completely, with some overlap. As it was, at the moment, too hot to work comfortably with the fingers, he pressed it into the mould with a wet file-handle, replacing this as soon as possible with the infinitely more efficient thumb. It was a somewhat tedious process, for every part of the surface had to be pressed into the mould so that no detail should be missed; but it was not until the hardening of the gutta-percha as it cooled rendered further manipulation useless that Pottermack laid it aside as finished and proceeded to operate in like manner on the other mould.

When both moulds were filled, he immersed them in the cold water in the bucket in order to cool and harden the gutta-percha more quickly, and leaving them there, he turned his attention to the over-shoes. The important question was as to their size. How did they compare with Lewson's shoes? He had assumed that they were as nearly as possible alike in size, but now, when he placed one of the over-shoes, sole upwards, beside the corresponding cast, he felt some misgivings. However, a few careful measurements with a tape-measure reassured him. The over-shoes were a trifle larger—an eighth of an inch wider and nearly a quarter of an inch longer than the casts, so that there would be a sixteenth overlap at the sides and an eighth at the toe and heel. That would be of no importance; or if it were, he could pare off the overlap.

Much encouraged, he fell to work on the over-shoes. He knew all about balata soles. The present ones—which were of one piece with the flat heels—he had stuck on with a powerful fusible cement. All that he had to do now was to warm them cautiously over the

Primus stove until the cement was softened and then peel them off;
and when he had done this, there were the flat leather soles, covered
with the sticky cement, all ready for the attachment of the gutta-
percha "squeezes."

There was still one possible snag ahead. The squeezes might
have stuck to the moulds; for gutta-percha is a sticky material when
hot. However, the moulds had been saturated with water and usually gutta-percha will not stick to a wet surface, so he hoped for the
best. Nevertheless it was with some anxiety that he fished one of the
moulds out of the bucket, and, grasping an overlapping edge of the
squeeze with a pair of flat-nosed pliers, gave a cautious and tentative
pull. As it showed no sign of yielding, he shifted to another part of
the overlap and made gentle traction on that, with no better result.
He then tried the piece of overlap that projected beyond the toe,
and here he had better luck; for, as he gave a firm, steady pull, the
squeeze separated visibly from the mould, and, with a little coaxing,
came out bodily.

Pottermack turned it over eagerly to see what result his labours
had yielded, and as his glance fell on the smooth, brown surface he
breathed a sigh of deep satisfaction. He could have asked for no better
result. The squeeze had not failed at a single point. There was the
horse with the little gash in its neck, the inscription and the makers'
mark; the circular heel with its sunk, five-pointed star, the little
marks of wear, and the central screw showing its slot quite distinctly.
Even the little grain of embedded gravel was there. The impression
was perfect. He had never seen the soles of Lewson's shoes, but he
knew now exactly what they looked like. For here before him was
an absolutely faithful facsimile.

Handling it with infinite tenderness—for gutta-percha, when
once softened, is slow to harden completely—he replaced it in the
bucket, and taking out the other mould, repeated the extracting

operation with the same patient care and with a similar happy result. It remained now only to pare off the overlap round the edges, shave off with a sharp knife one or two slight projections on the upper surface and wipe the latter perfectly dry. When this was done, the soles were ready for fixing on the over-shoes.

Placing the invaluable tin of cement on the bench near the Primus, Pottermack proceeded to warm the sole of one of the over-shoes over the flame. Then, scooping out a lump of tough cement, he transferred it to the warmed sole and spread it out evenly with a hot spatula. The next operation was more delicate and rather risky; for the upper surface of the gutta-percha sole had to be coated with cement without warming the mass of the sole enough to endanger the impression on its under surface. However, by loading the spatula with melted cement and wiping it swiftly over the surface, the perilous operation was completed without mishap. And now came the final stage. Fixing the over-shoe in the bench-vice, and once more passing the hot spatula over its cemented sole, Pottermack picked up the gutta-percha sole and carefully placed it in position on the over-shoe, adjusting it so that the overlaps at the sides and the toe were practically equal, the larger overlap at the heel being—by reason of the thickness of the latter—of no consequence.

When the second shoe had been dealt with in a similar manner and with a like success, and the pair placed on the bench, soles upward, to cool and harden, Pottermack emptied the bucket, and, carrying it in his hand, stole out of the workshop and made his way out of the walled garden into the orchard, where he advanced cautiously along the path. Presently the house came into view and he saw with satisfaction that the lower part was in darkness whereas lights were visible at two of the upper windows—those of the respective bedrooms of Mrs. Gadby and the maid. Thereupon he walked forward boldly, let himself silently into the house and tiptoed to the dining-room, where, having closed the door, he proceeded at once to transfer the ice and the ice-cold water from the tub to the bucket. Then, in the same silent manner, he went out into the garden, softly closing the door after him, and took his way back to the workshop.

Here his first proceeding was to take down from a shelf a large, deep porcelain dish, such as photographers use. This he placed on the bench and poured into it the iced water from the bucket. Then, taking up the shoes, one at a time, he lowered them slowly and carefully, soles downward, into the iced water and finished by packing the ice round them. And there he left them to cool and harden completely while he attended to one or two other important matters.

The first of these was the line of tell-tale footprints leading to the well. They had served their invaluable purpose and now it was time to get rid of them; which he did forthwith with the aid of a rake and a hard broom. Then there must be one or two footprints outside the gate that would need to be obliterated. He took the broom and rake, and, crossing to the gate, listened awhile, then softly opened it, listened again and peered out. Having satisfied himself that there was no one in sight, he stooped to scrutinize the ground and finally went down on his hands and knees. Sure enough, there were four footprints that told the story much too plainly for safety: two diverging from the main track towards the gate and two more pointing directly towards it. Their existence was a little disquieting at the first glance, for they might already have been seen; but a close scrutiny of the ground for signs of any more recent footprints reassured him. Evidently Lewson was the last person who had trodden that path. Having established this encouraging fact, Pottermack, still keeping inside his gate, passed the rake lightly over the four footprints and then smoothed the surface with the broom.

His preparations were now nearly complete. Reclosing the gate, he went back to the workshop to prepare his outfit. For though the "sugaring" expedition was but a pretext, he intended to carry it through with completely convincing realism. On that realism it was quite conceivable that his future safety might depend. Accordingly he proceeded to pack the large rucksack that he usually carried on these expeditions with the necessary appliances: a store of collecting-boxes, the killing-jar, a supply of pins, the folding-net, an air-tight metal pot which he filled with pieces of rag previously dipped into the sugaring mixture and reeking of beer and rum, and an electric inspection-lamp. When he had packed it, he laid the net-stick by its side and then turned his attention to the shoes.

The gutta-percha soles were now quite cold and hard. He dried them carefully with a soft rag, and as he did so, the little surrounding overlap caught his eye. It seemed to be of no consequence. It was very unlikely that it would leave any mark on the ground, unless he should meet with an exceptionally soft patch. Still, there had been no overlap on Lewson's shoes, and it was better to be on the safe side. Thus reflecting, he took from the tool-rack a shoemaker's knife, and having given it a rub or two on the emery board, neatly shaved away the overlap on each sole to a steep bevel. Now the impression would be perfect no matter what kind of ground he met with.

This was the finishing touch, and he was now ready to go forth. Slipping his arms through the straps of the rucksack, he picked up the net-stick, took down from a peg his working apron, tucked the shoes under his arm, switched off the light and went out, crossing the lawn direct to the side gate. Here he spread the apron on the ground, and, stepping on to it, listened for a few moments and then softly opened the gate. Having taken a cautious peep out to assure himself that there was no one in sight, he slipped on and fastened the over-shoes, and, taking the inspection-lamp from the rucksack, dropped the battery into his coat pocket and hooked the bull's-eye into a button-hole. Then, throwing the light for an instant on the path and marking the correct spot by his eye, he stepped out sideways, planting his right foot on the smoothly swept ground a pace in front of the last impression of Lewson's left foot.

Steadying himself with the net-stick, he pulled the gate to until the latch clicked; then he put down his left foot a good pace in advance and set forth on his pilgrimage, carefully adapting the length of his stride to match, as well as he could judge, that of his long-legged predecessor.

The country was profoundly quiet, and, though the moon peeped out now and again, the night was for the most part so dark that he had occasionally to switch on his lamp to make sure that he was keeping to the path. The state of affairs, however, that these occasional flashes revealed was highly encouraging, for though the beaten surface of the path showed numerous traces of human feet, these were mostly faint and ill-defined, and none of them looked very recent. They suggested that few wayfarers used this path, and that the very striking tracks that he was laying down might remain undisturbed and plainly visible for many days unless a heavy rain should fall and wash them away.

So Pottermack trudged on, stepping out with conscious effort and keeping his attention fixed on the regulation of his stride. About half a mile from home the path entered a small wood, and here the aid of the lamp was needed continuously. Here, too, the sodden state of the path caused Pottermack to congratulate himself on his wise caution in shaving off the overlaps. For in this soft earth they would have shown distinctly and might have attracted undesirable notice—that is, if any one should give the footprints more than the passing glance that would suffice for recognition; which was in the highest degree unlikely.

Presently the path emerged from the wood and meandered across a rough common, covered with gorse and heather. Eventually, as

Pottermack knew, it joined, nearly at a right angle, a by-road, which in its turn opened on the main London road. Here, he decided, the tracks could plausibly be lost; and as he drew near to the neighbourhood of the by-road he kept a sharp look-out for some indication of its whereabouts. At length he made out dimly a gate which he recognized as marking a little bridge across the roadside ditch. At once he stepped off the path into the heather, and, after walking on some twenty paces, halted, and unfastening the over-shoes, slipped them off. Then he took off the rucksack, turned out its contents, and having stowed the shoes at the bottom, repacked it and put it on again.

Hitherto he had not met or seen a soul since he started, and he was rather anxious not to meet any one until he was clear of this neighbourhood. His recent activities had perhaps made him a little over-conscious. Still, this was the night of the disappearance and here the tracks faded into the heather. If he were seen hereabouts, he might hereafter be questioned as to whether he had seen the missing man. No great harm in that, perhaps; but he had the feeling that it were much better for him not to be associated with the affair in any way. There were all sorts of possible snags. For instance, how did he get here without leaving any footprints on the path by which he would naturally have come? From which it will be seen that, if conscience was not making a coward of Mr. Pottermack, it was at least a little unduly stimulating his imagination. And yet it was as well to err on the right side.

Turning back, he strode on through the heather until he came once more to the path, which he crossed by a long jump that landed him in the heather on the farther side. He now struck across the common, making for a detached coppice that formed an outlier of the wood. As soon as he reached it he fell to work without delay on the completion of his programme, pinning the pieces of sugared rag on the trunks of half a dozen trees. Usually he gave the moths ample time to find the bait and assemble round it. But to-night, with that incriminating pair of shoes in his rucksack, his methods were more summary. By the time that he had pinned on the last rag, one or two moths had begun to flutter round the first, easily visible in the darkness by the uncanny, phosphorescent glow of their eyes. Pottermack unfolded his net, and, screwing it on to the stick, switched on his lamp and proceeded to make one or two captures, transferring the captives from the net to the killing-jar, and, after the necessary interval, thence to the collecting-boxes.

He was not feeling avaricious to-night. He wanted to get home and bring his task definitely to an end. He was even disposed to resent the indecent way in which the moths began to swarm round the rags. They seemed to be inviting him to make a night of it, as they were doing amidst the fumes of the rum. But he was not to be tempted. When he had pinned a dozen specimens in his collecting-box and put a few more in the lethal jar, he considered that he had done enough to account plausibly for his nocturnal expedition. Thereupon he packed up, and, leaving the lepidopterous revellers to the joys of intoxication, he turned away and strode off briskly in the direction of the by-road, carrying the net still screwed to the stick. A few minutes' rough walking brought him to the road, down which he turned in the direction of the town. In another ten minutes he reached the outskirts of the town and the road on which his house fronted. At this late hour it was as deserted as the country; indeed in its whole length he encountered but a single person—a jovial constable who greeted him with an indulgent smile as he fixed a twinkling eye on the butterfly net, and, having playfully enquired what Mr. Pottermack had got in that bag, hoped that he had had good sport, and wished him good-night. So Pottermack went on his way, faintly amused at the flutter into which the constable's facetious question had put him. For if it had chanced that the guardian of the law had been a stranger and had insisted on examining the bag, nothing could have been more apparently innocent than its contents. But the guilty man finds it hard to avoid projecting into the minds of others the secret knowledge that his own mind harbours.

When Pottermack at last let himself in at his front door and secured it with bolt and chain, he breathed a sigh of relief. The horrible chapter was closed. To-morrow he could clear away the last souvenirs of that hideous scene in the garden and then, in the peace and security of his new life, try to forget the price that he had paid for it. So he reflected as he carried the tub to the scullery and drew into it enough water to account for the vanished ice; as he washed at the sink, as he sat at the table consuming the arrears of his supper, and as, at length, he went up to bed, carrying the rucksack with him.

IV

THE PLACING OF THE SUN-DIAL

WHEN, AFTER BREAKFAST ON THE FOLLOWING MORNING, Mr. Pottermack betook himself, rucksack in hand, to the walled garden, he experienced, as he closed the door behind him and glanced round the enclosure, curiously mixed feelings. He was still shaken by the terrific events of the previous night, and, in his disturbed state, disposed to be pessimistic and vaguely apprehensive. Not that he regretted what he had done. Lewson had elected to make his life insupportable, and a man who does that, does it at his own risk. So Pottermack argued, and he reviewed the circumstances without the slightest twinge of remorse. Repugnant as the deed had been to him, and horrible as it had been in the doing—for he was by temperament a humane and kindly man—he had no sense of guilt. He had merely the feeling that he had been forced to do something extremely unpleasant.

When, however, he came to review the new circumstances, he was conscious of a vague uneasiness. Considered in advance, the making away with Lewson had been a dreadful necessity, accepted for the sake of the peace and security that it would purchase. But had that security been attained? The blackmailer, indeed, had gone for ever with his threats and his exactions. But that thing in the well— It was actually possible that Lewson dead might prove more formidable even than Lewson living. It was true that everything seemed to be quite safe and secret. He, Pottermack, had taken every possible precaution. But supposing that he had forgotten something; that he had overlooked some small but vital detail. It was quite conceivable. The thing had frequently happened. The annals of crime, and especially of murder, were full of fatal oversights.

So Mr. Pottermack cogitated as, having picked up the apron, he made his way to the workshop, where he set to work at once on the tasks that remained to be done. First he dealt with the shoes. As it would have been difficult and was quite unnecessary to remove the gutta-percha soles, he simply shaved off the heels, heated the surface and then stuck on the original soles of balata. Next he broke up the plaster moulds and casts into small fragments, which he carried out in the bucket and shot down the well. Those, he reflected with a sense of relief as he replaced the hurdle, were the last visible traces of the tragedy; but even as he turned away from the well, he saw that they were not. For, glancing at the summer-house, he observed the decanter, the siphon, and the tumbler still on the table. Of course, to no eye but his was there anything suspicious or unusual in their presence there. But the sight of them affected him disagreeably. Not only were they a vivid and unpleasant reminder of events which he wished to forget. They revived the doubts that had tended to fade away under the exhilarating influence of work. For here was something that he had overlooked. A thing of no importance, indeed, but still a detail that he had forgotten. Trivial as the oversight was, he felt his confidence in his foresight shaken.

He walked to the summer-house, and, setting down the bucket outside, entered and proceeded to clear away these traces. Opening the cupboard, he caught up the siphon and the decanter and stepped behind the table to put them on the shelves. As he did so, he felt something soft under his foot, and when he had closed the cupboard door he looked down to see what it was. And then his heart seemed to stand still. For the thing under his foot was a coat—and it was not his coat.

There is a very curious phenomenon which we may describe as deferred visual sensation. We see something which is plainly before our eyes, but yet, owing to mental preoccupation, we are unaware of it. The image is duly registered on the retina; the retina passes on its record to the brain; but there the impression remains latent until some association brings it to the surface of consciousness.

Now, this was what had happened to Pottermack. In the moment in which his glance fell on the coat there started up before him the vision of a bulky figure flourishing its fists and staggering backwards towards the well—the figure of a man in shirt-sleeves. In spite of the darkness, he had seen that figure quite distinctly; he even recalled that the shirt-sleeves were of a dark grey. But so intense had been his preoccupation with the dreadful business of the moment that the detail, physically seen, had passed into his memory without conscious recognition.

He was literally appalled. Here, already, was a second oversight; and this time it was one of vital importance. Had any one who knew Lewson been present when the coat was discovered, recognition would have been almost certain; for the material was of a strikingly conspicuous and distinctive pattern. Then the murder would have been out, and all his ingenious precautions against discovery would have risen up to testify to his guilt.

All his confidence, all of the sense of security that he had felt on his return home on the previous night, had evaporated in an instant. Two obvious things he had forgotten, and one of them might have been fatal. Indeed, there were three; for he had been within an ace of overlooking those incriminating footprints that might have led the searchers to his very gate. Was it possible that there was yet some other important fact that he had failed to take into account?

He realized that it was very possible indeed; that it might easily be that he should add yet another instance to the abundant records of murderers who, covering up their tracks with elaborate ingenuity, have yet left damning evidence plain for any investigator to see.

He picked up the coat, and, rolling it up loosely, considered what he should do with it. His first impulse was to drop it in the well. But he rejected the idea for several reasons. It would certainly float, and might possibly be seen by the mason when the sun-dial was fixed, especially if he should throw a light down. And then, if the well should, after all, be searched, the presence of a separate coat would be against the suggestion of accident. And it would be quite easy to burn it in the rubbish destructor. Moreover, in rolling the coat he had become aware of a bulky object in one of the pockets which recalled certain statements that Lewson had made. In the end, he tucked the coat under his arm and, catching up the bucket, took his way back to the workshop.

It was significant of Pottermack's state of mind that as soon as he was inside he locked the door; notwithstanding that he was alone in the walled garden and that both the gates were securely fastened. Moreover, before he began his inspection he unlocked a large drawer and left it open with the key in the lock, ready to thrust the coat out of sight in a moment. Then he unrolled the coat on the bench, and, putting his hand into the inside breast pocket, drew out a leather wallet. It bulged with papers of various kinds, mostly bills and letters, but to these Pottermack gave no attention. The one item in the contents that interested him was a compact bundle of banknotes. There were twenty of them, all five-pound notes, as he ascertained by going through the bundle; a hundred pounds in all—the exact sum that had been demanded of him. In fact, these notes were understudies of his expected contribution They had been "borrowed" by Lewson out of the current cash to meet some sudden call, and his,

Pottermack's, notes were to have been either paid in place of them or to have enabled Lewson to make good his loan in the morning.

It seemed a queer proceeding, and to Mr. Pottermack it was not very intelligible. But the motive was no concern of his; what was his concern was the train of consequences that would be set going. The obvious fact was that the little branch bank of which Lewson had had sole charge was now minus a hundred pounds in five-pound notes. That fact must inevitably come to light within a day or two; most probably this very day. Then the hue and cry would be out for the missing manager.

Well, that was all to the good. There would certainly be a hot search for Lewson. But the searchers would not be seeking the body of a murdered man. They would be on the look-out for an exceedingly live gentleman with a bundle of stolen notes in his pocket. As he considered the almost inevitable course of events, Pottermack's spirits rose appreciably. The borrowing of those notes had been most fortunate for him, for it turned what would have been an unaccountable disappearance into a perfectly accountable flight. It seemed an incredibly stupid proceeding, for if Pottermack had paid up, the borrowing would have been unnecessary; if he had not paid up, the "loan" could not have been made good. However, stupid or not, it had been done; and in the doing it Lewson had, for the first and last time, rendered his victim a real service.

When he had inspected the notes, Pottermack replaced them in the wallet, returned the latter to the pocket whence it had come, rolled up the coat and bestowed it in the drawer, which he closed and locked. The consumption of it in the rubbish destructor could be postponed for a time; and perhaps it might not come to that at all. For the finding of the notes had, to a great extent, restored Pottermack's confidence; and already there had appeared in his mind the germ of an idea—vague and formless at present—that the notes, and perhaps even the coat, might yet have further useful offices to perform.

As he had now completed his tasks and cleared away—as he hoped—the last traces of the previous night's doings, he thought it time that he should show himself to Mrs. Gadby in his normal, everyday aspect. Accordingly he took the rucksack, a setting-board, and a few other necessary appliances and made his way to the house, where he established himself in the dining-room at a table by the window and occupied the time in setting the moths which he had captured on the previous night. They were but a poor collection, with an unconscionable proportion of duplicates, but Pottermack pinned them all out impartially—even the damaged ones—on the setting-board. It was their number, not their quality, that would produce the necessary moral effect on Mrs. Gadby when she came in to lay the table for his mid-day dinner. So he worked away placidly with an outward air of complete absorption in his task; but all the while there kept recurring in his mind, like some infernal refrain, the disturbing question: Was there even now something that he had forgotten: something that his eye had missed but that other eyes might detect?

In the afternoon he strolled round to Mr. Gallett's yard to see if all was going well in regard to the preparations for setting up the sun-dial. He was anxious that there should be no delay, for though the presence of the dial would afford him no added security, he had an unreasonable feeling that the fixing of it would close the horrible incident. And he did very much want that sinister black hole hidden from sight for ever. Great, therefore, was his relief when he discovered Mr. Gallett and two of his men in the very act of loading a low cart with what was obviously the material for the job.

The jovial mason greeted him with a smile and a nod. "All ready, you see, Mr. Pottermack," said he, indicating the dial-pillar, now swathed in a canvas wrapping, and slapping one of the stone slabs that stood on edge by its side. "Could almost have done it to-day, but it's getting a bit late and we've got one or two other jobs to finish up here. But we'll have him round by nine o'clock to-morrow morning if that will do."

It would do admirably, Mr. Pottermack assured him, adding: "You will have to bring it in at the side gate. Do you know whereabouts that is?"

"I can't say as I do exactly," replied Gallett. "But I'll bring him to the front gate and then you can show me where he is to go."

To this Pottermack agreed, and they then strolled together to the gate, where Mr. Gallett halted, and, having looked up and down the street with a precautionary air, said in what he meant to be a low tone:

"Rummy report going round the town. Have you heard anything of it?"

"No," replied Pottermack, all agog in a moment. "What is it?"

"Why, they say that the manager of Perkins's Bank has hopped it. That's what they say, and I fancy there must be something in it, because I went there this morning to pay in a cheque and I found the place closed. Give me a rare turn, because I've got an account there. So I rang the bell and the caretaker he come and tells me that Mr. Lewson wasn't able to attend to-day but that there would be some one there later to carry on till he came back. And so there was, for I went round a couple of hours later and found the place open and business going on as usual. There was a youngish fellow at the counter, but there was an elderly gent—rather a foxy-looking customer—who seemed to be smelling round, taking down the books and looking into the drawers and cupboards. Looks a bit queer, don't you think?"

"It really does," Pottermack admitted. "The fact of the bank not being open at the usual time suggests that Mr. Lewisham—"

"Lewson is his name," Mr. Gallett corrected.

"Mr. Lewson. It suggests that he had absented himself without giving notice, which is really rather a remarkable thing for a manager to do."

"It is," said Gallett; "particularly as he lived on the premises."

"Did he, indeed?" exclaimed Pottermack. "That makes it still more remarkable. Quite mysterious, in fact."

"Very mysterious," said Gallett. "Looks as if he had mizzled; and if he has, why, he probably didn't go away with his pockets empty."

Pottermack shook his head gravely. "Still," he urged, "it is early to raise suspicions. He may possibly have been detained somewhere. He was at the bank yesterday?"

"Oh, yes; and seen in the town yesterday evening. Old Keeling, the postman, saw him about half-past seven and wished him goodnight. Says he saw him turn into the footpath that leads through Potter's Wood."

"Ha," said Pottermack. "Well, he may have lost his way in the wood, or been taken ill. Who knows? It is best not to jump at conclusions too hastily."

With this and a friendly nod he turned out of the yard and took his way homeward, cogitating profoundly. Events were moving even more quickly than he had anticipated, but they were moving in the right direction. Nevertheless, he recognized with something like a shudder how near he had been to disaster. But for the chance moonbeam that had lighted up the footprints in his garden, he would have overlooked those other tell-tale tracks outside. And again he asked himself uneasily if there could be something else that he had overlooked. He was tempted to take a walk into the country in the direction of the wood to see if there were yet any signs of a search; for, by Gallett's report, it appeared that the direction in which Lewson had gone, and even his route, was already known. But prudence bade him keep aloof and show no more than a stranger's interest in

the affair. Accordingly he went straight home; and since in his restless state he could not settle down to read, he betook himself to his
workshop and spent the rest of the day in sharpening chisels and
plane-irons and doing other useful, time-consuming jobs.

True to his word, Mr. Gallett appeared on the following morning
almost on the stroke of nine. Pottermack himself opened the door
to him and at once conducted him through the house out into the
orchard and thence to the walled garden. It was not without a certain
vague apprehensiveness that he unlocked the gate and admitted his
visitor, for since that fatal night no eye but his had looked on that
enclosure. It is true that on this very morning he had made a careful
tour of inspection and had satisfied himself that nothing was visible
that all the world might not see. Nevertheless, he was conscious of
a distinct sense of discomfort as he let the mason in, and still more
when he led him to the well.

"So this is where you wants him planted?" said Mr. Gallett, stepping up to the brink of the well and looking down it reflectively. "It
do seem a pity for to bung up a good well. And you say there's a tidy
depth of water in him."

"Yes," said Pottermack; "a fair depth. But it's a long way down
to it."

"So 'tis, seemingly," Gallett agreed. "The bucket would take a
bit of histing up." As he spoke, he felt in his pocket and drew out a
folded newspaper, and from another pocket he produced a box of
matches. In leisurely fashion he tore off a sheet of the paper, struck
a match, and, lighting a corner of the paper, let it fall, craning over
to watch its descent. Pottermack also craned over, with his heart in
his mouth, staring breathlessly at the flaming mass as it sank slowly,
lighting up the slimy walls of the well, growing smaller and fainter
as it descended, while a smaller, fainter spark rose from the depths
to meet it. At length they met and were in an instant extinguished;

and Pottermack breathed again. What a mercy he had not thrown the coat down!

"We'll have to bank up the earth a bit," said Mr. Gallett, "for the slabs to bed on. Don't want 'em to rest on the brickwork of the well or they may settle out of the level after a time. And if you've got a spade handy, we may as well do it now, 'cause we can't get to the side gate for a few minutes. There's a gent out there a-takin' photographs of the ground."

"Of the ground!" gasped Pottermack.

"Ay. The path, you know. Seems as there's some footmarks there—pretty plain ones they looked to me without a-photographin' of 'em. Well, it's them footmarks as he's a-takin'."

"But what for?" demanded Pottermack.

"Ah," said Mr. Gallett. "There you are. I don't know, but I've got my ideas. I see the police inspector a-watchin' of him—all on the broad grin he was too—and I suspect it's got something to do with that bank manager that I was tellin' you about."

"Ah, Mr. Lewis?"

"Lewson is his name. There's no news of him and he was seen coming this way on Wednesday night. Why, he must have passed this very gate."

"Dear me!" exclaimed Pottermack. "And as to his reasons for going away so suddenly. Is anything—er—?"

"Well, no," replied Gallett. "Nothing is known for certain. Of course, the bank people don't let on. But there's some talk in the town about some cash that's missing. May be all bunkum, though it's what you'd expect. Now, about that spade. Shall I call in my men or can we do it ourselves?"

Pottermack decided that they could do it themselves, and, having produced a couple of spades, he fell to work under Gallett's direction, raising a low platform for the stone slabs to rest on. A few minutes' work saw it finished to the mason's satisfaction, and all was now ready for the fixing of the dial.

"I wonder if that photographer chap has finished," said Mr. Gallett. "Shall we go and have a look?"

This was what Pottermack had been bursting to do, though he had heroically suppressed his curiosity; and even now he strolled indifferently to the gate and held it open for the mason to go out first.

"There he is," said Gallett, "and blow me if he isn't a-takin' of 'em all the way along. What can he be doing that for? The cove had only got two feet."

Mr. Pottermack looked out and was no less surprised than the worthy mason. But he did not share the latter's purely impersonal interest. On the contrary, what he saw occasioned certain uncomfortable stirrings in the depths of his consciousness. Some little distance up the path a spectacled youth of sage and sober aspect had set up a tripod to which a rather large camera of the box type was attached by a goose-neck bracket. The lens was directed towards the ground, and when the young man had made his exposure by means of a wire release, he opened a portfolio and made a mark or entry of some kind on what looked like a folded map. Then he turned a key on the camera, and, lifting it with its tripod, walked away briskly for some twenty or thirty yards, when he halted, fixed the tripod and repeated the operation. It really was a most astonishing performance.

"Well," said Mr. Gallett, "he's finished here, at any rate, so we can get on with our business now. I'll just run round and fetch the cart along."

He sauntered away towards the road, and Pottermack, left alone, resumed his observation of the photographer. The proceedings of that mysterious individual puzzled him not a little. Apparently he was taking a sample footprint about every twenty yards, no doubt selecting specially distinct impressions. But to what purpose? One or two photographs would have been understandable as permanent records of marks that a heavy shower might wash away and that would, in any case, soon disappear. But a series, running to a hundred or more, could have no ordinary utility. And yet it was not possible that that solemn young man could be taking all this trouble without some definite object. Now, what could that object be?

Pottermack was profoundly puzzled. Moreover, he was more than a little disturbed. Hitherto his chief anxiety had been lest the footprints should never be observed. Then he would have had all his trouble for nothing, and those invaluable tracks, leading suspicion far away from his own neighbourhood to an unascertainable destination, would have been lost. Well, there was no fear of that now. The footprints had not only been observed and identified, they were going to be submitted to minute scrutiny. He had not bargained for that. He had laid down his tracks expecting them to be scanned by the police or the members of a search party, to whom they would have been perfectly convincing. But how would they look in a photograph? Pottermack knew that photographs have an uncanny way of bringing out features that are invisible to the eye. Now could there be any such features in those counterfeit footprints? He could not imagine any. But then why was this young man taking all those photographs? With his secret knowledge of the real facts, Pottermack could not shake off an unreasoning fear that his ruse had been already discovered, or at least suspected.

His cogitations were interrupted by the arrival of the cart, which was halted and backed up against his gateway. Then there came the laying down of planks to enable the larger slab to be trundled on rollers to the edge of the platform. Pottermack stood by, anxious and restless, inwardly anathematizing the conscientious mason as he tried the surface of the platform again and again with his level. At last he was satisfied. Then the big base slab was brought on edge to the platform, adjusted with minute care and finally let down slowly into its place; and as it dropped the last inch with a gentle thud, Pottermack drew a deep breath and felt as if a weight, greater far than that of the slab, had been lifted from his heart.

In the remaining operations he had to feign an interest that he ought to have felt but did not. For him, the big base slab was what mattered. It shut that dreadful, yawning, black hole from his sight, as he hoped, for ever. The rest was mere accessory detail. But, as it would not do for him to let this appear, he assumed an earnest and critical attitude, particularly when it came to the setting up of the pillar on the centre of the upper slab.

"Now then," said Mr. Gallett as he spread out a thin bed of mortar on the marked centre, "how will you have him? Will you have the plinth parallel to the base or diagonal?"

"Oh, parallel, I think," replied Pottermack; "and I should like to have the word *spes* on the eastern side, which will bring the word *pax* to the western."

Mr. Gallett looked slightly dubious. "If you was thinking of setting him to the right time," said he, "you won't do it that way. You'll have to unscrew the dial-plate from the lead bed and have him fixed correct to time. But never mind about him now. We're a-dealing with the stone pillar."

"Yes," said Pottermack, "but I was considering the inscription. That is the way in which it was meant to be placed, I think"; and here he explained the significance of the motto.

"There now," said Mr. Gallett, "see what it is to be a scholar. And you're quite right too, sir: you can see by the way the lichen grew on it that this here *sole orto* was the north side. So we'll put him round to the north again, and then I expect the dial will be about right, if you aren't partickler to a quarter of an hour or so."

Accordingly the pillar was set up in its place and centred with elaborate care. Then, when the level of the slabs had been tested and a few slight adjustments made, the pillar was tried on all sides with the plumb-line and corrected to a hair's breadth.

"There you are, Mr. Pottermack," said Mr. Gallett, as he put the last touch to the mortar joint and stepped back to view the general effect of his work; "see that he isn't disturbed until the mortar has had time to set and he won't want touching again for a century or two. And an uncommon nice finish he'll give to the garden when you get a bit of smooth turf round him and a few flowers."

"Yes," said Pottermack, "you've made an extremely neat job of it, Mr. Gallett, and I'm very much obliged to you. When I get the turf laid and the flower borders set out, you must drop in and have a look at it."

The gratified mason, having suitably acknowledged these commendations of his work, gathered up his tools and appliances and departed with his myrmidons. Pottermack followed them out into the lane and watched the cart as it retired, obliterating the footprints which had given him so much occupation. When it had gone, he strolled up the path in the direction in which the photographer had gone, unconsciously keeping to the edge and noting with a sort of odd self-complacency the striking distinctness of the impressions of his gutta-percha soles. The mysterious operator was now out of sight, but he, too, had left his traces on the path, and these Pottermack studied with mingled curiosity and uneasiness. It was easy to see, by the marks of the tripod, which footprints had been photographed, and it was evident that care had been taken to select the sharpest and most perfect impressions. Pottermack had noticed, when he first looked out of the gate with Mr. Gallett, that the tripod had been set up exactly opposite the gateway and that the three marks surrounded the particularly fine impression that he had made when he stepped out sideways on to the smooth-swept path.

On these facts he reflected as he sauntered back to the gate, and entering, closed it behind him. What could be that photographer's object in his laborious proceeding? Who could it be that had set him to work? And what was it possible for a photograph to show that the eye might fail to see? These were the questions that he turned over uncomfortably in his mind and to which he could find no answer. Then his glance fell on the dial, resting immovable on its massive base, covering up the only visible reminder of the past, standing there to guard for ever his secret from the eyes of man. And at the sight of it he was comforted. With an effort he shook off his apprehensions and summoned his courage afresh. After all, what was there to fear? What could these photographs show that was not plainly visible? Nothing. There was nothing to show. The footprints were, it is true, counterfeits in a sense. But they were not imitations in the sense that a forged writing is an imitation. They were mechanical reproductions, necessarily true in every particular. In fact, they were actually Lewson's own footprints, though it happened that other feet than his were in the shoes. No. Nothing could be discovered for the simple reason that there was nothing to discover.

So Mr. Pottermack, with restored tranquillity and confidence, betook himself to the summer-house, and sitting down, looked out upon the garden and let his thoughts dwell upon what it should be when the little island of stone should be girt by a plot of emerald turf. As he sat, two sides of the sun-dial were visible to him, and on them he read the words *"decedente pax."* He repeated them to himself, drawing from them a new confidence and encouragement. Why should it not be so? The storms that had scattered the hopes of his youth had surely blown themselves out. His evil genius, who had first betrayed him and then threatened to destroy utterly his hardly earned prosperity and security; who had cast him into the depths and had fastened upon him when he struggled to the surface; the evil genius, the active cause of all his misfortunes, was gone for ever and would certainly trouble him no more.

Then why should the autumn of his life not be an Indian summer of peace and tranquil happiness? Why not?

V

DR. THORNDYKE LISTENS TO A STRANGE STORY

"AND THAT," SAID MR. STALKER, PICKING UP A WELL-WORN attaché-case and opening it on his knees, "finishes our little business and relieves you of my society."

"Say 'deprives,'" Thorndyke corrected. "That is, if you must really go."

"That is very delicate of you, doctor," Stalker replied as he stuffed a bundle of documents into the attaché-case; "and, by the way, it isn't quite the finish. There is another small matter which I had nearly forgotten; something that my nephew, Harold, asked me to hand to you. You have heard me speak of Harold—my sister's boy?"

"The inventive genius? Yes, I remember your telling me about him."

"Well, he asked me to pass this on to you; thought it might interest you."

He took from his case a flat disc which looked like a closely rolled coil of paper tape, secured with a rubber band, and passed it to Thorndyke, who took it, and, unrolling a few inches, glanced at it with a slightly puzzled smile.

"What is it?" he asked.

"I had better explain," replied Stalker. "You see, Harold has invented a recording camera which will take small photographs in a series and mark each one with its serial number, so that there can be no mistake about the sequence. It is a box camera and it takes quite a big roll of kinematograph film with a capacity of something like five hundred exposures. And the mechanism not only marks each negative with its number but also shows the number which is being exposed on a little dial on the outside of the camera. Quite a useful instrument, I should think, for certain purposes, though I can't, at the moment, think of a case to which it would be applicable."

"I can imagine certain cases, however," said Thorndyke, "in which it would be quite valuable. But with regard to these particular photographs?"

"They are, as you see, a series of footprints—the footprints of a man who absconded from a country bank and has not been seen since."

"But why did Harold take so many? There must be about a couple of hundred on this strip."

Stalker chuckled. "I don't think," said he, "that we need go far for the reason. Harold had got a camera that would take a numbered series and he had never had a chance to try it. Now here was an undoubted series of footprints on a footpath and they were those of an absconding man. It was a chance to show what the camera would do, and he took it. He professes to believe that these photographs might furnish an important clue to an investigator like yourself. But, of course, that is all nonsense. He just wanted to try his new camera. Still, he did the job quite thoroughly. He took a twenty-five inch ordnance map with him and marked each exposure on it, showing the exact position of that particular footprint. He made an exposure about every twenty yards. You will see, if you look at the map. I have the three sheets here. He told me to give them to you with the pho-tographs, so that you could examine them together if you wanted to—which I imagine you won't. Of course, the information they give is quite valueless. One or two photographs would have shown all that there was to show."

"I wouldn't say that," Thorndyke dissented. "The application of the method to the present case is, I must admit, not at all evident. One or two photographs would have been enough for simple identification. But I can imagine a case in which it might be of the highest importance to be able to prove that a man did actually follow a particular route, especially if a time factor were also available."

"Which it is, approximately, in the present instance. But it was already known that the man went that way at that time, so all this elaborate detail is merely flogging a dead horse. The problem is not which way did he go, but where is he now? Not that we care a great deal. He only took a hundred pounds with him—so far as we know at present—so the Bank is not particularly interested in him. Nor am I, officially, though I must confess to some curiosity about him. There are some rather odd features in the case. I am quite sorry that we can't afford to call you in to investigate them."

"I expect you are more competent than I am," said Thorndyke. "Banking affairs are rather out of my province."

"It isn't the banking aspect that I am thinking of," replied Stalker. "Our own accountants can deal with that. But there are some other queer features, and about one of them I am a little uncomfortable. It seems to suggest a miscarriage of justice in another case. But I mustn't take up your time with irrelevant gossip."

"But indeed you must," Thorndyke rejoined. "If you have got a queer case, I want to hear it. Remember, I live by queer cases."

"It is rather a long story," objected Stalker, evidently bursting to tell it nevertheless.

"So much the better," said Thorndyke. "We will have a bottle of wine and make an entertainment of it."

He retired from the room and presently reappeared with a bottle of Chambertin and a couple of glasses; and having filled the latter, he provided himself with a writing-pad, resumed his armchair and disposed himself to listen at his ease.

"I had better begin," said Stalker, "with an account of this present affair. The man who has absconded is a certain James Lewson, who was the manager of a little branch of Perkins's Bank down at Borley. He ran it by himself, living on the premises and being looked after by the caretaker's wife. It is quite a small affair—just a nucleus with an eye for the future, for Meux's do most of the business at Borley, such as it is—and easily run by one man; and everything has gone on quite smoothly there until last Wednesday week. On that day Lewson went out at about a quarter-past seven in the evening. The caretaker saw him go out at the back gate and thought that he looked as if he had been drinking, and on that account he sat up until past twelve o'clock to see him in safely. But he never came home, and as he had not returned by the morning, the caretaker telegraphed up to headquarters.

"Now I happened to be there when the telegram arrived—for I am still on the board of directors and do a bit of work there—and I suggested that old Jewsbury should go down to see what had been happening and take a young man with him to do the routine work while he was going through the books. And as Harold was the only one that could be spared, he was told off for the job. Of course, he fell in with it joyfully, for he thought he saw a possible chance of giving his camera a trial. Accordingly, down he went, with the camera in his trunk, all agog to find a series of some kind that wanted photographing. As soon as they arrived, Jewsbury saw at a glance that some of the cash was missing—a hundred pounds in five-pound Bank of England notes."

"And the keys?" asked Thorndyke.

"The safe key was missing too. But that had been anticipated, so Jewsbury had been provided with a master-key. The other keys were in the safe.

"Well, as soon as the robbery was discovered, Jewsbury had a talk with the caretaker and the police inspector, who had called to see him. From the caretaker, a steady old retired police sergeant, Jewsbury gathered that Lewson had been going to the bad for some time, taking a good deal more whisky than was good for him. But we needn't go into that. The police inspector reported that Lewson had been seen at about seven-thirty—that is, within a quarter of an hour of his leaving the bank—turning into a footpath that leads out into the country and eventually to the main London road. The inspector had examined the path and found on it a track of very distinct and characteristic footprints, which he was able to identify as Lewson's, not only by the description given by the caretaker, who usually cleaned Lewson's shoes, but by one or two fairly clear footprints in the garden near the back gate, by which Lewson went out. Thereupon, he returned to the footpath and followed the tracks out into the country, through a wood and across a heath until he came to a place where Lewson had left the path and gone off through the heather; and there, of course all traces of him were lost. The inspector went on and searched a by-road and went on to the London road, but not a single trace of him could he discover. At that point where he stepped off the footpath into the heather James Lewson vanished into thin air."

"Where is the railway station?" Thorndyke asked.

"In the town. There is a little branch station by the London road, but it is certain that Lewson did not go there, for there were no passengers at all on that evening. He must have gone off along the road on foot.

"Now, as soon as Harold heard of those footprints, he decided that his chance had come. The footprints would soon be trodden out or washed away by rain, and they ought to be recorded permanently. That was his view."

"And a perfectly sound one, too," remarked Thorndyke.

"Quite. But there was no need for a couple of hundred repetitions."

"Apparently not," Thorndyke agreed, "though it is impossible to be certain even of that. At any rate, a superabundance of evidence is a good deal better than a deficiency."

"Well, that is what Harold thought, or pretended to think, and in effect, he nipped off to the Post Office and got the large-scale ordnance maps that contained his field of operations. Then on the following morning he set to work, leaving Jewsbury to carry on. He began by photographing a pair of the footprints in the garden—they are numbers 1 and 2—and marking them on the map. Then he went off to the footpath and took a photograph about every twenty yards, selecting the most distinct footprints and writing down the number of the exposure on the map at the exact spot on which it was made. And so he followed the track into the country, through the wood, across the heath to what we may call the vanishing point. Number 197 is the last footprint that Lewson made before he turned off into the heather.

"So much for Harold and his doings. Now we come to the queer features of the case, and the first of them is the amount taken. A hundred pounds! Can you imagine a sane man, with a salary of six hundred a year, absconding with such a sum? The equivalent of two months' salary. The thing seems incredible. And why a hundred pounds only? Why didn't he take, at least, the whole of the available cash? It is incomprehensible. And in a few days his monthly salary would have been due. Why didn't he wait to collect that?

"But there is a partial explanation. Only the explanation is more incomprehensible than what it explains. By the evening post on the day on which Jewsbury arrived a letter was delivered, addressed to Lewson, and, under the circumstances, Jewsbury felt justified in opening it. Its contents were to this effect:

'DEAR LEWSON,—I expected you to come round last night, as you promised, to settle up. As you didn't come and have not written, I think it necessary to tell you plainly that this can't be allowed to go on. If the amount (£97, 13s. 4d.) is not paid within the next forty-eight hours, I shall have to take measures that will be unpleasant to both of us.—Yours faithfully,

LEWIS BATEMAN.'

Now this letter seemed to explain the small amount taken. It suggested that Lewson was being pressed for payment and that, as he had not got the wherewith to pay, he had taken the amount out of the cash, trusting to be able to replace it before the periodical audit. But if so, why had he not paid Bateman? And why had he absconded? The letter only deepens the mystery?"

"Is it an ascertained fact that he had not the wherewithal to pay?"

"I think I may say that it is. His own current account at the bank showed a balance of about thirty shillings and he had no deposit account. Looking over his account, Jewsbury noticed that he seemed to spend the whole of his income and was often overdrawn at the end of the month.

"But this letter brought into view another queer feature of the case. On enquiring of the police inspector, Jewsbury found that the man, Bateman, is a member of a firm of outside brokers who have offices in Moorgate Street. Bateman lives at Borley, and he and Lewson seemed to have been on more or less friendly terms. Accordingly, Jewsbury and the inspector called on him, and, under some pressure, he disclosed the nature of Lewson's dealing with his firm. It appeared that Lewson was a regular 'operator,' and that he was singularly unfortunate in his speculations and that he had a fatal habit of carrying over when he ought to have cut his loss and got out. As a result, he dropped quite large sums of money from time to time, and had lost heavily during the last few months. On the transactions of the last twelve months, Bateman reckoned—he hadn't his books with him, of course, at Borley—that Lewson had dropped over six hundred pounds; and in addition, he happened to know that Lewson had been plunging and losing on the turf.

"Now, where did Lewson get all this money? His account shows no income beyond his salary, and the debit side shows only his ordinary domestic expenditure. There are a good many cash drafts, some of which may have represented betting losses, but they couldn't represent the big sums that he lost through the bucket shop."

"He didn't pay the brokers by cheque, then?"

"No. Always in notes—five-pound notes; not that there is anything abnormal in that. As a bank manager, he would naturally wish to keep these transactions secret. It is the amount that creates the mystery. He spent the whole of his income in a normal though extravagant fashion, and he dropped over six hundred pounds in addition. Now, where did he get that six hundred pounds?"

"Is it certain that he had no outside source of income?" Thorndyke asked.

"Obviously he had. But since there is no sign of it on the credit side of his account, he must have received it in cash; which is a mighty queer circumstance when you consider the amount. Jewsbury is convinced that he must have been carrying on some kind of embezzlement, and I don't see what other explanation there can be. But if so, it has been done with extraordinary skill. Jewsbury has been through the books with the utmost rigour and with this suspicion in his mind, but he can't discover the slightest trace of any falsification. And mind you, Jewsbury is a first-class accountant and as sharp as a needle. So that is how the matter stands, and I must confess that I can make nothing of it."

Mr. Stalker paused, and, with a profoundly reflective air, took a sip from his glass, which Thorndyke had just refilled. The latter waited for some time with an expectant eye upon his guest and at length remarked:

"You were saying something about a miscarriage of justice."

"So I was," said Stalker. "But that is another story—unless it is a part of this story, which I begin to be afraid it is. However, you shall judge. I should like to hear what you think. It carries us back some fifteen years; that was before I took up the 'Griffin' company, and I was then assistant manager of Perkins', at the Cornhill office. About that time it was discovered that quite a long series of forgeries had been committed. They were very skilfully done and very cleverly managed, evidently by somebody who knew what customers' accounts it would be safe to operate on. It was found that a number of forged bearer cheques had been presented and paid over the counter; and it was further found that nearly all of them had been presented and paid at the counter of one man, a young fellow named Jeffrey Brandon. As soon as the discovery was made, it was decided—seeing that the forger was almost certainly an employee of the bank—to muster the staff and invite them all to turn out their pockets. And this was done on the following morning. When they had all arrived, and before the bank opened, they were mustered in the hall and the position of affairs explained to them; whereupon all of them, without being invited, expressed the wish to be searched. Accordingly, a detective officer who was in attendance searched each of them in turn, without any result. Then the detective suggested that the office coats, which most of them used and which were hanging in the lobby, should be fetched by the detective and the porter and searched in the presence of their owners. This also was done. Each man identified his own coat, and the detective searched it in his presence. All went well until we came to nearly the last coat—that belonging to

Jeffrey Brandon and identified by him as his. When the detective put his hand into the inside breast pocket, he found in it a letter-case; and on opening this and turning out its contents, he discovered in an inner compartment three bearer cheques. They were payable to three different—presumably fictitious—persons and were endorsed in the names of the payees in three apparently different handwritings.

"On the production of these cheques, Brandon showed the utmost astonishment. He admitted that the letter-case was his, but denied any knowledge of the cheques, declaring that they must have been put into the case by some one else—presumably the forger—while the coat was hanging in the lobby. Of course, this could not be accepted. No one but the senior staff knew even of the discovery of the forgery—at least, that was our belief at the time. And the search had been sprung on the staff without a moment's warning. Furthermore, there was the fact that nearly all the forged cheques had been paid at Brandon's counter. What followed was inevitable. Brandon was kept under observation at the bank until the ostensible drawers of the cheques had been communicated with by telegram or telephone; and when they had all denied having drawn any such cheques, he was arrested and charged before a magistrate. Of course, he was committed for trial; and when he was put in the dock at the Old Bailey the only defence he had to offer was a complete denial of any knowledge of the cheques and a repetition of his statement that they must have been put into his pocket by some other person for the purpose of incriminating him. It was not a very convincing defence, and it is not surprising that the jury would not accept it."

"And yet," Thorndyke remarked, "it was the only defence that was possible if he was innocent. And there was nothing inherently improbable in it."

"No. That was what I felt; and when he was found guilty and sentenced to five years' penal servitude, I was decidedly unhappy about the affair. For Brandon was a nice, bright, prepossessing youngster, and there was nothing whatever against him but this charge. And, later, I was made still more uncomfortable when I had reason to believe that the discovery of the forgeries had in some way become known, on the day before the search, to some members of the junior staff. So that what Brandon had said might easily have been true.

"However, that is the old story. And now as to its connection with the present one. Brandon had one specially intimate friend at the bank, and that friend's name was James Lewson. Now, we have never had anything against Lewson in all these years, or he would never have been a branch manager. But, from what we know of him now, he is, at least, an unscrupulous rascal; and, if Jewsbury is right, he is an embezzler and a thief. I can't rid myself of a horrible suspicion that James Lewson put those forged cheques into Brandon's pocket."

"If he did," said Thorndyke, "hanging would be a great deal too good for him."

"I quite agree with you," Stalker declared emphatically. "It would have been a dastardly crime. But I can't help suspecting him very gravely. I recall the look of absolute amazement on poor Brandon's face when those cheques were produced. It impressed me deeply at the time, but the recollection of it impresses me still more now. If Brandon was innocent, it was a truly shocking affair. It won't bear thinking of."

"No," Thorndyke agreed. "There is no tragedy more dreadful than the conviction of an innocent man. By the way, do you know what became of Brandon?"

"Indeed I do," replied Stalker. "The poor fellow is beyond the reach of any possible reparation, even if his innocence could be proved. He died in an attempt to escape from prison. I remember the circumstances only too clearly. Soon after his conviction he was sent to the convict prison at Colport. There, while he was working outside with a gang, he slipped past the civil guard and made off along the sea wall. He got quite a good start while they were searching for him in the wrong direction, but at last they picked up his tracks and set off in pursuit. And presently, on the seaward face of the wall, they found his clothes and the marks of his feet where he had walked out across the mud to the sea. They assumed that he had swum out to some passing vessel, and that is probably what he tried to do. But no tidings of him could be obtained from any of the anchored vessels or those that had passed up or down. Then, about six weeks later, the mystery was solved; for his body was found on the mud in a creek some miles farther down."

"About six weeks later," Thorndyke repeated. "What time of year was it?"

"He was found about the middle of August. Yes, I know what you are thinking. But, really, the question of identity hardly arose, although, no doubt, the corpse was examined as far as was possible. Still, the obvious facts were enough. A naked man was missing and the body of a nude man was found just where it was expected to wash ashore. I think we may take it that the body was Brandon's body. I only wish I could think otherwise."

"Yes," said Thorndyke. "It is a melancholy end to what sounds like a very tragic story. But I am afraid you are right. The body was almost certainly his."

"I think so," agreed Stalker. "And now, I hope I haven't taken up your time for nothing. You will admit that this Lewson case has some rather queer features."

"It certainly has," said Thorndyke. "It is most anomalous and puzzling from beginning to end."

"I suppose," said Stalker, "it would be hardly fair to ask for a few comments?"

"Why not?" demanded Thorndyke. "This is an entertainment, not a professional conference. If you want my views on the case, you are welcome to them; and I may say, in the first place, that I do not find myself quite in agreement with Jewsbury in regard to the embezzlement—of which, you notice, he can find no evidence. To me there is a strong suggestion of some outside source of income. We note that Lewson paid these large sums of money in cash—in five-pound notes. Now that may have been for secrecy. But where did he get all those notes? He paid no cheques into his account. He couldn't have stolen the notes from the bank's cash. There is a distinct suggestion that he received the money in the same form in which he paid it away. And his conduct on this occasion supports that view. He just baldly took a hundred pounds out of cash—in five-pound notes—to meet a sudden urgent call. One feels that he must have expected to be able to replace it almost at once. The idea that a man of his experience should have committed a simple, crude robbery like this is untenable. And then there is the amount: taken, almost certainly, for this specific purpose. The irresistible suggestion is that he merely borrowed this money in the confident expectation of obtaining the wherewith to put it back before it should be missed.

"Then there is the singular suggestion of a change of purpose. Apparently he started out to pay Bateman. Then why did he not pay him? He had the money. Instead, he suddenly turns off and walks out into the country. Why this change of plan? What had happened in the interval to cause him to change his plans in this remarkable manner? Had he discovered that he would not be able to replace the money? Even that would not explain his proceedings, for the natural thing would have been to return to the bank and put the notes back.

"Again, if he intended to abscond, why go away across the country on foot? He could easily have taken the train to town and disappeared there. But the idea of his absconding with that small amount of money is difficult to accept: and yet he undoubtedly did walk out into the country. And he has disappeared in a manner which is rather remarkable when one considers how easy a solitary pedestrian is to trace in the country. There is even something rather odd in his leaving the footpath and plunging into the heather, which must have been very inconvenient walking for a fugitive. Taking the case as a whole, I feel that I cannot accept the idea that he simply absconded with stolen money. Why he suddenly changed his plans and made off I am unable to guess, but I am certain that behind his extraordinary proceedings there is something more than meets the eye."

"That is precisely my feeling," said Stalker, "and the more so now that I have heard your summing-up of the case. I don't believe the man set out from home with the idea of absconding. I suspect that something happened after he left the house; that he got some sudden scare that sent him off into the country in that singular fashion. And now I must really take myself off. It has been a great pleasure to talk this case over with you. What about those things of Harold's? Shall I relieve you of them, now that you have seen them?"

"No," replied Thorndyke. "Leave them with me for the present. I should like to look them over before I hand them back."

"You don't imagine that Harold is right, do you? That these footprints may yield a clue to the man's disappearance?"

"No. I was not thinking of them in relation to the present case, but in regard to their general evidential bearing. As you know, I have given a great deal of attention and study to footprints. They sometimes yield a surprising amount of information, and as they can be accurately reproduced in the form of plaster casts, or even photographs, they can be produced in court and shown to the judge and the jury, who are thus able to observe for themselves instead of having to rely on the mere statements of witnesses.

"But footprints, as one meets with them in practice, have this peculiarity: that, although they are made in a series, they have to be examined separately as individual things. If we try to examine them on the ground as a series, we have to walk from one to another and trust largely to memory. But in these photographs of Harold's we can take in a whole series at a glance and compare any one specimen with any other. So what I propose to do is to look over these photographs and see if, apart from the individual characters which identify a footprint, there are any periodic or recurring characters which would make it worth while to use a camera of this type in practice. I want to ascertain, in fact, whether a consecutive series of footprints is anything more than a number of repetitions of a given footprint."

"I see. Of course, this is not a continuous series. There are long intervals."

"Yes. That is a disadvantage. Still, it is a series of a kind."

"True. And the maps?"

"I may as well keep them too. They show the distances between the successive footprints, which may be relevant, since the intervals are not all equal."

"Very well," said Stalker, picking up his attaché-case. "I admire your enthusiasm and the trouble you take, and I will tell Harold how seriously you take his productions. He will be deeply gratified."

"It was very good of him to send them, and you must thank him for me."

The two men shook hands, and when Thorndyke had escorted his guest to the landing and watched him disappear down the stairs, he returned to his chambers, closing the "oak" behind him and thereby secluding himself from the outer world.

VI

DR. THORNDYKE BECOMES INQUISITIVE

TEMPERAMENTALLY, DR. JOHN THORNDYKE PRESENTED A PECU-liarity which, at the first glance, seemed to involve a contradiction. He was an eminently friendly man; courteous, kindly and even genial in his intercourse with his fellow-creatures. Nor was his suave, amicable manner in any way artificial or consciously assumed. To every man his attitude of mind was instinctively friendly, and if he did not suffer fools gladly, he could, on occasion, endure them with almost inexhaustible patience.

And yet, with all his pleasant exterior and his really kindly nature, he was at heart a confirmed solitary. Of all company, his own thoughts were to him the most acceptable. After all, his case was not singular. To every intellectual man, solitude is not only a necessity, it is the condition to which his mental qualities are subject; and the man who cannot endure his own sole society has usually excellent reasons for his objection to it.

Hence, when Thorndyke closed the massive outer door and connected the bell-push with the laboratory floor above, there might have been detected in his manner a certain restfulness. He had enjoyed Stalker's visit. Particularly had he enjoyed the "queer case," which was to him what a problem is to an ardent chess player. But still, that was only speculation, whereas with the aid of Harold's photographs he hoped to settle one or two doubtful points relating to the characters of footprints which had from time to time arisen in his mind, and thereby to extend his actual knowledge.

With a leisurely and thoughtful air he moved a few things on the table to make a clear space, took out from a cupboard a surveyor's boxwood scale, a pair of needle-pointed spring dividers, a set of paper-weights, a note-block, and a simple microscope (formed of a watch-maker's doublet mounted on three legs) which he used for examining documents. Then he laid the three sheets of the ordnance map in their proper sequence on the table, with the roll of photographs by their side, drew up a chair and sat down to his task.

He began by running his eye along the path traversed by the fugitive, which was plainly marked by a row of dots, each dot having above it a microscopic number. Dots and numbers had originally been marked with a sharp-pointed pencil, but they had subsequently been inked in with red ink and a fine-pointed pen. From the maps he turned his attention to the photographs, unrolling a length of about nine inches and fixing the strip with a paper-weight at each end. The strip itself was an inch wide, and each photograph was an inch and a half long, and every one of the little oblongs contained the image of a footprint which occupied almost its entire length and which measured—as Thorndyke ascertained by taking the dimensions with his dividers—one inch and three-eighths. Small as the photographs were, they were microscopically sharp in definition, having evidently been taken with a lens of very fine quality; and in the corner of each picture was a minute number in white, which stood out clearly against the rather dark background.

Sliding the little microscope over one of the prints, Thorndyke examined it with slightly amused interest. For a fugitive's footprint it was a frank absurdity, so strikingly conspicuous and characteristic was it. If Mr. Lewson had had his name printed large upon the soles of his shoes he could hardly have given more assistance to his pursuers. The impression was that of a rubber sole on which, near the toe, was a framed label containing the makers' name, J. Bell and Co. Behind this was a panel, occupied by a prancing horse, and the Kentish motto, "Invicta," beneath the panel, implied that this was the prancing horse of Kent. The circular rubber heel was less distinctive, though even this was a little unusual, for its central device was a five-pointed star, whereas most star-pattern heels present six points. But not only were all the details of the pattern distinctly visible; even the little accidental markings, due to wear and damage, could be plainly made out. For instance, a little ridge could be seen across the horse's neck, corresponding to a cut or split in the rubber sole, and a tiny speck on the heel, which seemed to represent a particle of gravel embedded in the rubber.

When he had made an exhaustive examination of the one photograph, he turned back to numbers 1 and 2, which represented the footprints near the back gate of the bank, and which were not for his purpose part of the series. After a brief inspection of them, he placed one of the paper-weights on them, and, by means of another, exposed about eighteen inches of the strip. Next, he drew a vertical line down the middle of the note-block, dividing it into two parts, which he headed respectively "Right" and "Left." Then he began his comparative study with a careful examination of number 3, the first print photographed on the footpath.

Having finished with number 3, which was a right foot, he wrote down the number at the top of the "Right" column, in the middle of the space. Then he passed to number 5—the next right foot—and having examined it, wrote down its number. Next, he took, with the dividers, the distance between the dots marked 3 and 5 on the map, and, transferring the dividers to the boxwood scale, took off the distance in yards—forty-three yards—and wrote this down on the note-block opposite and at the left side of the number 5. From 5 he passed on to 7, 9, 11, 13, and so on, following the right foot along the strip until he had dealt with a couple of yards (the total length of the strip was a little over twenty-four feet), occasionally turning back to verify his comparisons, writing down the numbers in the middle of the column with the distances opposite to them on the left and jotting down in the space at the right a few brief notes embodying his observations. Then he returned to the beginning of the strip and dealt with the prints of the left foot in the same manner and for the same distance along the strip.

One would not have regarded it as a thrilling occupation. Indeed there was rather a suggestion of monotony in the endless recurrence of examination, comparison, and measurements of things which appeared to be merely mechanical repetitions of one another. Nor did the brief and scanty jottings in the "notes" column suggest that this tedious procedure was yielding any great wealth of information. Nevertheless, Thorndyke continued to work at his task methodically, attentively, and without any symptoms of boredom, until he had dealt with nearly half of the strip. But at this point his manner underwent a sudden and remarkable change. Hitherto he had carried on his work with the placid air of one who is engaged on a mildly interesting piece of routine work. Now he sat up stiffly, gazing at the strip of photographs before him with a frown of perplexity, even of incredulity. With intense attention, he re-examined the last half-dozen prints that he had dealt with; then, taking a right foot as a starting-point, he followed the strip rapidly, taking no measurements and making no notes, until he reached the end, where he found a slip of paper pasted to the strip and bearing the note: "Footprints cease here. Track turned off to left into heather. Length of foot, 12½ inches. Length of stride from heel to heel, 34 inches."

Having rapidly copied this note on to his block, Thorndyke resumed his examination with eager interest. Returning to the starting-point, he again examined a print of the left foot and then followed its successive prints to the final one at the end of the strip. Again he came back to the starting-point; but now, taking this as a centre, he began to move backwards and forwards, at first taking a dozen prints in each direction, then, by degrees, reducing the distance of his excursions until he came down to a single print of the right foot—a specially clear impression, marked with the number 93. This he again examined through the little microscope with the most intense scrutiny. Then, with a like concentrated attention, he examined first the preceding right-foot print, 91, and then the succeeding one, 95. Finally, he turned to the map to locate number 93, which he found near the middle of a wall—apparently the enclosing wall of a large garden or plantation—and exactly opposite a gate in that wall.

From this moment Thorndyke's interest in his original investigations seemed to become extinct. The little microscope, the scale, even the photographs themselves, were neglected and unnoticed, while he sat with his eyes fixed on the map—yet seeming to look through it rather than at it—evidently immersed in profound thought. For a long time he sat thus, immovable as a seated statue. At length he rose from his chair, and, mechanically filling his pipe, began slowly to pace up and down the room, and to any observer who knew him, had there been one, the intense gravity of his expression, the slight frown, the compressed lips, the downcast eyes, as well as the unlighted pipe that he grasped in his hand, would have testified that some problem of more than common intricacy was being turned over in his mind and its factors sorted out and collated.

He had been pacing the room for nearly half an hour when a key was softly inserted into the latch of the outer door. The door opened and closed quietly, and then a gentle tap on the knocker of the inner door heralded the entry of a small gentleman of somewhat clerical aspect and uncommon crinkliness of countenance, who greeted Thorndyke with a deprecating smile.

"I hope, sir," said he, "that I am not disturbing you, but I thought that I had better remind you that you have not had any supper."

"Dear me!" exclaimed Thorndyke. "What a memory you have, Polton. And to think that I, who am really the interested party, should have overlooked the fact. Well, what do you propose?"

Polton glanced at the table with a sympathetic eye. "You won't want your things disturbed, I expect, if you have got a job on hand. I had better put your supper in the little laboratory. It won't take more than five minutes."

"That will do admirably," said Thorndyke. "And, by the way, I think that adjourned inquest at Aylesbury is the day after to-morrow, isn't it?"

"Yes, sir, Thursday. I fixed the letter on the appointment board."

"Well, as there is nothing pressing on Friday, I think I will stay the night there and come back on Friday evening if nothing urgent turns up in the interval."

"Yes, sir. Will you want anything special in the research case?"

"I shall not take the research case," replied Thorndyke; "in fact, I don't know that I want anything excepting the one-inch ordnance map, unless I take that stick of yours."

Polton's face brightened. "I wish you would, sir," he said persuasively. "You have never tried it since I made it, and I am sure you will find it a most useful instrument."

"I am sure I shall," said Thorndyke; "and perhaps I might as well take the little telephoto camera, if you will have it charged."

"I will charge it to-night, sir, and overhaul the stick. And your supper will be ready in five minutes."

With this Polton disappeared silently as he had come, leaving his principal to his meditations.

*

On the following Friday morning, at about half-past ten, Dr. John Thorndyke might have been seen—if there had been any one to see him, which there was not—seated in a first-class smoking-compartment in the Aylesbury to London train. But he was evidently not going to London, for, as the train slowed down on approaching Borley station, he pocketed the folded ordnance map which he had been studying, stood up and took his stick down from the rack.

Now this stick was the only blot on Thorndyke's appearance. Apart from it his "turn-out" was entirely satisfactory and appropriate to his country surroundings without being either rustic or sporting. But that stick, with a tweed suit and a soft hat, struck a note of deepest discord. With a frock-coat and a top-hat it might have passed, though even then it would have called for a Falstaffian bearer. But as a country stick it really wouldn't do at all.

In the first place it was offensively straight—as straight as a length of metal tube. It was of an uncomely thickness, a full inch in diameter. As to the material, it might, by an exceedingly bad judge, have been mistaken for ebony. In fact, it was, as to its surface, strongly reminiscent of optician's black enamel. And the handle was no better. Of the same funereal hue and an unreasonable thickness, it had the stark mechanical regularity of an elbow-joint on a gas pipe, and, to make it worse, its end was finished by a sort of terminal cap. Moreover, on looking down the shaft of the stick, a close observer would have detected, about fifteen inches from the handle, a fine transverse crack, suggestive of a concealed joint. A sharp-eyed rural constable would have "spotted" it at a glance as a walking-stick gun; and he would have been wrong.

However, despite its aesthetic shortcomings, Thorndyke seemed to set some store by it, for he lifted it from the rack with evident care, and with the manner of lifting something heavier than an ordinary walking-stick; and when he stepped forth from the station, instead of holding it by its unlovely handle with its ferrule on the ground, he carried it "at the trail," grasping it by its middle.

On leaving the station precincts, Thorndyke set forth with the confident air of one who is on familiar ground, though, as a matter of fact, he had never been in the district before; but he had that power, which comes by practice, of memorizing a map that makes unvisited regions familiar and is apt to cause astonishment to the aboriginal inhabitants. Swinging along at an easy but rapid pace, he presently entered a quiet, semi-suburban road which he followed for a quarter of a mile, looking about him keenly, and identifying the features of the map as he went. At length he came to a kissing-gate which gave access to a footpath, and, turning into this, he strode away along the path, looking closely at its surface and once stopping and retracing his steps for a few yards to examine his own footprints.

A few hundred yards farther on he crossed another road, more definitely rural in character, and noted at the corner a pleasant-looking house of some age, standing back behind a well-kept garden, its front entrance sheltered by a wooden porch which was now almost hidden by a mass of climbing roses. The side wall of the garden abutted on the footpath and extended along it for a distance that suggested somewhat extensive grounds. At this point Thorndyke reduced his pace to a slow walk, scrutinizing the ground—on which he could detect, even now, occasional fragmentary traces of the familiar footprints of Harold's photographs—and noting how, since crossing the road, he had passed completely out of the last vestiges of the town into the open country.

He had traversed rather more than half the length of the wall when he came to a green-painted wooden gate, before which he halted for a few moments. There were, however, no features of interest to note beyond the facts that its loop handle was unprovided with a latch and that it was secured with a Yale lock. But as he stood looking at it with a deeply reflective air, he was aware of a sound proceeding from within—a pleasant sound, though curiously out of key with his own thoughts—the sound of some one whistling, very skilfully and melodiously, the old-fashioned air, "Alice, where art thou?" He smiled grimly, keenly appreciative of the whimsical incongruity of these cheerful, innocent strains with the circumstances that had brought him thither; then he turned away and walked slowly to the end of the wall where it was joined by another, which enclosed the end of the grounds. Here he halted and looked along the path towards a wood which was visible in the distance; then, turning, he looked back along the way by which he had come. In neither direction was there any one in sight, and Thorndyke noted that he had not met a single person since he had passed through the kissing-gate. Apparently this path was quite extraordinarily unfrequented.

Having made this observation, Thorndyke stepped off the path and walked a few paces along the end wall—which abutted on a field—to a spot where an apple tree in the grounds rose above the summit. Here he stopped, and, having glanced up at the wall—which was nearly seven feet high—grasped the uncomely stick with both hands, one on either side of the concealed joint, and gave a sharp twist. Immediately the stick became divided into two parts, the lower of which—that bearing the ferrule—Thorndyke stood against the wall. It could now be seen that the upper part terminated in a blackened brass half-cylinder, the flat face of which was occupied by a little circular glass window, and when Thorndyke had unscrewed the cap from the end of the handle, the latter was seen to be a metal tube, within which was another little glass window—the eye-piece. In effect, Polton's hideous walking-stick was a disguised periscope.

Taking up a position close to the wall, Thorndyke slowly raised the periscope until its end stood an inch or so above the top of the wall, with the little window looking into the enclosure. The eye-piece being now at a convenient level, he applied his eye to it, and immediately had the sensation of looking through a circular hole in the wall. Through this aperture (which was, of course, the aperture of the object-glass above him, reflected by a pair of prisms) he looked into a large garden, enclosed on all sides by the high wall and having apparently only two doors or gates, the one at the side, which he had already seen, and another which appeared to open into another garden nearer the house, and which, like the side gate, seemed to be fitted with a night-latch of the Yale type. On one side, partly concealed by a half-grown yew hedge, was a long, low building which, by the windows in its roof, appeared to be some kind of workshop; and by rotating the periscope it was possible to catch a glimpse of part of what seemed to be a summer-house in the corner opposite the workshop. Otherwise, excepting a narrow flower border and a few fruit trees ranged along the wall, the whole of the enclosure was occupied by a large lawn, the wide expanse of which was broken only by a sun-dial, beside which, at the moment, a man was standing; and on man and sun-dial, Thorndyke, after his swift preliminary survey, concentrated his attention.

The stone pillar of the dial was obviously ancient. Equally obviously the stone base on which it stood was brand new. Moreover, the part of the lawn immediately surrounding the base was yellow and faded as if it had been recently raised and relaid. The manifest inference was that the dial had but lately been placed in its present position; and this inference was supported by the occupation in which the man was engaged. On the stone base stood a Windsor chair, the seat of which bore one or two tools and a pair of spectacles. Thorndyke noted the spectacles with interest, observing that they had "curl sides" and were therefore habitually worn; and since they had been discarded while their owner consulted a book that he held, it seemed to follow that he must be near-sighted.

As Thorndyke watched, the man closed the book and laid it on the chair, when by its shape and size, its scarlet back and apple-green sides, it was easily recognizable as Whitaker's Almanack. Having laid down the book, the man drew out his watch, and, holding it in his hand, approached the pillar and grasped the gnomon of the dial; and now Thorndyke could see that the dial-plate had been unfixed from its bed, for it moved visibly as the gnomon was grasped. The nature of the operation was now quite clear. The man was re-setting the dial. He had taken out the Equation of Time from Whitaker and was now adjusting the dial-plate by means of his watch to show the correct Apparent Solar Time.

At this point—leaving the man standing beside the pillar, watch in hand—Thorndyke picked up the detached portion of the stick, and stepping along the wall, glanced up and down the path. So far as he could see—nearly a quarter of a mile in each direction—he had the path to himself; and, noting with some surprise and no little interest the remarkable paucity of wayfarers, he returned to his post and resumed his observations.

The man had now put away his watch and taken up a hammer and bradawl. Thorndyke noted the workmanlike character of the former—a rather heavy ball-pane hammer such as engineers use—and when the bradawl was inserted into one of the screw-holes of the dial-plate and driven home into the lead bed with a single tap, he observed the deftness with which the gentle, calculated blow was delivered with the rather ponderous tool. So, too, with the driving of the screw; it was done with the unmistakable ease and readiness of the skilled workman.

Having rapidly made these observations, Thorndyke drew from his hip pocket the little camera and opened it, setting the focus by the scale to the assumed distance—about sixty feet—fixing the wire release and setting the shutter to half a second—the shortest exposure that was advisable with a telephoto lens. Another peep through the periscope showed the man in the act of again inserting the bradawl, and, incidentally, presenting a well-lighted right profile; whereupon Thorndyke raised the camera and placed it on the top of the wall with the wire release hanging down and the lens pointed, as well as he could judge, at the sun-dial. Then, as the man poised the hammer preparatory to striking, he pressed the button of the release and immediately took down the camera and changed the film.

Once more he went to the corner of the wall and looked up and down the path. This time a man was visible—apparently a labourer—coming from the direction of the town. But he was a long distance away and was advancing at a pace so leisurely that Thorndyke decided to complete his business, if possible, before he should arrive. A glance through the periscope showed the man in the garden driving another screw. When he had driven it home, he stepped round the pillar to deal with the screws on the other side. As he inserted the bradawl and balanced the hammer, presenting now his left profile, Thorndyke lifted the camera to the top of the wall, made the exposure, took down the camera, and having changed the film, closed it and put it in his pocket. Then he joined up the two parts of the stick, fixed the cap on the eye-piece and came out on to the path, turning towards the town to meet the labourer. But the latter had now disappeared, having apparently turned into the road on which the house fronted. Having the path once more to himself, Thorndyke walked along it to the gate, where he paused and rapped on it smartly with his knuckles.

After a short interval, during which he repeated the summons, the gate was opened a few inches and the man whom he had seen within looked out with an air of slightly irritable enquiry.

"I must apologize for disturbing you," Thorndyke said with disarming suavity, "but I heard some one within, and there was no one about from whom I could make my enquiry."

"You are not disturbing me in the least," the other replied, not less suavely. "I shall be most happy to give you any information that I can. What was the enquiry that you wished to make?"

As he asked the question, the stranger stepped out on the path, drawing the gate to after him, and looked inquisitively at Thorndyke.

"I wanted to know," the latter replied, "whether this footpath leads to a wood—Potter's Wood, I think it is called. You see, I am a stranger to this neighbourhood."

On this the man seemed to look at him with heightened interest as he replied:

"Yes, it leads through the wood about half a mile farther on."

"And where does it lead to eventually?"

"It crosses a patch of heath and joins a by-road that runs from the town to the main London road. Was that where you wanted to go?"

"No," replied Thorndyke. "It is the path itself that I am concerned with. The fact is, I am making a sort of informal inspection in connection with the case of a man who disappeared a short time ago—the manager of a local branch of Perkins's Bank. I understand that he was last seen walking along this path."

"Ah," said the other, "I remember the affair. And is he still missing?"

"Yes. He has never been seen or heard of since he started along this path. What is the wood like? Is it a place in which a man might lose himself?"

The other shook his head. "No, it is only a small wood. A sound and sober man could not get lost in it. Of course, if a man were taken ill and strayed into the wood, he might die and lie hidden for months. Has the wood been searched?"

"I really can't say. It ought to have been."

"I thought," said the stranger, "that you might, perhaps, be connected with the police."

"No," replied Thorndyke. "I am a lawyer and I look after some of the affairs of the bank. One of the directors mentioned this disappearance to me a few days ago, and as I happened to be in the neighbourhood to-day, I thought I would come and take a look round. Perhaps you could show me where we are on my map. It is a little confusing to a stranger."

He drew out the folded map and handed it to his new acquaintance, who took it and pored over it as if he found it difficult to decipher. As he did so, Thorndyke took the opportunity to look him over with the most searching scrutiny; his face, his hair, his spectacles, his hands and his feet; and when he had inspected the left side of the face—which was the one presented to him—he crossed as if to look over the man's right shoulder and examined the face from that side.

"This dotted line seems to be the footpath," said the stranger, tracing it with the point of a pencil. "This black dot must be my house, and here is the wood with the dotted line running through it. I think that is quite clear."

"Perfectly clear, thank you," said Thorndyke, as the other handed him back the map. "I am very greatly obliged to you and I must again apologize for having disturbed you."

"Not at all," the stranger returned genially; "and I hope your inspection may be successful."

Thorndyke thanked him again, and with mutual bows they separated, the one retiring into his domain, the other setting forth in the direction of the wood.

For some minutes Thorndyke continued to walk at a rapid pace along the path. Only when a sharp turn carried him out of sight of the walled garden did he halt to jot down in his note-book a brief summary of his observations while they were fresh in his mind. Not that the notes were really necessary, for, even as he had made those observations, the significance of the facts that they supplied became apparent. Now, as he walked, he turned them over again and again.

What had he observed? Nothing very sensational, to be sure. He had seen a man who had recently set up in his garden a pillar dial on a broad stone base. The dial was old, but the base was new and seemed to have been specially constructed for its present purpose. The garden in which it had been set up was completely enclosed, was extremely secluded, was remote from its own or any other house, and was very thoroughly secured against any possible intrusion by two locked gates. The man himself was a skilled workman, or at least a very handy man; ingenious and resourceful, too, for he could time a sun-dial, a thing that not every handy man could do. Then he appeared to have some kind of workshop of a size suggesting good accommodation and facilities for work, and this workshop was in a secluded situation, very secure from observation. But in these facts there would seem to be nothing remarkable; only they were in singular harmony with certain other facts—very remarkable facts indeed—that Thorndyke had gleaned from an examination of Harold's absurd photographs.

And there was the man himself, and especially his spectacles. When Thorndyke had seen those spectacles lying on the chair while their owner drove in the screws, looked at his watch, and scrutinized the shadow on the dial, he had naturally assumed that the man was near-sighted; that he had taken off his "distance" glasses to get the advantage of his near sight for the near work. But when the man appeared at the gate, it was immediately evident that he was not near-sighted. The spectacles were convex bi-focal glasses, with an upper half of nearly plain glass and a lower segment distinctly convex, suited for long sight or "old sight." A near-sighted man could not have seen through them. But neither did their owner seem to need them, since he had taken them off just when they should have been most useful—for near work. Moreover, when Thorndyke had presented the map, the man had looked at it, not through the lower "reading" segment, but through the weak, upper, "distance" segment. In short, the man did not need those spectacles at all. So far from being a convenience, they were a positive inconvenience. Then, why did he wear them? Why had he put them on to come to the gate? There could be only one answer. People who wear useless and inconvenient spectacles do so in order to alter their appearance; as a species of disguise, in fact. Then it seemed as if this man had some reason for wishing to conceal his identity. But what could that reason be?

As to his appearance, he was a decidedly good-looking man, with an alert, intelligent face that was in harmony with his speech and bearing. His mouth and chin were concealed by a moustache and a short beard, but his nose was rather handsome and very striking, for it was of that rare type which is seen in the classical Greek sculptures. His ears were both well-shaped, but one of them—the right—was somewhat disfigured by a small "port-wine mark," which stained the lobule a deep purple. But it was quite small and really inconspicuous.

This was the sum of Thorndyke's observations, to which may be added that the man appeared to be prematurely grey and that his face, despite its cheerful geniality, had that indefinable character that may be detected in the faces of men who have passed through long periods of stress and mental suffering. Only one datum remained unascertained, and Thorndyke added it to his collection when, having traversed the wood and the heath, he returned to the town by way of the by-road. Encountering a postman on his round, he stopped him and enquired:

"I wonder if you can tell me who is living at 'The Chestnuts' now? You know the house I mean. It stands at the corner—"

"Oh, I know 'The Chestnuts,' sir. Colonel Barnett used to live there. But he went away nigh upon two years ago, and, after it had been empty for a month or two, it was bought by the gentleman who lives there now, Mr. Pottermack."

"That is a queer name," said Thorndyke. "How does he spell it?"

"P.o.t.t.e.r.m.a.c.k," the postman replied. "Marcus Pottermack, Esq. It is a queer name, sir. I've never met with it before. But he is a very pleasant gentleman, all the same."

Thorndyke thanked the postman for his information, on which he pondered as he made his way to the station. It was a very queer name. In fact, there was about it something rather artificial; something that was not entirely out of character with the unwanted spectacles.

VII

O N EACH OF THE TWO MEN WHO PARTED AT THE GATE THE brief interview produced its appropriate effects; in each it generated a certain train of thought which, later, manifested itself in certain actions. In Mr. Pottermack, as he softly reopened the gate to listen to the retreating footsteps, once even venturing to peep out at the tall figure that was striding away up the path, the encounter was productive of a dim uneasiness, a slight disturbance of the sense of security that had been growing on him since the night of the tragedy. For the first few days thereafter he had been on wires. All seemed to be going well, but he was constantly haunted by that ever-recurring question, "Was there anything vital that he had overlooked?"

The mysterious photographer, too, had been a disturbing element, occasioning anxious speculations on the motive or purpose of his inexplicable proceedings and on the possibility of something being brought to light by the photographs that was beyond the scope of human vision. But as the days had passed with no whisper of suspicion, as the local excitement died down and the incident faded into oblivion, his fears subsided, and by degrees he settled down into a feeling of comfortable security.

And after all, why not? In the first few days his own secret knowledge had prevented him from seeing the affair in its true perspective. But now, looking at it calmly with the eyes of those who had not that knowledge, what did Lewson's disappearance amount to?

It was a matter of no importance at all. A disreputable rascal had absconded with a hundred pounds that did not belong to him. He had disappeared and no one knew whither he had gone. Nor did any one particularly care. Doubtless the police would keep a look-out for him; but he was only a minor delinquent, and they would assuredly make no extraordinary efforts to trace him.

So Mr. Pottermack argued, and quite justly; and thus arguing came by degrees to the comfortable conclusion that the incident was closed and that he might now take up again the thread of his peaceful life, secure alike from the menace of the law and the abiding fear of impoverishment and treachery.

It was this new and pleasant feeling of security that had been disturbed by his encounter with the strange lawyer. Not that he was seriously alarmed. The man seemed harmless enough. He was not, apparently, making any real investigations but just a casual inspection of the neighbourhood, prompted, as it appeared, by a not very lively curiosity. And as a tracker he seemed to be of no account, since he could not even find his position on a one-inch map.

But for all that, the incident was slightly disquieting. Pottermack had assumed that the Lewson affair was closed. But now it seemed that it was not closed. And it was a curious coincidence that this man should have knocked at *his* gate, should have selected *him* for these enquiries. No doubt it was but chance; but still, there was the coincidence. Again, there was the man himself. He had seemed foolish about the map. But he did not look at all like a foolish man. On the contrary, his whole aspect and bearing had a suggestion of power, of acute intellect and quiet strength of character. As Pottermack recalled his appearance and manner he found himself asking again and again: Was there anything behind this seemingly chance encounter? Had this lawyer seen those photographs, and if so, had he found in them anything more than met the eye? Could he have had any special reason for knocking at this particular gate? And what on earth could he be doing with that walking-stick gun?

Reflections such as these pervaded Mr. Pottermack's consciousness as he went about his various occupations. They did not seriously disturb his peace of mind, but still they did create a certain degree of unrest, and this presently revived in his mind certain plans which he had considered and rejected; plans for further establishing his security by shifting the field of possible inquiry yet farther from his own neighbourhood.

On Thorndyke the effects of the meeting were quite different. He had come doubting if a certain surmise that he had formed could possibly be correct. He had gone away with his doubts dispelled and his surmise converted into definite belief. The only unsolved question that remained in his mind was, "Who was Marcus Pottermack?" The answer that suggested itself was improbable in the extreme. But it was the only one that he could produce, and if it were wrong he was at the end of his unassisted resources.

The first necessity, therefore, was to eliminate the improbable—or else to confirm it. Then he would know where he stood and could consider what action he would take. Accordingly he began by working up the scanty material that he had collected. The photographs, when developed and enlarged by Polton, yielded two very fair portraits of Mr. Pottermack showing clearly the right and left profiles respectively; and while Polton was dealing with these, his principal made a systematic, but not very hopeful, inspection of the map in search of possible finger-prints. He had made a mental note of the way in which Pottermack had held the map, and even of the spots which his finger-tips had touched, and on these he now began cautiously to operate with two fine powders, a black and a white, applying each to its appropriate background.

The results were poor enough, but yet they were better than

he had expected. Pottermack had held the map in his left hand, the better to manipulate the pencil with which he pointed, and his thumb had been planted on a green patch which represented a wood. Here the white powder settled and showed a print which, poor as it was, would present no difficulties to the experts and which would be more distinct in a photograph, as the background would then appear darker. The prints of the finger-tips which the black powder brought out on the white background were more imperfect and were further confused by the black lettering. Still, Thorndyke had them all carefully photographed and enlarged to twice the natural size, and, having blocked out on the negative the surrounding lettering (to avoid giving any information that might be better withheld), had prints made and mounted on card.

With these in his letter-case and the two portraits in his pocket, he set forth one morning for New Scotland Yard, proposing to seek the assistance of his old friend, Mr. Superintendent Miller, or, if he should not be available, that of the officer in charge of criminal records. However, it happened fortunately that the Superintendent was in his office, and thither Thorndyke, having sent in his card, was presently conducted.

"Well, doctor," said Miller, shaking hands heartily, "here you are, gravelled as usual. Now what sort of mess do you want us to help you out of?"

Thorndyke produced his letter-case, and, extracting the photographs, handed them to the Superintendent.

"Here," he said, "are three finger-prints; apparently the thumb and first two fingers of the left hand."

"Ha," said Miller, inspecting the three photographs critically. "Why 'apparently'?"

"I mean," explained Thorndyke, "that that was what I inferred from their position on the original document."

"Which seems to have been a map," remarked Miller, with a faint grin. "Well, I expect you know. Shall I take it that they are the thumb and index and middle finger of the left hand?"

"I think you may," said Thorndyke.

"*I* think I may," agreed Miller; "and now the question is: What about it? I suppose you want us to tell you whose finger-prints they are; and you want to gammon us that you don't know already. And I suppose—as I see you have been faking the negative—that you don't want to give us any information?"

"In effect," replied Thorndyke, "you have, with your usual acuteness, diagnosed the position exactly. I don't much want to give any details, but I will tell you this much. If my suspicions are correct, these are the finger-prints of a man who has been dead some years."

"Dead!" exclaimed Miller. "Good Lord, doctor, what a vindictive man you are! But you don't suppose that we follow the criminal class into the next world, do you?"

"I have been assuming that you don't destroy records. If you do, you are unlike any government officials that I have ever met. But I hope I was right."

"In the main, you were. We don't keep the whole set of documents of a dead man, but we have a set of skeleton files on which the personal documents—the finger-prints, photographs and description—are preserved. So I expect we shall be able to tell you what you want to know."

"I am sorry," said Thorndyke, "that they are such wretchedly poor prints. You don't think that they are too imperfect to identify, I hope."

Miller inspected the photographs afresh. "I don't see much amiss with them," said he. "You can't expect a crook to go about with a roller and inking-plate in his pocket so as to give you nice sharp prints. These are better than a good many that our people have to work from. And besides, there are three digits from one hand. That gives you part of the formula straight away. No, the experts won't make any trouble about these. But supposing these prints are not on the file?"

"Then we shall take it that I suspected the wrong man."

"Quite so. But, if I am not mistaken, your concern is to prove whose finger-prints they are in order that you can say whose finger-prints they are not. Now, supposing that we don't find them on the files of the dead men, would it help you if we tried the current files—the records of the crooks who are still in business? Or would you rather not?"

"If it would not be giving you too much trouble," said Thorndyke, "I should be very much obliged if you would."

"No trouble at all," said Miller, adding with a sly smile: "only it occurred to me that it might be embarrassing to you if we found your respected client's finger-prints on the live register."

"That would be a highly interesting development," said Thorndyke, "though I don't think it a likely one. But it is just as well to exhaust the possibilities."

"Quite," agreed Miller; and thereupon he wrote the brief particulars on a slip of paper which he put into an envelope with the photographs, and, having rung a bell, handed the envelope to the messenger who appeared in response to the summons.

"I don't suppose we shall have to keep you waiting very long," said the Superintendent. "They have an extraordinarily ingenious system of filing. Out of all the thousands of finger-prints that they have, they can pounce on the one that is wanted in the course of a few minutes. It seems incredible, and yet it is essentially simple—just a matter of classification and ringing the changes on different combinations of types."

"You are speaking of completely legible prints?" suggested Thorndyke.

"Yes, the sort of prints that we get sent in from local prisons for identification of a man who has been arrested under a false name. Of course, when we get a single imperfect print found by the police at a place where a crime has been committed, a bit more time has to be spent. Then we have not only got to place the print, but we've got to make mighty sure that it is the right one, because an arrest and a prosecution hangs on it. You don't want to arrest a man and then, when you come to take his finger-prints properly, find that they are the wrong ones. So, in the case of an imperfect print, you have got to do some careful ridge-tracing and counting and systematic checking of individual ridge-characters, such as bifurcations and islands. But, even so, they don't take so very long over it. The practised eye picks out at a glance details that an unpractised eye can hardly recognize even when they are pointed out."

The Superintendent was proceeding to dilate, with professional enthusiasm, on the wonders of finger-print technique and the efficiency of the Department when his eulogies were confirmed by the entrance of an officer carrying a sheaf of papers and Thorndyke's photographs, which he delivered into Miller's hands.

"Well, doctor," said the Superintendent, after a brief glance at the documents, "here is your information. Jeffrey Brandon is the name of the late lamented. Will that do for you?"

"Yes," replied Thorndyke, "that is the name I expected to hear."

"Good," said Miller. "I see they have kept the whole of his papers for some reason. I will just glance through them while you are doing Thomas Didymus with the finger-prints. But it is quite obvious, if you compare your photographs with the rolled impressions, that the ridge-patterns are identical."

He handed Thorndyke the finger-print sheet, to which were attached the photograph and personal description, and sat down at the table to look over the other documents, while Thorndyke walked over to the window to get a better light. But he did not concern himself with the finger-prints beyond a very brief inspection. It was the photograph that interested him. It showed, on the same print, a right profile and a full face; of which he concentrated his attention on the former. A rather remarkable profile it was, strikingly handsome and curiously classical in outline, rather recalling the head of Antinous in the British Museum. Thorndyke examined it minutely, and then—his back being turned to Miller—he drew from his waistcoat pocket the right profile of Mr. Pottermack and placed it beside the prison photograph.

A single glance made it clear that the two photographs represented the same face. Though one showed a clean-shaven young man with the full lips and strong, rounded chin completely revealed, while the other was a portrait of a bearded, spectacled, middle-aged man, yet they were unmistakably the same. The remarkable nose and brow and the shapely ear were identical in the two photographs; and in both, the lobe of the ear was marked at its tip by a dark spot.

From the photograph he turned to the description. Not that it was necessary to seek further proof; and he did, in fact, merely glance through the particulars. But that rapid glance gathered fresh confirmation. "Height 5 feet 6½ inches, hair chestnut, eyes darkish grey, small port-wine mark on lobe of right ear," etc. All the details of Jeffrey Brandon's personal characteristics applied perfectly to Mr. Marcus Pottermack.

"I don't quite see," said Miller, as he took the papers from Thorndyke and laid them on the others, "why they kept all these documents. The conviction doesn't look to me very satisfactory—I don't like these cases where the prosecution has all its eggs in one basket, with the possible chance that they may be bad eggs; and it was a devil of a sentence for a first offence. But as the poor beggar is dead, and no reconsideration of either the conviction or the sentence is possible, there doesn't seem much object in preserving the records. Still, there may have been some reason at the time."

In his own mind, Thorndyke was of opinion that there might have been a very good reason. But he did not communicate this opinion. He had obtained the information that he had sought and was not at all desirous of troubling still waters; and his experience having taught him that Mr. Superintendent Miller was an exceedingly "noticing" gentleman, he thought it best to avoid further discussion and take his departure, after having expressed his appreciation of the assistance that he had received.

Nevertheless, for some time after he had gone, the Superintendent remained wrapped in profound thought; and that his cogitations were in some way concerned with the departed visitor would have been suggested by the circumstance that he sauntered to the window and looked down with a speculative eye on that visitor as he strode across the courtyard towards the Whitehall gate.

Meanwhile Thorndyke's mind was no less busy. As he wended his way Templewards he reviewed the situation in all its bearings. The wildly improbable had turned out to be true. He had made a prodigiously long shot and he had hit the mark; which was gratifying inasmuch as it justified a previous rather hypothetical train of reasoning. Marcus Pottermack, Esq., was undoubtedly the late Jeffrey Brandon. There was now no question about that. The only question that remained was what was to be done in the matter; and that question would have been easier to decide if he had been in possession of more facts. He had heard Mr. Stalker's opinion of the conviction, based on intimate knowledge of the circumstances, and he had heard that of the Superintendent, based on an immense experience of prosecutions. He was inclined to agree with them both; and the more so inasmuch as he had certain knowledge which they had not.

In the end, he decided to take no action at present, but to keep a watchful eye for further developments.

VIII

MR. POTTERMACK SEEKS ADVENTURE

IN THE LAST CHAPTER IT WAS STATED THAT ONE OF THE EFFECTS of Thorndyke's appearance at the side gate of "The Chestnuts," Borley, was to revive in the mind of its tenant certain projects which had been considered and rejected. But perhaps the word "rejected" overstates the case. For the continued existence in a locked drawer in Mr. Pottermack's workshop of a coat which had once been James Lewson's and a bundle of twenty five-pound notes implied a purpose which had been abandoned only conditionally and subject to possible reconsideration.

Again and again, as the destructor which stood in the corner beyond the tool-shed smoked and flared as he fed it with combustible rubbish, had he been on the point of flinging into it the coat and the banknotes and thereby reducing to unrecognizable ash the last visible traces of the tragedy. And every time his hand had been stayed by the thought that possibly, in some circumstances as yet unforeseen, these mementoes of that night of horror might yet be made to play a useful part. So, not without many a twinge of uneasiness, he had let these incriminating objects lie hidden in the locked drawer. And now, as it seemed to him, the circumstances had arisen in which some of them, at least, might be turned to account.

What were those circumstances? Simply the state of mind of the strange lawyer. To the people of Borley, including the police, Lewson was a man who had absconded and vanished. His tracks had shown him striking out across country towards the London road. Those tracks, it is true, broke off short on the heath and had not re-appeared elsewhere, but no one doubted that he had gone clear away from the vicinity of Borley and was now in hiding at a safe distance from his old haunts. The natives of the district had never given Mr. Pottermack a moment's anxiety. But with this lawyer the case was different. The disturbing thing about him was that his curiosity, tepid as it was, concerned itself, not with the man who had vanished but with the locality from which he disappeared. But curiosity of that kind, Mr. Pottermack felt, was a thing that was not to be encouraged. On the contrary, it had better be diverted into a more wholesome channel. In short, the time had come when it would be desirable that James Lewson should make his appearance, if only by proxy, in some district as far removed as possible from the neighbourhood of "The Chestnuts," Borley.

So it came about that Mr. Pottermack prepared to set forth along that perilous track beaten smooth by the feet of those who do not know when to let well alone.

For some days after having come to his decision in general terms he was at a loss for a detailed plan. Somehow, the stolen notes had got to be put into circulation. But not by him. The numbers of those notes were known, and, as soon as they began to circulate, some, at least, of them would be identified and would be rigorously traced. The problem was how to get rid of them in a plausible manner without appearing in the transaction; and for some time he could think of no better plan than that of simply dropping them in a quiet London street, a plan which he summarily rejected as not meeting the necessities of the case. The fruitful suggestion eventually came from a newsboy who was roaring "Egbert Bruce's Finals" outside the station. In an instant, Mr. Pottermack realized that here was the perfect plan, and having purchased a paper, took it home to extract the details on which he proposed to base his strategic scheme.

The "finals" related to a somewhat unselect race-meeting which was to take place in a couple of days' time at Illingham in Surrey, a place conveniently accessible from Borley and yet remote enough to render it unlikely that he would be seen there by any of his fellow-townsmen. Not that his presence there would be in any way suspicious or incriminating, but, still, the less people knew about his movements the better.

On the appointed day he set forth betimes, neatly but suitably dressed and all agog for the adventure, tame though it promised to be if it worked according to plan. To Mrs. Gadby he had explained—quite truthfully—that he was going to London; and if she had wanted confirmation of the statement, it could have been supplied by sundry natives of the town with whom he exchanged greetings on the platform as he waited for the London train.

But despite his geniality, he made a point of selecting an empty first-class compartment and shutting himself in. He had no hankering for human companionship. For beneath the exhilaration engendered by this little adventure was an appreciable tinge of nervousness. No foreseeable contingency threatened his safety; but it is an undeniable fact that a man who carries, buttoned up in his inside breast pocket, twenty stolen banknotes, of which the numbers are known to the police, and of his possession of which he could give no credible account, is not without some reason for nervousness. And that was Mr. Pottermack's position. Just before starting, he had disinterred the whole bundle of those fatal notes and stuffed them into a compartment of the letter-case which he usually carried in his breast pocket. He had also hunted up another letter-case, aged, outworn and shabby, into which he had put a half-dozen ten-shilling notes for the day's expenses and stowed it in the outside hip pocket of his jacket.

As soon as the train had fairly started, he proceeded to make certain rearrangements related to his plan of campaign. Taking out the two letter-wallets—which we may distinguish as the inner and the outer—he laid them on the seat beside him. From the inner wallet he took out five of the stolen notes and placed them loosely in a compartment of the other wallet with their ends projecting so that they were plainly visible when it was open; and from the outer wallet he transferred four of the ten-shilling notes to the inner (he had paid for his ticket in silver). Then he returned the two wallets to their respective pockets and buttoned up his coat.

From Marylebone Station he walked to Baker Street, where he took a train for Waterloo and arrived to find the great station filled with a seething crowd of race-goers. Not, on the whole, a prepossessing crowd, though all sorts and conditions of men were represented. But Mr. Pottermack was not hypercritical. At the over-smart, horsey persons, the raffish sporting men with race-glasses slung over their shoulders, the men of mystery with handbags or leather satchels, he glanced with benevolent interest. They had their uses in the economy of nature—in fact, he hoped to make use of some of them himself. So tolerant, indeed, was he that he even greeted with a kindly smile the notices pasted up urging passengers to beware of pickpockets. For in that respect his condition was unique. In spite of the wallet in his outside pocket, he enjoyed complete immunity; and as he joined the queue at the booking-office window, he reflected with grim amusement that, of all that throng, he was probably the only person who had come expressly to have his pocket picked.

As he approached the window he drew the wallet from his outside pocket, and, opening it, inspected its interior with an air of indecision, took out one of the banknotes, put it back, and, finally dipping into the other compartment, fished out a ten-shilling note. Holding this in one hand and the open wallet in the other, he at last came opposite the window, where he purchased his ticket and moved on to make way for a large, red-faced man who seemed to be in a hurry. As he walked on slowly towards the barrier, pocketing the wallet as he went, the crowd surged impatiently past him; but watching that crowd as it swept on ahead, he could see no sign of the red-faced man. That gentleman's hurry seemed suddenly to have evaporated, and it was only when Pottermack was entering his carriage and turned to look back that he observed his roseate friend immediately behind him. Instantly he entered the nearly full compartment, and as he took his seat he was careful to leave a vacant place on his right hand; and when the red-faced man, closely following him, plumped down into the vacant space and at once began to exercise his elbows, he smiled inwardly with the satisfaction of the fortunate angler who "sees his quill or cork down sink." In short, he felt a comfortable certainty that he had "got a bite."

It was now a matter of deep regret to him that he had neglected to provide himself at the bookstall with something to read. A newspaper would have been so helpful to his friend on the right. However, the deficiency was made up to a practicable extent by a couple of men who faced each other from the two corners to his left, and who, having spread a small rug across their joint knees, were good enough to give a demonstration for the benefit of the company at large of the immemorial three-card trick. Towards them Pottermack craned with an expression of eager interest that aroused in them an unjustified optimism. With intense concentration the operator continued over and over again to perform dummy turns, and the professional "mug," who sat opposite to Pottermack, continued with blatant perversity to spot the obviously wrong card every time, and pay up his losses with groans of surprise, while the fourth confederate, on Pottermack's left, nudged him from time to time and solicited in a whisper his opinion as to which was really the right card. It is needless to say that his opinion turned out invariably to be correct, but still he resisted the whispered entreaties of his neighbour to try his luck "seeing that he was such a dab at spotting 'em." Under other circumstances he would have invested the ten-shilling note for the sake of publicity. As things were, he did not dare to touch the wallet, or even put his hand to the pocket wherein it reposed. Premature discovery would have been fatal.

As the train sped on and consumed the miles of the short journey, the operator's invitations to Pottermack to try his luck became more urgent and less polite; until at length, as the destination drew near, they degenerated into mere objurgation and epithets of contempt. At length the train slowed down at the platform. Every one stood up and all together tried to squeeze through the narrow doorway, Pottermack himself emerging with unexpected velocity, propelled by a vigorous shove from behind. At the same moment his hat was lightly flicked off his head and fell among the feet of the crowd. He would have stooped to recover it, but the necessity was forestalled by an expert kick which sent it soaring aloft; and hardly had it descended when it rose again and yet again until, having taken its erratic flight over the fence, it came at last to rest in the station-master's garden. By the time it had been retrieved with the aid of the sympathetic station-master, the last of the passengers had filed through the barrier and Pottermack brought up the extreme rear like a belated straggler.

As soon as he had had time to recover from these agitating experiences his thoughts flew to the wallet and he thrust his hand into his outside pocket. To his unspeakable surprise, the wallet was still there. As he made the discovery he was aware of a pang of disappointment, even of a sense of injury. He had put his trust in the red-faced man, and behold! that rubicund impostor had betrayed him. It looked as if this plan of his was not so easy as it had appeared.

But when he came to the turnstile of the enclosure and drew out the wallet to extract the ten-shilling note—and incidentally to display its other contents—he realized that he had done the red-faced man an injustice. The ten-shilling note, indeed, was there, tucked away at the bottom of its compartment, but otherwise the wallet was empty. Pottermack could hardly believe his eyes. For a few moments he stood staring at it in astonishment until an impatient poke in the back and an imperative command to "pass along, please," recalled him to the present proceedings, when he swept up and pocketed his change and strolled away into the enclosure, meditating respectfully on the skill and tact of his red-faced acquaintance and wishing that he had made the discovery sooner. For, now, the wallet would need to be recharged for the benefit of the next artist. This he could have done easily in the empty station, but in the crowd which surrounded him the matter presented difficulties. He could not do it unobserved, and it would appear a somewhat odd proceeding—especially to the eye of a plain-clothes policeman. There must be a good number of those useful officials in the crowd, and it was of vital importance that he should not attract the attention of any of them.

He looked round in some bewilderment, seeking a secluded spot in which he could refill the outer wallet unnoticed. A vain quest! Every part of the enclosure, excepting the actual course, was filled with a seething multitude, varying in density but all-pervading. Here and there, a closely packed mass indicated some juggler, mountebank, thimble artist, or card expert, and some distance away a Punch and Judy show rose above the heads of the crowd, the sound of its drum and Pan's pipes and the unmistakable voice of the hero penetrating the general hubbub. Towards this exhibition Pottermack was directing his course when shouts of laughter proceeding from the interior of a small but dense crowd suggested that something amusing was happening there; whereupon Pottermack, renouncing the delights of Punch and Judy, began cautiously to elbow his way towards the centre of attraction.

At this moment a bell rang in the distance, and instantly the whole crowd was in motion, surging towards the course. And then began a most singular hurly-burly in Pottermack's immediate neighbourhood. An unseen foot trod heavily on his toes, and at the same moment he received a violent shove that sent him staggering to the right against a seedy-looking person who thumped him in the ribs and sent him reeling back to the left. Before he could recover his balance some one butted him in the back with such violence that he flew forward and impinged heavily on a small man in a straw hat—very much in it, in fact, for it had been banged down right over his eyes—who was beginning to protest angrily when some unseen force from behind propelled him towards Pottermack and another violent collision occurred. Thereafter Pottermack had but a confused consciousness of being pushed, pulled, thumped, pinched, and generally hustled until his head swam. And then, quite suddenly, the crowd streamed away towards the course and Pottermack was left alone with the straw-hatted man, who stood a few yards away, struggling to extract himself from his hat and at the same time feverishly searching his pockets. By the well-known process of suggestion, this latter action communicated itself to Mr. Pottermack, who proceeded to make a hasty survey of his own pockets, which resulted in the discovery that, though the inside wallet, securely buttoned in, was still intact, the outside, empty one had this time disappeared, and most of his small change with it.

Strange are the inconsistencies of the human mind. But a little while ago he had been willing to make a free gift of that wallet to his red-faced fellow-traveller. Now that it was gone he was quite appreciably annoyed. He had planned to recharge it with a fresh consignment to be planted in a desirable quarter, and its loss left him with the necessity of making some other plausible arrangements, and at the moment he could not think of any. To put the notes loose in his pocket seemed to be but inviting failure, for, to the sense of touch from without, the pocket would appear to be empty.

As he was thus cogitating, he caught the eye of the straw-hatted gentleman fixed upon him with unmistakable and undissembled suspicion. This was unpleasant, but one must make allowances. The man was, no doubt, rather upset. With a genial smile, Mr. Pottermack approached the stranger and expressed the rather optimistic hope that he had not suffered any loss; but the only reply that his enquiry elicited was an inarticulate grunt.

"They have been through my pockets," said Mr. Pottermack cheerfully, "but I am glad to say that they took nothing of any value."

"Ha," said the straw-hatted gentleman.

"Yes," pursued Pottermack, "they must have found me rather disappointing."

"Oh," said the other in a tone of sour indifference.

"Yes," said Pottermack, "all they got from me was an empty letter-case and a little loose silver."

"Ah," said the straw-hatted man.

"I hope," Pottermack repeated, beginning slightly to lose patience, "that you have not lost anything of considerable value."

For a moment or two the other made no reply. At length, fixing a baleful eye on Pottermack, he answered with significant emphasis: "If you want to know what they took, you'd better ask them"; and with this he turned away.

Pottermack also turned away—in the opposite direction, and some inward voice whispered to him that it were well to evacuate the neighbourhood of the man in the straw hat.

He strolled away, gradually increasing his pace, until he reached the outskirts of the crowd that had gathered at the margin of the course. By a sound of cheering he judged that some ridiculous horses were careering along somewhere beyond the range of his vision. But they were of no interest to him. They did, however, furnish him with a pretext for diving into the crowd and struggling towards the source of the noise, and this he did, regardless of the unseemly comments that he provoked and the thumps and prods that he received in his progress. When, as it seemed, he had become immovably embedded, he drew a deep breath and turned to look back. For a few blissful moments he believed that he had effected a masterly retreat and escaped finally from his suspicious fellow-victim; but suddenly there emerged into view a too-familiar battered straw hat, moving slowly through the resisting multitude, and moving in a bee-line in his direction.

Then it was that Mr. Pottermack became seized with sudden panic. And no wonder. His previous experiences of the law had taught him that mere innocence is of no avail; and now, simply to be charged involved the risk of recognition and inevitable return to a convict prison. But apart from that, his position was one of extreme peril. On his person at this very moment were fifteen stolen notes of which he could give no account, but which connected him with that thing that reposed under the sun-dial. At the best, those notes might fairly send him to penal servitude; at the worst, to the gallows.

It is therefore no matter for surprise that the sight of that ominous straw hat sent a sudden chill down his spine. But Mr. Pottermack was no coward. Unforeseen as the danger was, he kept his nerve and made no outward sign of the terror that was clutching at his heart. Calmly he continued to worm his way through the crowd, glancing back now and again to note his distance from that relentless hat, and ever looking for a chance to get rid of those fatal notes. For, if once he could get clear of those, he would be ready to face with courage and composure the lesser risk. But no chance ever came.

Openly to jettison the notes in the midst of the crowd would have been fatal. He would have been instantly written down a detected and pursued pickpocket.

While his mind was busy with these considerations his body was being skilfully piloted along the line of least resistance in the crowd. Now and again he made excursions into the less dense regions on the outskirts, thereby securing a gain in distance, only to plunge once more into the thick of the throng in the faint hope of being lost sight of. But this hope was never realized. On the whole, he maintained his distance from his pursuer and even slightly increased it. Sometimes for the space of a minute or more the absurd sleuth was lost to his view; but just as his hopes were beginning to revive, that accursed hat would make its reappearance and reduce him, if not to despair, at least to the most acute anxiety.

In the course of one of his excursions into the thinner part of the crowd, he noticed that, some distance ahead, a bold curve of the course brought it comparatively near to the entrance to the enclosure. He could see a steady stream of people still pouring in through the entrance turnstile, but that which gave exit from the ground was practically free. No one seemed to be leaving the enclosure at present, so the way out was quite unobstructed. Noting this fact with a new hope, he plunged once more into the dense crowd and set a course through it nearly parallel to the railings. When he had worked his way to a point nearly opposite to the entrance, he looked back to ascertain the whereabouts of his follower. The straw-hatted man was plainly visible, tightly jammed in the thickest part of the crowd and apparently not on amicable terms with his immediate neighbours. Pottermack decided that this was his chance and proceeded to take it. Skilfully extricating himself from the throng, he walked briskly towards the gates and made for the exit turnstile. As there was no one else leaving the ground, he passed out unhindered, pausing only for a moment to take a quick glance back. But what he saw in that glance was by no means reassuring. The straw-hatted man was, indeed, still tightly jammed in the thick of the crowd; but at his side was a policeman to whom he appeared to be making a statement as he pointed excitedly towards the turnstile. And both informer and constable seemed to be watching his departure.

Pottermack waited to see no more. Striding away from the entrance, he came to a road on which was a signpost pointing to the station. The railway being the obvious means of escape, he turned in the opposite direction, which apparently led into the country. A short distance along the road, he encountered an aged man, engaged in trimming the hedge, who officiously wished him good-afternoon and whom he secretly anathematized for being there. A little farther on, round a sharp turn in the road, he came to a stile which gave access to a little-used footpath which crossed a small meadow. Vaulting over the stile, he set out along the footpath at a sharp walk. His impulse was to run, but he restrained it, realizing that a running man would attract attention where a mere walker might pass unobserved, or at least unnoticed. However, he quickly came to the farther side of the meadow, where another stile gave on a narrow by-lane. Here Pottermack paused for a moment, doubtful which way to turn; but the fugitive's instinct to get as far as possible from the pursuers decided the question. He turned in the direction that led away from the race-course.

Walking quickly along the lane for a minute or two, he came to a sudden turn and saw that, a short distance ahead, the lane opened into a road. At the same moment there rose among a group of elms on his right the tower of a church; and here the hedgerow gave place to a brick wall, broken by a wicket-gate, through which he looked into a green and pleasant churchyard. The road before him he surmised to be the one that he had left by the stile, and his surmise received most alarming confirmation. For, even at the very moment when he was entering the wicket, two figures walked rapidly across the end of the lane. One of them was a tall, military-looking man who swung along with easy but enormous strides; the other, who kept up with him with difficulty, was a small man in a battered straw hat.

With a gasp of horror, Pottermack darted in through the wicket and looked round wildly for possible cover. Then he saw that the church door was open, and, impelled, possibly, by some vague idea of sanctuary, bolted in. For a moment he stood at the threshold looking into the peaceful, silent interior, forgetting in his agitation even to take off his hat. There was no one in the church; but immediately confronting the intruder, securely bolted to a stone column, was a small iron-bound chest. On its front were painted the words "Poor Box," and above it, an inscription on a board informed Mr. Pottermack that "The Lord loveth a Cheerful Giver."

Well, He had one that time. No sooner had Mr. Pottermack's eyes lighted on that box than he had whipped out his wallet and extracted the notes. With trembling fingers he folded them up in twos and threes and poked them through the slit; and when the final pair—as if protesting against his extravagant munificence—stuck in the opening and refused to go in, he adroitly persuaded them with a penny, which he pushed through and dropped in by way of an additional thank-offering. As that penny dropped down with a faint, papery rustle, he put away his wallet and drew a deep breath. Mr. Pottermack was his own man again.

Of course, there was the straw-hatted man. But now that those incriminating notes were gone, so great was the revulsion that he could truly say, in the words of the late S. Pepys—or at least in a polite paraphrase of them—that he "valued him not a straw." The entire conditions were changed. But as he turned with a new buoyancy of spirit to leave the church, there came to him a sudden recollection of the red-faced man's skill and ingenuity which caused him to thrust his hands into his pockets. And it was just as well that he did, for he brought up from his left-hand coat pocket a battered silver pencil-holder that was certainly not his and that advertised the identity of its legitimate owner by three initial letters legibly engraved on its flat end.

On this—having flung the pencil-holder out through the porch doorway into the high grass of the churchyard—he turned back into the building and made a systematic survey of his pockets, emptying each one in turn on to the cushioned seat of a pew. When he had ascertained beyond all doubt that none of them contained any article of property other than his own, he went forth with a light heart and retraced his steps through the wicket out into the lane, and, turning to the right, walked on towards the road. It had been his intention to return along it to the station, but when he came out of the lane, he found himself at the entrance to a village street and quite near to a comfortable-looking inn which hung out the sign of "The Farmer's Boy." The sight of the homely hostelry reminded him that it was now well past his usual luncheon hour and made him aware of a fine, healthy appetite.

It appeared, on enquiry, that there was a cold sirloin in cut and a nice, quiet parlour in which to consume it. Pottermack smiled with anticipatory gusto at the report and gave his orders; and within a few minutes found himself in the parlour aforesaid, seated at a table covered with a clean white cloth on which was an abundant sample of the sirloin, a hunk of bread, a slab of cheese, a plate of biscuits and a jovial, pot-bellied brown jug crowned with a cap of foam.

Mr. Pottermack enjoyed his lunch amazingly. The beef was excellent, the beer was of the best, and their combined effect was further to raise his spirits and lower his estimate of the straw-hatted man. He realized now that his initial panic had been due to those ill-omened notes; to the fact that a false charge might reveal the material for a real one of infinitely greater gravity. Now that he was clear of them, the fact that he was a man of substance and known position would be a sufficient answer to any mere casual suspicion. His confidence was completely restored, and he even speculated with detached interest on the possible chance of encountering his pursuers on his way back to the station.

He had finished the beef to the last morsel and was regarding with tepid interest the slab of high-complexioned cheese when the door opened and revealed two figures at the threshold, both of whom halted with their eyes fixed on him intently. After a moment's inspection, the shorter—who wore a battered straw hat—pointed to him and affirmed in impressive tones: "That's the man."

On this, the taller stranger took a couple of steps forward and said, as if repeating a formula: "I am a police officer" (it was a perfectly unnecessary statement. No one could have supposed that he was anything else). "This—er—gentleman informs me that you picked his pocket."

"Does he really?" said Pottermack, regarding him with mild surprise and pouring himself out another glass of beer.

"Yes, he does; and the question is, what have you got to say about it? It is my duty to caution you—"

"Not at all," said Pottermack. "The question is, what has *he* got to say about it? Has he given you any particulars?"

"No. He says you picked his pocket. That's all."

"Did he see me pick his pocket?"

The officer turned to the accuser. "Did you?" he asked.

"No, of course I didn't," snapped the other. "Pickpockets don't usually let you see what they are up to."

"Did he feel me pick his pocket?" Pottermack asked, with the air of a cross-examining counsel.

"Did you?" the officer asked, looking dubiously at the accuser.

"How could I," protested the latter, "when I was being pulled and shoved and hustled in the crowd?"

"Ha," said Pottermack, taking a sip of beer. "He didn't see me pick his pocket, he didn't feel me pick his pocket. Now, how did he arrive at the conclusion that I *did* pick his pocket?"

The officer turned almost threateningly on the accuser.

"How did you?" he demanded.

"Well," stammered the straw-hatted man, "there was a gang of pickpockets and he was among them."

"But so were you," retorted Pottermack. "How do I know that you didn't pick *my* pocket? Somebody did."

"Oh!" said the officer. "Had your pocket picked too? What did they take of yours?"

"Mighty little—just a few oddments of small change. I kept my coat buttoned."

There was a slightly embarrassed silence, during which the officer, not for the first time, ran an appraising eye over the accused. His experience of pickpockets was extensive and peculiar, but it did not include any persons of Pottermack's type. He turned and directed a dubious and enquiring look at the accuser.

"Well," said the latter, "here he is. Aren't you going to take him into custody?"

"Not unless you can give me something to go on," replied the officer. "The station inspector wouldn't accept a charge of this sort."

"At any rate," said the accuser, "I suppose you will take his name and address?"

The officer grinned sardonically at the artless suggestion but agreed that it might be as well, and produced a large, funereal note-book.

"What is your name?" he asked.

"Marcus Pottermack," the owner of that name replied, adding: "my address is 'The Chestnuts,' Borley, Buckinghamshire."

The officer wrote down these particulars, and then, closing the note-book, put it away with a very definite air of finality, remarking: "That's about all that we can do at present." But this did not at all meet the views of the straw-hatted man, who protested plaintively:

"And you mean to say that you are going to let him walk off with my gold watch and my note-case with five pounds in it? You are not even going to search him?"

"You can't search people who haven't been charged," the officer growled; but here Pottermack interposed.

"There is no need," he said suavely, "for you to be hampered by mere technical difficulties. I know it is quite irregular, but if it would give you any satisfaction just to run through my pockets, I haven't the slightest objection."

The officer was obviously relieved. "Of course, sir, if you volunteer that is a different matter, and it would clear things up."

Accordingly, Pottermack rose and presented himself for the operation, while the straw-hatted man approached and watched with devouring eyes. The officer began with the wallet, noted the initials, M. P., on the cover, opened and considered the orderly arrangement of the stamps, cards and other contents; took out a visiting-card, read it and put it back, and finally laid the wallet on the table. Then he explored all the other pockets systematically and thoroughly, depositing the treasure trove from each on the table beside the wallet. When he had finished, he thanked Mr. Pottermack for his help, and turning to the accuser, demanded gruffly:

"Well, are you satisfied now?"

"I should be better satisfied," the other man answered, "if I had got back my watch and my note-case. But I suppose he passed them on to one of his confederates."

Then the officer lost patience. "Look here," said he, "you are behaving like a fool. You come to a race-meeting, like a blooming mug, with a gold watch sticking out, asking for trouble, and when you get what you asked for, you let the crooks hop off with the goods while you go dandering about after a perfectly respectable gentleman. You bring me trapesing out here on a wild goose chase, and when it turns out that there isn't any wild goose, you make silly, insulting remarks. You ought to have more sense at your age. Now, I'll just take your name and address and then you'd better clear off."

Once more he produced the Black Maria note-book, and when he had entered the particulars he dismissed the straw-hatted man, who slunk off, dejected but still muttering.

Left alone with the late accused, the officer became genially and politely apologetic. But Pottermack would have none of his apologies. The affair had gone off to his complete satisfaction, and, in spite of some rather half-hearted protests, he insisted on celebrating the happy conclusion by the replenishment of the brown jug. Finally, the accused and the minion of the law emerged from the inn together and took their way back along the road to the station, beguiling the time by amicable converse on the subject of crooks and their ways and the peculiar mentality of the straw-hatted man.

It was a triumphant end to what had threatened to be a most disastrous incident. But yet, when he came to consider it at leisure, Pottermack was by no means satisfied. The expedition had been a failure, and he now wished, heartily, that he had left well alone and simply burnt the notes. His intention had been to distribute them in small parcels among various pickpockets, whereby they would have been thrown into circulation with the certainty that it would have been impossible to trace them. That scheme had failed utterly. There they were, fifteen stolen notes, in the poor-box of Illingham church. When the reverend incumbent found them, he would certainly be surprised, and, no doubt, gratified. Of course, he would pay them into his bank; and then the murder would be out. The munificent gift would resolve itself into the dump of a hunted and hard-pressed pickpocket; and Mr. Pottermack's name and address was in the note-book of the plain-clothes constable.

Of course, there was no means of connecting him directly with the dump. But there was the unfortunate coincidence that both he and the stolen notes were connected with Borley, Buckinghamshire. That coincidence could hardly fail to be noticed; and, added to his known proximity to the church, it might create a very awkward situation. In short, Mr. Pottermack had brought his pigs to the wrong market. He had planned to remove the area of investigation from his own neighbourhood to one at a safe and comfortable distance; instead of which, he had laid down a clue leading straight to his own door.

It was a lamentable affair. As he sat in the homeward train with an unread evening paper on his knee, he found himself recalling the refrain of the old revivalist hymn and asking himself "Oh, what shall the harvest be?"

IX

PROVIDENCE INTERVENES

IN HIS CAPACITY OF MEDICO-LEGAL ADVISER TO THE "GRIFFIN" Life Assurance Company, Thorndyke saw a good deal of Mr. Stalker, who, in addition to his connection with Perkins's Bank, held the post of Managing Director of the "Griffin." For if the Bank had but rarely any occasion to seek Thorndyke's advice, the Assurance Office was almost daily confronted with problems which called for expert guidance. It thus happened that, about three weeks after the date of the Illingham Races, Thorndyke looked in at Mr. Stalker's office in response to a telephone message to discuss the discrepancies between a proposal form and the medical evidence given at an inquest on the late proposer. The matter of this discussion does not concern us and need not be detailed here. It occupied some considerable time, and when Thorndyke had stated his conclusions, he rose to take his departure. As he turned towards the door, Mr. Stalker held up a detaining hand.

"By the way, doctor," said he, "I think you were rather interested in that curious case of disappearance that I told you about—one of our branch managers, you may remember."

"I remember," said Thorndyke; "James Lewson of your Borley branch."

"That's the man," Stalker assented, adding: "I believe you keep a card index in your head."

"And the best place to keep it," retorted Thorndyke. "But what about Lewson? Has he been run to earth?"

"No; but the notes that he took with him have. You remember that he went off with a hundred pounds—twenty five-pound notes, of all of which we were able to ascertain the numbers. Now, the numbers of those notes were at once given to the police, who circulated the information in all the likely quarters and kept a sharp look-out for their appearance. Yet in all this time, up to a week or two ago, there was not a sign of one of them. Then a most odd thing happened. The whole lot of them made their appearance almost simultaneously."

"Very remarkable," commented Thorndyke.

"Very," agreed Stalker. "But there is something still more queer about the affair. Of course, each note, as it was reported, was rigorously traced. As a rule there was no difficulty—up to a certain point. And at that point the trail broke off short, and that point was the possession of the note by a person known to the police. In every case in which tracing was possible, the trail led back to an unquestionable crook."

"And were the crooks unable to say where they got the notes?"

"Oh, not at all. They were able, in every case, to give the most lucid and convincing accounts of the way in which they came into possession of the notes. Only, unfortunately, not one of them could give 'a local habitation and a name.' They had all received the notes from total strangers."

"They probably had," said Thorndyke, "without the stranger's concurrence."

"Exactly. But you see the oddity of the affair—at least, I expect you do. Remember that, although the individual notes were reported at different times, on tracing them to their origin it looks almost as if the whole of them had come into circulation on the same day; about three weeks ago. Now, what does that suggest to you?"

"The obvious suggestion," replied Thorndyke, "seems to be that Lewson had been robbed; that some fortunate thief had managed to relieve him of the whole consignment at one *coup*. The only other explanation—and it is far less probable—is that Lewson deliberately jettisoned an incriminating cargo."

"Yes," Stalker agreed doubtfully, "that is a possibility; but, as you say, it is very much less probable. For if he had simply thrown them away, there would be no reason why they should have been so invariably traceable to a member of the criminal class; and surely, out of the whole lot, there would have been one or two honest persons who would admit to having found them. No, I feel pretty certain that Lewson has been robbed, and if he has, he must be in a mighty poor way. One is almost tempted to feel sorry for him."

"He has certainly made a terrible hash of his affairs," said Thorndyke; and with this, the subject having been exhausted, he picked up his hat and stick and took his departure.

But as he wended his way back to the Temple he cogitated profoundly on what Stalker had told him; and very surprised would Mr. Stalker have been if he could have been let into the matter of those cogitations. For, as to what had really happened, Thorndyke could make an approximate guess, though guesses were not very satisfying to a man of his exact habit of mind. But he had been expecting those notes to reappear, and he had expected that when they did reappear it would prove impossible to trace them to their real source.

Nevertheless, though events had befallen, so to speak, according to plan, he speculated curiously on the possible circumstances which had determined the issue of the whole consignment at once; and on arrival at his chambers he made certain notes in his private shorthand which he bestowed in a small portfolio labelled "James Lewson," which, in its turn, reposed, safely under lock and key, in the cabinet in which he kept his confidential documents.

Meanwhile, Mr. Pottermack was passing through a period of tribulation and gnawing anxiety. Again and again did he curse the

folly that had impelled him, when everything seemed to have settled down so comfortably, to launch those notes into the world
to start a fresh train of trouble. Again and again did he follow in
imagination what appeared to be the inevitable course of events.
With horrid vividness did his fancy reconstruct the scenes of that
calamitous comedy; the astonished parson lifting the treasure with
incredulous joy from the poor-box; the local bank manager carrying the notes round to the police station; the plain-clothes constable triumphantly producing his note-book and pointing to the
significant word "Borley"; and finally, the wooden-faced detective
officer confronting him in his dining-room and asking embarrassing
questions. Sometimes his imagination went farther, and, becoming
morbid, pictured Mr. Gallett, the mason, volunteering evidence, with
a resulting exploration of the well. But this was only when he was
unusually depressed.

In his more optimistic moods he presented the other side of the
case. If enquiries were made, he would, naturally, deny all knowledge of the notes. And who was to contradict him? There was not a
particle of evidence that could connect him with them directly—at
least, he believed there was not. But still, deep down in his consciousness was the knowledge that he *was* connected with them; that he
had taken them from the dead man's pocket and he *had* dumped
them in the church. And Mr. Pottermack was no more immune
than the rest of us from the truth that "conscience does make
cowards of us all."

So, in those troublous times, by day and by night, in his walks
abroad and in his solitude at home, he lived in a state of continual
apprehension. The fat was in the fire and he waited with constantly
strained ears to catch the sound of its sizzling; and though, as the
days and then the weeks went by and no sound of sizzling became
audible, the acuteness of his anxiety wore off, still his peace of mind

was gone utterly and he walked in the shadow of dangers unknown and incalculable. And so he might have gone on indefinitely but for one of those trivial chances that have befallen most of us and that sometimes produce results so absurdly disproportionate to their own insignificance.

The occasion of this fortunate chance was a long, solitary walk through the beautiful Buckinghamshire lanes. Of late, in his disturbed state of mind, which yielded neither to the charms of his garden nor the allurements of his workshop, Mr. Pottermack had developed into an inveterate pedestrian; and on this particular day he had taken a long round, which brought him at length, tired and hungry, to the town of Aylesbury, where, at a frowsy restaurant in a by-street, he sat him down to rest and feed. It was a frugal meal that he ordered, for with the joy of living had gone his zest for food. Indeed, to such depths of despondency had he sunk that he actually scandalized the foreign proprietor by asking for a glass of water.

Now, it happened that on an adjacent chair was an evening paper. It was weeks old, badly crumpled and none too clean. Almost automatically, Mr. Pottermack reached out for it, laid it on the table beside him and smoothed out its crumpled pages. Not that he had any hankering for news; but, like most of us, he had contracted the pernicious habit of miscellaneous reading—which is often but an idle substitute for thought—and he scanned the ill-printed columns in mere boredom. He was not in the least interested in the Hackney Man who had kicked a cat and been fined forty shillings. No doubt it served him right—and the cat too, perhaps—but it was no affair of his, Pottermack's. Nevertheless he let an inattentive eye ramble aimlessly up and down the page, lightly scanning the trivial vulgarities that headed the paragraphs, while in the background of his consciousness, hovering, as it were, about the threshold, lurked the everlasting theme of those accursed notes.

Suddenly his roving eye came to a dead stop, for it had alighted on the word "Illingham." With suddenly sharpened attention, he turned back to the heading and read:

"SACRILEGE IN A SURREY CHURCH

"A robbery of a kind that is now becoming increasingly common occurred late in the afternoon of last Tuesday at the picturesque and venerable church of Illingham. This was the day of the races on the adjacent course, and it is believed that the outrage was committed by some of the doubtful characters who are always to be found at race-meetings. At any rate, when the sexton entered to close the church in the evening, he found that the lid of the poor-box had been wrenched open, and, of course, the contents, whatever they may have been, abstracted. The rector is greatly distressed at the occurrence, not on account of what has been stolen—for he remarked, with a pensive smile, that the loss is probably limited to the cost of repairing the box—but because he holds strong opinions on the duty of a clergyman to leave his church open for private prayer and meditation, and he fears that he may be compelled to close it in future, at least on race-days."

Mr. Pottermack read this paragraph through, first with ravenous haste and then again, slowly and with the minutest attention. It was incredible. He could hardly believe the evidence of his eyes. Yet there it was, a clear and unmistakable message, of which the marvellous significance was to be grasped by him alone of all the world. Providence—which is reported to make some queer selections for its favourites—had stepped in and mercifully repaired his error.

In a moment he was a new man, or rather the old man restored. For he was saved. Now could he go abroad with a confident step and look the world in the face. Now could he take his ease at home in peace and security; could return with gusto to his garden and know once more the joys of labour in his workshop. With a fresh zest he fell to upon the remainder of his meal. He even electrified the proprietor by calling for coffee and a green Chartreuse. And when he at length went forth refreshed, to take the road homeward, he seemed to walk upon air.

X

THE FORTUNATE ENDING OF THE GREAT NOTE ADVENTURE, which had at one time looked so threatening, had a profound effect on Mr. Pottermack's state of mind, and through this on his subsequent actions. Wherever the notes might be circulating, they were, he felt confident, well out of his neighbourhood; and since they had all fallen into the hands of thieves, he was equally confident that they would prove untraceable. So far as he was concerned, they had served their purpose. The field of inquiry concerning Lewson's disappearance was now shifted from Borley to the localities in which those notes had made their appearance.

Thus, to Mr. Pottermack it appeared that he was finally rid of Lewson, alive or dead. The incident was closed. He could now consign the whole horrible affair to oblivion, forget it if he could, or at least remember it only as a hideous experience which he had passed through and finished with, just as he might remember certain other experiences which belonged to the unhappy past. Now he might give his whole attention to the future. He was still a comparatively young man, despite the grizzled hair upon his temples. And Fortune was deeply in his debt. It was time that he began to collect from her some of the arrears.

Now, whenever Mr. Pottermack let his thoughts stray into the future, the picture that his fancy painted was wont to present a certain constant deviation from the present. It was not that the surroundings were different. Still in imagination he saw himself rambling through the lovely Buckinghamshire lanes, busying himself in his workshop or whiling away the pleasant hours in the walled garden among his flowers and his fruit trees. But in those pictures of the sunny future that was to indemnify him for the gloomy past there were always two figures; and one of them was that of the comely, gracious young widow who had already brought so much sunshine into his rather solitary life.

During the last few strenuous weeks he had seen little of her, indeed he had hardly seen her at all. Now that he could put behind him for ever the events that had filled those weeks, now that he was free from the haunting menace of the blackmailer's incalculable actions and could settle down to a stable life with his future in his own hands, the time had arrived when he might begin to mould that future in accordance with his heart's desire.

Thus reflecting on the afternoon following his visit to Aylesbury, he proceeded to make the first move. Having smartened himself up in a modest way, he took down from his shelves a favourite volume to serve as a pretext for a call, and set forth with it in his pocket towards the quiet lane on the fringe of the town wherein Mrs. Alice Bellard had her habitation. And a very pleasant habitation it was, though, indeed, it was no more than an old-fashioned country cottage, built to supply the simple needs of some rural worker or village crafts-man. But houses, like dogs, have a way of reflecting the personalities of their owners; and this little dwelling, modest as it was, conveyed to the beholder a subtle sense of industry, of ordered care, and a somewhat fastidious taste.

Pottermack stood for a few moments with his hand on the little wooden gate, looking up with an appreciative eye at the ripe red brickwork, the golden tiles of the roof, and the little stone tablet with the initials of the first owners and the date, 1761. Then he opened the latch and walked slowly up the path. Through the open window came the sound of a piano rendering, with no little skill and feeling, one of Chopin's preludes. He waited at the door, listening, until the final notes of the piece were played, when he turned and rapped out a flourish on the brightly burnished brass knocker.

Almost immediately the door opened, revealing a girl of about sixteen, who greeted him with a friendly smile, and forthwith, without question or comment, inducted him to the sitting-room, where Mrs. Bellard had just risen from the piano-stool.

"I am afraid," said he, as they shook hands, "that I am interrupting your playing—in fact, I know I am. I was half inclined to wait out in the garden and enjoy your performance without disturbing you."

"That would have been foolish of you," she replied, "when there is a nice, comfortable armchair in which you can sit and smoke your pipe and listen at your ease—if you want to."

"I do, most certainly," said he. "But first, lest I should forget it, let me hand you this book. I mentioned it to you once—*The Harvest of a Quiet Eye*. It is by a nice old west country parson and I think you will like it."

"I am sure I shall if you do," she said. "We seem to agree in most things."

"So we do," assented Pottermack, "even to our favourite brands of snail. Which reminds me that the pleasures of the chase seem to have been rather neglected of late."

"Yes, I have been quite busy lately furbishing up the house. But I have nearly finished. In a few days I shall have everything straight and tidy, and then a-snailing we will go."

"We will," he agreed, "and if we find that we are exhausting the subject of molluscs, we might, perhaps, give a passing thought to the question of beetles. They are practically inexhaustible and they are not so hackneyed as butterflies and moths, and not so troublesome to keep. And they are really very beautiful and interesting creatures."

"I suppose they are," she said a little doubtfully, "when you have got over your prejudice against their undeniable tendency to crawliness. But I am afraid you will have to do the slaughtering. I really couldn't kill the poor little wretches."

"Oh, I will do that cheerfully," said Pottermack, "if you will make the captures."

"Very well; then, on that understanding I will consider the beetle question. And now, would you really like me to play to you a little?"

"I should like it immensely. I seem to hear so little music nowadays, and you play so delightfully. But are you sure you don't mind?"

She laughed softly as she sat down at the piano. "Mind, indeed!" she exclaimed. "Did you ever know a musician who wasn't only too delighted to play to a sympathetic listener? It is the whole joy and reward of the art. Now, you just sit in that chair and fill your pipe, and I will play to you some of the things that I like playing to myself and that you have got to like too."

Obediently Pottermack seated himself in the easy-chair and reflectively filled his pipe while he watched the skilful hands moving gracefully with effortless precision over the keyboard. At first she kept to regular pianoforte music, mostly that of Chopin: one or two of the shorter nocturnes, a prelude and a polonaise, and a couple of Mendelssohn's "Lieder." But presently she began to ramble away reminiscently among all sorts of unconventional trifles: old-fashioned songs, country dances, scraps of church music, and even one or two time-honoured hymn tunes. And as she played these simple melodies, softly, tastefully, and with infinite feeling, she glanced furtively from time to time at her visitor until, seeing that he was no longer looking at her, but was gazing dreamily out of the window, she let her eyes rest steadily on his face. There was something very curious in that long, steady look; a strange mingling of sadness, of pity and tenderness and of yearning affection with a certain vague anxiety as if something in his face was puzzling her. The eyes that dwelt on him with such soft regard yet seemed to ask a question.

And Pottermack, sitting motionless as a statue, grasping his unlighted pipe, let the simple, homely melodies filter into his soul and deliver their message of remembrance. His thoughts were at once near and far away; near to the woman at his side, yet far away from the quiet room and the sunlit garden on which his eyes seemed to rest. Let us for a while leave him to his reverie, and if we may not follow his thoughts, at least—in order that we may the better enter into the inwardness of this history—transport ourselves into the scenes that memory is calling up before his eyes.

Fifteen years ago there was no such person as Marcus Pottermack. The sober, middle-aged man, grey-headed, bearded, spectacled, who sits dreaming in the widow's parlour, was a handsome, sprightly youth of twenty-two—Jeffrey Brandon by name—who, with his shapely, clean-shaven face and his striking Grecian nose, had the look and manner of a young Olympian. And his personality matched his appearance. Amiable and kindly by nature, with a gay and buoyant temperament that commended him alike to friends and strangers, his keen intelligence, his industry and energy promised well for his worldly success in the future.

Young as he was, he had been, at this time, engaged for two years. And here again he was more than commonly fortunate. It was not merely that the maiden of his choice was comely, sweet-natured, clever and accomplished; or that she was a girl of character and spirit; or even that she had certain modest expectations. The essence of the good fortune lay in the fact that Jeffrey Brandon and Alice Bentley were not merely lovers; they were staunch friends and sympathetic companions, with so many interests in common that it was incredible that they should ever tire of each other's society.

One of their chief interests—perhaps the greatest—was music. They were both enthusiasts. But whereas Jeffrey's accomplishments went no farther than a good ear, a pleasant baritone voice and the power of singing a part at sight, Alice was really a musician. Her skill at the piano was of the professional class; she was a fair organist, and in addition she had a good and well-trained contralto voice. Naturally enough, it happened that they drifted into the choir of the little friendly Evangelical church that they attended together, and this gave them a new and delightful occupation. Now and again Alice would take a service at the organ; and then there were practice nights and preparations for special services, musical festivals or informal sacred concerts which kept them busy with the activities that they both loved. And so their lives ran on, serenely, peacefully, filled with quiet enjoyment of the satisfying present, with the promise of a yet more happy future when they should be married and in full possession of each other.

And then, in a moment, the whole fabric of their happiness collapsed like a house of cards. As if in an incomprehensible nightmare, the elements of that tragedy unfolded: the amazing accusation, the still more amazing discovery; the trial at the Old Bailey Sessions, the conviction, the sentence; the bitter, despairing farewell, and, last of all, the frowning portals of the convict prison.

Of course, Alice Bentley scouted the idea of her lover's guilt. She roundly declared that the whole affair was a plot, a wicked and foolish miscarriage of justice, and she announced her intention of meeting him at the prison gate when he should be set free, to claim him as her promised husband, that she might try to make up to him by her devotion and sympathy what he had suffered from the world's injustice. And when it was coldly pointed out to her that he had had a fair trial and had been found guilty by a jury of his fellow-countrymen, she broke away indignantly and thereafter withdrew herself from the society of these fair-weather friends.

Meanwhile, the unfortunate Jeffrey, meditating in his prison cell, had come with no less resolution to his decision. In so far as was possible he would bear the burden of his misfortune alone. Deeply, passionately as he loved the dear girl who, almost alone of all the world, still believed in his innocence, he must cast her out of his life for ever. He gloried in her loyalty, but he could not accept her sacrifice. Alice—his Alice—should never marry a convict. For that was what he was: a convicted thief and forger; and nothing but a miracle could alter his position. The fact that he was innocent was beside the mark, since his innocence was known only to himself and one other—the nameless villain who had set this infamous trap for him. To all the rest of the world he was a guilty man; and the world was right according to the known facts. He had had a fair trial, a perfectly fair trial. The prosecution had not been vindictive, the judge had summed up fairly, and the jury had found him guilty; and the jury had been right. On the evidence before them, they could have found no other verdict. He had no complaint against them. No one could have guessed that all the evidence was false and illusory. From which it followed that he must go through life stamped as a convicted thief, and as such could never be a possible husband for Alice Bentley.

But he realized very clearly that Alice, certain as she was of his innocence, would utterly refuse to accept this view. To her he was a martyr, and as such she would proclaim him before all the world. On his release, she would insist on the restoration of the *status quo ante*. Of that he felt certain; and hour after hour, in his abundant solitude, he sought vainly a solution of the problem. How should he meet her demand? Letters he knew would be useless. She would wait for the day of his release, and then— The prospect of having, after all, to refuse her love, to repudiate her loyalty, was one that wrung his heart to contemplate.

And then, in the most unforeseen way, the problem was solved. His escape from the gang was totally unpremeditated. He just saw a chance, when the attention of the civil guard was relaxed, and took it instantly. When he found the absent bather's clothes upon the shore and hastily assumed them in place of his prison suit, he suspected that the bather was already dead, and the report which he read in the next day's paper confirmed this belief. But during the next few weeks, as he tramped across country to Liverpool—subsisting, not without qualms, on the little money that he had found in the unknown bather's pockets, eked out by an occasional odd job—he watched the papers eagerly for further news. For six long weeks he found nothing either to alarm or reassure him. Indeed, it was not until he had secured a job as deck-hand on an American tramp steamer and was on the point of departure that he learned the welcome tidings. On the very night before the ship was due to sail, he was sitting in the forecastle, watching an evening paper that was passing round from hand to hand, when the man who was reading it held it towards him, pointing with a grimy forefinger to a particular paragraph.

"I call that damned hard luck, I do," said he. "Just you read it, mate, and see what you think of it."

Jeffrey took the paper, and, glancing at the indicated paragraph, suddenly sat up with a start. It was the report of an inquest on the body of a man who had been found drowned; which body had been identified as that of Jeffrey Brandon, a convict who had recently escaped from Colport Gaol. He read it through slowly, and then, with an inarticulate mumble, handed the paper back to his sympathetic messmate. For some minutes he sat dazed, hardly able to realize this sudden change in his condition. That the bather's body would, sooner or later, be found he had never doubted. But he had expected that the finding of it and its identification would solve the mystery of his escape and immediately give rise to a hue and cry. Never had he dreamed that the body could be identified as his.

But now that this incredible thing had happened, he would be simply written off and forgotten. He was free. And not only was he free; Alice was free too. Now he would quietly pass out of her life without bitterness or misunderstanding; not forgotten, indeed, but cherished only, in the years to come, with loving remembrance.

Nevertheless, when at daybreak on the morrow the good ship *Potomac* of New Orleans crossed the Mersey bar, the new deck-hand, Joe Watson, looked back at the receding land with a heavy heart and a moistening eye. The world was all before him. But it was an empty world. All that could make life gracious and desirable was slipping away farther with each turn of the propeller, and a waste of waters was stretching out between him and his heart's desire.

His life in America need not be followed in detail. He was of the type that almost inevitably prospers in that country. Energetic, industrious, handy, ready to put his heart into any job that offered; an excellent accountant with a sound knowledge of banking business and general finance, he was not long in finding a position in which he could prove his worth. And he had undeniably good luck. Within a year of his landing, almost penniless, he had managed, by hard work and the most drastic economy, to scrape together a tiny nest-egg of capital. Then he met with a young American, nearly as poor as himself but of the stuff of which millionaires are made; a man of inexhaustible energy, quick, shrewd and resolute, and possessed by a devouring ambition to be rich. But notwithstanding his avidity for wealth, Joseph Walden was singularly free from the vices of his class. He looked to become rich by work, good management, thrift, and a reputation for straight dealing. He was a man of strict integrity, and, if a little blunt and outspoken, was still a good friend and a pleasant companion.

With his shrewd judgment, Walden saw at once that his new friend would make an ideal collaborator in a business venture. Each had special qualifications that the other lacked, and the two together would form a highly efficient combination. Accordingly the two young men pooled their resources and embarked under the style and title of the Walden Pottermack Company. (Jeffrey had abandoned the name of Joe Watson on coming ashore, and, moved by some whimsical sentiment, had adopted as his godparent the ship which had carried him away to freedom and the new life. With a slight variation of spelling, he was now Marcus Pottermack.)

For some time the new firm struggled on under all the difficulties that attend insufficient capital. But the two partners held together in absolute unison. They neglected no chances, they spared no effort, they accepted willingly the barest profits, and they practised thrift to the point of penury. And slowly the tension of poverty relaxed. The little snowball of their capital began to grow, imperceptibly at first, but then with a constantly increasing acceleration—for wealth, like population, tends to increase by geometrical progression. In a year or two the struggles were over and the Company was a well-established concern. A few more years and the snowball had rolled up to quite impressive dimensions. The Walden Pottermack Company had become a leading business house, and the partners men of respectable substance.

It was at this point that the difference between the two men began to make itself apparent. To the American, the established prosperity of the firm meant the attainment of the threshold of big business with the prospect of really big money. His fixed intention was to push the success for all that it was worth, to march on to greater and yet greater things, even unto millionairedom. Pottermack, on the other hand, began to feel that he had enough. Great wealth held out no allurements for him. Nor did he, like Walden, enjoy the sport of winning and piling it up. At first he had worked hard for a mere livelihood; then for a competence that should presently enable him to live his own life. And now, as he counted up his savings, it seemed to him that he had achieved his end. With what he had he could purchase all that he desired and that was purchasable.

It was not purchasable in America. Grateful as he was to the country that had sheltered him and taken him to her heart as one of her own sons, yet he found himself from time to time turning a wistful eye towards the land beyond the great ocean. More and more, as the time went on, he was conscious of a hankering for things that America could not give; for the sweet English countryside, the immemorial villages with their ancient churches, their oast-houses and thatched barns, for all the lingering remains of an older civilization.

And there was another element of unrest. All through the years the image of Alice had never ceased to haunt him. At first it was but as the cherished memory of a loved one who had died and passed out of his life for ever. But as the years ran on there came a subtle change. Gradually he began to think of their separation, not as something final and irretrievable but as admitting in a vague and shadowy way of the idea of reunion this side of the grave. It was very nebulous and indefinite, but it clung to him persistently, and ever the idea grew more definite. The circumstances were, indeed, changed utterly. When he left her, he was a convict, infamous in the eyes of all the world. But the convict, Jeffrey Brandon, was dead and forgotten, whereas he, Marcus Pottermack, was a man of position and repute. The case was entirely altered.

So he would argue with himself in moments of expansiveness. And then he would cast away his dreams, chiding himself for his folly and telling himself that, doubtless, she had long since married and settled down; that dead he was and dead he must remain, and not seek to rise again like some unquiet spirit to trouble the living.

Nevertheless, the leaven continued to work, and the end of it was that Mr. Pottermack wound up his business affairs and made arrangements for his retirement. His partner regretfully agreed to take over his interest in the company—which he did on terms that were not merely just but generous—and thus his commercial life came to an end. A week or two later he took his passage for England.

Now, nebulous and shadowy as his ideas had been with reference to Alice, partaking rather of the nature of day-dreams than of thoughts implying any settled purpose, no sooner had he landed in the Old Country than he became possessed by a craving, at least to hear of her, to make certain that she was still alive, if possible to see her. He could not conceal from himself some faint hope that she might still be unmarried. And if she were—well, then it would be time for him to consider what he would do.

His first proceeding was to establish himself in lodgings in the old neighbourhood, where he spent his days loitering about the streets that she had been used to frequent. On Sundays he attended the church with scrupulous regularity, modestly occupying a back seat and lingering in the porch as the congregation filed out. Many familiar faces he noted, changed more or less by the passage of time; but no one recognized in the grey-haired, bearded, spectacled stranger the handsome youth whom they had known in the years gone by. Indeed, how should they, when that youth had died, cut off in the midst of his career of crime?

He would have liked to make some discreet enquiries, but no enquiries would have been discreet. Above all things, it was necessary for him to preserve his character as a stranger from America. And so he could do no more than keep his vigil in the streets and at the church, watching with hungry eyes for the beloved face—and watching in vain.

And then at last, after weeks of patient searching with ever-dwindling hope, he had his reward. It was on Easter Sunday, a day which had, in old times, been kept as the chief musical festival of the year. Apparently the custom was still maintained, for the church was unusually full and there was evidently a special choir. Mr. Pottermack's hopes revived, though he braced himself for another disappointment. Surely, he thought, if she ever comes to this church, she will come to-day.

And this time he was not disappointed. He had not long been seated on the modest bench near the door when a woman, soberly dressed in black, entered and walked past him up the aisle, where she paused for a few moments looking about her somewhat with the air of a stranger. He knew her in a moment by her figure, her gait, and the poise of her head. But if he had had any doubt, it would have been instantly dispelled when she entered a pew, and, before sitting down, glanced back quickly at the people behind her.

For Pottermack it was a tremendous moment. It was as if he were looking on the face of one risen from the dead. For some minutes after she had sat down and become hidden from his sight by the people behind her he felt dazed and half-incredulous of the wonderful vision that he had seen. But as the effects of the shock passed, he began to consider the present position. That single instantaneous glance had shown him that she had aged a little more than the lapse of time accounted for. She looked graver than of old, perhaps even a thought sombre, and something matronly and middle-aged in the fashion of her dress made disquieting suggestions.

When the long service was ended, Pottermack waited on his bench watching her come down the aisle and noting that she neither spoke to nor seemed to recognize any one. As soon as she had passed his bench, he rose and joined the throng behind her. His intention was to follow her and discover, if possible, where she lived. But as they came into the crowded porch he heard an elderly woman exclaim in a markedly loud tone:

"Why, surely it is Miss Bentley!"

"Yes," was the reply in the well-remembered voice. "At least, I was Miss Bentley when you knew me. Nowadays I am Mrs. Bellard."

Pottermack, standing close behind her and staring at a notice-board, drew a deep breath. Only in that moment of bitter disappointment did he realize how much he had hoped.

"Oh, indeed," said the loud-spoken woman. "Mrs. Bennett—it was Bennett that you said?"

"No, Bellard—B.e.l.l.a.r.d."

"Oh, Bellard. Yes. And so you are married. I have often wondered what became of you when you stopped coming to the church after—er—all those years ago. I hope your good husband is well."

"I lost my husband four years ago," Mrs. Bellard replied in a somewhat dry, matter-of-fact tone.

Pottermack's heart gave a bound and he listened harder than ever.

"Dear, dear!" exclaimed the other woman. "What a dreadfully sad thing! And are there any children?"

"No; no children."

"Ah, indeed. But perhaps it is as well, though it must be lonely for you. Are you living in London?"

"No," replied Mrs. Bellard, "I have only just come up for the week-end. I live at Borley in Buckinghamshire—not far from Aylesbury."

"Do you? It must be frightfully dull for you living all alone right down in the country. I do hope you have found comfortable lodgings."

Mrs. Bellard laughed softly. "You are pitying me more than you need, Mrs. Goodman. I am not dull at all, and I don't have to live in lodgings. I have a house to myself. It is only a very small one, but it is big enough and it is my own; so I am secure of a shelter for the rest of my life."

Here the two women drifted out of distinct ear-shot, though their voices continued to be audible as they walked away, for they both spoke in raised tones, Mrs. Goodman being, apparently, a little dull of hearing. But Pottermack had heard enough. Drawing out his pocket-book, he carefully entered the name and the address, such as it was, glancing at the notice-board as if he were copying some particulars from it. Then he emerged from the porch and walked after the two women; and when they separated, he followed Mrs. Bellard at a discreet distance, not that he now had any curiosity as to her present place of abode, but merely that he might pleasure his eyes with the sight of her trim figure tripping youthfully along the dull suburban street.

Mr. Pottermack's joy and triumph were tempered with a certain curiosity, especially with regard to the late Mr. Bellard. But his cogitations were not permitted to hinder the necessary action. Having no time-table, it being Sunday, he made his way to Marylebone Station to get a list of the week-day trains; and at that station he presented himself on the following morning at an unearthly hour, suitcase in hand, to catch the first train to Borley. Arrived at the little town, he at once took a room at the Railway Inn, from whence he was able conveniently to issue forth and stroll down the station approach as each of the London trains came in.

It was late in the afternoon when, among the small crowd of passengers who came out of the station, he saw her, stepping forward briskly and carrying a good-sized handbag. He turned, and, walking back slowly up the approach, let her pass him and draw a good distance ahead. He kept her in sight without difficulty in the sparsely peopled streets until, at the outskirts of the town, she turned into a quiet by-lane and disappeared. Thereupon he quickened his pace and entered the lane just in time to see her opening the garden gate of a pleasant-looking cottage, at the open door of which a youthful maidservant stood, greeting her with a welcoming grin. Pottermack walked slowly past the little house, noting the name, "Lavender Cottage," painted on the gate, and went on to the top of the lane, where he turned and retraced his steps, indulging himself as he passed the second time with a long and approving look at the shrine which held the object of his worship.

On his return to the inn he proceeded to make enquiries as to a reliable house-agent, in response to which he was given, not only the name of a recommended agent but certain other more valuable information. For the landlord, interested in a prospective new resident, was questioning Pottermack as to the class of house that he was seeking when the landlady interposed.

"What about 'The Chestnuts,' Tom, where Colonel Barnett used to live? That's empty and for sale—been empty for months. And it's a good house though rather out-of-the-way. Perhaps that might suit this gentleman."

Further details convinced Mr. Pottermack that it would, and the upshot was that on the very next day, after a careful inspection, the deposit was paid to the agents, Messrs. Hook and Walker, and a local solicitor was instructed to carry out the conveyance. Within a week the principal builder of the town had sent in his estimates for repairs and decoration, and Mr. Pottermack was wrestling with the problem of household furnishing amidst a veritable library of catalogues.

But these activities did not distract him from his ultimate object. Realizing that, as a stranger to the town, his chance of getting a regular introduction to Mrs. Bellard was infinitely remote, he decided to waive the conventions and take a short-cut. But the vital question was, Would she recognize him? It was a question that perplexed

him profoundly and that he debated endlessly without reaching any
conclusion. Of course, under normal circumstances there would be
no question at all. Obviously, in spite of his beard, his spectacles,
and his grey hair, she would recognize him instantly. But the circumstances were very far from normal. To her, he was a person who
had died some fifteen years ago. And the news of his death would
have come to her, not as a mere rumour or vague report, but as an
ascertained fact. He had been found dead and identified by those
who knew him well. She could never have had a moment's doubt
that he was dead.

How, then, would she react to the conflict between her knowledge
and the evidence of her senses? Which of the two alternative impos-
sibilities would she accept? That a dead man might come to life again
or that one human being might bear so miraculous a resemblance to
another? He could form no opinion. But of one thing he felt confident. She would certainly be deeply impressed by the resemblance,
and that state of mind would easily cover anything unconventional
in the manner of their meeting.

His plan was simple to crudeness. At odd times, in the intervals
of his labours, he made it his business to pass the entrance of the
lane—Malthouse Lane was its name—from whence he could see
her house. For several days no opportunity presented itself. But one
morning, a little more than a week after his arrival, on glancing up
the lane, he perceived a manifestly feminine hat above the shrubs in
her garden. Thereupon he turned boldly into the little thoroughfare
and walked on until he was opposite the cottage, when he could
see her, equipped with gardening gloves and a rather juvenile fork,
tidying up the borders. Unobserved by her, he stepped up to the
wooden palings, and, lifting his hat, enquired apologetically if she
could inform him whether, if he followed the lane, he would come
to the Aylesbury road.

At the first sound of his voice she started up and gazed at him with an expression of the utmost astonishment; nor was her astonishment diminished when she looked at his face. For an appreciable time she stood quite still and rigid, with her eyes fixed on him and her lips parted as if she had seen a spectre. After an interval, Pottermack—who was more or less prepared, though his heart was thumping almost audibly— repeated his question, with apologies for intruding on her; whereupon, recovering herself with an effort, she came across to the palings and began to give him some directions in a breathless, agitated voice, while the gloved hand that she rested on the palings trembled visibly.

Pottermack listened deferentially and then ventured to explain his position: that he was a stranger, about to settle in the district and anxious to make himself acquainted with his new surroundings. As this was received quite graciously, he went on to comment in admiring terms on the appearance of the cottage and its happy situation in this pleasant leafy lane. Through this channel they drifted into amicable conversation concerning the town and the surrounding country, and as they talked—Pottermack designedly keeping his face partially turned away from her—she continued to watch him with a devouring gaze and with a curious expression of bewilderment and incredulity mingled with something reminiscent, far away and dreamy. Finally, encouraged by his success, Pottermack proceeded to expound the embryonic state of his household, and enquired if by any chance she happened to know of a reliable middle-aged woman who would take charge of it.

"How many are you in family?" Mrs. Bellard asked with ill-concealed eagerness.

"My entire family," he replied, "is covered by one rather shabby hat."

"Then you ought to have no difficulty in finding a housekeeper. I do, in fact," she continued, "know of a woman who might suit you, a middle-aged widow named Gadby—quite a Dickens name, isn't it? I know very little about her abilities, but I do know that she is a pleasant, good-natured, and highly respectable woman. If you like, and will give me your address, I will send her to see you."

Mr. Pottermack jumped at the offer, and having written down his name and his address at the inn (at the former of which she glanced with eager curiosity), he thanked her warmly, and, wishing her good-morning with a flourish of the shabby hat, went on his way rejoicing. That same evening, Mrs. Gadby called at the inn and was promptly engaged; and a very fortunate transaction the engagement proved. For, not only did she turn out to be an incomparable servant, but she constituted herself a link between her employer and her patroness. Not that the link was extremely necessary, for whenever Pottermack chanced to meet Mrs. Bellard—and it was surprising how often it happened—she greeted him frankly as an acknowledged acquaintance; so that gradually—and not so very gradually either—their footing as acquaintances ripened into that of friends. And so, as the weeks passed and their friendship grew up into a pleasant, sympathetic intimacy, Mr. Pottermack felt that all was going well and that the time was at hand when he should collect some of the arrears that were outstanding in his account with Fortune.

But Fortune had not done with him yet.

The card that she held up her sleeve was played a few weeks after he had entered into occupation of his new house and was beginning to be comfortably settled. He was standing by the counter of a shop where he had made some purchases when he became aware of some person standing behind him and somewhat to his left. He could not see the person excepting as a vague shadow, but he had the feeling that he was being closely scrutinized. It was not a pleasant feeling, for, altered as he was, some inopportune recognition was always possible; and when the person moved from the left side to the right, Mr.

Pottermack began to grow distinctly apprehensive. His right ear bore a little purple birth-mark that was highly distinctive, and the movement of the unknown observer associated itself very disagreeably in his mind with this mark. After enduring the scrutiny for some time with growing uneasiness, he turned and glanced at the face of the scrutinizer. Then he received a very distinct shock, but at the same time was a little reassured. For the stranger was not a stranger at all, but his old friend and fellow-clerk, James Lewson.

Involuntarily his face must have given some sign of recognition, but this he instantly suppressed. He had no fear of his old friend, but still, he had renounced his old identity and had no intention of acknowledging it. He had entered on a new life with a new personality. Accordingly, after a brief glance, as indifferent as he could make it, he turned back to the counter and concluded his business. And Lewson, for his part, made no outward sign of recognition, so that Pottermack began to hope that he had merely noticed an odd resemblance, without any suspicion of actual identity. After all, that was what one would expect, seeing that the Jeffrey Brandon whom he resembled had been dead nearly fifteen years.

But when he left the shop and went his way through the streets on other business, he soon discovered that Lewson was shadowing him closely. Once or twice he put the matter to the test by doubling back or darting through obscure passages and by-ways; and when he still found Lewson doggedly clinging to his skirts, he had to accept the conviction that he had been recognized and deal with the position to the best of his discretion. Accordingly, he made straight for home; but instead of entering by the front door, he took the path that skirted the long wall of his garden and let himself in by the small side gate, which he left unlatched behind him. A minute later, Lewson pushed it open and looked in; then, seeing that the garden was unoccupied save by Pottermack, he entered and shut the gate.

"Well, Jeff," he said genially, as he faced Pottermack, "so here you are. A brand—or shall we say a Brandon—snatched from the burning. I always wondered if you had managed to do a mizzle, you are such an uncommonly downy bird."

Pottermack made a last, despairing effort. "Pardon me," said he, "but I fancy you must be mistaking me for—"

"Oh, rats," interrupted Lewson. "Won't do, old chap. Besides, I saw that you recognized me. No use pretending that you don't know your old pal, and certainly no use pretending that he doesn't know you."

Pottermack realized the unwelcome truth and, like a wise man, bowed to the inevitable.

"I suppose it isn't," he admitted, "and, for that matter, I don't know that there is any reason why I should. But you will understand that—"

"Oh, I understand well enough," said Lewson. "Don't imagine that I am offended. Naturally you are not out for digging up your old acquaintances, especially as you seem to have feathered your nest pretty well. Where have you been all these years?"

"In the States. I only came back a few weeks ago."

"Ah, you'd have been wiser to stay there. But I suppose you made a pile and have come home to spend it."

"Well, hardly a pile," said Pottermack, "but I have saved enough to live on in a quiet way. I am not expensive in my habits."

"Lucky beggar!" said Lewson, glancing around with greedy eyes. "Is this your own place?"

"Yes, I have just bought it and moved in. Got it remarkably cheap, too."

"Did you? Well, I say again, lucky beggar. It's quite a lordly little estate."

"Yes, I am very pleased with it. There's a good house and quite a lot of land, as you see. I hope to live very comfortably here."

"You ought to, if you don't get blown on; and you never need be if you are a wise man."

"No, I hope not," said Pottermack, a little uneasily. He had been looking at his old friend and was disagreeably impressed by the change that the years had wrought. He was by no means happy to know that his secret was shared with this unprepossessing stranger—for such he, virtually, was. But still he was totally unprepared for what was to follow.

"It was a lucky chance for me," remarked Lewson, "that I happened to drop in at that shop. Best morning's work that I have done for a long time."

"Indeed!" said Pottermack, looking a little puzzled.

"Yes. I reckon that chance was worth a thousand pounds to me."

"Was it really? I don't quite see how."

"Don't you?" demanded Lewson, with a sudden change of manner. "Then I'll explain. I presume you don't want the Scotland Yard people to know that you are alive and living here like a lord?"

"Naturally I don't."

"Of course you don't. And if you show a proper and liberal spirit towards your old pal, they are never likely to know."

"But," gasped Pottermack, "I don't think I quite understand what you mean."

"You are devilish thick-headed if you don't," said Lewson. "Then I'll put it in a nutshell. You hand me over a thousand pounds and I give you a solemn undertaking to keep my mouth shut for ever."

"And if I don't?"

"Then I hop off to Scotland Yard and earn a small gratuity by giving them the straight tip."

Pottermack recoiled from him in horror. He was thunderstruck. It was appalling to find that this man, whom he had known as an apparently decent youth, had sunk so low. He had actually descended to blackmail—the lowest, the meanest, and the shabbiest of crimes. But it was not the blackmail alone that filled Pottermack's soul with loathing of the wretch who stood before him. In the moment in which Lewson made his demand, Pottermack knew the name of the villain who had forged those cheques and had set the dastardly trap in which he, Pottermack, was, in effect, still held.

For some moments he was too much shocked to reply. When at length he did, it was merely to settle the terms of the transaction. He had no choice. He realized that this was no empty threat. The gleam of malice in Lewson's eye was unmistakable. It expressed the inveterate hatred that a thoroughly base man feels towards one on whom he has inflicted an unforgivable injury.

"Will a crossed cheque do for you?" he asked.

"Good Lord! no!" was the reply; "nor an open one either. No cheques for me. Hard cash is what I should prefer, but as that might be difficult to manage I'll take it in notes—five-pound notes."

"What, a thousand pounds!" exclaimed Pottermack. "What on earth will the people at the bank think?"

Lewson sniggered. "What would they think, old chap, if I turned up with an open cheque for a thousand pounds? Wouldn't they take an interest in the endorsement? No, dear boy, you get the notes—fivers, mind. They know you. And look here, Jeff. This is a strictly private transaction. Neither of us wants it to leak out. It will be much safer for us both if we remain tee-total strangers. If we should meet anywhere, you needn't take off your hat. I shan't. We don't know one another. I don't even know your name. By the way, what *is* your name?"

"Marcus Pottermack."

"God, what a name! However, I'll forget it if I can. You agree with me?"

"Certainly," replied Pottermack with unmistakable sincerity. "But where and how am I to hand you over the money?"

"I was coming to that," said Lewson. "I will come along here and collect it on Thursday night—that will give you time to get the notes. I shall come after dark, about nine o'clock. You had better leave this gate unlatched, and then, if I see that the coast is clear, I can pop in unobserved. Will that do?"

Pottermack nodded. "But there is one thing more, Lewson," said he. "This is a single, final transaction. I pay you a thousand pounds to purchase your silence and secrecy for ever!"

"That is so. *In saecula saeculorum.*"

"There will be no further demands?"

"Certainly not," Lewson replied indignantly. "Do you think I don't know what a square deal is? I've given you my solemn promise and you can trust me to keep it."

Pottermack pursued the matter no farther; and as the calamitous business was now concluded, he softly opened the gate, and, having ascertained that no one was in sight, he let his visitor out and watched the big, burly figure swaggering townwards along the little path that bordered his wall.

Closing the gate, he turned back into the garden, his heart filled with bitterness and despair. His dream was at an end. Never, while this horse-leech hung on to him, could he ask Alice Bellard to be his wife. For his prophetic soul told him only too truly that this was but a beginning; that the blackmailer would come again and again and yet again, always to go away still holding the thing that he had sold.

And so it befell; and so the pitiless extortion might have gone on to its end in the ruin and impoverishment of the victim but for the timely appearance of the sun-dial in Mr. Gallett's yard.

XI

THE SOUND OF THE PIANO FADED AWAY IN A GRADUAL diminuendo and at last stopped. A brief interval of silence followed.

Then Mr. Pottermack, withdrawing his gaze from the infinite distance beyond the garden, turned to look at his hostess and found her regarding him with a slightly quizzical smile.

"You haven't lit your pipe after all, Mr. Pottermack," said she.

"No," he replied. "My savage breast was so effectually soothed by your music that tobacco would have been superfluous. Besides, my pipe would have gone out. It always does when my attention is very completely occupied."

"And was it? I almost thought you were dozing."

"I was dreaming," said he; "day-dreaming; but wide awake and listening. It is curious," he continued after a pause, "what power music has to awaken associations. There is nothing like it, excepting, perhaps, scents. Music and odours, things utterly unlike anything but themselves, seem to have a power of arousing dormant memories that is quite lacking in representative things such as pictures and statues."

"So it would seem," said Mrs. Bellard, "that I have been, in a fashion, performing the function of an opium pipe in successful competition with the tobacco article. But it is too late to mend matters now. I can hear Anne approaching with the tea-things."

Almost as she spoke, the door opened and the maid entered, carrying a tray with anxious care, and proceeded to set out the tea-things with the manner of one performing a solemn rite. When she had gone and the tea was poured out, Mrs. Bellard resumed the conversation.

"I began to think you had struck me off your visiting list. What have you been doing with yourself all this time?"

"Well," Pottermack replied evasively—for, obviously, he could not go into details—"I have been a good deal occupied. There have been a lot of things to do; the sun-dial, for instance. I told you about the sun-dial, didn't I?"

"Yes, but that was a long time ago. You said you were going to show it to me when it was set up, but you never have. You haven't even shown it to Mrs. Gadby. She is quite hurt about it."

"Dear me!" exclaimed Pottermack; "how self-centred we old bachelors get! But this neglect must be remedied at once. When can you come and see it? Could you come round and have tea with me to-morrow?"

"Yes. I should like to; but I can't come very early. Will a quarter to five do?"

"Of course it will. We can have tea first and then make a leisurely survey of the sun-dial and the various other things that I have to show you."

Thus the arrangement was made, very much to Mr. Pottermack's satisfaction, for it enabled him to postpone to the morrow a certain very momentous question which he had thought of raising this very afternoon, but which now appeared a little inopportune. For a delicate question must be approached cautiously through suitable channels, and no such means of approach had presented themselves or seemed likely to. Accordingly, relieved of the necessity of looking for an opening, Mr. Pottermack was able to give his whole attention to making himself agreeable, and eventually took his departure in the best of spirits, looking forward with confidence to the prospects of the morrow.

The tea, as arranged by Mrs. Gadby in the pleasant dining-room of "The Chestnuts," was a triumphant success. It would have been an even greater success if the fair visitor had happened to have been on short commons for the preceding week. But the preposterous abundance at least furnished the occasion of mirth, besides serving as an outlet for Mrs. Gadby's feelings of regard and admiration towards the guest and a demonstration of welcome.

"It is really very nice of her," said Mrs. Bellard, glancing smilingly round the loaded table, "and tactful too. It is a compliment to us both. It implies that she has cause to be grateful to me for introducing her here, and you are that cause. I expect she has a pretty comfortable time."

"I hope so," said Pottermack. "I have, thanks to her and to you. And she keeps the house in the most perfect order. Would you like to look over it presently?"

"Naturally I should. Did you ever meet a woman who was not devoured by curiosity in regard to a bachelor's household arrangements? But I am really more interested in the part of the premises that is outside Mrs. Gadby's domain; the part that reflects your own personality. I want especially to see your workshop. Am I to be allowed to?"

"Undoubtedly you are; in fact, if we have finished, as it seems we have, you shall be introduced to it forthwith."

They rose, and, passing out at the back door, walked together up the long path through the kitchen garden and orchard until they came to the gate of the walled garden, which Pottermack unlocked with his Yale key.

"This is very impressive and mysterious," said Mrs. Bellard as the gate closed and the spring-latch snapped. "I am quite proud to be admitted into this holy of holies. It is a delightful garden," she continued, letting her eyes travel round the great oblong enclosure, "so perfectly peaceful and quiet and remote. Here one is cut off from all the world, which is rather restful at times."

Mr. Pottermack agreed, and reflected that the present was one of those times. "When I want to be alone," he remarked, "I like to be definitely alone and secure from interruption."

"Well, you are secure enough here, shut in from the sight of any human eye. Why, you might commit a murder and no one would be any the wiser."

"So I might," agreed Mr. Pottermack, rather taken aback. "I hadn't thought of that advantage, and, of course, you understand that the place wasn't laid out with that purpose in view. What do you think of the sun-dial?"

"I was just looking at it and thinking what a charming finish it gives to the garden. It is delightful, and will be still more so when the new stone has weathered down to the tone of the old. And I think you told me that there is a well underneath. That adds a sort of deliciously horrible interest to it."

"Why horrible?" Pottermack enquired uncomfortably.

"Oh, don't you think wells are rather gruesome things? I do. There is one in my garden, and it gives the creeps whenever I lower the bucket and watch it sinking down, down that black hole and vanishing into the bowels of the earth."

"Yes," said Pottermack, "I have that feeling myself. Probably most town-bred people have. And they are really rather dangerous, especially when they are unguarded as this one was. That was why I took the opportunity to cover it up."

By this time they were close up to the dial, and Mrs. Bellard walked round it to read the motto. "Why do they always write these things in Latin?" she asked.

"Partly for the sake of brevity," he replied. "Here are five Latin words. The equivalent in English is: 'At the rising of the sun, hope: at the going down thereof, peace.'"

"It is a beautiful motto," she said, looking wistfully and a little sadly at the stone pillar. "The first part is what we all know by experience; the second is what we pray for to compensate us for the sorrows and disillusionments of the years that come between. But now let us go and look at the workshop."

Pottermack conducted her behind the yew hedge into the range of well-lighted workrooms, where he exhibited, not without a touch of pride, his very complete outfit. But the fair widow's enthusiastic interest in the tools and appliances rather surprised him; for women are apt to look on the instruments of masculine handicraft with a slightly supercilious eye. No general survey satisfied her. He had to display his "plant" in detail and explain and demonstrate the use of each appliance: the joiner's bench with its quick-grip vice; the metalwork bench with its anvil and stakes and the big brazing-jet; the miniature forge, the lathe, the emery-wheel, and the bench-drill. She examined them all with the closest attention and with a singularly intelligent grasp of their purposes and modes of action. Pottermack became so absorbed in the pleasure of exhibiting his treasures that, for the moment, he almost forgot his main purpose.

"I am glad I have seen the place where you work," she said, as they came out into the garden. "Now I can picture you to myself among your workshop gods, busy and happy. You are happy when you are working there, aren't you?"

She asked the question with so much concern that Pottermack was fain to reply:

"Every workman, I think, is happy when he is working. Of course, I mean a skilled man, working with his hands and his brain, creating something, even if it is only a simple thing. Yes, I am happy when I am doing a job, especially if it is a little difficult."

"I understand; if it calls for a little extra planning and thought. But are you, in general, a happy man? Do you find life pleasant? You always seem very cheerful, and yet sometimes I wonder if you really enjoy life."

Pottermack reflected a few moments. "You are thinking," said he, "of my solitary and apparently friendless state, though I am not friendless at all, seeing that I have you—the dearest and kindest friend that a man could wish for. But in a sense you are right. My life is an incomplete affair, and these activities of mine, pleasant as they are, serve but as makeshifts to fill a blank. But it could easily be made complete. A word from you would be enough. If you were my wife there would be nothing left in the world for me to covet. I should be a perfectly happy man."

He paused and looked at her, and was a little disconcerted to see that her eyes had filled and that she was looking down with an evident expression of distress. As she made no answer, he continued, more eagerly:

"Why should it not be, Alice? We are the very best of friends— really devoted and affectionate friends. We like the same things and the same ways of life. We have the same interests, the same pleasures. We should try to make one another happy, and I am sure we should succeed. Won't you say the word, dear, and let us join hands to go our ways together for the rest of our lives?"

She turned and looked in his face with brimming eyes and laid her hand on his arm.

"Dear friend," she said, "dearest Marcus, I would say yes, joyfully, thankfully, if only it were possible. I have given you my friendship, my most loving friendship, and that is all I have to give. It is impossible for me to be your wife."

Pottermack gazed at her in dismay. "But," he asked huskily, "why is it impossible? What hinders?"

"My husband hinders," she replied in a low voice.

"Your husband!" gasped Pottermack.

"Yes. You have believed, as every one here believes, that I am a widow. I am not. My husband is still alive. I cannot and will not live with him or even acknowledge him. But he lives, to inflict one more injury on me by standing between you and me. Come," she continued, as Pottermack, numb with amazement, gazed at her in silence, "let us go and sit down in the summer-house and I will tell you the whole pitiful story."

She walked across the lawn, and Pottermack accompanied her with half-unconscious reluctance. Since that fatal night he had made little use of the summer-house. Its associations repelled him. Even now he would, by choice, have avoided it; and it was with a certain vague discomfort that he saw his beloved friend seat herself in the chair that had stood vacant since that night when Lewson had sat in it.

"I will tell you my story," she began, "from the time when I was a girl, or perhaps I should say a young woman. At that time I was engaged to a young man named Jeffrey Brandon. We were devotedly attached to each other. As to Jeffrey, I need say no more than that you are—allowing for the difference of age—quite extraordinarily like him; like in features, in voice, in tastes, and in nature. If Jeffrey had been alive now, he would have been exactly like you. That is what attracted me to you from the first.

"We were extremely happy—perfectly happy—in our mutual affection, and we were all-sufficient to one another. I thought myself the most fortunate of girls, and so I was; for we were only waiting until I should come into a small property that was likely to fall to me shortly, when we should have had enough to marry upon comfortably. And then, in a moment, our happiness was shattered utterly. A most dreadful thing happened. A series of forgeries was discovered at the bank where Jeffrey was employed. Suspicion was made to fall upon him. He was prosecuted, convicted—on false evidence, of course—and sentenced to a term of penal servitude.

"As soon as he was convicted, he formally released me from our engagement, but I need not say that I had no intention of giving him up. However, the question never arose. Poor Jeffrey escaped from prison, and in trying to swim out to some ship in the river was drowned. Later, his body was recovered and taken to the prison, where an inquest was held. I went down, and by special permission attended the funeral and laid a wreath on the grave in the prison cemetery. And that was the end of my romance.

"When Jeffrey died, I made up my mind that I was a spinster for life; and so I ought to have been. But things fell out otherwise. Besides me, Jeffrey had one intimate friend, a fellow-clerk at the bank, named James Lewson. Of course, I knew him fairly intimately, and after Jeffrey's conviction I saw a good deal of him. Indeed, we became quite friendly—which we had hardly been before—by reason of the firm belief that he expressed in Jeffrey's innocence. Every one else took the poor boy's guilt for granted, so, naturally, I was drawn to the one loyal friend. Then, when Jeffrey died and was lost to me for ever, he took every opportunity of offering me comfort and consolation; and he did it so tactfully, was so filled with grief for our lost friend and so eager to talk of him and keep his memory green between us, that we became greater friends than ever.

"After a time, his friendship took on a more affectionate and demonstrative character, and finally he asked me plainly to marry him. Of course, I said no; in fact, I was rather shocked at the proposal, for I still felt that I belonged to Jeffrey. But he was quietly persistent. He took no offence, but he did not pretend to accept my refusal as final. Especially he urged on me that Jeffrey would have wished that

I should not be left to go through life alone, but that I should be cherished and protected by his own loyal and devoted friend.

"Gradually his arguments overcame my repugnance to the idea of the marriage, though it was still distasteful to me, and when he asked for my consent as a recognition and reward of his loyalty to Jeffrey, I at last gave way. It appeared ungrateful to go on refusing him; and after all, nothing seemed to matter much now that Jeffrey was gone. The end of it was that we were married just before he started to take up an appointment in a branch of the bank at Leeds.

"It was not long before the disillusionment came, and when it did come, I was astonished that I could have been so deceived. Very soon I began to realize that it was not love of me that had made him such a persistent suitor. It was the knowledge that he had gathered of the little fortune that was coming to me. His greediness for money was incredible; and yet he was utterly unable to hold it. It ran through his hands like water. He had a fair salary, but yet we were always poor and usually in debt. For he was an inveterate gambler—a gambler of that hopeless type that must inevitably lose. He usually did lose at once, for he was a reckless plunger, but if by chance he made a *coup*, he immediately plunged with his winnings and lost them. It was no wonder that he was always in difficulties.

"When, at last, my little property came to me, he was deeply disappointed; for it was tied up securely in the form of a trust, and my uncle, who is a solicitor, was the managing trustee. And a very careful trustee he was, and not at all well impressed by my husband. James Lewson had hoped to get control of the entire capital, instead of which he had to apply to me for money when he was in difficulties and I had to manage my trustee as best I could. But in spite of this, most of the income that I received went to pay my husband's debts and losses.

"Meanwhile our relations grew more and more unsatisfactory. The disappointment due to the trust, and the irritation at having to ask me for money and explain the reasons for his need of it, made him sullen and morose, and even, at times, coarsely abusive. But there was something more. From the first I had been dismayed at his freedom in the matter of drink. But the habit grew upon him rapidly, and it was in connection with this that the climax of our disagreement came about and led to our separation.

"I understand that drink has different effects on different types of men. On James Lewson its effects began with the loss of all traces of refinement and a tendency to coarse facetiousness. The next stage was that of noisy swagger and boasting, and then he soon became quarrelsome and even brutal. There were one or two occasions when he threatened to become actually violent. Now it happened more than once that, when he had drunk himself into a state of boastful exaltation, he spoke of Jeffrey in a tone of such disrespect and even contempt that I had to leave the room to avoid an open, vulgar quarrel. But on the final occasion he went much farther. He began by jeering at my infatuation for 'that nincompoop,' as he called him, and when I, naturally, became furiously angry and was walking out of the room, he called me back, and, laughing in my face, actually boasted to me—to me!—that his was the master mind that had planned and carried out the forgeries and then set up 'that mug, Jeff,' as the man of straw for the lawyers to knock down.

"I was absolutely thunderstruck. At first I thought that it was mere drunken fooling. But then he went on to give corroborative details, chuckling with idiotic self-complacency, until at last I realized that it was true; that this fuddled brute was the dastardly traitor who had sent my Jeffrey to his death.

"Then I left him. At once I packed a small suitcase and went out and took a room at an hotel in the town. The next day I returned and had an interview with him. He was mightily flustered and apologetic. He remembered quite well what he had said, but tried to persuade me that it was a mere drunken joke and that it was all a fabrication, invented to annoy me. But I knew better. In the interval I had thought matters over, and I saw how perfectly his confession explained everything and agreed with what I now knew of him; his insatiable greed for money, his unscrupulousness, his wild gambling, and the reckless way in which he contracted debts. I brushed aside his explanations and denials and presented my ultimatum, of which the terms were these:

"We should separate at once and completely, and henceforth be as total strangers, not recognizing one another if we should ever meet. I should take my mother's maiden name, Bellard, and assume the status of a widow. He should refrain from molesting me or claiming any sort of acquaintance or relationship with me.

"If he agreed to these terms, I undertook to pay him a quarterly allowance and to take no action in respect of what I had learned. If he refused, I should instruct my uncle to commence proceedings to obtain a judicial separation and I should state in open court all that I knew. I should communicate these facts to the directors of the bank; and if, in my uncle's opinion, any prosecution were possible—for perjury or any other offence connected with the forgeries—I should instruct him to prosecute.

"My ultimatum took him aback completely. At first he tried to bluster, then he became pathetic and tried to wheedle. But in the end, when he saw that I was not to be moved from my resolution, he gave way. I could see that my threats had scared him badly, though, in fact, I don't believe that I could have done anything. But perhaps he knew better. There may have been some other matters of which I had no knowledge. At any rate, he agreed, with the one stipulation, that the quarterly allowance should be paid in notes and not by a cheque.

"As soon as I had settled the terms of the separation I moved to Aylesbury, where my mother's people had lived, and stayed there in lodgings while I looked for a small, cheap house. At length I found the cottage at Borley, and there I have lived ever since, as comfortably as my rather straitened means would let me. For, of course, the allowance has been rather a strain, though I have paid it cheerfully as the price of my freedom; and I may say that James Lewson has kept to the terms of our agreement with one exception—an exception that I expected. He has not been satisfied with the allowance. From time to time, and with increasing frequency, he has applied for loans—which, of course, meant gifts—to help him out of some temporary difficulty; and sometimes—but not always—I have been weak enough to supply him.

"But I was not to be left completely in peace. When I had been settled in Borley for about a year, I received a letter from him informing me that 'by a strange coincidence' he had been appointed to the managership of the Borley branch of the Bank. Of course, I knew that it was no coincidence at all. He had engineered the transfer himself."

"With what object, do you suppose?" asked Pottermack.

"It may have been mere malice," she replied, "just to cause me annoyance without breaking the terms of the agreement. But my impression is that it was done with the deliberate purpose of keeping me in a state of nervous unrest so that I should be the more easily prevailed on to comply with his applications for money. At any rate, those applications became more frequent and more urgent after he came to live here, and once he threw out a hint about calling at my house for an answer. But I put a stop to that at once."

"Did you ever meet him in Borley?" Pottermack asked.

"Yes, once or twice. But I passed him in the street without a glance of recognition and he made no attempt to molest me. I think he had a wholesome fear of me. And, of course, I kept out of his way as much as I could. But it was an immense relief to me when he went away. You heard of his disappearance, I suppose? It was the talk of the town at the time."

"Oh yes," replied Pottermack. "My friend, Mr. Gallett, the mason, was almost the first to announce the discovery. But I little thought when I heard of it how much it meant to you—and to me. What do you suppose has become of him?"

"I can't imagine. It is a most mysterious affair. There is no reason that I can think of why he should have absconded at all. I can only suppose that he had done something which he expected to be found out but which has not come to light. Perhaps the most mysterious thing about it is that he has never applied to me for money. He would know quite well that I should at least have sent him his allowance, and that he could depend on me not to betray him, profoundly as I detest him."

Mr. Pottermack cogitated anxiously. He loathed the idea of deceiving this noble, loyal-hearted woman. Yet what could he do? He was committed irrevocably to a certain line of action, and in committing himself he had unconsciously committed her. He had embarked on a course of deception and had no choice but to follow it. And with regard to the future, he could honestly assure himself that whatever made for his happiness would make for hers.

"Do you think he may have gone abroad?" he asked.

"It is impossible to say," she replied. "I have no reason to suppose he has, excepting his extraordinary silence."

"It is even possible," Pottermack suggested in a slightly husky voice, "that he may be dead."

"Yes," she admitted, "that is possible, and it would certainly account for his silence. But is it any use guessing?"

"I was only thinking," said Pottermack, "that if he should happen to have died, that would—er—dispose of our difficulties."

"Not unless we knew that he was dead. On the contrary. If he should have died and his death should remain undiscovered, or, what is the same thing, if he should have died without having been identified, then I should be bound to him beyond any possible hope of release."

Pottermack drew a deep breath, and unconsciously his glance fell on the sun-dial.

"But," he asked in a low tone, "if it should ever become known as an ascertained fact that he was dead? Then, dear Alice, would you say yes?"

"But have I not said it already?" she exclaimed. "Did I not tell you that, if I were free, I would gladly, thankfully take you for my husband? Then, if that is not enough, I say it again. Not that it is of much use to say it, seeing that there is no reason to suppose that he is dead or likely to die. I only wish there were. It may sound callous to express such a wish, but it would be mere hypocrisy to pretend to any other feeling. He ruined poor Jeffrey's life and he has ruined mine."

"I wouldn't say that," Pottermack protested gently. "The sands of your life have yet a long time to run. There is still time for us both to salve some happy years from the wreckage of the past."

"So there is," she agreed. "I was wrong. It is only a part of my life that has been utterly spoiled. And if you, too, have been through stormy weather—as I, somehow, think you have—we must join forces and help one another with the salvage work. But we shall have to be content to be friends, since marriage is out of our reach."

"My dear," said Pottermack, "if you say that you would be willing to have me for your husband, that is all I ask."

They went forth from the summer-house and walked slowly, hand in hand, round the old garden; and Pottermack, anxious to conceal his bitter disappointment, chatted cheerfully about his fruit trees and the flowers that he meant to plant in the sunny borders. Very soon they seemed to be back on the old footing, only with a new note of affection and intimacy which made itself evident when Pottermack, with his hand on the latch of the gate, drew his companion to him and kissed her before they passed through together into the orchard.

He walked with her back to the cottage and said good-bye at the little wooden gate.

"I hope, dear," she whispered, as she held his hand for a moment, "that you are not very, very disappointed."

"I am not thinking of disappointments," he replied cheerily. "I am gloating over the blessings that I enjoy already and hoping that Fortune may have something to add to them later on."

But despite his assumed cheeriness of manner, Mr. Pottermack took his way homeward in a profoundly depressed state of mind. The dream of settled happiness that had haunted him for years, vague and unreal at first but ever growing more definite and vivid, had been shattered in the very moment when it seemed to have become a reality. He thought bitterly of the later years in America when his purpose of seeking his lost love had been forming, almost unrecognized by himself as a thing actually intended; of his long search in London with its ultimate triumph; of the patient pursuit of the beloved object to this place and the purchase of his house; of the long untiring effort, always bringing him nearer and nearer to success. And then, when he seemed to have conquered every difficulty, to have his treasure within his very grasp, behold an obstacle undreamed of and apparently insuperable.

It was maddening; and the most exasperating feature of it was that the obstacle was of his own creating. Like most men who have committed a fatal blunder, Mr. Pottermack was impelled to chew the bitter cud of the might-have-been. If he had only known! How easy it would have been to arrange things suitably! Looking back, he now saw how unnecessary had been all that laborious business of the gutta-percha soles. It had been the result of mere panic. He could see that now. And he could have met the conditions so much more simply and satisfactorily. Supposing he had just made a few footprints in the soft earth leading to the well—he could have done that with the plaster casts—flung down the coat by the brink and gone out on the following morning and informed the police. There would have been no risk of suspicion. Why should there have been? He would have told a perfectly convincing story. He could have related how he had gone out in the evening, leaving his gate unlocked, had returned in the dark and found it ajar; had discovered in the morning strange footprints and a coat, suggesting that some stranger had strayed into the garden and, in the darkness, had fallen down the well. It would have been a perfectly natural and straightforward story. Nobody would have doubted it or connected him with the accident. Then the well would have been emptied, the body recovered and the incident closed for ever.

As it was, the situation was one of exasperating irony. He was in a dilemma from which there seemed to be no escape. He alone, of all the world, knew that Alice Bellard was free to marry him; and that knowledge he must carry locked up in his breast for the remainder of his life.

XII

THE UNDERSTUDY

R EADERS WHO HAVE FOLLOWED THIS HISTORY TO ITS PRESENT
stage will have realized by this time that Mr. Pottermack was a
gentleman of uncommon tenacity of purpose. To the weaker vessels the sudden appearance of an apparently insuperable obstacle is
the occasion for abandoning hope and throwing up the sponge. But
Mr. Pottermack was of a tougher fibre. To him a difficulty was not
a matter for wringing of hands but for active search for a solution.

Hence it happened that the black despair that enveloped and
pervaded him after his proposal to Alice Bellard soon began to dis-
perse under the influence of his natural resiliency. From profitless
reflections on the might-have-been he turned to the consideration
of the may-be. He began to examine the obstacle critically, not as
a final extinguisher of his hopes, but as a problem to be dealt with.

Now what did that problem amount to? He, Marcus Pottermack,
desired to marry Alice Bellard. That had been the darling wish and
purpose of his life and he had no intention of abandoning it. She,
on her side, wished to marry him, but she believed that her husband
was still alive. He, Pottermack, knew that the said husband was
dead, but he could not disclose his knowledge. Yet, until the fact of
the husband's death was disclosed, the marriage was impossible and
must remain so for ever. For there is this unsatisfactory peculiarity
about a dead man: that it is hopeless to look forward to the possibility of his dying. Thus the problem, put in a nutshell, amounted

to this: that James Lewson, being dead *de facto*, had got to be made dead *de jure*.

But how was this to be done? It is hardly necessary to say that, at first, a number of wild-cat schemes floated through Mr. Pottermack's mind, though they found no lodgment there. For instance, he actually considered the feasibility of dismounting the sun-dial, fishing up the body and planting it in some place where it might be found. Of course, the plan was physically impossible even if he could have faced the horrors of its execution.

Then he turned his attention to the now invaluable coat. He conceived the idea of depositing it at the edge of a cliff or on the brink of a river or dock. But this would not have served the required purpose. Doubtless it would have raised a suspicion that the owner was dead. But suspicion was of no use. Absolute certainty was what was needed to turn the wife into a widow. In connection with this idea, he studied the law relating to Presumption of Death; but when he learned that, about 1850, the Court of Queen's Bench had refused to presume the death of a person who was known to have been alive in the year 1027, he decided that the staying power of the law was considerably greater than his own and finally abandoned the idea.

Nevertheless his resolution remained unshaken. Somehow James Lewson would have to be given the proper, recognized status of a dead man. Though no practicable scheme presented itself, the problem was ever present in his mind. By day and by night, in his work in the garden, in his walks through the quiet lanes, even in the fair widow's pleasant sitting-room, his thoughts were constantly busy with the vain search for some solution; and so they might have continued indefinitely but for a chance circumstance that supplied him with a new suggestion. And even then, the suggestion was so indirect and so little related to the nature of his problem that he had nearly missed it.

From time to time, Mr. Pottermack was in the habit of paying a visit to London for the purpose of making various purchases, particularly of tools and materials. On one of these occasions, happening to be in the neighbourhood of Covent Garden, and realizing suddenly that the day was Friday, it occurred to him to look in at the auction rooms in King Street, hard by, and see what was going. For the Friday sales of "miscellaneous property" are of special interest to those who use tools, appliances, or scientific instruments, and Pottermack had on one or two previous occasions picked up some very useful bargains.

But this time he seemed to have drawn a blank; for when he ran his eye over the catalogue which was fixed to the doorpost he found, to his disgust, that the principal feature was "The valuable collection brought together by a well-known Egyptologist, lately deceased." He was on the point of turning away when he noticed, near the end of the catalogue, "another property" consisting of a quantity of model-maker's tools and appliances; whereupon he entered the office, and, having provided himself with a catalogue, made his way to the inner room where the tools were on view. These he looked over critically, marking here and there a "Lot" which might be worth buying if it should go, cheaply enough. Then, having finished his actual business, he proceeded rather aimlessly to browse round the room, catalogue in hand, glancing at the various items of the Egyptologist's collection.

There is always something impressive about the relics of Ancient Egypt. Their vast antiquity, the evidence that they present of strange knowledge and a rather uncanny skill, with suggestions of a state of mind by no means primitive, yet utterly unlike our own, gives them a certain weird quality that makes itself felt by most observers. Pottermack was distinctly aware of it. As he looked over the collection of venerable objects—the ushabti figures, the wooden head-rests, the pre-dynastic painted vases, the jar-sealings, the flint implements and copper tools and weapons—he had the feeling that the place was unworthy of them. Particularly in regard to the wooden and stone steles, the portrait statuettes, the canopic jars and other pious memorials of the dead, did he feel that their presence here, offered for sale in the public market, was an affront to their sacred character. As to the coffins, and above all the mummies, their exposure here seemed to him positively indecent. Here were the actual bodies of deceased ladies and gentlemen, persons of rank and station in their day, as the inscriptions testified, catalogued as mere curios, with the auctioneer's ticket pasted on their very coffins or even on their funeral vesture.

Mr. Pottermack halted by a large open box into which a much-damaged mummy had been crammed and lay, partly doubled up, amidst a litter of broken wood. The ticket, stuck on the linen bandage in which the body was swathed, marked it as "Lot 15"; and reference to the catalogue elicited the further particulars; "Mummy of an official with portions of wooden coffin (a.f.)"; while a label attached to the mummy identified the deceased as "Khama-Heru, a libationer of the 19th or 20th dynasty."

Mr. Pottermack stood by the box, looking down distastefully, almost resentfully, at the shapeless figure, wrapped in its bulky swathings, and looking like a gigantic rag doll that had been bundled into a rubbish-box. That great rag doll had once been a respected attendant at feasts and solemn ceremonials. Presently it would be put up "with all faults" and probably knocked down for a few shillings to some speculative curio dealer. And as he reflected thus, the words of Sir Thomas Browne floated through his mind: "The Egyptian mummies which Time or Cambyses hath spared, Avarice now consumeth." Vain, indeed, were the efforts of the pious Mizraim to achieve even physical immortality.

He had turned away and was beginning to move slowly towards the door. And then, suddenly, in a moment of time, two separate ideas, apparently unrelated, linked themselves together and evolved a third. And a very strange one that newly evolved idea was. Mr. Pottermack was quite startled. As it flashed into his mind, he stopped dead, and then, retracing his steps, halted once more beside the box. But now, as he looked down on the great rag doll that had once been Khama-Heru, no distaste or resentment was in his eye, but rather an eager curiosity that estimated and measured and sought for details. He inspected critically the fracture where the brittle corpse had been doubled up to jam it in the box; the spot where part of a shrivelled nose peeped through a hole in the rotten linen. The history of this thing interested him no more. What it had been was no concern of his. Its importance to him was in what it was now. It was a dead body—a dead human body; the body of a man; of a tall man, so far as he could judge.

He made a pencil mark on his catalogue opposite Lot 15, and then, having glanced at his watch, walked out into King Street, there to pace up and down until it should be time for the auction to begin; and meanwhile to try to fashion this startling but rather nebulous idea into a more definite shape; to decide, in short, the part which the late Khama-Heru could be given to play in his slightly involved affairs.

The actual acquirement of the gruesome relic presented no difficulties. It is true that the auctioneer made some conscientious efforts to invest Lot 15 with some semblance of value. But his plausible suggestions as to the "trifling restorations" that might be necessary aroused no enthusiasm. He had to start the bidding himself— at ten shillings; and at fifteen the hammer descended to confirm Mr. Pottermack in the lawful possession of a deceased libationer. Thereupon the money was handed in and the box handed out, and when it had its lid nailed on and a length of cord tied round it, it was

conveyed out to the pavement, whence it was presently transferred
to the roof of a cab and in due course transported to Marylebone
Station to await the next train to Borley.

The advent of Khama-Heru, deceased, to "The Chestnuts,"
Borley, inaugurated a radical change in Mr. Pottermack's habits and
mental state. Gone was the restless indecision that had kept him
mooning about, thinking everlastingly and getting nothing done.
Now, his mind was, in a measure, at rest. He had a job, and if all the
details of that job were not yet clear to him, still he could, as in any
other job, get on with the part that he knew had to be done while
he was planning out the remainder.

The first problem was to dispose of the box—and of the occupant when he should emerge. In the first place, it had been conveyed
through the side gate to the workshop, where it at present reposed.
But this would never do, especially when the emergence should
take place. For, of late, Alice Bellard had taken to bringing him little
commissions and sitting by him in the workshop babbling cheerfully
while he carried them out. Which was exceedingly pleasant. But two
is company, and, assuredly, Khama-Heru would have made a very
undesirable third. And there was another point. At present, in his box
with the fragments of the coffin and the auctioneer's ticket, K.-H. was
harmless enough; a mere fifteen shillings' worth of miscellaneous
property. But after a few "trifling restorations" (of a rather different
kind from those contemplated by the auctioneer) the said K.-H.
would present a highly compromising appearance. Arrangements
would have to be made for keeping him in strict retirement.

The conditions were met fairly well by emptying the tool-house.
The roller and the lawn-mower could rest safely outside under a
tarpaulin, and the garden tools could be stowed at the end of the
metal-shop. When this had been done and the tool-house door fitted
with a really safe lock, Pottermack dragged the box thither; and

having taken off the lid, strengthened it, and fitted it with a pair of stout hinges and a good lever lock, he felt that he had made things secure for the present. The tool-house was furnished with a long bench for the storage of flower-pots, and, as it was lighted only by a window in the roof, he would be able to work there conveniently and safe from observation.

His first proceeding was to unroll the mummy, to unwind the countless yards of rotten linen bandage with which it had been covered. He wanted to see what the mummy itself was like and whether it was complete. But when he had got all the wrappings off and looked at the thing as it lay on the bench, he was appalled at its appearance. In its wrappings it had been gruesome enough—a great, horrible rag doll; but divested of those wrappings it was ghastly. For now it revealed itself frankly for what it was—a dead man; dry, shrivelled, unnatural, but still undeniably the dead body of a man.

Pottermack stood by the bench gazing at it distastefully and with something of the compunction that he had felt in the auction room. But it was of no use being squeamish. He had bought the thing for a specific and most necessary purpose, and that purpose had got to be carried into effect. Gulping down his qualms, therefore, he set himself to make a systematic examination.

Apparently the body was quite complete. The abdomen looked a little queer, but probably that was due to the drying, though there were unmistakable signs of its having been opened. Both legs were partially broken off at the hip-joints, just hanging on loosely by a few strings of dried flesh. But the bones seemed quite uninjured. The head was in the same condition as the legs, detached from the spine save for one or two strands of dry muscle, and at the moment rolled over on its side with its face turned towards Pottermack. And a grisly face it was; for despite the shrivelled nose, the papery ears, the sunken eyes, and the horrid sardonic grin, it had a recognizable human

expression. Looking at it with shuddering interest, Pottermack felt
that he could form a fairly clear idea as to what Khama-Heru must
have looked like when alive.

Careful measurement with a two-foot rule showed that the
body was just under five feet nine inches in length. Allowing for
shrinkage in drying, his height had probably been well over five feet
ten; enough to make him a passable understudy for James Lewson.
Unfortunately, there was no facial resemblance whatever, but this,
Pottermack hoped, would be of no consequence. The dimensions
were what really mattered. But, of course, the body was useless
for Pottermack's purpose in its present rigid, brittle state, and the
important question was how far it could be softened and rendered
flexible. Pottermack decided to make a tentative experiment on one
shoulder by leaving it for an hour or two under several thicknesses of
wet rag; which he did, with results that were, on the whole, satisfactory. The moistened flesh and skin swelled up appreciably and took
on a much more natural appearance, and the arm now moved freely
at the shoulder-joint. But it was evident that this treatment must not
be applied prematurely, or other, less desirable changes would set in.
He accordingly allowed the moistened area to dry thoroughly and
then put the mummy away in its box, there to remain hidden until
the other preparations had been completed.

These were of two kinds. First, the understudy had to be provided with a "make-up" which would be perfectly convincing under
somewhat rigorous conditions; and secondly, a suitable setting had
to be found for the little drama in which the understudy should play
his part. Both gave Mr. Pottermack considerable occupation.

In connection with the make-up, it happened most fortunately
that he had preserved the copy of the local paper containing the
announcement of the disappearance with the description of the missing man issued by the police. With native caution, Mr. Pottermack

had used the paper to line a drawer, and he now drew it forth and studied its remarkably full details. The coat was in his possession; most fortunately, since it was of a conspicuous pattern and would have been almost impossible to duplicate. The other clothing—the pinhead worsted waistcoat and trousers, the plain grey cotton shirt, the collar, neck-tie, and underclothing—was all of a kind that could be easily matched from the description, aided in some cases by his own memory; and the shoes, which were described minutely, could be duplicated with ease at any large shoe-retailers, while as to the rubber soles, they were of a pattern that were turned out by the thousand.

Nevertheless, the outfit for the deceased gave him endless trouble and occasioned numerous visits to London. The clothing called for tactful manœuvring, since it was obviously not for his own wear. The "Invicta" sole manufacturers had to be found through the directory, and the circular heels, with their five-pointed stars, involved a long and troublesome search; for most of the star-pattern heels have six-pointed stars. And even when the outfit had been obtained the work was not at an end. For all the things were new. They had to be "conditioned" before they would be ready for the final act. The garments had to be worn, and worn roughly (in the garden and workshop, since their size made them entirely unpresentable), to produce marks of wear and convincing creases. The shoes, when the soles had been stuck on and a knife-cut made across the neck of the horse on the right sole, had to be taken out for long nocturnal walks on rough roads, having been previously fitted with two pairs of inner cork soles to prevent them from dropping off. The underclothing would require to be marked, but this Pottermack prudently put off until the last moment. Still, all these preparatory activities took up a good deal of time and gave a considerable amount of trouble. Not that time was of any importance. There was no hurry. Now that Pottermack had a plan his mind was at rest.

Moreover, he had certain distractions, besides his frequent visits to Lavender Cottage. For, in addition to these preparations connected with the costume of the actor, there were others concerned with the scene of the drama. A suitable setting had to be found for James Lewson's next—and, as Pottermack devoutly hoped, final—appearance.

The place must of necessity be close at hand and ought to be on the line of Lewson's known route. This left, practically, the choice between the heath and the wood. The former he rejected as too exposed for his purpose and too much frequented to be perfectly convincing. Of the wood he knew little excepting that few persons seemed ever to enter it, probably for the reason that had led him to avoid it; that, owing to its neglected state, it was choked by almost impenetrable undergrowth.

Now he decided to explore it thoroughly, and since the path which meandered through it divided it into two nearly equal parts, he proposed to make a systematic exploration of each part separately.

He began with the part that lay to the left of the path, which was, if possible, less frequented than the other. Choosing a place where the undergrowth was least dense, he plunged in and began to burrow through the bushes, stooping low to avoid the matted twigs and branches and keeping an eye on a pocket-compass that he held in his left hand. It was a wearisome and uncomfortable mode of progression, and had the disadvantage that, doubled up as he was, he could see little but the compass and the ground at his feet. And it nearly brought him to disaster; for he had been blundering along thus for about ten minutes in as near to a straight line as was possible, when he suddenly found himself at the edge of what looked like a low cliff. Another step forward and he would have been over the brink.

He stopped short, and, straightening his back, drew aside the branches of the tall bushes and looked down. Beneath him was what had evidently been a gravel-pit; but it must have been disused for many years, for its floor was covered, not only with bushes but trees of quite a respectable size. It seemed to him that this place was worth a closer examination. And since the pit had been produced by excavation, there must obviously be some passage-way to the bottom, up and down which the carts had passed when the gravel was being dug.

Accordingly he began to make his way cautiously along the brink, keeping a safe distance from the possibly crumbling edge. He had proceeded thus for a couple of hundred yards when he came to the edge of a sunken cart-track, and following this, soon reached the entrance. Walking down the rough track, in which the deep cart-ruts could still be made out, he reached the floor of the pit and paused to look around; but the trees that had grown up and the high bushes made it impossible to see across. He therefore embarked on a circumnavigation of the pit, wading through beds of tall nettles that grew luxuriantly right up to the cliff-like face of the gravel.

He had made nearly half the circuit of the pit when he perceived, some distance ahead, a large wooden gate which guarded the entrance to a tunnel or excavation of some kind. It had two leaves, in one of which he could see, as he came nearer, a wicket which stood half open. Approaching and peering in through the opening, he found the cavity to be an artificial cave dug in the hard gravel, apparently to serve as a cart-shelter, for the floor was marked by a pair of wide ruts and the remains of a broken sway-bar lay close to one side.

Deeply interested in this excavation, Mr. Pottermack pulled open the wicket-gate—in the lock of which a rusty key still remained— and stepping in through the opening, looked critically around the interior. That it had been for many years disused, so far as its original purpose was concerned, followed from the state of the pit and the absence of any signs of recent digging. But yet the cave itself showed traces of comparatively recent occupation; and those traces threw considerable light on the character of the occupants. A sooty streak up one wall, fading away on the roof, and a heap of wood-ashes mixed with fragments of charcoal, told of not one fire but a series of fires lit on the same spot. Beside the long-extinct embers lay a rusty "billy," originally made from a bully-beef tin fitted with a wire handle; fragments of unsavoury rags and a pair of decayed boots spoke of changes of costume that could certainly not have been premature; while numbers of bird and rabbit bones strewn around hinted at petty poaching, with, perchance, a fortunate snatch now and again in the vicinity of a farmyard.

Mr. Pottermack viewed these relics of the unknown nomad with profound attention. Like most resourceful men, he was quick to take a suggestion. And here, in the pit, the cavern, and these unmistakable relics, was a ready-made story. His own scheme had hardly advanced beyond the stage of sketchy outline. He knew broadly what he intended, but the details had not yet been filled in. Now he could complete the sketch in such detail that nothing would remain but the bare execution; and even that had been robbed of its chief difficulties by the discovery of this cavern.

He paced slowly up and down the echoing chamber, letting his imagination picture the dramatic climax and congratulating himself on this fortunate discovery. How astonishingly well it all came together! The place and the circumstances might have been designed for the very purpose. No need now to puzzle out a plausible cause of death. The empty poison-bottle and the discharged pistol-bullet, which he had considered alternatively, could now be discarded. The cause of death would be obvious. He had nearly broken his own neck coming here in broad daylight. If he had come in the dark, he would have broken it to a certainty.

Then there were the vanished notes and the necessarily empty pockets—necessarily empty, since, as he did not know what they had contained, he would not dare to introduce contents. He had hoped that a reasonable inference would be drawn. But now no inference would be needed. Even the most guileless village constable, when he had seen those fowl and rabbit bones, would understand how deceased's pockets came to be empty.

From reflections on the great *dénouement* Pottermack recalled his thoughts to the practical details of procedure. He proposed forthwith to take over the reversion of the late resident's tenancy. But he could not leave it in its present unguarded state. When the time came for him to occupy it he would require "the use and enjoyment of the said messuage and premises" in the strictest privacy. It would never do to have casual callers dropping in there in his absence. He must see how the place could be made secure.

Inspection of the entrance showed that the large gates were fastened on the inside by massive bars of wood thrust through great iron staples. Consequently, when the wicket-gate was locked the cave was absolutely secure from intrusion. The important question now was as to the lock of the wicket-gate. Was it possible to turn the key? A few strenuous wrenches answered the question in the negative. It is true that, by a strong effort, the rusty key could be made to turn backwards, but by no effort whatever could it be made to shoot the bolt. Key and lock were both encrusted with the rust of years.

There was only one thing to be done. The key must be taken away and scraped clean. Then, with the aid of oil or paraffin, it would probably be possible to make the lock work. By putting out all his strength, Pottermack managed to turn the key backwards far enough to enable him to pull it out of the lock; whereupon, having dropped it in his pocket, he retraced his steps to the entrance to the pit and walked up the sloping cart-track until it emerged on the level, when he halted, and having consulted his compass, set forth, holding it in his hand, and trying by means of the ruts to find the track along which the carts used to pass to and fro across the road.

As the matter was of considerable importance (since the cave was to be the scene of some momentous operations and it was necessary for him to be able to find his way to it with ease and certainty), he took his time over the survey, tracing the ruts until they faded away into the younger undergrowth, and thereafter identifying the overgrown track by the absence of large bushes or trees. From time to time he jotted down a note of the compass-bearing and sliced off with his knife a piece of bark from one of the larger branches of a bush or the trunk of a sapling, and so proceeded methodically, leaving an inconspicuously blazed trail behind him until at last he came out on to the path. Here he paused and looked about him for a landmark, his natural caution restraining him from making an artificial mark; nor was this necessary, for exactly opposite to the point where he had emerged, a good-sized beech tree stood back only a few yards from the path.

Having taken a good look at the tree, that he might recognize it at the next visit, he pocketed his compass and started homewards, counting his paces as he went until he reached the place where the path entered the wood, when he halted and wrote down in his pocket-book the number of paces. That done, his exploration was finished for the time being. The rest of the day he devoted to cleaning the key, to drawing on a card a little sketch-map of his route from the notes in his pocket-book, and to one or two odd jobs connected with the great scheme.

We need not follow his proceedings in minute detail. On the following day, having furnished himself with the cleaned key, a small spanner, a bottle of paraffin mixed with oil, and one or two feathers, he returned to the cave, finding his way thither without difficulty by the aid of his map. There he made a determined attack on the rusty lock, oiling its interior parts freely and turning the key—also oiled—by means of the spanner. At length its corroded bolt shot out with a reluctant groan; and when this, too, had been oiled and shot back and forth a few times, Pottermack shut the wicket, locked it and came away with the key in his pocket, with the comfortable feeling that he now had a secure place in which the highly compromising final operations could be carried out in reasonable safety.

And now the time drew nigh for those final operations to be proceeded with. The costume was complete and its various items had been brought by wear and rough usage to a suitable condition. The waning summer hinted at the approach of autumn and the weather would presently be such as to render woodland expeditions, especially of a nocturnal kind, disagreeable and difficult. And then Pottermack, though not in any way hustled, was beginning to look forward a little eagerly to the end of this troublesome, secret business. He yearned to feel that the tableau was set and that he could wait quietly for the *dénouement*. Also, he was getting to feel very strongly that he would be glad to be relieved of the society of Khama-Heru.

But meanwhile that ancient libationer became daily a more and more undesirable tenant. For the time had come for the course of treatment that should render him at once more convincing and more portable. His condition when first unrolled from his wrappings was that of a wooden effigy, hard and stiff as a board. In that state he could never be got into his clothes, nor could he be transported to the cave under the necessary conditions of secrecy; nor could he effectively impersonate the late James Lewson. The work that the embalmers had done so well would have to be undone. After all, he had had some four thousand years of physical immortality, so the embalmers' fees would not have been thrown away.

There was no difficulty about the treatment. Pottermack simply wrapped the mummy in several thicknesses of wet rag, poured a can of water over it, and, having enclosed it in an outer covering of tarpaulin, left it to macerate for forty-eight hours. When, at the end of that time, he uncovered it, he was at once encouraged and appalled. The last trace of the museum atmosphere was dissipated. It was a mummy no more but just an unburied corpse. The dry muscles had absorbed the moisture and swelled up to an unexpected bulk; the parchment-like skin had grown soft and sodden, and the skeleton hands had filled out and looked almost natural save for the queer, dirty orange colour of the finger-nails. And even that, when Pottermack had observed it with a strong suspicion that it was an artificial stain, disappeared almost completely after a cautious application of chlorinated soda. In short, Khama-Heru seemed already to call aloud for the coroner. All, then, was going well so far. But Pottermack realized only too clearly that the part that was done was the easy part. The real difficulties had now to be faced; and when he considered those difficulties, when he reflected on the hideous risks that he would have to run, the awful consequences of a possible miscarriage of his plans, he stood aghast.

But still with unshaken resolution he set himself to plotting out the details of the next move.

XIII

THE SETTING OF THE TABLEAU

THE TASK WHICH CONFRONTED MR. POTTERMACK IN THE IMME-
diate future involved a series of operations of greatly varying
difficulty. The materials for the "tableau" had to be transported from
the workshop and tool-house to the cave in the gravel-pit. Thither
they would be conveyed in instalments and left safely under lock and
key until they were all there, ready to be "assembled." In the case
of the clothing, the conveyance would be attended by no difficulties
and little risk. It could be done quite safely by daylight. But the instalments of Khama-Heru, particularly the larger ones, would have to
be transported, not merely after dark, but so late as to make it practically certain that he would have the path and the wood to himself.

The latter fact had been evident from the beginning, and in
view of it, Pottermack had provided himself with a night-marching
compass (having a two-inch luminous dial and direction-pointer) and
an electric lamp of the police pattern; so that he was now ready to
begin; and as he had decided to convey the clothing first, he com-
menced operations by making a careful survey of the separate items
and putting the necessary finishing touches to them.

It was now for the first time that he made a thorough examination
of Lewson's coat and of the contents of the letter-case. And it was
just as well that he did; for among those contents was a recent letter
from Alice, refusing a "loan" (probably that letter had precipitated
the catastrophe). It was unsigned and bore no address, but still it

might have given trouble, even if no one but himself should have been able to identify the very characteristic handwriting. Accordingly he burned it forthwith and went still more carefully through the remaining papers; but there was nothing more that interested him. They consisted chiefly of tradesmen's bills, demands for money owing, notes of racing transactions, a letter from his broker, and a few visiting-cards—his own—all of which Pottermack returned to their receptacle. The other pockets contained only a handkerchief, marked "J. Lewson," a leather cigarette-case, and a loose key which looked like a safe key. The key he transferred to the trousers pocket, the cigarette-case he burned, and the handkerchief he retained as a guide to the next operation, that of marking the underclothing. This he did with great care, following his copy closely and placing the marks in accordance with the particulars in the police description, using a special ink of guaranteed durability.

When the "properties" were ready for removal he considered the question of time. This need not be a nocturnal expedition. There would be nothing suspicious in his appearance, and he had, in fact, during his exploration of the wood, not met or seen a single person. Still, it might be better to make his visit to the pit after dusk, when, even if he should be seen, he would not be recognized, and the nature of his proceedings there would not be clearly observable.

Accordingly he prepared for his start with the first instalment as the sun was getting low in the west. Lewson's coat he put on in lieu of his own, covering it with a roomy showerproof overcoat. The trousers and waistcoat he stowed neatly at the bottom of his rucksack with his moth-collecting kit and folding-net above them. Then, with the net-staff in his hand, he let himself out of the side gate just as the crimson disc of the sun began to dive behind a bank of slaty cloud.

The expedition was quite uneventful. He tramped along the path in the gloaming, a solitary figure in the evening landscape; he followed it into the wood and along to the now familiar beech tree; and in all the way he met not a soul. He turned off on the almost indistinguishable track, finding no need for his sketch-map and only glancing now and again at the inconspicuous blazings on bush and sapling. By the time he reached the entrance to the pit, the dusk had closed in; but even now there was light enough for him to find his way down the sloping cart-track, and even to note that, apparently since his last visit, inasmuch as he had not noticed it before, a small tree had toppled over the edge of the cliff, bringing down with it a little avalanche of stones and gravel. He looked up and made a slight detour, picking his way cautiously among the fallen stones; and, preoccupied as he was, that fallen tree and those heaped and scattered stones started a train of thought of which he was hardly conscious at the time.

When he had shed Lewson's coat and by the light of a little, dim pocket-lamp unpacked the trousers and waistcoat, he threw them down in a corner at the back of the cave. Apprehensively he glanced round for some trace of recent visitors (though he knew there could have been none); then he extinguished the lamp, passed out through the wicket, shut the little gate, locked it, and, having pocketed the key, turned away with a sigh of relief. The first instalment was delivered. It wasn't much, but still, he had made a beginning.

On his way back through the wood he made use of the night-compass; not that he seemed greatly to need it, for he found his way with an ease that surprised him. But it was obviously a useful instrument and it was well that he should acquire experience in its management, for there were circumstances that might possibly arise in which it would be invaluable. It would be a fearsome experience to be lost at night in the wood—especially with one of the later instalments.

The easy success of this first expedition had a beneficial moral effect, and with each of the succeeding journeys the strangeness of the experience wore off more and more. Even in the twilight he threaded the blazed track through the wood quite readily without reference to the blazings; and the return in the dark, with the glowing compass in his hand, was hardly more difficult. Half a dozen of these evening jaunts found the entire costume—clothes, shoes, cap, socks, underclothing—stored under lock and key in the cave—waiting for the arrival of the wearer.

But now came the really formidable part of the undertaking, and as Pottermack contemplated those next few journeys he quailed. There was now no question of setting forth in the gloaming; these journeys would have to be made in the very dead of night. So he felt; and even as he yielded to the feeling as to something inevitable, he knew that the reason for it was largely psychological; that it was determined by his own mental state rather than by external circumstances. Admittedly, a human head is an awkward thing to pack neatly in a rucksack. Still, it is of no great size. Its longest diameter, including the lower jaw, is no more than nine or ten inches. A half-quartern loaf and a bottle of beer would make a bigger bulge; yet with these, Pottermack would have gone abroad gaily, never dreaming of having his burden challenged.

He knew all this. And yet as he took up the head (it came off in his hands owing to the frayed-out condition of the softened muscle and ligament) a thrill of horror ran through him at the thought of that journey. The thing seemed to grin derisively in his face as he carried it from the tool-house to the workshop; and when he laid it down on the sheet of brown paper on the bench, the jaws fell open as if it were about to utter a yell.

He wrapped it up hastily and thrust it into the rucksack, and then, by way of feeble and futile precaution, stuffed the sugaring-tin and collecting-box on top. With creeping flesh he slung the package on his back, and, grasping the net-stick, went out across the garden to the gate. He was frankly terrified. When he had passed out of the gate, he stood for some seconds irresolute, unwilling to shut it behind him; and when at last he closed it softly, the click of the spring-latch shutting him out definitely gave him such a qualm that he could hardly resist the impulse to reopen the gate, or, at least, to leave the key in the lock ready for instant use.

Once started, he strode forward at a rapid pace, restraining himself by an effort from breaking into a run. It was a pitch-dark night, near to new moon and overcast as well; so dark that he could barely see the path in the open, and only a slightly intenser gloom told him when he had entered the wood. Here he began to count his paces and strain his eyes into the blackness ahead; for, anticipating some nervousness on this journey, he had taken the precaution when returning from the last to spread a sheet of newspaper at the foot of the beech tree (which formed his "departure" for the cart-track and the gravel-pit) and weight it with a large stone. For this patch of light on the dark background he looked eagerly as he stumbled forward, peering into utter blackness and feeling his way along the path with his feet; and when he had counted out the distance and still saw no sign of it, he halted, and, listening fearfully to the stealthy night sounds of the wood, looked anxiously both ahead and behind him.

Nothing whatever could be seen. But perhaps it was too dark for even a white object to show. Perhaps he had counted wrong, or possibly in his haste he had "stepped out" or "stepped short." Reluctantly he drew out his little pocket-lamp (he did not dare to use the powerful inspection-lamp, though he had it with him) and let its feeble glimmer travel around him. Somehow the trees and bushes looked unfamiliar; but doubtless everything would look unfamiliar in that deceptive glimmer. Still, he had begun to know this path pretty well, even by night. Eventually he turned back and slowly retraced his steps, throwing the dim lamplight on the path ahead. Presently, out of the greenish gloom with its bewildering shadows there sprang a spot of white; and hurrying forward, he recognized with a sigh of relief the sheet of paper lying at the foot of the beech.

From this point he had no more difficulty. Plunging forward into the cellar-like darkness, he went on confidently, guided by the trusty compass which glowed only the more brightly for the impenetrable gloom around. Now and again he stopped to let the swinging dial come to rest and to verify his position by a momentary flash of the lamp. Soon he felt the familiar ruts beneath his feet and came out into the mitigated obscurity of the open track; then, following it down the slope, found his way through the nettles under the cliff, over the remains of the avalanche, until he reached the gate of the cave. A few minutes more and he had discharged his ghastly cargo, locked it into its new abode, and started, free at last from his horrid incubus, on the homeward journey, noting with a certain exasperation how, now that it was of no consequence, he made his way through the wood almost as easily as he would have done by daylight.

But it had been a harrowing experience. Short as had been the journey and light the burden, he stumbled in at his gate as wearily as if he had tramped a dozen miles with a sack of flour on his back. And yet it was but the first and by far the easiest of these midnight expeditions. He realized that clearly enough as he stole silently into the house while a neighbouring church clock struck two. There were three more instalments; and of the last one he would not allow himself to think.

But events seldom fall out precisely as we forecast them. The next two "trips" gave Pottermack less trouble than had the first, though they were undeniably more risky. The safe conveyance of the first instalment gave him confidence, and the trifling, but disconcerting, hitch in finding the "departure" mark suggested measures to prevent its repetition. Still, it was as well that he had transported the easiest load first, for the two succeeding ones made call enough on his courage and resolution. For whereas the head had merely created a conspicuous bulge in the rucksack, the legs refused to be concealed at all. Doubled up as completely as the softened muscles and ligaments permitted, each made an unshapely, elongated parcel over twenty inches in length, of which nearly half projected from the mouth of the rucksack.

However, the two journeys were made without any mishap. As on the previous occasions, Pottermack met nobody either on the path or in the wood, and this circumstance helped him to brace up his nerves for the conveyance of the final instalment. Indeed, the chance of his meeting any person at one or two in the morning in this place, which was unfrequented even by day, was infinitely remote. At those hours one could probably have walked the whole length of the town without encountering a single human being other than the constables on night duty; and it was certain that no constable would be prowling about the deserted countryside or groping his way through the wood.

So Pottermack argued, and reasonably enough; but still he shied at that last instalment. The headless trunk alone was some twenty-six inches long, and, with the attached arms, was a bulky mass. No disguise was possible in its conveyance. It would have to be put into a sack and frankly carried on his shoulder. Of course, if he met nobody, this was of no consequence apart from the inconvenience and exertion; and again he assured himself that he would meet nobody. There was nobody to meet. But still—well, there was no margin for the unexpected. The appearance of a man carrying a sack at one o'clock in the morning was a good deal more than suspicious. No rural constable or keeper would let him pass. And a single glance into that sack—

However, it was useless to rack his nerves with disquieting suppositions. There was pretty certainly not a human creature abroad in the whole countryside, and at any rate the thing had got to be taken to the cave. Quivering with disgust and apprehension, he persuaded the limp torso into the sack that he had obtained for it, tied up the mouth, and, hoisting it on his shoulder, put out into the darkness.

As soon as he had closed the gate he set off at a quick walk. He had no inclination to run this time, for his burden was of a very substantial weight from the moisture that it had absorbed. From time to time he had to halt and transfer it from one shoulder to the other. He would have liked to put it down and rest for a few moments, but did not dare while he was in the open. An unconquerable terror urged him forward to the shelter of the wood and forbade him to slacken his pace, though his knees were trembling and the sweat trickled down his face. Yet he kept sufficient presence of mind to make sure of his "departure," counting his paces from the entrance to the wood and showing the glimmer of his little lamp as his counting warned him of his approach to the beech tree. Soon its light fell on the sheet of paper, and, with a sigh of relief, he turned off the path into the old cart-track.

Once off the path, his extreme terror subsided and he followed the track confidently with only an occasional flash of his lamp to pick up a blaze on bush or tree and verify his direction. He even contemplated a brief rest, and he had, in fact, halted and was about to lower his burden from his shoulders when his ear seemed to catch a faint sound of movement somewhere within the wood. Instantly all his terrors revived. His limbs trembled and his hair seemed to stir under his cap as he stood stock-still with mouth agape, listening with almost agonized intentness.

Presently he heard the sound again; the sound of something moving through the undergrowth. And then it became quite distinct and clearly recognizable as footfalls—the footsteps of two persons at least, moving rather slowly and stealthily; and by the increasing distinctness of the sounds, it was evident that they were coming in his direction. The instant that he recognized this, Pottermack stole softly off the track into the dense wood until he came to a young beech tree, at the foot of which he silently deposited the sack, leaning it against the bole of the tree. Then in the same stealthy manner he crept away a dozen paces or so and again halted and listened. But now the sounds had unaccountably ceased; and to Pottermack the profound silence that had followed them was sinister and alarming. Suddenly there came to him distinctly a hoarse whisper:

"Joe, there's some one in the wood!"

Again the deathly silence descended. Then the sack, which must have been stood up insecurely, slipped from the bole of the tree and rolled over among the dead leaves.

"J'ear that?" came the hushed voice of the unseen whisperer.

Pottermack listened intently, craning forward in an effort to locate the owner of the voice. In fact, he craned a little too far and had to move one foot to recover his balance. But the toe of that foot caught against a straggling root and tripped him up, so that he staggered forward a couple of paces, not noisily, but still very audibly.

Instantly the silence of the wood was dissipated. A startled voice exclaimed: "Gawd! Look out!" and then Joseph and his companion took to undissembled flight, bursting through the undergrowth and crashing into the bushes like a couple of startled elephants. Pottermack made a noisy pretence of pursuit which accelerated the pace of the fugitives; then he stood still, listening with grateful ears to the hurried tramplings as they gradually grew faint in the distance.

When they had nearly died away, he turned, and re-entering the dense wood, made his way, with the aid of the little lamp, towards the beech where he had put down the sack. But the beech was not exactly where he had supposed it to be, and it took him a couple of minutes of frantic searching to locate it. At last the feeble rays of his lamp fell on the slender trunk, and he hurried forward eagerly to retrieve his treasure. But when he reached the tree and cast the light of his lamp on the buttressed roots, the sack was nowhere to be seen. He gazed in astonishment at the roots and the ground beyond, but the sack was certainly not there. It was very strange. He had heard the sack fall over and roll off the roots, but it could not have rolled out of sight. Was it possible that the poachers, or whatever they were, could have picked it up and carried it away? That seemed quite impossible, for the voice had come from the opposite direction. And then the simple explanation dawned on him. This was the wrong tree.

As he realized this, his self-possession forsook him completely. With frantic haste he began to circle round, thrusting through the undergrowth, peering with starting eyes at the ground carpeted with last year's leaves on which the light fell from his lamp. Again and again a tall, slender trunk lured him on to a fresh disappointment. He seemed to be bewitched. The place appeared to be full of beech trees—as in fact it was, being a beech wood. And with each failure he became more wildly terrified and distraught. All sense of direction and position was gone. He was just blindly seeking an unknown tree in a pitch-dark wood.

Suddenly he realized the horrid truth. He was lost. He had no idea whatever as to his whereabouts. He could not even guess in which direction the track lay, and as to his hideous but precious burden, he might have strayed half a mile away from it. He stopped short and tried to pull himself together. This sort of thing would never do. He might wander on, at this rate, until daylight or topple unawares into the pit and break his neck. There was only one thing to be done. He must get back to the path and take a fresh departure.

As this simple solution occurred to him, his self-possession became somewhat restored and he was able to consider his position more calmly. Producing his compass and opening it, he stood quite still until the dial came to rest. Then he turned slowly, so as not to set it swinging again, until the luminous "lubber-line" pointed due west. He had only to keep it pointing in that direction and it would infallibly lead him to the path, which ran nearly north and south. So, with renewed confidence, he began to walk forward, keeping his eye fixed on that invaluable direction-line.

He had been walking thus some three or four minutes, progressing slowly of necessity since he had to push straight forward through the undergrowth, when he tripped over some bulky object and butted rather heavily into the trunk of a tree. Picking himself up, a little shaken by the impact, he snatched out his lamp and threw its light on the object over which he had stumbled. And then he could hardly repress a shout of joy.

It was the sack.

How differently do we view things under different circumstances. When Pottermack had started, the very touch of that sack with its damp, yielding inmate had sent shudders of loathing down his spine. Now he caught it up joyfully, he could almost have embraced it, and as he set forward in the new direction he steadied it fondly on his shoulder. For he had not only found the sack, he had recovered his position. A dozen paces to the north brought him to the spot from whence he had stepped off the track into the wood. Now he had but to turn east and resume his interrupted journey.

But the meeting with those two men had shaken his confidence. He stole on nervously along the cart-track, and when he reached the pit, he peered apprehensively into the darkness on every side, half expecting to detect some lurking figure watching him from among the high nettles. Only when he had at last deposited his burden in the cave and locked and tried the wicket was his mind even moderately at rest; and even then, throughout the homeward journey his thoughts occupied themselves in picturing, with perverse ingenuity, all the mischances that might possibly have befallen him and that might yet lie in wait to defeat his plans in the very moment of their accomplishment.

He arrived home tired, shaken, and dispirited, inclined rather to let his thoughts dwell on the difficulties and dangers that lay ahead than to congratulate himself on those that he had surmounted. As he crept noiselessly up to bed and thought of the gruesome task that had yet to be accomplished, he resolved to give himself a day or two's rest to steady his nerves before he embarked on it. But the following day saw a change of mind. Refreshed even by the short night's sleep, as soon as he had risen he began to be possessed by a devouring anxiety to finish this horrible business and be done with it. Besides which, common sense told him that the presence of the body and the clothes in the cave constituted a very serious danger. If they should be discovered, very awkward enquiries might be set on foot, and at the best his scheme would be "blown on" and rendered impossible for ever after.

A long nap in the afternoon further revived him, and as the evening wore on he began to be impatient to get on the road. This time there were no special preparations to make and no risks in the actual journeys, either going or returning. The recollection of those two men occasioned some passing thoughts of means of defence, for they had obviously been out for no good, as their precipitate retreat showed. He even considered taking a revolver, but his thorough-going British dislike of lethal weapons, which his long residence in the States had accentuated rather than diminished, made him reject the idea. The net-staff was quite a good weapon, especially in the dark; and, in fact, he was not particularly nervous about those men, or any others, so long as he bore no incriminating burden.

When at last he started, just after midnight, he carried the ruck-sack slung from his shoulders and the stout net-stick in his hand. But the former contained nothing but a *bona fide* collecting outfit, including the inspection-lamp, so even a police patrol had no terrors for him. Naturally, it followed that he neither met, saw, nor heard a single person either on the path or in the wood. Swinging easily along the now familiar way, he made his departure almost by instinct and threaded the cart-track with hardly a glance at the compass. And all too soon—as it seemed to him—he found himself at the gate of the cave with the last horrid task immediately confronting him.

It was even worse than he had expected, for he had never dared to let his imagination fill in all the dreadful details. But now, when he had locked himself in and hung the inspection-lamp on a nail in the gate so that a broad beam of light fell on the grisly heap, he stood, shivering and appalled, struggling to brace up his courage to begin. And at last he brought himself to the sticking point and fell to work.

We need not share his agonies. It was a loathly business. The dis-membered parts had to be inducted separately into their garments, leaving the "assembling" for a later stage; and the sheer physical dif-ficulty of persuading those limp, flabby, unhelpful members into the closer-fitting articles of clothing was at once an aggravation and a distraction from the horror of the task. And with it all, it was neces-sary to keep the attention wide awake. For there must be no mistakes. A time would come when the clothing would be submitted to criti-cal examination and the slightest error might rouse fatal suspicions. So Pottermack told himself as, with trembling fingers, he buttoned the waistcoat on the headless, legless torso; only to discover, as he fastened the last button, that he had forgotten the braces.

At length the actual clothing was completed. The legs, encased in underclothing, trousers, socks and shoes, lay on the floor, sprawling in hideous, unnatural contortion; the trunk, fully dressed even to collar and neck-tie, reposed on its back with its arms flung out and the brown, claw-like hands protruding from the sleeves; while, hard by, the head seemed to grin with sardonic amusement at the cloth cap that sat incongruously on its ancient cranium. All was now ready for the "assembling."

This presented less difficulty, but the result was far from satisfactory. For no kind of fastening was permissible. The legs were joined to the trunk by the trousers only, secured precariously by the braces. As to the head, it admitted of no junction, but would have to be placed in position as best it could. However, bad as the "assemblage" was, it would answer well enough if there were no premature discovery.

Having seen everything ready for the final act, Pottermack switched off the lamp and stood awhile to let his eyes grow accustomed to the darkness before he should venture outside. It was not a situation that was helpful to a man whose nerves were already on edge. All sorts of sinister suggestions awakened in his mind in connection with the ghastly figure that sprawled unseen within a few inches of his feet. And then he became acutely sensible of the sepulchral silence of the place; a silence which was yet penetrated by sounds from without, especially by the hootings of a company of owls, whose derisive "hoo-hoos" seemed particularly addressed to him with something of a menacing quality. At length, finding the suspense unbearable, he unlocked the wicket and looked out. By now his eyes had recovered from the glare of the lamp sufficiently for him to be able to see the nearer objects distinctly and to make out the shadowy mass of the cliff close at hand. He peered into the gloom on all sides and listened intently. Nothing seemed to be moving, nor could his ear detect aught but the natural sounds of the woods.

He turned back into the cave, and, guided by a momentary glimmer of his small lamp, carefully gathered up the limp, headless effigy and lifted it with infinite precaution not to disturb the insecure fastenings that held its parts together. Thus he carried it tenderly out through the wicket, and, stepping cautiously over the rough ground and through the rank vegetation, bore it to "the appointed place"— the place where the fallen tree and the scattered stones and gravel marked the site of the "avalanche." Here, close by the tree, he laid it down, and, having inspected it rapidly by the light of the lamp and made a few readjustments, he went back and fetched out the head. This he laid in position by what was left of the neck and supported it in the chosen posture by packing handfuls of gravel round it. When the arrangement was completed he threw the feeble glimmer of the lamp on it once more and looked it over quickly. Then, satisfied that its appearance was as convincing as he could make it, he gathered a few stones and laid them on it, sprinkled over it a handful or two of gravel, and, finally, pulled the high nettles down over it until it was almost hidden from view.

And with that, his task was finished. Now, all he had to do was to get clear of the neighbourhood and wait for whatever might happen. With a sigh of relief he turned away and re-entered the cave, for the last time, as he hoped. Shutting himself in once more, he made a thorough examination of the place by the light of the inspection-lamp to make sure that he had left no traces of his tenancy. The remains of the tramp's fire, the billy, and the fowl and rabbit bones, he left intact; and, having satisfied himself that there was nothing else, he slipped on his rucksack, picked up his net-stick and went out, leaving the wicket gate ajar with the key in the outside of the lock as he had found it.

Very different were his feelings this night as he wended home-wards through the woods from what they had been on the night before. Now he cared not whom he might meet—though he was better pleased that he met nobody. His task was done. All the troublesome secrecy and scheming was over, and all the danger was at an end. His premises were purged of every relic of that night of horror and release. Now he could go back to his normal life and resume his normal occupations. And as to the future; at the worst, a premature discovery might expose the fraud and spoil his plans. But no one would connect him with the fraud. He had given no name to the auctioneer. If suspicion fell on any one, it would fall on the fugitive, James Lewson.

But it was infinitely unlikely that the fraud would be detected. And if it were not, if all went well, James Lewson would be given a decent, reasonable death, and, in due course, a suitable burial. And—again in due course—Alice Bellard would become Mrs. Pottermack.

XIV

THE DISCOVERY

IT WILL NOT APPEAR SURPRISING THAT FOR SOME DAYS AFTER his final expedition Mr. Pottermack's thoughts were almost exclusively occupied by the product of that night's labour. Indeed, his interest in it was so absorbing that on the very next day he was impelled to pay it a visit of inspection. He did not, however, go down to the gravel-pit, but, approaching it from above, found his way easily to that part of the brink from which the tree had fallen, carrying the "avalanche" with it. Here, going down on hands and knees, he crept to the extreme edge and peered over. There was not much to see. There lay the fallen tree, there was the great bed of nettles, and in the midst of it an obscure shape displaying at one end a pair of shoes and at the other, part of a shabby cap.

It was surprisingly inconspicuous. The tall nettles, which he had pulled down across it, concealed the face and broke the continuity of the figure so that its nature was not evident at the first glance. This was eminently satisfactory, for it multiplied the improbabilities of early discovery. It was unlikely that any one would come here at all, but if some person should chance to stray hither, still it was unlikely that the body would be observed.

Considerably reassured, Mr. Pottermack backed away from the insecure edge and went his way, and thereafter firmly resisted the strong impulse to repeat his visit. But, as we have said, that grim figure, though out of sight, was by no means out of mind; and for the next week or two Mr. Pottermack was uncomfortably on the qui vive for the rumour of discovery. But as the weeks went by and still the body lay undiscovered, his mind settled down more and more to a state of placid expectancy.

The summer came to an end with a month of steady rain that made the woods impossible for wayfarers despite the gravel soil. The autumn set in mild and damp. Hedgerow elms broke out into patches of yellow, and the beeches in the wood, after a few tentative changes, burst out into a glory of scarlet and crimson and orange. But their glory was short-lived. A sudden sharp frost held them in its grip for a day or two; and when it lifted, the trees were bare. Their gay mantles had fallen to form a carpet for the earth at their feet.

Then came the autumn gales, driving the fallen leaves hither and thither, but sooner or later driving most of them into the gravel-pit, whence there was no escape. And there they accumulated in drifts and mounds, moving restlessly round their prison as the winds eddied beneath the cliffs, and piling up in sheltered places, smothering the nettles and flattening them down by their weight.

Once, at this time, Mr. Pottermack was moved to call on the disguised libationer. But when he crawled to the edge of the pit and looked down, the figure was invisible. Even the nettles were hidden. All that was to be seen was a great russet bank, embedding the fallen tree, and revealing to the expert eye a barely perceptible elongated prominence.

These months of waiting were to Pottermack full of peace and quiet happiness. He was not impatient. The future was rich in promise and it was not so far ahead but that it seemed well within reach. He had no present anxieties, for the danger of premature discovery was past, and every month that rolled away added its contribution of security as to the final result. So he went his way and lived his life, care-free and soberly cheerful.

There were, indeed, times when he was troubled with twinges of compunction with regard to his beloved friend, for whom these Titanic labours had been undertaken. For Alice Bellard was acutely aware of the unsatisfactory nature of their relationship. She realized that simple, almost conventional friendship is no sort of answer to passionate love, and she made it clear to Pottermack that it was an abiding grief to her that she had no more to give. He yearned to disillusion her; to let her share his confident hopes that all would yet be well. But how could he? It was unavoidable that, in deceiving all the world, he must deceive her.

But, in fact, he was not deceiving her. He was merely conveying to her the actual truth by an indirect and slightly illusory method. So he argued in regard to his ultimate purpose; and as to this intervening period—well, obviously he could not make her an accessory to his illegal actions. So he had to put up, as best he could, with her grateful acknowledgments of his patience and resignation, his cheerful acceptance of the inevitable; feeling all the time an arrant humbug as he realized how far he had been from any such acceptance.

Thus, in quiet content and with rising hopes, he watched the seasons pass; saw the countryside mantled with snow, heard "the ring of gliding steel" on ice-bound ponds and streams, and walked with smoking breath on the hard-frozen roads. And still, as the sands of time trickled out slowly, he waited, now hardly expectant and not at all impatient but rather disposed to favour a little further delay. But presently the winter drew off her forces, reluctantly, like a defeated army, with rearguard actions of hail and rain and howling gales. And then the days began to lengthen, the sunbeams to shed a sensible warmth; the birds ventured on tentative twitterings and the buds made it clear that they were getting ready for business. In short, the spring was close at hand; and with the coming of spring, Mr. Pottermack's fancy lightly turned to thoughts of inquests.

For the time had come. The long months of waiting had been all to the good. They had given the crude understudy time to mature, to assimilate itself to its setting and to take on the style of the principal actor. But the preparatory stage must not be unduly prolonged or it might defeat its own end. There might come a stage at which the transformation would be so complete as not only to prevent the detection of the imposture but to render identification even of the counterfeit impossible. Hence, as the spring sunshine brightened and the buds began to burst, Mr. Pottermack's expectancy revived, not untinged with anxiety. Hopefully his thoughts dwelt on primrose-gatherers and rambling juveniles in search of birds' nests and eggs; and when still no news was heard from the gravel-pit, he began seriously to consider the abandonment of his purely passive attitude and the adoption of some active measures to bring about the discovery.

It was a difficult problem. The one thing that was quite clear to him was that he must on no account appear personally in the matter. He could not say exactly why. But he had that feeling, and probably he was right. But if he could not appear in it himself, how was the thing to be managed? That was the question that he put to himself a hundred times in a day, but to which he could find no answer. And as events fell out, no answer had, after all, to be found, for a contingency that he had never contemplated arose and solved his problem for him.

It happened that on a fine sunny day after a spell of wet he was moved to take a walk along the path through the wood, which he had not done for a week or two. He was conscious of a rather strong desire to pay a visit to the pit and see for himself how matters were progressing, but he had no intention of yielding to this weakness; for the nearer the discovery, the more necessary it was for him to keep well in the background. Accordingly he trudged on, propounding to himself again and again that seemingly unanswerable question, and meanwhile picking up half-unconsciously the old landmarks.

He had approached within a few yards of the well-remembered "departure" beech tree when he suddenly caught sight of a new feature that brought him instantly to a stand. Right across the path, cutting deep into the soft loam of the surface, was a pair of cart-ruts with a row of large hoof-marks between them. They were obviously quite fresh, and it was clear, by the depth and width of the ruts and by the number of hoof-prints and the fact that they pointed in both directions, that they had been made by more than one cart, or at least by more than one journey to and fro of a single cart.

As he was standing eagerly examining them and speculating on what they portended, a hollow rumbling on his right heralded the approach of an empty cart from the west. A few moments later it came into sight through an opening just beyond the beech, the carter, dismounted, leading his horse by the bridle. Seeing Pottermack, he touched his hat and civilly wished him "good morning."

"Now, where might you be off to?" Pottermack enquired genially.

"To the old gravel-pit, sir," was the reply. "'Tis many a year since any gravel was dug there. But Mr. Barber he's a-makin' a lot of this here concrate stuff for to put into the foundations of the new houses what he's buildin', and he thought as it were foolishness to send for gravel to a distance when there's a-plenty close at hand. So we're a-openin' up the old pit."

"Where about is the pit?" asked Pottermack. "Is it far from here?"

"Far! Lor' bless yer, no, sir. Just a matter of a few hundred yards. If you like to walk along with me, I'll show you the place."

Pottermack accepted the offer promptly, and as the man started his horse with a friendly "gee-up," he walked alongside, following the new ruts down the familiar track—less familiar now that the great hoofs and the wide cart wheels had cleared an open space—until they came out at the top of the rough road that led down to the pit. Here Pottermack halted, wishing his friend "good morning," and stood watching the cart as it rumbled down the slope and skirted the floor of the pit towards a spot where a bright-coloured patch on the weathered "face" showed the position of the new working.

Here Pottermack could see two men loosening the gravel with picks and two more shovelling the fallen stuff into a cart that was now nearly full. The place where they were at work was on the right side of the pit, as Pottermack stood, and nearly opposite to the cave, the gates of which he could see somewhat to his left. Standing there, he made a rapid mental note of the relative positions, and then, turning about, made his way back to the path, cogitating profoundly as he went.

How long would it be before one of those men made the momentous discovery? Or was it possible that they might miss it altogether? The British labourer is not by nature highly observant, nor has he an excessively active curiosity. Nearly the whole width of the pit separated them from the remains. No occasion need arise for them to stray away from the spot where their business lay. But it would be exasperating if they should work there for a week or two and then go away leaving the discovery still to be made.

However, it was of no use to be pessimistic. There was a fair probability that one of them would at least go round to the cave. Quite possibly it might again be put to its original use as a cart-shelter. For his part, he could do no more than wait upon the will of Fortune and meanwhile hold himself prepared for whatever might befall. But in spite of the latter discreet resolution, the discovery, when it came, rather took him by surprise. He was lingering luxuriously over his after-breakfast pipe some four or five days after his meeting with the carter, idly turning over the leaves of a new book, while his thoughts circled about the workers in the pit and balanced the chances of their stumbling upon that gruesome figure under the cliff, when a familiar knock at the front door dispelled his reverie in an instant and turned his thoughts to more pleasant topics. He had risen and was about to go to the door himself, but was anticipated by Mrs. Gadby, who, a few moments later, announced and ushered in Mrs. Bellard.

Pottermack advanced to greet her, but was instantly struck by something strange and disquieting in her appearance and manner. She stopped close by the door until the housekeeper's footsteps had died away, then, coming close to him, exclaimed almost in a whisper:

"Marcus, have you heard? About James, I mean?"

"James!" repeated Pottermack helplessly, his wits for the moment paralysed by the suddenness of the disclosure; then, pulling himself together with a violent effort, he asked: "You don't mean to say that fellow has turned up again?"

"Then you haven't heard. He is dead, Marcus. They found his body yesterday evening. The news is all over the town this morning."

"My word!" exclaimed Pottermack. "This is news with a vengeance! Where was he found?"

"Quite near here. In a gravel-pit in Potter's Wood. He must have fallen into it the very night that he went away."

"Good gracious!" ejaculated Pottermack. "What an astonishing thing! Then he must have been lying there all these months! But—er—I suppose there is no doubt that it is Lewson's body?"

"Oh, not the least. Of course the body itself was quite unrecognizable. They say it actually dropped to pieces when they tried to pick it up. Isn't it horrible? But the police were able to identify it by the clothes and some letters and visiting-cards in the pockets. Otherwise there was practically nothing left but the bones. It makes me shudder to think of it."

"Yes," Pottermack admitted calmly, his self-possession being now restored, "it does sound rather unpleasant. But it might have been worse. He might have turned up alive. Now you are rid of him for good."

"Yes, I know," said she; "and I can't pretend that it isn't a great relief to know that he is dead. But still—what ought I to do, Marcus?"

"Do!" Pottermack repeated in astonishment.

"Yes. I feel that I ought to do something. After all, he was my husband."

"And a shocking bad husband at that. But I don't understand what you mean. What do you suppose you ought to do?"

"Well, don't you think that somebody—somebody belonging to him—ought to come forward to—to identify him?"

"But," exclaimed Pottermack, "you said that there is nothing left of him but his bones. Now, my dear, you know you can't identify his bones. You've never seen them. Besides, he has been identified already."

"Well, say, to acknowledge him."

"But, my dear Alice, why on earth should you acknowledge him, when you had, years ago, repudiated him, and even taken another name to avoid being in any way associated with him?

"No, no, my dear, you just keep quiet and let things take their course. This is one of those cases in which a still tongue shows a wise head. Think of all the scandal and gossip that you would start if you were to come forward and announce yourself as Mrs. Lewson. You would never be able to go on living here. I take it that no one in this place knows who you are?"

"Not a soul."

"And how many people altogether know that you were married to him?"

"Very few, and those practically all strangers. We lived a very solitary life at Leeds."

"Very well. Then the least said the soonest mended. Besides," he added, as another highly important consideration burst on him, "there is our future to think of. You are still willing to marry me, dear, aren't you?"

"Yes, Marcus, of course I am. But please don't let us talk about it now."

"I don't want to, my dear, but we have to settle this other matter. The position is now that we can get married whenever we please."

"Yes, there is no obstacle now."

"Then, Alice dearest, don't let us make obstacles. But we shall if we make known the fact that you were Lewson's wife. Just think of the position. Here were you and your husband in the same town, posing as total strangers. And here were you and I, intimate friends and generally looked upon almost as an engaged couple. Now, suppose that we marry in the reasonably near future. That alone would occasion a good deal of comment. But suppose that it should turn out that Lewson met his death by foul means. What do you imagine people would say then?"

"Good heavens!" exclaimed Alice. "I had never thought of that. Of course, people—or at any rate, some people—would say that we had conspired to get him out of the way. And really, that is what it would look like. I *am* glad I came and consulted you."

Pottermack drew a deep breath. So that danger was past. Not that it had been a very obvious danger. But instinct warned him—and it was a perfectly sound instinct—to avoid at all costs having his personality in any way connected with that of James Lewson. Now he would be able to watch the course of events at his ease, and to all appearance from the detached standpoint of a total stranger. Nor was Alice less relieved. Some obscure sense of loyalty had seemed to impel her to proclaim her relationship to the dead wastrel. But she was not unwilling to be convinced of her mistake; and when presently she went away, her heart was all the lighter for feeling herself excused from the necessity of laying bare to the public gaze the sordid details of her domestic tragedy.

When she was gone, Pottermack reflected on the situation and considered what he had better do. Caution conflicted with inclination. He was on the very tiptoe of curiosity, but yet he felt that he must show no undue interest in the affair. Nevertheless, it was desirable that he should know, if possible, what had really happened and what was going to be done about it. Accordingly he decided to go forth and perambulate the town and passively permit the local quidnuncs to supply him with the latest details.

He did not, however, add much to his knowledge excepting in one important respect, which was that the date of the inquest was already fixed. It was to take place at three o'clock in the afternoon on the next day but one; and having regard to the public interest in the case, the inquiry was to be held in the Town Hall. When he had ascertained this fact, and that the public would have free access to the hall during the proceedings, he went home and resolved to manifest no further interest in the case until those proceedings should open.

But the interval was one of intense though suppressed excitement. He could settle to nothing either in the workshop or in the garden. He could only seek relief in interminable tramps along the country roads. His mind seethed with mingled anxiety and hope. For the inquest was the final scene of this strange drama of which he was at once author and stage manager; and it was the goal of all his endeavours. If it went off successfully, James Lewson would be finished with for ever; he would be dead, buried, and duly registered at Somerset House; and Marcus Pottermack could murmur "Nunc dimittis" and go his way in peace.

Naturally enough, he was punctual, and more than punctual, in his attendance at the Town Hall on the appointed day, for he arrived at the entrance nearly half an hour before the time announced for the opening of the inquiry. However, he was not alone. There were others still more punctual and equally anxious to secure good places. In fact, there was quite a substantial crowd of early place-seekers which grew from moment to moment. But their punctuality failed to serve its purpose, since the main doors were still closed and a constable stationed in front of them barred all access. Some of them strayed into the little square or yard adjoining, apparently for the satisfaction of looking at the closed door of the mortuary on its farther side.

Pottermack circulated among the crowd, speaking to no one but listening to the disjointed scraps of conversation that came his way. His state of mind was very peculiar. He was acutely anxious, excited, and expectant. But behind these natural feelings he had a queer sense of aloofness, of superiority to these simple mortals around him, including the coroner and the police. For he knew all about it, whereas they would presently grope their way laboriously to a conclusion, and a wrong conclusion at that. He knew whose were the remains lying in the mortuary. He could have told them that they were about to mistake the scanty vestiges of a libationer of the nineteenth or twentieth dynasty for the body of the late James Lewson. So it was that he listened with a sort of indulgent complacency to the eager discussions concerning the mysterious end of the deceased branch manager.

Presently a report began to circulate that a gentleman had been admitted to the mortuary by the sergeant, and, as the crowd forthwith surged along in that direction, he allowed himself willingly to be carried with it. Arrived at the little square, the would-be spectators developed a regular gyratory movement down one side and up the other, being kept on the move by audible requests to "pass along, please." In due course Pottermack came in sight of the mortuary door, now half open and guarded by a police-sergeant who struggled vainly to combine the incompatible qualities of majestic impassivity and a devouring curiosity as to what was going on inside.

At length Pottermack reached the point at which he could see in through the half-open door, and at the first glance his "superiority complex" underwent sudden dissolution. A tall man, whose back was partly turned towards him, held in his hand a shoe, the sole of which he was examining with concentrated attention. Pottermack stopped dead, gazing at him in consternation. Then the sergeant sang out his oft-repeated command and Pottermack was aware of increasing pressure from behind. But at the very instant when he was complying with the sergeant's injunction to "pass along," the tall man turned his head to look out at the door and their eyes met. And at the sight of the man's face Pottermack could have shrieked aloud.

It was the strange lawyer.

For some moments Pottermack's faculties were completely paralysed by this apparition. He drifted on passively with the crowd in a state of numb dismay. Presently, however, as the effects of the shock passed off and his wits began to revive, some of his confidence revived with them. After all, what was there to be so alarmed about? The man was only a lawyer, and he had seemed harmless enough when they had talked together at the gate. True, he had seemed to be displaying an unholy interest in the soles of those shoes. But what of that? Those soles were all correct, even to the gash in the horse's neck. They were, in fact, the most convincing and unassailable part of the make-up.

But, encourage himself as he would, the unexpected appearance of this lawyer had given his nerves a nasty jar. It suggested a number of rather disquieting questions. For instance, how came this man to turn up at this "psychological moment" like a vulture sniffing from afar a dead camel in the desert? Why was he looking at those soles with such extraordinary interest? Was it possible that he had seen those photographs? And if so, might they have shown something that was invisible to the unaided eye?

These questions came crowding into Mr. Pottermack's mind, each one more disquieting than the others. But always he came back to the most disquieting one of all. How, in the name of Beelzebub, came this lawyer to make his appearance in the Borley mortuary at this critical and most inopportune moment?

It was natural that Mr. Pottermack should ask himself this very pertinent question; for, in truth, it did appear a singular coincidence. And inasmuch as coincidences usually seem to demand some explanation, we may venture to pursue the question that the reader may attain to the enlightenment that was denied to Mr. Pottermack.

XV

T HE REPERCUSSIONS OF MR. POTTERMACK'S ACTIVITIES MADE themselves felt at a greater distance than he had bargained for. By the agency of an enterprising local reporter they became communicated to the daily press, and thereby to the world at large, including Number 5A King's Bench Walk, Inner Temple, London, E.C., and the principal occupant thereof. The actual purveyor of intelligence to the latter was Mr. Nathaniel Polton, and the communication took place in the afternoon of the day following the discovery. At this time Dr. Thorndyke was seated at the table with an open brief before him, jotting down a few suggestions for his colleague, Mr. Anstey, when to him entered Nathaniel Polton aforesaid, with a tray of tea-things in one hand and the evening paper in the other. Having set down the tray, he presented the paper, neatly folded into a small oblong, with a few introductory words.

"There is a rather curious case reported in the *Evening Post*, sir. Looks rather like something in our line. I thought you might be interested to see it, so I've brought you the paper."

"Very good of you, Polton," said Thorndyke, holding out his hand with slightly exaggerated eagerness. "Curious cases are always worth our attention."

Accordingly he proceeded to give his attention to the marked paragraph; but at the first glance at the heading, the interest which he had assumed out of courtesy to his henchman became real and intense. Polton noted the change, and his lined face crinkled up into a smile of satisfaction as he watched his employer reading the paragraph through with a concentration that, even to him, seemed hardly warranted by the matter. For, after all, there was no mystery about the affair, so far as he could see. It was just curious and rather gruesome. And Polton had distinct liking for the gruesome. So, apparently, had the reporter, for he used that very word to lend attraction to his heading. Thus:—

"GRUESOME DISCOVERY AT BORLEY.

"Yesterday afternoon some labourers who were digging gravel in a pit in Potter's Wood, Borley, near Aylesbury, made a shocking discovery. When going round the pit to inspect a disused cart-shelter, they were horrified at coming suddenly upon the much-decomposed body of a man lying at the foot of the perpendicular 'face,' down which he had apparently fallen some months previously. Later it was ascertained that the dead man is a certain James Lewson, the late manager of the local branch of Perkins's Bank, who disappeared mysteriously about nine months ago. An inquest on the body is to be held at the Town Hall, Borley, on Thursday next at 3 p.m., when the mystery of the disappearance and death will no doubt be elucidated."

"A very singular case, Polton," said Thorndyke, as he returned the paper to its owner. "Thank you for drawing my attention to it."

"There doesn't seem to be any mystery as to how the man met his death," remarked Polton, cunningly throwing out this remark in the hope of eliciting some illuminating comments. "He seems to have just tumbled into the pit and broken his neck."

"That is what is suggested," Thorndyke agreed. "But there are all sorts of other possibilities. It would be quite interesting to attend the inquest and hear the evidence."

"There is no reason why you shouldn't, sir," said Polton. "You've got no arrangements for Thursday that can't easily be put off."

"No, that is true," Thorndyke rejoined. "I must think it over and consider whether it would be worth giving up the time."

But he did not think it over, for the reason that he had already made up his mind. Even as he read the paragraph, it was clear to him that here was a case that called aloud for investigation.

The call was twofold. In the first place he was profoundly interested in all the circumstances surrounding the disappearance of James Lewson. In any event he would have wished to make his understanding of the case complete. But there was another and a more urgent reason for inquiry. Hitherto his attitude had been simply spectatorial. Neither as a citizen nor as an officer of the law had he felt called upon to interfere. Now it became incumbent on him to test the moral validity of his position; to ascertain whether that detached attitude was admissible in these new circumstances.

The discovery had taken him completely by surprise. Some developments he had rather expected. The appearance of the stolen notes, for instance, had not surprised him at all. It had seemed quite "according to plan"; just a manœuvre to shift the area of inquiry. But this new development admitted of no such explanation; for if it was an "arrangement" of some kind, what could be the motive? There appeared to be none.

He was profoundly puzzled. If this was really James Lewson's body, then the whole of his elaborate scheme of reasoning was fallacious. But it was not fallacious. For it had led him to the conclusion that Mr. Marcus Pottermack was Jeffrey Brandon, deceased.

And investigation had proved beyond a doubt that that conclusion was correct. But a hypothesis which, on being applied, yields a new truth—and one that is conditional upon its very terms—must be true. But again, if his reasoning was correct, this could not be Lewson's body.

But if it was not Lewson's body, whose body was it? And how came it to be dressed in Lewson's clothes—if they really were Lewson's clothes and not a carefully substituted make-up? It was here that the question of public policy arose. For here was undoubtedly a dead person. If that person proved to be James Lewson, there was nothing more to be said. But if he were not James Lewson, then it became his, Thorndyke's, duty as a citizen and a barrister to ascertain who he was and how his body came to be dressed in Lewson's clothes; or, at least, to set going inquiries to that effect.

That evening he rapidly reviewed the material on which his reasoning had been based. Then, unrolling the strip of photographs, he selected a pair of the most distinct—showing a right and a left foot—and, with the aid of the little document microscope, made an enlarged drawing of each on squared paper to a scale of three inches to the foot, i.e. a quarter of the natural size. The drawings, however, were little more than outlines, showing none of the detail of the soles; but the dimensions were accurately rendered, excepting those of the screws which secured the heels, which were drawn disproportionately large and the position of the slots marked in with special care and exactness.

With these drawings in his pocket and the roll of photographs in his attaché-case for reference if any unforeseen question should arise, Thorndyke started forth on the Thursday morning en route for Borley. He did not anticipate any difficulties. An inquest which he had attended at Aylesbury some months previously had made him acquainted with the coroner who would probably conduct this inquiry; but in any case, the production of his card would secure him the necessary facilities.

It turned out, however, that his acquaintance was to conduct the proceedings, though he had not yet arrived when Thorndyke presented himself at the Town Hall nearly an hour before the time when the inquest was due to open. But the police officer on duty, after a glance at his card, showed him up to the coroner's room and provided him with a newspaper wherewith to while away the time of waiting; which Thorndyke made a show of reading, as a precaution against possible attempts at conversation, until the officer had retired, when he brought forth the two drawings and occupied himself in memorizing the dimensions and other salient characteristics of the footprints.

He had been waiting close upon twenty minutes when he heard a quick step upon the stair and the coroner entered the room with extended hand.

"How do you do, doctor?" he exclaimed, shaking Thorndyke's hand warmly. "This is indeed an unexpected pleasure. Have you come down to lend us a hand in solving the mystery?"

"Is there a mystery?" Thorndyke asked.

"Well, no, there isn't," was the reply, "excepting how the poor fellow came to be wandering about the wood in the dark. But I take it, from your being here, that you are in some way interested or concerned in the case."

"Not in the case," replied Thorndyke. "Only in the body. And my interest in that is rather academic. I understand that it is known to have been lying exposed in the open for nine months. Now, I have never had an opportunity of inspecting a body that has been exposed completely in the open for so long. Accordingly, as I happened to be in the neighbourhood, I thought that I would ask your kind permission just to look it over and make a few notes as to its condition."

"I see; so that you may know exactly what a nine-months-old exposed body looks like, with a view to future contingencies. But of course, my dear doctor, I shall be delighted to help you to this modest extent. Would you like to make your inspection now?"

"How will that suit you?"

"Perfectly. The jury will be going in to view the remains in about half an hour, but they won't interfere with your proceedings. But you will probably be finished by then. Are you coming to the inquest?"

"I may as well, as I have nothing special to do for an hour or two; and the evidence may help me to amplify my notes."

"Very well," said the coroner, "then I will see that a chair is kept for you. And now I will tell Sergeant Tatnell to take you to the mortuary and see that you are not disturbed while you are making your notes."

Hereupon, the sergeant, being called in and given his instructions, took Thorndyke in custody and conducted him down a flight of stairs to a side door which opened on a small square, on the opposite side of which was the mortuary. A considerable crowd had already collected in front of the Town Hall and at the entrance of the square, and by its members Thorndyke's emergence with the sergeant by no means passed unnoticed; and when the latter proceeded to unlock the mortuary door and admit the former, there was a general movement of the crowd into the square with a tendency to converge on the mortuary door.

The sergeant, having admitted Thorndyke, gazed at him hungrily as he pointed out the rather obvious whereabouts of the corpse and the clothing. Then, with evident reluctance, he retired, leaving the door half open and stationing himself on guard in a position which commanded an unobstructed view of the interior. Thorndyke would rather have had the door closed, but he realized the sergeant's state of mind and viewed it not unsympathetically. And a spectator or two was of no consequence since he was merely making an inspection.

As the sergeant had obligingly explained, the body was in the open shell or coffin which rested on one of the tables, while the clothing was laid out on an adjoining table in a manner slightly reminiscent of a rummage sale or a stall in the Petticoat Lane Market. Having put down his attaché-case, Thorndyke began his inspection with the clothing, and, bearing in mind the sergeant's eye, which was following his every movement, he first looked over the garments, one by one, until he came naturally to the shoes. These he inspected from various points of view, and when he had minutely examined the uppers he picked up the right shoe, and, turning it over, looked at the heel. And in the instant that his glance fell on it his question was answered.

It was not Lewson's shoe.

Putting it down, he picked up the left shoe and inspected it in the same manner. It gave the same answer as the right had done, and each confirmed the other with the force of cumulative evidence. These were not James Lewson's shoes. There was no need to apply the measurements that he had marked on his diagrams. The single fact which he had elicited settled the matter.

It was quite a plain and obvious fact, too, though it had escaped the police for the simple reason that they were not looking for it. It was just a discrepancy in the position of the screws. But it was absolutely conclusive. For the central screw by which a circular rubber heel is secured is of necessity a fixture. When once it is driven in, it remains immovable so long as the heel continues in position. For if the screw turns in the slightest degree, its hold is loosened, it unscrews from its hole and the heel comes off. But these heels had not come off. They were quite firmly attached, as Thorndyke ascertained by grasping them and as was proved by the extent to which they were worn down. Therefore the screws could not have moved.

But yet their slots were at a totally different angle from the slots of the screws in Lewson's shoes.

He was standing with the shoe in his hand when a sharply spoken command from the sergeant to "pass along, please" caused him half-unconsciously to turn his head. As he did so, he became aware of Mr. Pottermack gazing at him through the half-open door with an expression of something very like consternation. The glance was only momentary, for, even as their eyes met, Pottermack moved away in obedience to the sergeant's command, reinforced by a vigorous *vis a tergo* applied by the spectators in his rear.

Thorndyke smiled grimly at the coincidence—which was hardly a coincidence at all—and then returned to the consideration of the shoes. He had thoroughly memorized his drawings, but still, his rigorously exact mind demanded verification. Accordingly he placed both shoes sole uppermost and—with his back to the sergeant—produced the drawings from his pocket for comparison with the shoes. Of course he had made no mistake. In the drawing of the right foot, the slot of the screw was at a right angle to the long axis of the shoe—in the position of the hands of a clock at a quarter to three; in the right shoe before him, the slot was oblique—in the position of the clock-hands at five minutes past seven. So with the left; in the drawing it was in the position of ten minutes to four; in the mortuary shoe it was in that of twenty minutes to two.

The proof was conclusive, and it justified Thorndyke's forecast. For he had assumed that if the shoes on the discovered body were counterfeits, the one detail which the counterfeiter would overlook or neglect would be the position of the screw-slots; while, by the ordinary laws of probability, it was infinitely unlikely that the positions of the slots would happen to match in both feet by mere chance.

But, this point being settled, a more important one arose. If the shoes were not Lewson's shoes, the body was probably not Lewson's body. And if it were not, then it was the body of some other person; which conclusion would raise the further question, How was that body obtained? This was the vitally important issue, for it would appear that the having possession of a dead human body almost necessarily implies the previous perpetration of some highly criminal act.

So Thorndyke reflected, a little anxiously, as he stood by the open shell, looking down on the scanty remains of what had once been a man. His position was somewhat difficult, for, since he had never seen Lewson and knew nothing of his personal characteristics beyond his approximate age and what he had inferred from the footprints—that he was a man approaching six feet in height, which appeared to be also true of the body in the shell—he had no effective means of identification. Nevertheless, it was possible that a careful examination might bring into view some distinctive characters that would furnish a basis for further inquiry when the witnesses should presently be called.

Thus encouraging himself, he began to look over the gruesome occupant of the shell more critically. And now, as his eye travelled over it, he began to be conscious of an indefinite something in its aspect that was not quite congruous with the ostensible circumstances. It seemed to have wasted in a somewhat unusual manner. Then his attention was attracted by the very peculiar appearance of the toe-nails. They showed a distinct orange-yellow coloration which was obviously abnormal, and when he turned for comparison to the finger-nails, traces of the same unnatural colour were detectable though much less distinct.

Here was a definite suggestion. Following it up, he turned his attention to the teeth, and at once the suggestion was confirmed. These were the teeth of no modern civilized European. The crowns of the molars, cuspless and ground down to a level surface, spoke of the gritty meal from a hand-quern and other refractory food-stuffs beyond the powers of degenerate civilized man. Still following the clue, Thorndyke peered into the nasal cavities, the entrance to which had been exposed by the almost complete disappearance of the nose. With the aid of a tiny pocket electric lamp, he was able to make out on both sides extensive fractures of the inner bones—the turbinates and ethmoid. In the language of the children's game, he was "getting warm"; and when he had made a close and prolonged examination of the little that was left of the abdomen, his last lingering doubts were set at rest.

He stood up, at length, with a grim but appreciative smile, and recapitulated his findings. Here was a body, found in a gravel-pit, clothed in the habiliments of one James Lewson. The toe- and finger-nails were stained with henna; the teeth were the characteristic teeth of somewhat primitive man; the ethmoid and turbinate bones were fractured in a manner incomprehensible in connection with any known natural agency but in precisely the manner in which they would have been damaged by the embalmer's hook; there was not the faintest trace of any abdominal viscera, and there did appear to be—though this was not certain, owing to the wasted condition of the remains—some signs of an incision in the abdominal wall; and finally, the hair showed evidence of chemical corrosion, not to be accounted for by any mere exposure to the weather. In short, this body displayed a group of distinctive features which, taken collectively, were characteristic of, and peculiar to, an Egyptian mummy; and that it was an Egyptian mummy he felt no doubt whatever.

He hailed the conclusion with a sigh of relief. He had come here prepared to intervene at the inquest and challenge the identity of the corpse if he had found any evidence of the perpetration of a crime. But he would have been profoundly reluctant to intervene. Now there was no need to intervene, since there was no reason to suppose that any crime had been committed. Possession of an Egyptian mummy does not imply any criminal act. Admittedly, these proceedings of Mr. Pottermack's were highly irregular. But that was a different matter. Allowance had to be made for special circumstances.

Nevertheless, Thorndyke was not a little puzzled. Acting on his invariable principle, he had disregarded the apparent absence of motive and had steadily pursued the visible facts. But now the question of motive arose as a separate problem. What could be the purpose that lay behind this quaint and ingenious personation of a dead man? Some motive there must have been, and a powerful motive too. Its strength could be measured by the enormous amount of patient and laborious preparation that the result must have entailed, to say nothing of the risk. What could that motive have been? It did not, apparently, arise out of the original circumstances. There must be something else that had not yet come into view. Perhaps the evidence at the inquest might throw some light upon it.

At any rate, no crime had been committed, and as to this dummy inquest, there was no harm in it. On the contrary, it was all to the good. For it would establish and put on record a fact which otherwise would have gone unascertained and unrecorded, but which ought, on public grounds, to be duly certified and recorded.

As Thorndyke reached this comfortable conclusion, the sergeant announced the approach of the jury to view the body; whereupon he picked up his attaché-case, and, emerging from the mortuary, made his way to the court-room and took possession of a chair which a constable was holding in reserve for him, close to that which was to be occupied by the coroner.

XVI

EXIT KHAMA-HERU

HAVING TAKEN HIS SEAT—AND WISHED THAT IT HAD BEEN A little farther from the coroner's—Thorndyke glanced round the large court-room, noting the unusual number of spectators and estimating from it the intense local interest in the inquiry. And as his eye roamed round, it presently alighted on Mr. Pottermack, who had secured a seat in a favourable position near the front and was endeavouring, quite unsuccessfully, to appear unaware of Thorndyke's arrival. So unsuccessful, indeed, were his efforts that inevitably their eyes met, and then there was nothing for it but to acknowledge as graciously as he could the lawyer's friendly nod of recognition.

Pottermack's state of mind was one of agonized expectation. He struggled manfully enough to summon up some sort of confidence. He told himself that this fellow was only a lawyer, and that lawyers know nothing about bodies. Now, if he had been a doctor it might have been a different matter. But there was that accursed shoe. He had certainly looked at that as if he saw something unusual about it; and there was no reason why a lawyer shouldn't know something about shoes. Yet what could he have seen in it? There was nothing to see. It was a genuine shoe, and the soles and heels were unquestionably correct in every detail. He, Pottermack, could hardly have distinguished them from the originals himself.

So his feelings oscillated miserably between unreasonable hope and an all too reasonable alarm. He would have got up and gone out but that even his terrors urged him to stay at all costs and hear what this lawyer should say when his turn came to give evidence. And thus, though he longed to escape, he remained glued to his chair, waiting, waiting for the mine to blow up; and whenever his roving glance fell, as it constantly did from minute to minute, on the sphinx-like countenance of that inopportune lawyer, a cold chill ran down his spine.

Thorndyke, catching from time to time that wandering, apprehensive glance, was fully alive to Mr. Pottermack's condition and felt a humane regret that it was impossible to reassure him and put an end to his sufferings. He realized how sinister a significance his unexpected arrival would seem to bear to the eyes of the self-conscious gamester, sitting there trembling for the success of his last venture. And the position was made even worse when the coroner, re-entering with the jury, stopped to confer with him before taking his seat.

"You had a good look at the body, doctor?" he asked, stooping and speaking almost in a whisper. "I wonder if it would be fair for me to ask you a question?"

"Let us hear the question," Thorndyke replied cautiously.

"Well, it is this: the medical witness that I am calling is the police surgeon's locum tenens. I don't know anything about him, but I suspect that he hasn't had much experience. He tells me that he can find nothing definite to indicate the cause of death, but that there are no signs of violence. What do you say to that?"

"It is exactly what I should have said myself if I had been in his place," Thorndyke replied. "I saw nothing that gave any hint as to the cause of death. You will have to settle that question on evidence other than medical."

"Thank you, thank you," said the coroner. "You have set my mind completely at rest. Now I will get on with the inquiry. It needn't take very long."

He retired to his chair at the head of the long table, on one side of which sat the jury and on the other one or two reporters, and having seen that his writing materials were in order, prepared to begin. And Thorndyke, once more meeting Mr. Pottermack's eye, found it fixed on him with an expression of expectant horror.

"The inquiry, gentlemen," the coroner began, "which we are about to conduct concerns the most regrettable death of a fellow-townsman of yours, Mr. James Lewson, who, as you probably know, disappeared rather mysteriously on the night of the 23rd of last July. Quite by chance, his dead body was discovered last Monday afternoon, and it will be our duty to inquire and determine how, when, and where he met with his death. I need not trouble you with a long preliminary statement, as the testimony of the witnesses will supply you with the facts and you will be entitled to put any questions that you may wish to amplify them. We had better begin with the discovery of the body and take events in their chronological order. Joseph Crick."

In response to this summons a massively built labourer rose and advanced sheepishly to the table. Having been sworn, he deposed that his name was Joseph Crick and that he was a labourer in the employ of Mr. Barber, a local builder.

"Well, Crick," said the coroner, "now tell us how you came to discover this body."

The witness cast an embarrassed glance at the eager jurymen, and, having wiped his mouth with the back of his hand, began: "'Twere last Monday afternoon—"

"That was the thirteenth of April," the coroner interposed.

"Maybe 'twere," the witness agreed cautiously, "I dunno. But 'twere last Monday afternoon. Me and Jim Wurdle had been workin' in the pit a-fillin' the carts with gravel. We'd filled the last cart and seen her off, and then, as it were gettin' on for knockin'-off time, we lights our pipes and goes for a stroll round the pit to have a look at the old shelter-place where they used to keep the carts in the winter. We'd got round to the gate and Jim Wurdle was a-lookin' in when I happened to notice a tree that had fell down from the top of the face. And then I see something layin' by the tree what had got a cap at one end and a pair of shoes at the other. Give me a regler start, it did. So I says to Jim Wurdle, I says, Jim, I says, that's a funny-lookin' thing over yonder long-side the tree, I says. Looks like some one a-layin' down there, I says. So Jim Wurdle he looks at it and he says, 'right you are, mate,' he says, 'so it do,' he says. So we walked over to have a look at it and then we see as 'twere a dead man, or leastways a man's skillinton. Give us a rare turn, it did, to see it a-layin' there in its shabby old clothes with the beedles a-crawlin' about on it."

"And what did you do then?" asked the coroner.

"We sung out to the other chaps t'other side of the pit and told them about it, and then we set off for the town as hard as we could go until we come to the police station, where we see Sergeant Tatnell and told him about it; and he sent us back to the pit to wait for him and show him where it were."

When the coroner had written down Crick's statement he glanced at the jury and enquired: "Do you wish to ask the witness any questions, gentlemen?" And as nobody expressed any such wish, he dismissed Crick and called James Wurdle, who, in effect, repeated the evidence of the previous witness and was in his turn dismissed.

The next witness was Inspector Barnaby of the local police force, a shrewd-looking man of about fifty, who gave his evidence in the concise, exact manner proper to a police officer.

"On Monday last, the thirteenth of April, at five twenty-one p.m., it was reported to me by Sergeant Tatnell that the dead body of a man had been discovered in the gravel-pit in Potter's Wood. I obtained an empty shell from the mortuary, and, having put it on a wheeled stretcher, proceeded with Sergeant Tatnell to the gravel-pit, where the previous witnesses showed us the place where the body was lying. We found the body lying at the foot of the gravel-face close to a tree that had fallen from the top. I examined it carefully before moving it. It was lying in a sprawling posture, not like that of a sleeping man but like that of a man who had fallen heavily. There were a few stones and some gravel on the body, but most of the gravel which had come down with the tree was underneath. The body was in an advanced stage of decay; so much so that it began to fall to pieces when we lifted it to put it into the shell. The head actually dropped off, and we had great trouble in preventing the legs from separating."

An audible shudder ran round the court at this description and the coroner murmured, "Horrible! horrible!" But the inspector proceeded in matter-of-fact tones:

"We conveyed the remains to the mortuary, where I removed the clothing from the body and examined it with a view to ascertaining the identity of deceased. The underclothing was marked clearly 'J. Lewson,' and in the breast pocket of the coat I found a letter-case with the initials 'J. L.' stamped on the cover. Inside it were a number of visiting-cards bearing the name 'Mr. James Lewson' and the address 'Perkins's Bank, Borley, Bucks,' and some letters addressed to James Lewson, Esquire, at that address. In one of the trousers pockets I found a key, which looked like a safe key, and as there seemed to be no doubt that the body was that of Mr. Lewson, the late manager of the Borley branch of Perkins's Bank, I cleaned the rust off the key and showed it to Mr. Hunt, the present manager, who tried it in the lock of the safe and found that it entered and seemed to fit perfectly."

"Did it shoot the bolt of the lock?" one of the jurors asked.

"No," replied the inspector, "because, after Mr. Lewson went away and took the key with him, the manager had the levers of the lock altered and a pair of new keys made. But the old duplicate key was there, and when we compared it with the key from the body, it was obvious that the two keys were identical in pattern."

"Did you take any other measures to identify the body?" the coroner asked.

"Yes, sir. I checked the clothing carefully, garment by garment, by the description that we issued when Mr. Lewson disappeared, and it corresponded to the description in every respect. Then I got the caretaker from the bank to look it over, and he identified the clothes and shoes as those worn by Mr. Lewson on the night when he disappeared."

"Excellent," said the coroner. "Most thorough and most conclusive. I think, gentlemen, that we can fairly take it as an established fact that the body is that of Mr. James Lewson. And now, Inspector, to return to the clothing; you have mentioned two articles found by you in deceased's pockets. What else did you find?"

"Nothing, sir. With the exception of those two articles—which I handed to you—the pockets were all completely empty."

"And the letter-case?"

"That contained nothing but letters, bills, cards, and a few stamps; nothing but what was in it when I gave it to you."

Here the coroner opened his attaché-case, and, taking from it the letter-wallet, the letters, cards, bills, and other contents, placed them, together with the key, on a wooden office tray which he pushed along the table for the jurymen's inspection. While they were curiously poring over the tray, he continued his examination.

"Then you found nothing of value on the person of deceased?"

"With the exception of the stamps, nothing whatsoever. The pockets were absolutely empty."

"Do you happen to know if deceased, at the time of his disappearance, had any valuable property about him?"

"Yes, sir. It is nearly certain that when he went away at about eight o'clock on the night of Wednesday, the twenty-third of last July, he had on his person one hundred pounds in five-pound Bank of England notes."

"When you say that it is nearly certain, what does that certainty amount to?"

"It is based on the fact that after he had gone, banknotes to that amount were found to be missing from the bank."

"And is it known what became of those notes?"

"Yes, sir. Their numbers were known and they have now all been recovered. As soon as they appeared in circulation they were traced; and in nearly every case traced to some person who was known to the police."

"Is it certain that these notes were taken by deceased and not by some other person?"

"Yes, practically certain. Deceased was in sole charge, and he had one key on his person and the other locked in the safe, where it was found when the lock was picked. But, if you will allow me, sir, I should like to say, in justice to deceased, that he had, apparently, no intention of stealing these notes, as was thought at first. Certain facts came to light later which seemed to show that he had merely borrowed this money to meet a sudden urgent call and that he meant to replace it."

"I am sure every one will be very glad to hear that," said the coroner. "We need not go into the circumstances that you mention, as they do not seem relevant to this inquiry. But these notes raise an important point. If they were on his person when he went away and they were not on his body when it was found, and if, moreover, they are known to have been in circulation since his death, the question of robbery arises, and with it the further question of possible murder. Can you give us any help in considering those questions?"

"I have formed certain opinions, sir, but, of course, it is a matter of guesswork."

"Never mind, Inspector. A coroner's court is not bound by the strict rules of evidence; and, besides, yours is an expert opinion. Let us hear what view you take of the matter."

"Well, sir, my opinion is that deceased met his death by accident the night that he went away. I think that he fell into the pit in the dark, dislodging a lot of gravel and pulling the small tree down with him. Both the body and the tree were on top of the heap of gravel, but yet there was a good deal of gravel and some stones on the body."

The coroner nodded and the witness proceeded:

"Then I think that, about a month later, some tramp found the body and went through the pockets, and when he discovered the notes, he cleared off and said nothing about having seen the body."

"Have you any specific reasons for this very definite theory?"

"Yes, sir. First, there is clear evidence that the pit has been frequented by one or more tramps. Quite close to where the body was discovered is an old cart-shelter, dug out of the gravel, and that shelter has been used from time to time by some tramp or tramps as a residence. I found in it a quantity of wood ashes and charcoal and large sooty deposits on the wall and roof, showing that many fires had been lit there. I also found an old billy, or boiling-can, a lot of rags and tramps' raffle and a quantity of small bones—mostly rabbits' and fowls' bones. So tramps have certainly been there.

"Then the state of deceased's pockets suggests a tramp's robbery. It was not only the valuables that were taken. He had made a clean sweep of everything. Not a thing was left. Not even a pipe or a packet of cigarettes or even a match-box."

"And as to the time that you mentioned?"

"I am judging by the notes. A sharp look-out was kept for them from the first. A very sharp look-out. But for fully a month after the disappearance not one of them came to light. And then, suddenly, they began to come in one after the other and even in batches, as if the whole lot had been thrown into circulation at once. But if it had been a case of robbery with violence, the robber would have got rid of the notes immediately, before the hue and cry started."

"So you consider that the possibility of robbery with murder may be ruled out?"

"On the facts known to me, sir, I do—subject, of course, to the medical evidence."

"Exactly," said the coroner. "But in any case you have given us most valuable assistance. Is there any point, gentlemen, that is not quite clear, or any question that you wish to put to the inspector? No questions? Very well. Thank you, Inspector."

The next witness called was the police surgeon's deputy, a young-ish Irishman of somewhat convivial aspect. Having been sworn, he deposed that his name was Desmond M'Alarney, that he was a Doctor of Medicine and at present acting as locum tenens for the police surgeon, who was absent on leave.

"Well, doctor," said the coroner, "I believe that you have made a careful examination of the body of deceased. Is that so?"

"I have made a most careful examination, sir," was the reply, "though as to calling it a body, I would rather describe it as a skeleton."

"Very well!" the coroner agreed good-humouredly, "call it what you like. Perhaps we may refer to it as the remains."

"Ye may," replied the witness, "and mighty small remains, by the same token. But such as they are, I have examined them with the greatest care."

"And did your examination enable you to form any opinion as to the cause of death?"

"It did not."

"Did you find any injuries or signs of violence?"

"I did not."

"Were any of the bones fractured or injured in any way?"

"They were not."

"Can you give us no suggestion as to the probable cause of death?"

"I would suggest, sir, that a twenty-foot drop into a gravel-pit is a mighty probable cause of death."

"No doubt," said the coroner. "But that is hardly a matter of medical evidence."

"'Tis none the worse for that," the witness replied cheerfully.

"Can you say, definitely, that deceased did not meet his death by any kind of homicidal violence?"

"I can not. When a body is rejuiced to a skeleton, all traces of violence are lost so long as there has been no breaking of bones. He might have been strangled or smothered or stabbed or had his throat cut without leaving any marks on the skeleton. I can only say that I found no indications of any kind of homicidal violence or any violence whatsoever."

"The inspector has suggested that deceased met his death by accident—that is by the effects of the fall, and that appears to be your opinion too. Now, if that were the case, what would probably be the immediate cause of death?"

"There are several possible causes, but the most probable would be shock, contusion of the brain, or dislocation of the neck."

"Would any of those conditions leave recognizable traces?"

"Contusion of the brain and dislocation of the neck could be recognized in the fresh body but not in a skeleton like this. Of course, if the dislocation were accompanied—as it very often is—by fracture of the little neck-bone known as the odontoid process of the axis, that could be seen in the skeleton. But there is no such fracture in the skeleton of deceased. I looked for it particularly."

"Then we understand that you found nothing definite to indicate the cause of death?"

"That is so, sir."

"Do you consider that the appearance of the body, in a medical sense, is consistent with a belief that deceased was killed by the effects of the fall?"

"I do, sir."

"Then," said the coroner, "that seems to be about all that we can say as to the cause of death. Do the jury wish to put any questions to the medical witness? If not, we need not detain the doctor any longer."

As Dr. M'Alarney picked up an uncommonly smart hat and retired, the coroner glanced quickly over his notes and then proceeded to address the jury.

"I need not occupy your time, gentlemen, with a long summing-up. You have heard the evidence and probably have already arrived at your conclusions. There are certain mysterious circumstances in the case, as, for instance, how deceased came to be wandering about in the wood at night. But these questions do not concern us. We have to consider only how deceased met his death, and as the doctor justly remarked, the fact that the body was found at the bottom of a gravel-pit, having evidently fallen some eighteen or twenty feet, offers a pretty obvious explanation. The only suspicious circumstance was that deceased had clearly been robbed either before or after death. But you have heard the opinion of a very able and experienced police inspector, and the excellent reasons that he gave for that opinion. So I need say no more, but will now leave you to consider your verdict."

During the short interval occupied by the discussions of the jurymen among themselves, two members of the audience were engaged busily in reviewing the evidence in its relation to the almost inevitable verdict. To Thorndyke the proceedings offered an interesting study in the perverting effect upon the judgment of an unconscious bias, engendered by the suggestive power of a known set of circumstances. All the evidence that had been given was true. All the inferences from that evidence were sound and proper inferences, so far as they went. Yet the final conclusion which was going to be arrived at would be wildly erroneous, for the simple reason that all the parties to the inquiry had come to it already convinced as to the principal fact—the identity of the deceased person—which had accordingly been left unverified.

As to Pottermack, his state of mind at the close of the inquiry was one of astonished relief. All through the proceedings he had sat in tremulous expectancy, with a furtive eye on the strange lawyer, wondering when that lawyer's turn would come to give his evidence and what he would have to say. That the stranger had detected some part, at least, of the fraud he had at first little doubt, and he expected no less than to hear the identity of the body challenged. But, as the time ran on and witness after witness came forward guilelessly and disgorged the bait for the nourishment of the jury, his fears gradually subsided and his confidence began to revive. And now that the inquiry was really over and they had all gobbled the bait and got it comfortably into their gizzards; now that it was evident that this lawyer had nothing to say, after all, in spite of his preposterous porings over those admirable shoes, Mr. Pottermack was disposed just a little to despise himself for having been so easily frightened. The "superiority complex" began to reassert itself. Here he sat, looking upon a thoroughly bamboozled assembly, including a most experienced police inspector, a coroner, a lawyer, and a doctor. He alone of all that assembly, indeed of the whole world, knew all about it.

But perhaps his alarm had been excusable. We get into the habit of attaching too much importance to these lawyers and doctors. We credit them with knowing a great deal more than they do. But, at any rate, in this case it was all to the good. And as Mr. Pottermack summed up in this satisfactory fashion, the foreman of the jury announced that the verdict had been agreed on.

"And what is your finding, gentlemen, on the evidence that you have heard?" the coroner asked.

"We find that the deceased, James Lewson, met his death on the night of the twenty-third of last July by falling into a gravel-pit in Potter's Wood."

"Yes," said the coroner. "That amounts to a verdict of Death by Misadventure. And a very proper verdict, too, in my opinion. I must thank you, gentlemen, for your attendance and for the careful consideration which you have given to this inquiry, and I may take this opportunity of telling you what I am sure you will be glad to hear, that the directors of Perkins's Bank have generously undertaken to have the funeral conducted at their expense."

As the hall slowly emptied, Thorndyke lingered by the table to exchange a few rather colourless comments on the case with the coroner. At length, after a cordial handshake, he took his departure, and, joining the last stragglers, made his way slowly out of the main doorway, glancing among the dispersing crowd as he emerged; and presently his roving glance alighted on Mr. Pottermack at the outskirts of the throng, loitering irresolutely as if undecided which way to go.

The truth is that the elation at the triumphant success of his plan had begotten in that gentleman a spirit of mischief. Under the influence of the "superiority complex" he was possessed with a desire to exchange a few remarks with the strange lawyer; perhaps to "draw" him on the subject of the inquest; possibly even to "pull his leg"—not hard, of course, which would be a liberty, but just a gentle and discreet tweak. Accordingly he hovered about opposite the hall, waiting to see which way the lawyer should go; and as

Thorndyke unostentatiously steered in his direction, the meeting came about quite naturally, just as the lawyer was turning—rather to Mr. Pottermack's surprise—away from the direction of the station.

"I don't suppose you remember me," he began. But Thorndyke interrupted promptly: "Of course I remember you, Mr. Pottermack, and am very pleased to meet you again."

Pottermack, considerably taken aback by the mention of his name, shook the proffered hand and cogitated rapidly. How the deuce did the fellow know that his name was Pottermack? He hadn't told him.

"Thank you," he said. "I am very pleased, too, and rather surprised. But perhaps you are professionally interested in this inquiry."

"Not officially," replied Thorndyke. "I saw a notice in the paper of what looked like an interesting case, and, being in the neighbourhood, I dropped in to see and hear what was going on."

"And did you find it an interesting case?" Pottermack asked.

"Very. Didn't you?"

"Well," replied Pottermack, "I didn't bring an expert eye to it as you did, so I may have missed some of the points. But there did seem to be some rather queer features in it. I wonder which of them in particular you found so interesting?"

This last question he threw out by way of a tentative preliminary to the process of "drawing" the lawyer, and he waited expectantly for the reply.

Thorndyke reflected a few moments before answering it. At length he replied:

"There was such a wealth of curious matter that I find it difficult to single out any one point in particular. The case interested me as a whole, and especially by reason of the singular parallelism that it presented to another most remarkable case which was related to me in great detail by a legal friend of mine, in whose practice it occurred."

"Indeed," said Mr. Pottermack, still intent on tractive operations; "and what were the special features in that case?"

"There were many very curious features in that case," Thorndyke replied in a reminiscent tone. "Perhaps the most remarkable was an ingenious fraud perpetrated by one of the parties, who dressed an Egyptian mummy in a recognizable suit of clothes and deposited it in a gravel-pit."

"Good gracious!" gasped Pottermack, and the "superiority complex" died a sudden death.

"Yes," Thorndyke continued with the same reminiscent air, observing that his companion was for the moment speechless, "it was a most singular case. My legal friend used to refer to it, in a whimsical fashion, as the case of the dead man who was alive and the live man who was dead."

"B-but," Pottermack stammered, with chattering teeth, "that sounds like a c-contradiction."

"It does," Thorndyke agreed, "and of course it is. What he actually meant was that it was a case of a living man who was believed to be dead, and a dead man who was believed to be alive—until the mummy came to light."

Pottermack made no rejoinder. He was still dumb with amazement and consternation. He had a confused feeling of unreality as if he were walking in a dream. With a queer sort of incredulous curiosity he looked up at the calm, inscrutable face of the tall stranger who walked by his side and asked himself who and what this man could be. Was he, in truth, a lawyer—or was he the Devil? Stranger as he certainly was, he had some intimate knowledge of his—Pottermack's—most secret actions; knowledge which could surely be possessed by no mere mortal. It seemed beyond belief.

With a violent effort he pulled himself together and made an attempt to continue the conversation. For it was borne in on him that he must, at all costs, find out what those cryptic phrases meant and how much this person—lawyer or devil—really knew. After all, he did not seem to be a malignant or hostile devil.

"That must have been a most extraordinary case," he observed at length. "I am—er—quite intrigued by what you have told me. Would it be possible or admissible for you to give me a few details?"

"I don't know why not," said Thorndyke, "excepting that it is rather a long story, and I need not say highly confidential. But if you know of some place where we could discuss it in strict privacy, I should be pleased to tell you the story as it was told to me. I am sure it would interest you. But I make one stipulation."

"What is that?" Pottermack asked.

"It is that you, too, shall search your memory, and if you can recall any analogous circumstances as having arisen within your experience or knowledge, you shall produce them so that we can make comparisons."

Pottermack reflected for a few moments, but only a few. For his native common sense told him that neither secrecy nor reservation was going to serve him.

"Very well," he said, "I agree; though until I have heard your story I cannot judge how far I shall be able to match it from my limited experience. But if you will come and take tea with me in my garden, where we shall be quite alone, I will do my best to set my memory to work when I have heard what you have to tell."

"Excellent," said Thorndyke. "I accept your invitation with great pleasure. And I observe that some common impulse seems to have directed us towards your house, and even towards the very gate at which I had the good fortune to make your acquaintance."

In effect, as they had been talking, they had struck into the footpath and now approached the gate of the walled garden.

XVII

M R. POTTERMACK INSERTED THE SMALL, THIN KEY INTO THE Yale lock of the gate and turned it while Thorndyke watched him with a faint smile.

"Admirable things, these Yale locks," the latter remarked as he followed his host in through the narrow gateway and cast a comprehensive glance round the walled garden, "so long as you don't lose the key. It is a hopeless job trying to pick one."

"Did you ever try?" asked Pottermack.

"Yes, and had to give it up. But I see you appreciate their virtues. That looks like one on the farther gate."

"It is," Pottermack admitted. "I keep this part of the garden for my own sole use and I like to be secure from interruption."

"I sympathize with you," said Thorndyke. "Security from interruption is always pleasant, and there are occasions when it is indispensable."

Pottermack looked at him quickly but did not pursue the topic.

"If you will excuse me for a minute," he said, "I will run and tell my housekeeper to get us some tea. You would rather have it out here than in the house, wouldn't you?"

"Much rather," replied Thorndyke. "We wish to be private, and here we are with two good Yale locks to keep eavesdroppers at bay."

While his host was absent he paced slowly up and down the lawn, observing everything with keen interest but making no particular inspections. Above the yew hedge he could see the skylighted roof of what appeared to be a studio or workshop, and in the opposite corner of the garden a roomy, comfortable summer-house. From these objects he turned his attention to the sun-dial, looking it over critically and strolling round it to read the motto. He was thus engaged when his host returned with the news that tea was being prepared and would follow almost immediately.

"I was admiring your sun-dial, Mr. Pottermack," said Thorndyke. "It is a great adornment to the garden and a singularly happy and appropriate one; for the flowers, like the dial, number only the sunny hours. And it will look still better when time has softened the contrast between the old pillar and the new base."

"Yes," Pottermack agreed, a trifle uneasily, "the base will be all the better for a little weathering. How do you like the motto?"

"Very much," replied Thorndyke. "A pleasant, optimistic motto, and new to me. I don't think I have ever met with it before. But it is a proper sun-dial motto: 'Hope in the morning, Peace at eventide.' Most of us have known the first and all of us look forward to the last. Should I be wrong if I were to assume that there is a well underneath?"

"N-no," stammered Pottermack, "you would not. It is an old well that had been disused and covered up. I discovered it by accident when I was levelling the ground for the sun-dial and very nearly fell into it. So I decided to put the sun-dial over it to prevent any accidents in the future. And mighty glad I was to see it safely covered up."

"You must have been," said Thorndyke. "While it was uncovered it must have been a constant anxiety to you."

"It was," Pottermack agreed, with a nervous glance at his guest.

"That would be about the latter part of last July," Thorndyke suggested with the air of one recalling a half-forgotten event; and Mr. Pottermack breathlessly admitted that it probably was.

Here they were interrupted by the arrival of Mrs. Gadby, for whom the gate had been left open, followed by a young maid, both laden with the materials for tea on a scale suggestive of a Sunday School treat. The housekeeper glanced curiously at the tall, imposing stranger, wondering inwardly why he could not come to the dining-room like a Christian. In due course the load of provisions was transferred to the somewhat inadequate table in the summer-house and the two servants then retired, Mrs. Gadby ostentatiously shutting the gate behind her. As its lock clicked, Mr. Pottermack ushered his guest into the summer-house, offering him the chair once occupied by James Lewson and since studiously avoided by its owner.

When the hospitable preliminaries had been disposed of and the tea poured out, Thorndyke opened the actual proceedings with only the briefest preamble.

"I expect, Mr. Pottermack, you are impatient to hear about that case which seemed to pique your curiosity so much, and as the shadow is creeping round your dial, we mustn't waste time, especially as there is a good deal to tell. I will begin with an outline sketch of the case, in the form of a plain narrative, which will enable you to judge whether anything at all like it has ever come to your knowledge.

"The story as told to me by my legal friend dealt with the histories of two men, whom we will call respectively Mr. Black and Mr. White. At the beginning of the story they appear to have been rather intimate friends, and both were employed at a bank, which we will call Alsop's Bank. After they had been there some time—I don't know exactly how long—a series of forgeries occurred, evidently committed by some member of the staff of the bank. I need not go into details. For our purpose the important fact is that suspicion fell upon Mr. White. The evidence against him was striking, and, if genuine, convincing and conclusive. But to my friend it appeared decidedly unsatisfactory. He was strongly disposed to suspect that

the crime was actually committed by Mr. Black and that he fabricated
the evidence against Mr. White. But, however that may have been,
the Court accepted the evidence. The jury found Mr. White guilty
and the judge sentenced him to five years' penal servitude.

"It was a harsh sentence, but that does not concern us, as Mr.
White did not serve the full term. After about a year of it, he escaped
and made his way to the shore of an estuary, and there his clothes
were found and a set of footprints across the sand leading into the
water. Some six weeks later a nude body was washed up on the shore
and was identified as his body. An inquest was held and it was decided
that he had been accidentally drowned. Accordingly he was written
off the prison books and the records at Scotland Yard as a dead man.

"But he was not dead. The body which was found was probably
that of some bather whose clothes Mr. White had appropriated in
exchange for his own prison clothes. Thus he was able to get away
without hindrance and take up a new life elsewhere, no doubt
under an assumed name. Probably he went abroad, but this is only
surmise. From the moment of his escape from prison he vanishes
from our ken, and for the space of about fifteen years remains invisible, his existence apparently unknown to any of his former friends
or acquaintances.

"This closes the first part of the history; the part which deals with
the person whom my friend whimsically described as 'the dead man
who was alive.' And now, perhaps, Mr. Pottermack, you can tell me
whether you have ever heard of a case in any way analogous to this one."

Mr. Pottermack reflected for a few moments. Throughout
Thorndyke's recital he had sat with the feeling of one in a dream.
The sense of unreality had again taken possession of him. He had
listened with a queer sort of incredulous curiosity to the quiet voice
of this inscrutable stranger, relating to him with the calm assurance
of some wizard or clairvoyant the innermost secrets of his own life;

describing actions and events which he, Pottermack, felt certain could not possibly be known to any human creature but himself. It was all so unbelievable that any sense of danger, of imminent disaster, was merged in an absorbing wonder. But one thing was quite clear to him. Any attempt to deceive or mislead this mysterious stranger would be utterly futile. Accordingly he replied:

"By a most strange coincidence it happens that a case came to my knowledge which was point by point almost identical with yours. But there was one difference. In my case, the guilt of the person who corresponds to your Mr. Black was not problematical at all. He admitted it. He even boasted of it and of the clever way in which he had set up Mr. White as the dummy to take all the thumps."

"Indeed!" exclaimed Thorndyke. "That is extremely interesting. We must bear that point in mind when we come to examine the details. Now I go on to the second part of the narrative; the part that deals with the 'live man who was dead.'

"After the lapse of some fifteen years, Mr. White came to the surface, so to speak. He made his appearance in a small country town, and from his apparently comfortable circumstances he seemed to have prospered in the interval. But here he encountered a streak of bad luck. By some malignant chance, it happened that Mr. Black was installed as manager of the branch bank in that very town, and naturally enough they met. Even then all might have been well but for an unaccountable piece of carelessness on Mr. White's part. He had, by growing a beard and taking to the use of spectacles, made a considerable change in his appearance. But he had neglected one point. He had, it appears, on his right ear a small birth-mark. It was not at all conspicuous, but when once observed it was absolutely distinctive."

"But," exclaimed Pottermack, "I don't understand you. You say he neglected this mark. But what could he possibly have done to conceal it?"

"He could have had it obliterated," replied Thorndyke. "The operation is quite simple in the case of a small mark. The more widespread 'port-wine mark' is less easy to treat; but a small spot, such as I understand that this was, can be dealt with quite easily and effectively. Some skin surgeons specialize in the operation. One of them I happen to know personally: Mr. Julian Parsons, the dermatologist to St. Margaret's Hospital."

"Ha," said Mr. Pottermack.

"But," continued Thorndyke, "to return to our story. Mr. White had left his birth-mark untreated, and that was probably his undoing. Mr. Black would doubtless have been struck by the resemblance, but the birth-mark definitely established the identity. At any rate, Mr. Black recognized him and forthwith began to levy blackmail. Of course, Mr. White was an ideal subject for a blackmailer's operations. He was absolutely defenceless, for he could not invoke the aid of the law by reason of his unexpired sentence. He had to pay, or go back to prison—or take some private measures.

"At first, it appears that he accepted the position and paid. Probably he submitted to be bled repeatedly, for there is reason to believe that quite considerable sums of money passed. But eventually Mr. White must have realized what most blackmailers' victims have to realize: that there is no end to this sort of thing. The blackmailer is always ready to begin over again. At any rate, Mr. White adopted the only practicable alternative to paying out indefinitely. He got Mr. Black alone in a secluded garden in which there was a disused well. Probably Mr. Black came there voluntarily to make fresh demands. But however that may have been, Mr. Black went, dead or alive, down into the well."

"In the case which came to my knowledge," said Pottermack, "it was to some extent accidental. He had become rather violent, and in the course of what amounted to a fight he fell across the opening of the well, striking his head heavily on the brick coping, and dropped down in a state of insensibility."

"Ah," said Thorndyke, "that may be considered, as you say, to some extent accidental. But probably to a rather small extent. I think we may take it that he would have gone down that well in any case. What do you say?"

"I think I am inclined to agree with you," replied Pottermack.

"At all events," said Thorndyke, "down the well he went. And there seemed to be an end of the blackmailer. But it was not quite the end, and the sequel introduces a most interesting feature into the case.

"It appears that the path by which Mr. Black approached Mr. White's premises was an earth path, and owing to the peculiar qualities of the soil in that locality, it took the most extraordinarily clear impressions of the feet that trod on it. Now, it happened that Mr. Black was wearing shoes with rubber soles and heels of a strikingly distinctive pattern, which left on the earth path impressions of the most glaringly conspicuous and distinctive character. The result was a set of footprints, obviously and certainly those of Mr. Black, leading directly to Mr. White's gate and stopping there. This was a most dangerous state of affairs, for as soon as the hue and cry was raised—which it would be immediately in the case of a bank manager—the missing Black would be traced by his footprints to Mr. White's gate. And then the murder would be out.

"Now what was Mr. White to do? He could not obliterate those footprints in any practicable manner. So he did the next best—or even better—thing. He continued them past his gate, out into the country and across a heath, on the farther side of which he allowed them discreetly to fade away into the heather.

"It was an admirable plan, and it succeeded perfectly. When the hue and cry was raised, the police followed those tracks like bloodhounds until they lost them on the heath. A photographer with a special camera patiently took samples of the footprints along the whole route, from the place where they started to where they were lost on the heath. But no one suspected Mr. White. He did not come into the picture at all. It seemed that he had now nothing to do but to lie low and let the affair pass into oblivion.

"But he did nothing of the kind. Instead, he embarked on a most unaccountable proceeding. Months after the disappearance of Mr. Black, when the affair had become nearly forgotten, he proceeded deliberately to revive it. He obtained an Egyptian mummy, and having dressed it in Mr. Black's clothes, or in clothes that had been specially prepared to counterfeit those of Mr. Black, he deposited it in a gravel-pit. His reasons for doing this are unknown to my legal friend and are difficult to imagine. But whatever the object may have been, it was attained, for in due course the mummy was discovered and identified as the body of Mr. Black, an inquest was held and the mystery of the disappearance finally disposed of.

"That is a bare outline of the case, Mr. Pottermack; just sufficient to enable us to discuss it and compare it with the one that you have in mind."

"It is a very remarkable case," said Pottermack, "and the most remarkable feature in it is its close resemblance to the one of which I came to hear. In fact, they are so much alike that—"

"Exactly," interrupted Thorndyke. "The same thought had occurred to us both—that your case and the one related by my legal friend are in reality one and the same."

"Yes," agreed Pottermack, "I think they must be. But what is puzzling me is how your legal friend came by the knowledge of these facts, which would seem to have been known to no one but the principal actor."

"That is what we are going to consider," said Thorndyke. "But before we begin our analysis, there is one point that I should like to clear up. You said that Mr. Black had explicitly admitted his guilt in regard to those forgeries. To whom did he make that admission?"

"To his wife," replied Pottermack.

"His wife!" exclaimed Thorndyke. "But it was assumed that he was a bachelor."

"The facts," said Pottermack, "are rather singular. I had better fill in this piece of detail, which apparently escaped your legal friend's investigations.

"Mr. White, in the days before his troubles befell, was engaged to be married to a very charming girl to whom he was completely devoted and who was equally devoted to him. After Mr. White's reported death, Mr. Black sought her friendship and later tried to induce her to marry him. He urged that he had been Mr. White's most intimate friend and that their marriage was what the deceased would have wished. Eventually she yielded to his persuasion and married him, rather reluctantly, since her feeling towards him was merely that of a friend. What his feeling was towards her it is difficult to say. She had some independent means, and it is probable that her property was the principal attraction. That is what the subsequent history suggests.

"The marriage was a failure from the first. Black sponged on his wife, gambled with her money and was constantly in debt and difficulties. Also he drank to an unpleasant extent. But she put up with all this until one day he let out that he had committed the forgeries, and even boasted of his smartness in putting the suspicion on White. Then she left him, and, assuming another name, went away to live by herself, passing herself off as a widow."

"And as to her husband? How came he to allow this?"

"First, she frightened him by threatening to denounce him; but she also made him an allowance on condition that he should not molest her. He seems to have been rather scared by her threats and he wanted the money, so he took the allowance and as much more as he could squeeze out of her, and agreed to her terms.

"Later Mr. White returned to England from America. As he had now quite shed his old identity and was a man of good reputation and comfortably off, he sought her out in the hopes of possibly renewing their old relations. That, in fact, was what brought him to England. Eventually he discovered her, apparently a widow, and had no difficulty in making her acquaintance."

"Did she recognize him?"

"I think we must assume that she did. But nothing was said. They maintained the fiction that they were new acquaintances. So they became friends. Finally he asked her to marry him, and it was then that he learned, to his amazement, that she had married Mr. Black."

Thorndyke's face had suddenly become grave. He cast a searching glance at Mr. Pottermack and demanded: "When was this proposal of marriage made? I mean, was it before or after the incident of the well?"

"Oh, after, of course. No marriage could have been thought of by Mr. White while he was under the thumb of the blackmailer, with the choice of ruin or the prison before him. It was only when the affair was over and everything seemed to be settling down quietly that the marriage seemed to have become possible."

Thorndyke's face cleared and a grim smile spread over it. "I see," he chuckled. "A quaint situation for Mr. White. Now, of course, one understands the mummy. His function was to produce a death certificate. Very ingenious. And now I gather that you would like an exposition of the evidence in this case?"

"Yes," replied Pottermack. "Your legal friend seems to have had knowledge of certain actions of Mr. White's which I should have supposed could not possibly have been known to any person in the world but Mr. White himself. I should like to hear how he came by that knowledge if you would be so kind as to enlighten me."

"Very well," said Thorndyke, "then we will proceed to consider the evidence in this case; and I must impress on you, Mr. Pottermack, the necessity of discriminating clearly between what my legal friend knew and what he inferred, and of observing the point at which inference becomes converted into knowledge by verification or new matter.

"To begin with what my friend knew, on the authority of a director of Mr. Black's bank. He knew that Mr. Black had disappeared under very mysterious circumstances. That he had received an urgent and threatening demand from a creditor for the payment of a certain sum of money. That before starting that night he had taken from the monies belonging to the bank a sum of money in notes exactly equal to the amount demanded from him. The reasonable inference was that he set out intending to call on that creditor and pay that money; instead of which, he appeared to have walked straight out of the town into the country, where all trace of him was lost.

"Then my friend learned from the director that, whereas the books of the bank showed Mr. Black's known income and ordinary expenditure, there was evidence of his having paid away large sums of money on gambling transactions, always in cash—mostly five-pound notes; that these sums greatly exceeded his known income, and that his account showed no trace of their having been received. Since he must have received that money before he could have paid it away, he must clearly have had some unknown source of income; and since he had paid it away in cash, and there was no trace of his having received any cheques to these amounts, the inference was that he had received it in cash. I need not remind you, Mr. Pottermack, that the receipt of large sums of money in notes or specie is a very significant and rather suspicious circumstance."

"Might not these sums represent his winnings?" Pottermack asked.

"They might, but they did not, for all the transactions that were traced resulted in losses. Apparently he was the type of infatuated gambler who always loses in the end. So much for Mr. Black. Next, my friend learned from the director the circumstances of the forgeries, and he formed the opinion—which was also that of the director—that Mr. White had been a victim of a miscarriage of justice and that the real culprit had been Mr. Black. He also learned the particulars of Mr. White's escape from prison and alleged death. But he differed from the director in that, being a lawyer with special experience, he did not accept that death as an established fact, but only as a probability, reserving in his mind the possibility of a mistaken identity of the body and that Mr. White might have escaped and be still alive.

"Thus, you see, Mr. Pottermack, that my friend started with a good deal of knowledge of this case and the parties to it. And now we come to some facts of another kind which carry us on to the stage of inference. The director who furnished my friend with the information that I have summarized also put into his hands a long series of photographs of the footprints of Mr. Black, taken by an employé of the bank on the second morning after the disappearance."

"For what purpose?" asked Mr. Pottermack.

"Principally, I suspect, to try a new camera of a special type, but ostensibly to help the investigators to discover what had become of the missing man. They were handed to my friend for his inspection and opinion as to their value for this purpose. Of course, at the first glance they appeared to be of no value at all, but as my friend happens to be deeply interested in footprints as material for evidence, he retained them for further examination in relation to a particular point which he wished to clear up. That point was whether a series of footprints is anything more than a mere multiple of a single footprint; whether it might be possible to extract from a series any kind of evidence that would not be furnished by an individual footprint.

"Evidently, those photographs offered an exceptional opportunity for settling this question. They were in the form of a long paper ribbon on which were nearly two hundred numbered photographs of footprints, and they were accompanied by a twenty-five inch ordnance map on which each footprint was indicated by a numbered dot. The row of dots started at the bank, and then, after a blank interval, entered and followed a footpath which passed along a wall in which was a gate, and which enclosed a large garden or plantation; beyond the wall the dots continued, still on the footpath, between some fields, through a wood and across a heath, on the farther side of which they stopped. A note at the end of the ribbon stated that here the missing man had turned off the path into the heather and that no further traces of him could be found."

"Well," remarked Pottermack, "the police could see all that for themselves. It doesn't seem as if the photographs gave any further information."

"It does not," Thorndyke agreed. "And yet a careful examination of those photographs led my friend to the conviction that the missing man had entered the gate in the wall and had never come out again."

"But," exclaimed Pottermack, "I understood you to say that the footprints continued past the wall, through the wood and out across the heath."

"So they did. But a careful scrutiny of the photographs convinced my friend that this was not a single series of footprints, made by one man, but two series, made by two different men. The first series started from the bank and ended at the gate. The second series started from the gate and ended on the heath."

"Then the footprints were not all alike?"

"That," replied Thorndyke, "depends on what we mean by 'alike.' If you had taken any one footprint from any part of the whole series and compared it with any other corresponding footprint—right or left—in any other part of the series, you would have said that they were undoubtedly prints of the same foot."

"Do I understand you to mean that every footprint in the whole series was exactly like every other footprint of the same side?"

"Yes. Every right footprint was exactly like every other right footprint, and the same with the left. That is, considered as individual footprints."

"Then I don't see how your friend could have made out that the whole series of footprints, all indistinguishably alike, consisted of two different series, made by two different men."

Thorndyke chuckled. "It is quite a subtle point," he said, "and yet perfectly simple. I am a little surprised that it had not occurred to Mr. White, who seems to have been an acute and ingenious man. You see, the difference was not between the individual footprints but between certain periodic characters in the two series."

"I don't think I quite follow you," said Pottermack.

"Well, let us follow my legal friend's procedure. I have told you that his object in examining these photographs was to ascertain whether footprints in series present any periodic or recurrent characters that might be of evidential importance. Now, a glance at these photographs showed him that these footprints must almost certainly present at least one such character. They were the prints of shoes with rubber soles of a highly distinctive pattern and circular rubber heels. Now, Mr. Pottermack, why does a man wear circular rubber heels?"

"Usually, I suppose, because if he wears ordinary leather heels he wears them down all on one side."

"And how do the circular heels help him?"

"In the case of circular heels," Pottermack replied promptly, "the wear does not occur all at one point, but is distributed round the whole circumf—"

He stopped abruptly with his mouth slightly open and looked at Thorndyke.

"Exactly," said the latter, "you see the point. A circular heel is secured to the shoe by a single, central screw. But it is not a complete fixture. As the wearer walks, the oblique impact as it meets the ground causes it to creep round; very slowly when the heel is new and tightly screwed on, more rapidly as it wears thinner and the central screw-hole wears larger. Of course, my friend knew this, but he now had an opportunity of making his knowledge more exact and settling certain doubtful points as to rapidity and direction of rotation. Accordingly he proceeded, with the ribbon of photographs and the ordnance map before him, to follow the track methodically, noting down the distances and the rate and direction of rotation of each heel.

"His industry was rewarded and justified within the first dozen observations, for it brought to light a fact of considerable importance, though it does not happen to be relevant to our case. He found that both heels revolved in the same direction—clock-wise—though, of course, since they were in what we may call 'looking-glass' relation, they ought to have revolved in opposite directions."

"Yes," said Pottermack, "it is curious, but I don't see what its importance is."

"Its importance in an evidential sense," replied Thorndyke, "is this: the anomaly of rotation was evidently not due to the shoes but to some peculiarity in the gait of the wearer. The same shoes on the feet of another person would almost certainly have behaved differently. Hence the character of the rotation might become a test point in a question of personal identity. However, that is by the way. What concerns us is that my friend established the fact that both heels were rotating quite regularly and rather rapidly. Each of them made a complete rotation in about a hundred and fifty yards.

"My friend, however, did not accept this result as final, but continued his observations to ascertain if this regular rate of rotation was maintained along the whole of the track. So he went on methodically until he had examined nearly half of the ribbon. And then a most astonishing thing happened. Both the heels suddenly ceased to revolve. They stopped dead, and both at the same place.

"Now, the thing being apparently an impossibility, my friend thought that he must have made some error of observation. Accordingly he went over this part of the ribbon again. But the same result emerged. Then, abandoning his measurements, he went rapidly along the whole remaining length of the ribbon to the very end, but still with the same result. Throughout the whole of that distance, neither heel showed the slightest sign of rotation. So it came to this: the photographs from number 1 to number 92 showed both heels rotating regularly about once in every hundred and fifty yards; from number 93 to number 197 they showed the heels completely stationary.

"My friend was profoundly puzzled. On the showing of the photographs, the heels of this man's shoes, which had been turning quite freely and regularly as he walked, had, in an instant, become immovably fixed. And both at the same moment. He tried to think of some possible explanation, but he could think of none. The thing was utterly incomprehensible. Then he turned to the ordnance map to see if anything in the environment could throw any light on the mystery. Searching along the row of dots for number 93 he at length found it—exactly opposite the gate in the wall.

"This was a decidedly startling discovery. It was impossible to ignore the coincidence. The position was that this man's heels had been turning freely until he reached the gate; after passing the gate his heels had become permanently fixed. The obvious suggestion was that this mysterious change in the condition of the heels was in some way connected with the gate. But what could be the nature of the connection? And what could be the nature of the change in the shoes?

"To the first question the suggested answer was that the man might have gone in at the gate; and while he was inside, something might have happened to his shoes which caused the heels to become fixed. But still the difficulty of the shoes remained. What could cause revolving heels to become fixed? To this question my friend could find no answer. The possibility that the heels had been taken off and screwed on again more tightly would not have explained their complete immobility; and, in fact, they had not been. The screws showed plainly in many of the photographs, and the position of their slots in all was identical. The footprints in the second series—those past the gate—were in every respect the exact counterparts of those in the first series—those from the town to the gate. The only condition that my friend could think of as agreeing with the physical facts was that which would have occurred if the prints in the second series had been made, not by the shoes themselves but by some sort of reproductions of them, such as plaster casts or casts in some other material."

"That sounds rather a far-fetched suggestion," remarked Pottermack.

"It does," Thorndyke agreed; "and in fact my friend did not entertain it seriously at first. He merely noted that the appearances were exactly such as would be produced by making impressions with casts; in which, of course, since the soles and heels would be all in one piece, no movement of the heels would be possible. But, Mr. Pottermack, we must bear in mind whose footprints these were. They were the footprints of a man who had disappeared in the most mysterious and unaccountable manner. The whole affair was highly abnormal. No reasonable explanation was possible either of the disappearance or of the singular character of the footprints. But in the absence of a reasonable explanation, it is admissible to consider an unreasonable one, if it agrees with the known facts. The cast theory did agree with the physical facts, and, on reflection, my friend decided to adopt it as a working hypothesis and see what came of it.

"Now, if the footprints from the gate to the heath were counterfeits of Black's footprints, made with shoes the soles and heels of which were mechanical reproductions of the soles and heels of Black's shoes, it followed that the wearer of these shoes was not Black, but some other person, in which case Black's own footprints ended at the gate. This at once got rid of the most unaccountable feature of the disappearance—the nocturnal flight out into the country; for if his footprints ended at the gate he must have gone in. But there was nothing at all abnormal about his calling at a house quite close to, and, in fact, almost in the town, from which he could have easily gone to keep his appointment with his creditor. Thus far, the hypothesis seemed to simplify matters.

"But it not only followed that Black must have gone in at the gate, it followed that he could never have come out. For the footprints that went on were not his, and there were no footprints going back towards the town."

"He might have come out another way; by the front door, for instance," Pottermack suggested.

"So he might," Thorndyke agreed, "under different circumstances. But the counterfeit footprints showed that he did not. For if the continuing footprints were counterfeits, made by some other person, what could have been their purpose? Clearly their purpose could have been no other than that of concealing the fact that Black had gone in at the gate. But if he had come out of the premises, there could have been no reason for concealing the fact that he had gone in.

"If, however, he did not come out, then, obviously, he remained inside. But in what condition? Was he alive and in hiding? Evidently not. In the first place, he had no occasion to hide, since he could have gone back to the bank and replaced the money. But the conclusive evidence that he was not in hiding was the counterfeit footprints. No mechanical reproduction of the shoes would have been necessary if Black had been there. Black's own shoes would have been borrowed and used to make the false footprints. But, obviously, the whole set of circumstances was against the supposition that he could be alive. If the evidence was accepted that he went in and was never seen again, the most obvious inference was that he had been made away with. And this inference was strongly supported by the troublesome and elaborate measures that had been taken to conceal the fact that he had gone in at the gate. Accordingly my friend adopted the view, provisionally, that Mr. Black had been made away with by some person inside the gate, hereinafter referred to as the tenant.

"But the adoption of this view at once raised two questions. First, how came it to be necessary to make reproductions of the dead man's shoes? Why did not the tenant simply take the shoes off the corpse and put them on his own feet? If he had done this, if he had made the false footprints with the dead man's own shoes, the illusion would have been perfect. No detection would have been possible. Why had he not done it? The shoes themselves could have presented no difficulty. They were large shoes, and large shoes can, with suitable preparation, be worn even by a small man.

"The answer that suggested itself was that, for some reason, the shoes were not available; that by the time that the necessity for the false footprints had been perceived, the shoes had in some way become inaccessible. But how could they have become inaccessible? Could the body have been buried? Apparently not. For it would have been much less trouble to dig up a body and recover the shoes than to make a pair of reproductions of them. Could it have been burned? Evidently not. Apart from the extreme difficulty of the operation, there had not been time. The false footprints were made on the very night of the disappearance, since they were traced by the police the next morning.

"The possibility that the body might have been conveyed away off the premises had to be borne in mind. But it was highly improbable, for many obvious reasons; and it did not dispose of the difficulty. For it would surely have been easier and quicker to go—at night—and retrieve the shoes than to make the counterfeits. Indeed, when my friend considered the immense labour that the making of those reproductions must have entailed, to say nothing of the great expenditure of time, just when every moment was precious, he felt that nothing but the absolute physical impossibility of getting access to the original shoes would explain their having been made.

"Now, what conditions would have rendered those shoes totally inaccessible? Remember the circumstances. Inasmuch as the sham footprints were found on the following morning, they must have been made that night. But before they could be made, the counterfeit soles must have been made, and the making of them must have been a long and tedious piece of work. It therefore followed that the tenant must have begun work on them almost immediately after the death of Mr. Black. From this it followed that the body of Mr. Black must have been immediately disposed of in such a way as at once to become inaccessible.

"What methods of disposing of a body would fulfil these conditions? My friend could think of only three, all very much alike: the dropping of the body down a dene-hole, or into a cess-pit, or into a disused well. Any of these methods would at once put the body completely out of reach. And all these methods had a special probability in this particular case. The great difficulty that confronts the would-be murderer is the disposal of the body. Hence the knowledge that there was available a means of immediately, securely, and permanently hiding the body might be the determining factor of the murder. Accordingly, my friend was strongly inclined to assume that one of these three methods was the one actually employed.

"As to the particular method, the question was of no great importance. Still, my friend considered it. The idea of a dene-hole was at once excluded on geological grounds. Dene-holes are peculiar to the chalk. But this was not a chalk district.

"The cess-pit was possible but not very probable; for if in use, it would be subject to periodical clearance, which would make it quite unsuitable as a hiding-place, while cess-pits which become superseded by drainage are usually filled in and definitely covered up. A well, on the other hand, is often kept open for occasional and special use after the laying on of a pipe service."

"Your friend," remarked Pottermack, "seems to have taken it for granted that a well actually existed."

"Not entirely," said Thorndyke. "He looked up an older map and found that this house had formerly been a farm-house, so that it must once have had a well; and as it now fronts on a road in which other houses have been built and which is virtually a street, it is pretty certainly connected with the water-service. So that it was practically certain that there was a well, and that well would almost certainly be out of use.

"And now, having deduced a reason why the counterfeit soles should have been necessary, he had to consider another question. If the original shoes were inaccessible, how could it have been possible to make the counterfeits, which were, apparently, casts of the originals? At first it looked like an impossibility. But a little reflection showed that the footprints themselves supplied the answer. Mr. Black's own footprints on the path were such perfect impressions that a little good plaster poured into selected samples of them would have furnished casts which would have been exact reproductions of the soles and heels of Mr. Black's shoes. Possibly there were equally good footprints inside the premises, but that is of no consequence. Those on the footpath would have answered the purpose perfectly.

"I may say that my friend tested this conclusion and got some slight confirmation. For if the false footprints were impressions of reproductions, not of the original shoes but of some other footprints, one would expect to find the accidental characters of those particular footprints as well as those of the shoes which produced them. And this appeared to be the case. In one of the points of the star on the left heel a small particle of earth seemed to have adhered. This was not to be found in Black's own footprints, but it was visible in all the footprints of the second series, from the gate to the heath. And the fact that it never changed along the whole series suggested that it was really a part of the cast, due to an imperfection in the footprint from which it was made.

"That brings us to an end of my friend's train of reasoning in regard to the actual events connected with Mr. Black's disappearance. His conclusions were, you observe, that Mr. Black went in at the gate; that he was thereafter made away with by some person inside whom we have called the tenant; that his body was deposited by the tenant in some inaccessible place, probably a disused well; and that the tenant then made a set of false footprints to disguise the fact that Mr. Black had gone in at the gate.

"The questions that remained to be considered were: first, What could be the tenant's motive for making away with Mr. Black? and second, Who was the tenant? But before we deal with his inferences on those points, I should like to hear any observations which you may have to make on what I have told you."

Mr. Pottermack pondered awhile on what he had heard, and as he reflected, he laid a disparaging hand on the teapot.

"It is rather cool," he remarked apologetically; "but such as it is, can I give you another cup?"

"Prolonged exposition," Thorndyke replied with a smile, "is apt to have a cooling effect upon tea. But it also creates a demand for liquid refreshment. Thank you, I think another cup would cheer, and we can dispense with the inebriation."

Mr. Pottermack refilled both the cups and put down the teapot, still cogitating profoundly.

XVIII

THE SUN-DIAL HAS THE LAST WORD

"YOUR LEGAL FRIEND," MR. POTTERMACK SAID AT LENGTH, "must be a man of extraordinary subtlety and ingenuity if he deduced all that you have told me from the mere peculiarities of a set of footprints, and only photographs at that. But what strikes me about it is that his reconstruction was, after all, pure speculation. There were too many 'ifs.'"

"But, my dear Mr. Pottermack," exclaimed Thorndyke, "it was all 'ifs.' The whole train of reasoning was on the plane of hypothesis, pure and simple. He did not, at this stage, assume that it was actually true, but merely true conditionally on the facts being what they appeared to be. But what does a scientific man do when he sets up a working hypothesis? He deduces from it its consequences, and he continues to pursue these so long as they are consistent with the facts known to him. Sooner or later, this process brings him either to an impossibility or a contradiction—in which case he abandons the hypothesis—or to a question of fact which is capable of being settled conclusively, yes or no.

"Well, this is what my friend did. So far we have seen him pursuing a particular hypothesis and deducing from it certain consequences. The whole thing might have been fallacious. But it was consistent, and the consequences were compatible with the known facts. Presently we shall come to the question of fact—the 'crucial experiment' which determines yes or no, whether the hypothesis is true or false. But we have to follow the hypothetical method a little farther first.

"The questions that remained to be considered were: first, What could have been the tenant's motive for killing Mr. Black? and second, Who was the tenant? My friend took the questions in this order because the motive might be arrived at by reasoning, and, if so arrived at, might throw light on the personality of the tenant; whereas the identity of the tenant, taken by itself, was a matter of fact capable of being ascertained by enquiry, but not by reasoning apart from the motive.

"Now, what motives suggest themselves? First, we must note that my friend assumed that the homicide was committed by the tenant himself, that is, by the proprietor of the premises and not by a servant or other person. That is a reasonable inference from the facts that the person, whoever he was, appeared to have command of all the means and materials necessary for making the counterfeits, and also that he must have had full control of the premises, both at the time and in the future, in order to hide the body and ensure that it should remain hidden. Well, what motive could a man in this position have had to kill Mr. Black?

"There is the motive of robbery, but the circumstances seem to exclude it as not reasonably probable. It is true that Black had a hundred pounds on his person, but there is no reason to suppose that any one knew that he had; and in any case, so small a sum, relatively, furnishes a quite insufficient motive for murder in the case of an apparently well-to-do man such as the tenant. My friend decided that robbery, though possible, was highly improbable.

"The possibilities that Black's death might have been the result of a quarrel or of some act of private vengeance had to be borne in mind, but there were no means of forming any opinions for or against them. They had to be left as mere speculative possibilities.

But there was another possibility which occurred to my friend, the probabilities of which were susceptible of being argued, and to this he turned his attention. It was based upon the application of certain facts actually known and which we will now consider.

"First, he noted that Mr. Black came to this place voluntarily, and that he came expressly to visit the premises within the gate is proved by the fact that this is the last house on that path. Beyond it is the country. There is no other human habitation to which he could have been bound. Now Mr. Black was, at this moment, in acute financial difficulties. He had borrowed a hundred pounds from the bank's money, and this hundred pounds he was about to pay away to meet an urgent demand. But that hundred pounds would have to be replaced, and it was of the utmost importance that it should be replaced without delay. For if a surprise inspection should have occurred before it was replaced, he stood to be charged with robbery. The circumstances, therefore, seemed to suggest that he had taken it with the expectation of being able to replace it almost immediately.

"Now, you will remember that it transpired after his disappearance that Mr. Black had some mysterious unknown source of income; that he had received on several occasions large sums of money, which had apparently come to him in the form of cash and had been paid away in the same form—always in five-pound notes. These monies did not appear in his banking account or in any other account. They were unrecorded—and, consequently, their total amount is not known. But the sums that he is known to have received were ascertained by means of the discovery of certain payments that he had made. I need not point out to you the great and sinister significance of these facts. When a man who has a banking account receives large payments in cash, and when, instead of paying them into his account, he pays them away in cash, it is practically certain that the monies that he has received are connected with some secret transaction, and that transaction is almost certainly an illicit one. But of all such transactions, by far the commonest is blackmail. In fact, one would hardly be exaggerating if one were to say that evidence of secret payments of large sums in coin or notes is presumptive evidence of blackmail. Accordingly my friend strongly suspected Mr. Black of being a blackmailer.

"And now, assuming this to be correct, see how admirably the assumption fits the circumstances. Mr. Black is at the moment financially desperate. He has taken certain money, which is not his, to pay an urgent and threatening creditor. Instead of going direct to that creditor, he comes first to this house. But he does not enter by the front door. He goes to a gate which opens on an unfrequented lane and which gives entrance to a remote part of the grounds, and he does this late in the evening. There is a manifestly secret air about the whole proceeding.

"And now let us make another assumption."

"What, another!" protested Pottermack.

"Yes, another; just to see if it will fit the circumstances as the others have done. Let us assume that the tenant was the person from whom Mr. Black had been extorting those mysterious payments; the victim whom he had been blackmailing. That he had called in on his way to his creditor to see if he could squeeze him for yet another hundred, so that the notes could be replaced before they could be missed. That the victim, being now at the end of his patience and having an opportunity of safely making away with his persecutor, took that opportunity and made away with him. Is it not obvious that we have a perfectly consistent scheme of the probable course of events?"

"It is all pure conjecture," objected Pottermack.

"It is all pure hypothesis," Thorndyke admitted, "but you see that it all hangs together, it all fits the circumstances completely. We have not come to any inconsistency or impossibility. And it is all intrinsically probable in the special conditions; for you must not forget that we are dealing with a set of circumstances that admits of no normal explanation.

"And now for the last question. Assuming that Mr. Black was a blackmailer and that the tenant was his victim, was it possible to give that victim a name? Here my friend was handicapped by the fact that Mr. Black was a complete stranger, of whose domestic affairs and friends and acquaintances he had no knowledge. With one exception. He had knowledge of one of Mr. Black's friends. That friend, it is true, was alleged to be dead. But it was by no means certain that he was dead. And if he were not dead, he was a perfectly ideal subject for blackmail, for he was an escaped convict with a considerable term of penal servitude still to run. My friend was, of course, thinking of Mr. White. If he should have attained to something approaching affluence and should be living in prosperous and socially desirable circumstances, he would allow himself to be bled to an unlimited extent rather than suffer public disgrace and be sent back to prison. And the person who would be, of all others, the most likely to recognize him and in the best position to blackmail him would be his old friend Mr. Black.

"Bearing these facts in mind, my friend was disposed to waive the *prima facie* improbability and assume, provisionally, that the tenant was Mr. White. It was certainly rather a long shot."

"It was indeed," said Pottermack. "Your friend was a regular Robin Hood."

"And yet," Thorndyke rejoined, "the balance of probability was in favour of that assumption. For against the various circumstances that suggested that the tenant was Mr. White there was to be set only one single improbability, and that not at all an impressive one:

the improbability that a body—found drowned after six weeks'
immersion and therefore really unrecognizable—should have been
wrongly identified. However, my friend did feel that (to continue the
metaphor, since you seem to approve of it) the time had come to step
forward and have a look at the target. The long train of hypothetical
reasoning had at length brought him to a proposition the truth of
which could be definitely tested. The tenant's identity with Mr. White
was a matter of fact which could be proved or disproved beyond all
doubt. Of course, the test would not be a real *experimentum crucis*,
because it would act in only one direction. If it should turn out that
the tenant was not Mr. White, that would not invalidate the other
conclusions, but if it should turn out that he was Mr. White, that
fact would very strongly confirm those conclusions.

"My friend, then, left his photographs and his ordnance map and
made a journey to the scene of these strange events to inspect the
place and the man with his own eyes. First he examined the path
and the exterior of the premises, and then he made a survey of the
grounds enclosed by the wall."

"How did he do that?" enquired Pottermack. "It was a pretty high
wall—at least, so I understand."

"He made use of an ancient optical instrument which has been
recently revived in an improved form under the name of 'periscope.'
The old instrument had two mirrors; the modern one has two
total-reflection prisms in a narrow tube. By projecting the upper or
objective end of the tube above the top of the wall, my friend was
able, on looking into the eye-piece, to get an excellent view of the
premises. What he saw was a large garden, completely enclosed by
four high walls in which were two small gates, each provided with a
night-latch and therefore capable of being opened only from within
or by means of a latchkey. A very secure and secluded garden. On
one side of it was a range of out-buildings which, by the glazed lights

in their roofs, appeared to be studios or workshops. Near one end of the lawn was a sun-dial on a very wide stone base. The width of the base was rather remarkable, being much greater than is usual in a garden dial. A glance at it showed that the dial had been quite recently set up, for, though the stone pillar was old, the base stones were brand new. Moreover, the turf around it had been very recently laid and some of the earth was still bare. Further proof of its newness was furnished by a gentleman who was, at the moment, engaged, with the aid of Whitaker's Almanack and his watch, in fixing the dial-plate in correct azimuth.

"This gentleman—the mysterious tenant—naturally engaged my friend's attention. There were several interesting points to be noted concerning him. The tools that he used were workmen's tools, not amateurs', and he used them with the unmistakable skill of a man accustomed to tools. Then he had laid aside his spectacles, which were 'curl-sided' and therefore habitually worn. It followed, then, that he was near-sighted; for if he had been old-sighted or long-sighted he would have needed the spectacles especially for the close and minute work that he was doing.

"When he had made these observations, my friend proceeded to take a couple of photographs—a right and a left profile."

"How did he manage that?" demanded the astonished Pottermack.

"By placing his camera on the top of the wall. It was a special, small camera, fitted with a four-point-five Ross-Zeiss lens and a cord release. Of course, he made the exposure with the aid of the periscope.

"When he had exposed the photographs, he decided to have a nearer view of the tenant. Accordingly he went round and knocked at the gate, which was presently opened by the gentleman of the sun-dial, who was now wearing his spectacles. Looking at those spectacles, my friend made a very curious discovery. The man was not near-sighted, for the glasses were convex bi-focals, the upper part nearly plain glass. Now, if he had not needed those spectacles for near work, he certainly could not need them for distance. Then, obviously, he did not need them at all. But, if so, why was he wearing them? The only possible explanation was that they were worn for their effect on his appearance; in short, for the purpose of disguise.

"As this gentleman was answering some questions about the locality my friend handed him a folded map. This he did with two objects: that he might get a good look at him unobserved, and that he might possibly obtain some prints of his finger-tips. As to the first, he was able to make a mental note of the tenant's salient characteristics and to observe, among other peculiarities, a purplish mark on the lobe of the right ear of the kind known to surgeons as a capillary nævus."

"And the finger-prints?" Pottermack asked eagerly.

"They were rather a failure, but not quite. When my friend developed them up, though very poor specimens, they were distinct enough to be recognizable by an expert.

"Now you will have noticed that everything that my friend observed was consistent with, and tended to confirm, the conclusions that he had arrived at by hypothetical reasoning. But the actual test still remained to be applied. Was the tenant Mr. White or was he not? In order to settle this question, my friend made enlargements of the photographs of the tenant and also of the finger-prints, and, with these in his pocket, paid a visit to Scotland Yard."

At the mention of the ill-omened name Pottermack started and a sudden pallor spread over his face. But he uttered no sound, and Thorndyke continued:

"There he presented the finger-prints as probably those of a deceased person, photographed from a document, and asked for an expert opinion on them. He gave no particulars and was not asked for any; but the experts made their examination and reported that the finger-prints were those of a convict named White who had died some fifteen years previously. My friend had, further, the opportunity of inspecting the prison photographs of the deceased White and of reading the personal description. Needless to say, they agreed completely in every particular, even to the capillary nævus on the ear.

"Here, then, my legal friend emerged from the region of hypothesis into that of established fact. The position now was that the person whom we have called 'the tenant' was undoubtedly the convict, White, who was universally believed to be dead. And since this fact had been arrived at by the train of reasoning that I have recited, there could be no doubt that the other, intermediate, conclusions were correct; that, in fact, the hypothesis as a whole was substantially true. Do you agree with that view?"

"There seems to be no escape from it," replied Pottermack; and after a brief pause he asked, a little tremulously: "And what action did your legal friend take?"

"In respect of the identity of the tenant? He took no action. He now considered it perfectly clear that Mr. White ought never to have been a convict at all. That unfortunate gentleman had been the victim of a miscarriage of justice. It would have been actually against public policy to disclose his existence and occasion a further miscarriage.

"With regard to the killing of Mr. Black, the position was slightly different. If it comes to the knowledge of any citizen—and especially a barrister, who is an officer of justice—that a crime has been committed, it is the duty of that citizen to communicate his knowledge to the proper authorities. But my friend had not come by any such knowledge. He had formed the opinion—based on certain inferences from certain facts—that Mr. Black had been killed. But a man is not under any obligation to communicate his opinions.

"This may seem a little casuistical. But my friend was a lawyer, and lawyers are perhaps slightly inclined to casuistry. And in this case there were certain features that encouraged this casuistical tendency. We must take it, I think, that a man who suffers a wrong for which the law provides a remedy and in respect of which it offers him protection is morally and legally bound to take the legal remedy and place himself under the protection of the law. But if the law offers him no remedy and no protection, he would appear to be entitled to resume the natural right to protect himself as best he can. That, at any rate, is my friend's view.

"Of course, the discovery of the alleged body of Mr. Black in the gravel-pit seemed to put an entirely new complexion on the affair. My friend was greatly perturbed by the news. It was hardly conceivable that it could really be Mr. Black's body. But it was some person's body, and the deliberate 'planting' of a dead human body seemed almost inevitably to involve a previous crime. Accordingly, my friend started off, hot-foot, to investigate. When the deceased turned out to be a mummy, his concern with the discovery came to an end. There was no need for him to interfere in the case. It was a harmless deception and even useful, for it informed the world at large that Mr. Black was dead.

"That, Mr. Pottermack, is the history of the dead man who was alive and the live man who was dead; and I think you will agree with me and my legal friend that it is a most curious and interesting case."

Pottermack nodded, but for some time remained silent. At length, in a tone the quietness of which failed to disguise the suppressed anxiety, he said:

"But you have not quite finished your story."

"Have I not?" said Thorndyke. "What have I forgotten?"

"You have not told me what became of Mr. White."

"Oh, Mr. White. Well, I think we can read from here upon your sun-dial a few words that put his remaining history in a nutshell. *Sole decedente pax*. He had the mark removed from his ear, he married his old love and lived happy ever after."

"Thank you," said Mr. Pottermack, and suddenly turned away his head.

THE END

ALSO AVAILABLE
IN THE BRITISH LIBRARY
CRIME CLASSICS SERIES

Big Ben Strikes Eleven	DAVID MAGARSHACK
Death of an Author	E. C. R. LORAC
The Black Spectacles	JOHN DICKSON CARR
Death of a Bookseller	BERNARD J. FARMER
The Wheel Spins	ETHEL LINA WHITE
Someone from the Past	MARGOT BENNETT
Who Killed Father Christmas?	ED. MARTIN EDWARDS
Twice Round the Clock	BILLIE HOUSTON
The White Priory Murders	CARTER DICKSON
The Port of London Murders	JOSEPHINE BELL
Murder in the Basement	ANTHONY BERKELEY
Fear Stalks the Village	ETHEL LINA WHITE
The Cornish Coast Murder	JOHN BUDE
Suddenly at His Residence	CHRISTIANNA BRAND
The Edinburgh Mystery	ED. MARTIN EDWARDS
Checkmate to Murder	E. C. R. LORAC
The Spoilt Kill	MARY KELLY
Smallbone Deceased	MICHAEL GILBERT
The Story of Classic Crime in 100 Books	MARTIN EDWARDS
The Pocket Detective: 100+ Puzzles	KATE JACKSON
The Pocket Detective 2: 100+ More Puzzles	KATE JACKSON

Many of our titles are also available
in eBook, large print and audio editions